THE RISE

OF A KING

Book One of EtharWorld Series

DeWitt C. Tremaine

ISBN: 978-1-966954-48-4 (paperback)
ISBN: 978-1-966954-49-1 (hardcover)
ISBN: 978-1-966954-50-7 (epub)

Library of Congress Control Number: 2025910283

Book Titles by

DeWitt C. Tremaine

Ethar World Series:

1. The Rise of a King – Book One of the Ethar World Series

2. A Time for Change - Book Two of the Ethar World Series

3. A Touch of Earth - Book Three of the Ethar World Series

4. Savage Continent - Book Four of the Ethar World Series

5. A Journey - Book Five of the Ethar World Series

6. Tallund - Book Six of the Ethar World Series

7. Telsa - Book Seven of the Ethar World Series

8. When Nothing Happens - Book Eight of the Ethar World Series

9. From Kendlar and Back Again – Book Nine in the Ethar World Series

Touch of Earth Saga:

1. Touch of Earth Saga 1 Heroes

2. Touch of Earth Saga 2 Secret Camp

3. Touch of Earth Saga 3 Janet

4. Touch of Earth Saga 4 Candy

5. Touch of Earth Saga 5 Mira

6. Touch of Earth Saga 6 Samuel

Dedication

To my children; may I prove worthy of their love.

CHAPTER 01

Through the Rabbit Hole

Time changes all things. Even the perception of time itself seems to change with time from a constant to perhaps a relative constant. As with all things we perceive the concept of what is constant changes as we learn to perceive things at new levels. Shiheel was busy in his laboratory on the planet Ethar. He was an alien to this world. He was an Eftite and they moved to this world about five hundred years ago. He was a scientist and studied information purely for the sake of knowledge.

He discovered from history that this world once had a natural dimensional bridge with a world called Earth. The Never-Ending Poem seemed to predict his involvement, but as with any prophecy there is lots of room for interpretation. As with lengthy wordy prophesies it is always easy to fit things that have happened into the endless predictions that were written. Seeing the future is a funny thing; if you see it, you can change it, and if you do change it, that does not mean it was never really the future you saw. No matter, the verses of the poem implied he is going to bring a hero to Ethar from Earth. Shiheel was going to try even if it was not for the prophesy. If it were for no other reason than his desire to study the science of the matter Shiheel would pursue building the bridge.

The portal he was working on was developed and ready to use. He had completed the last details a week ago. He had been using it to study possible candidates. The prophesy stated that the one brought from Earth would wield great power on Ethar. From what he could tell there was no real magic on Earth. As far as physical power, there was no one on Earth that he could see that would be able to compete with what was already on Ethar. He concluded then that the power referred to had to fall in the category of knowledge. This was an assumption on his part and he did not like making assumption.

There were troubles stirring on Ethar, so he knew he needed to either decide or wait until a later time before continuing his experiments. The Elven kingdom might be a starting point for bringing in this outsider and his ideas. He decided to push things forward and not wait. The portal was untested and the barriers of power that it passed through could affect creatures that were brought from Earth to Ethar. He was confident it would not affect him, but he was an Eftite and Eftites were an energy-based life form even while they hold a physical form. Even if it did affect him, he was from a world that was at least familiar with the possibilities.

He checked his list. He had a room ready for guests. He had a kitchen, another amenity for visitors since he used energy-matter conversion for his own sustenance. His visitor could have free reign of his lab and library. The equipment was as ready as it was going to be, although untested. His original plan was to test it in a remote location before actually using it. It was very rare for him to not have success on the first completed try. With the pressure of time he had confidence the portal would work.

Once he started the opening or the portal there no was turning back. His selected candidate was alone and asleep. He initialized the device and the patterns started weaving. He continuously calibrated and adjusted settings, as the portal wormed its way through the fabric of the time and dimensional barriers, breaking free of Ethar and then locating the barrier to Earth. The process would take a few hours, but the portal would flex with the movements of the dimensions after it was established. If the barriers truly were in possession of their own sentient nature and intelligence, as some implied, then he must have their permission to do what he is doing. Any force applied contrary to what he was doing would collapse the attempt, and it would be months before he could try again.

Shiheel looked at his watch. He was going to be late. As long as his candidate was not too resistant, he should still be able to make the meeting in the city of Talmorg, and still have time to present everything he had promised.

*   *   *   *   *   *   *

Talmorg was the high Elven prince, son of Erron Elkinshane. Their last name was very old and described the duties of their lineage. Elkin was their native tongue for Elves and shane would be defined as lord or ruler. An extended definition of shane would be something more like high servants by way of leading and guiding the Elven people with authority and command. Talmorg was the crowned prince, named after his grandfather and the founder of the Walled City of Talmorg.

Talmorg was currently working on a large political project, to unite the various kingdoms of the southern portion of the northern continent.

This area was more commonly referred to as the south lands by the people of the Northern Continent. His effort was to form unity by means of a voluntary alliance not by military might. There had been many smaller projects leading to this, the safety and the security for everyone was involved. This was the first-time political efforts of this nature had been made to unite any land occupied by multiple races. Lands had been united in the past, but by one race dominating others with military might and that just did not last. He wanted citizens not subjects.

Military domination always leads to rebellion and continuous fighting, no matter how fair or reasonable the ruling nation may be. Talmorg hoped for a peaceful unity, one that could lead to protecting roads and trade routes from brigands and bandits. He also hoped for enough unity to promote a unified defense force against outside threats, primarily from the north, but also any other threats that might impose themselves. Talmorg figured if they were working together for a common good, they were less likely to fight between themselves.

The Kingdom of Talmorg and the other Elf led city-states were the strongest and most secure. Challenges to these locations had turned to political approaches when it became evident that no military approach would be strong enough to pose a threat. They tried to be reasonable and fair in their dealings. It was their goal to promote harmony.

*   *   *   *   *   *   *

Eric awoke with a start for no apparent reason. He lay awake for several minutes listening with an eerie sense that something was wrong, but could not place what it was. All he heard was silence, a disturbing and penetrating silence, a silence that he could see and feel in the darkness. When he could not relax and go back to sleep, he got up and slipped into his smoking jacket. He did not bother turning any lights on until he stepped into the bathroom. He looked in the mirror, yawned, stretched and splashed his face with cold water.

It must still be quite early, he thought, as he prepared to shave. Bonny was not home, her mom was sick again, this had been a bad year for her especially lately. It seemed Bonny had to spend more than half her time over helping her mom. They tried to talk her mom into moving in with them, but she insisted that she would be all right and that coming and living with them was a 'silly idea'.

Eric thought about Bonny as he shaved. She was one of the more attractive women he had ever been with. She was not just a physically attractive lady, with her rich red hair dominating her soft porcelain facial features, she was also smart. Bonny was one of the few women he had ever been with that being six feet and a half inch was close to his own height. He could not imagine his own success without her. She had everything he would want in a wife, but they were not ready for that commitment. Honestly, he was afraid of it, though he did not know why. In his mind he looked into her bright blue eyes, set with perfection in the divine features of her face. Her high cheekbones supported smooth skin that hinted of freckles. He opened his eyes and his vision of perfection was replaced by his own face. He looked into his own hazel eyes and wondered why he was still waiting, what was he waiting for.

When Eric was done shaving, he picked up his watch from the side of the sink. It was Saturday, what was he going to be doing today? He had been planning on going to the University to tutor Jamis in his software development class, but Jamis called last night, he would not be able to make it this Saturday. It seemed he did not have to do anything today, and here he was getting up before the sun. What time was it anyway? He did not usually get up when it was still this dark out. He looked at his watch, now on his wrist which read Sat 9:04 Feb 6 1993, it could not be that late, not nine. The sun would have been shining through the bedroom windows a couple of hours earlier, if it was already nine. Surely his watch had not suddenly decided to gain a couple of hours either. Eric had spent good money on his precision Swiss watch and he had just taken it in for routine maintenance last week. It had checked out fine, nothing was wrong with it. Eric went into the living room, to turn the TV on and double check, but was disturbed to see the wall clock agreed with his watch. Eric considered the possibility that he had slept the entire day away and it was evening, but then Bonny would have been home, or at least called or stopped by. He also could not believe that the day had gone by without a phone call that would have pulled him from sleep.

He went straight to the window and looked out. White, all he could see was white, pressed up against the window. Eric turned on the TV for comfort, the foreboding feeling that something was wrong had risen up and been answered. How deep was it? He went to the front door, into the foyer and opened the outside door, to see another white wall, yet the snow did not cave in. It was packed well enough to hold its form, and it was deep enough that the sun barely glowed or glittered through. Eric had lived farther north before and seen heavy snowfall, but this was ridiculous. He considered the possibility that it may be still overcast enough to prevent much light from getting through. He went back into the living room, out of need he sat down, choosing the couch and stared into the Television, to think. Some talk show was on, but what caught his attention was the print rolling across the bottom of the TV screen:

...WEATHER.WARNING.....UNUSUAL.AND.UNPREDICTED. SNOWFALL.....DRIFTS.UP.TO.TWENTY.FEET.AND.STILL. FALLING....REPORTS.AT.PRESENT.LIMITED..LOCAL.AND. STATE.AREA....EXTENSIVENESS.UNKNOWN......STAY. TUNED.FOR.FURTHER.UPDATES....WEATHER.WARNING.... UNUSUAL.AND.UNPREDICTED.SNOW....

He breathed deeply, oddly he did not feel as alone, but he could not help feeling like it was all just a dream. It had to be a dream, this could not have happened without some kind of warning. Even if it was a government weather experiment, regardless of which government, it takes time to make major changes in the weather. He would wake up now at any minute and laugh at himself for even believing this was possible, everyone would get a good laugh at this one. He got up and went into the kitchen, time for some coffee and a good breakfast. If it was a dream he might just as well enjoy it, if it was real, he had to do something to suppress the edges panic trying to well up inside.

About forty minutes had passed, and he was sitting down eating his breakfast of eggs, bacon, hotcakes and sipping on his coffee, when a knock came from the door. That settles it he had to be dreaming, nobody could possibly have walked up to the door in this kind of weather. The knock came again, so he got up and went to the door, the knock came twice more on his way there. He gingerly pulled back the door with new hope and anticipation, expecting a five-foot rabbit with a stopwatch to come running through declaring he was late.

Even with his fanciful imagination, nothing could have prepared him for what he saw, when he opened the door. There was an oval portal cut through the snow. What he saw standing in it was not human. The creature stood about three and a half feet tall, its head looked like it was made out of light blue metal with a dull luster. It had two dark blue crystalline gridded facets where it should have had eyes. There was a third facet that was similar to the others, but lacked the distinction of color in the center of its forehead.

The creature had no apparent nose or ears and a small slit for a mouth. Its body had the appearance of heavy tanned leather of a medium brown shade. Its groin section was wrapped in the same type of metallic substance as its head. It had two elbows on each arm and two knees on each leg, which seemed to allow them to fold in a very compact fashion. Each hand had an additional thumb opposite from a normal thumb, likewise six toes on its feet, which appeared to have as much dexterity as its hands, almost like a chimpanzee in that sense. The ground the creature was standing just outside his doorway, was not Eric's front yard, but rather some kind of strange green volcanic rock the view of which was limited to what he could see through the oval opening in the wall of snow.

Stupefied, Eric stood staring with intent disbelief, at what was beyond the door he held open. He stuck his foot back to hold the door open and very carefully stuck his right hand halfway to the elbow in the snow next to the strange oval opening. When he could not see it through the opening, he reached around with his left hand through the opening where all he could see was just the rolling ridges of porous green stone behind the alien being standing there. His left arm felt like he had stuck it into something a little denser than air that moved almost like water. He could not find his arm and quickly yanked them both back, grabbing the door knob for balance. It was one thing to know the concept of a magic portal or a wormhole, it was a whole different matter unexpectedly seeing one.

He stood holding tight to the door knob with his left hand, until, the creature spoke. When it spoke, Eric noticed it did so without moving its mouth. "May I come in please? It would be a relief to sit for a little while, or do you leave all your guests standing in the door? We do have a few matters to discuss."

Eric still in a state of surprise managed a feeble "ah... Sure." He had not noticed it before with his attention on the portal, but as the creature walked by into his home, it had a tail a little longer than its legs.

The tail split into what could almost be called, three fingers at the end about five inches long, and looked very powerful. They passed through the living room Eric trailing behind slightly. "Please sit down." He said, more out of habit of courtesy than anything else as he glanced back and forth between the door and the strangest creature he ever let in his house.

The strange little creature turned the chair sideways to the dining table, but seemed to have no difficulty sitting. The chair was the right level to match his higher set of knees and he used his tail to conveniently pull the chair toward the table as he sat down. Eric also noticed that the height of the table was relatively convenient to the stranger, he easily cleared the top of it with his double set of elbows. Eric felt as though he had gone beyond panic and wonder, skipping stunned the moment the door had opened, now everything had a bewildered clarity to it.

He considered himself to be a very educated, and a very well-read man, yet in all his education, and in all his reading he had never seen anything that fit the appearance of this creature, real or fictitious. He considered for a moment that what he was looking at could be some kind of environmental suit, but dismissed the thought being more certain the creature he was looking at was just what he saw wearing nothing at all. The creature looked like a cross between many different things. It had characteristics that were unique to it alone, yet with a blending so odd that it could not be placed in any known category, aside from an animal maybe as opposed to plant.

Eric struggled with his inability to find a place for what he saw, even in science fiction, or fantasy, which genre was his favorite reading. There was no explanation or place in his knowledge of science, history, legend or myth for the stranger. Eric had spent most of his life in school, longer than most people would think of spending. He was a professional student, until he met Bonny, who had encouraged him to develop his life in more productive avenues. He had done nothing but go to school and she had felt he needed to get out in the working world, to see what "real life" was all about.

He never could find a job where he could encompass the use of all the education he had received. He could find some jobs using various narrow segments of his knowledge, physics, but not including anthropology, or biology, but not computer science, or medicine, but not history. The combinations varied, but never all inclusive. It seemed he had studied everything that he possibly could. He was a member of Mensa. He could have gone anywhere and done anything he wanted with his mind and he was always being flooded with opportunities. He was quite versatile, but there is where the problem came in. Eric, with all his knowledge, aptitude, education and ability, could never decide what he wanted to be 'when he grew up'. So as things turned out, what he finally did was, he got a job as a janitor at the local college, taught a couple classes and used whatever time he could to further his studies. Eric was caught in the hidden dilemma that posed a stumbling block for almost every genius that had a balanced aptitude in everything, the lack of direction to focus persistence. He wound up using his education for tutoring, and for his own private and entertainment excursions, although at times that even brought him a sizable income. He had taken the job as a janitor, because it gave him full access to the college facilities, without any curricular bounds or requirements. The manual labor also gave him opportunity to contemplate other things while working.

Now Eric's thinking started to shift, even if this was a dream, this stranger would be a great addition to his fantasy game that he had plugged into the college computer system. Eric had actually donated enough to expand the computer system so the game would not interfere with normal activity. Eighty nine percent of the people in the school played the game, including the college dean. They had their own characters in the game and enjoyed the challenges he set forth, the new twists, the new angles, the ever-changing world of fantasy, oddities which he contrived and added without breaching the laws and nature of the game. Each player could have up to eight characters in play at the same time and interact with other players in the world. Most stuck with playing one or two at a time.

Eric felt his mind coming back to the situation at hand and decided he wanted to know everything he could about this new and different stranger in his house even if it was just a dream. So, pushing to the side his breakfast plate, he faced the creature sat down and said, "I do not believe we have been properly introduced, my name is, Eric." He did so, leaving a pause sufficient for the other to give a proper and courteous response. To his pleasure the other complied.

Like a statue at a wax museum, the other began to speak, again without gesturing or moving its mouth. "Why hello. It's nice to see you are finished staring through the walls of thought and back to yourself. I am Shiheel. I am from another world in time, space and dimension. The kingdom I came here from is much the same as your fantasy novels and books, your myths, legends and fairytales. Almost all that lives in the world where I live, lives in your fantasies, with the exception of my kind, we are aliens to that world also. Some of your stories are taken from our histories, yet as I said I am alien to them also.

My people traveled a long time and distance, to arrive in their world and some of us chose to settle there. Our home worlds were destroyed when our star became a supernova. Our sun has been gone now for a long time, generations." The creature went on still not moving its mouth and gesturing about as much as the marble statues Eric had on his front lawn. Eric thought it was an odd way to speak without moving one's mouth, but continued to listen. Eric felt almost like he was sitting in on a history lecture where he should be taking notes. The creature went on with the history of his people and their disbursement through the galaxies in their dimension. How he and many others of his people chose to live in the world he now lived in, a world of Elves, Dwarves, Trolls and Goblins. It was a magical, mysterious world in constant change, a world where good and evil were always battling in one way or another. The world was called Ethar, a place where he felt functional and useful, where his natural powers were considered magical, though normal energy was their true nature. He explained that his original home was a six-planet system and his race was called Eftites evolved from an energy-based creature. There were many other types of creatures of varying intelligence and physical nature on his home worlds, his being the foremost, not that they dominated, but rather lived peaceably one with another.

Eric interrupted to ask, "Which planet did you live on?" fiddling with the fork off his plate and glancing in his now empty coffee cup.

"All of them, a predominance among our planets is the result of natural abilities, not studied science, though I also do much studying. We Eftites are high energy beings, dependent on our natural ability to convert matter and energy. We do not consume as others do, we derive our sustenance from either matter or energy converting it to what we need. This has also given us the ability to convert matter and energy either way. As a result, we can change the very substance of things at will, which gives us a great advantage over many other races." Shiheel went on explaining many things to Eric, new in concept and idea, much of which was as strange to Eric, as the creature itself. Eric caught most of what Shiheel was saying, as he wrestled to keep his own thoughts under control. Then Shiheel stopped with a long and uncomfortable pause, before speaking again to Eric, "Well, enough about me. Now I need to talk to you about returning with me, which is why I came here to see you."

If he was dreaming, why were they at his dining table instead of already being sucked into this world of fantasy? Eric was not sure he wanted to know or hear this, so to procrastinate he asked, "Would you like a cup of coffee?"

As he asked, he considered the possibilities, thinking this could be a fun or an interesting adventure. If it was, did he want it? This could also be some kind of trap. The stranger's total lack of motion made it impossible to second guess its feelings, or try to read from body language whether it was speaking the truth. He was not afraid of high-risk adventure, but even with that he normally knew what he would be dealing with and how to prepare for it, he could not prepare for something he knew nothing about.

Yet it could be interesting to go into a world that bore similarity to the game he had developed and set up, but it could also be very dangerous. A world similar to that game that had become so popular it became a primary source of income had serious risks involved. Though he ran it for free at the University, many companies were buying rights to sell the game on a home scale, to include systems similar to a cable hook up in the home, with a nationwide system, run out of centralized computers. People met and shared from different corners of the country by playing the game, a major portion of the characters in the game were now, player characters, though non-player characters were computer bred to keep the game in balance. Some of the systems were going worldwide. But what confronted Eric now would be an experience more intense, more involved than just a game. This creature was asking him to go to this other world, and he was not sure he wanted to leave the security and comfort of his own world. Even in the game the player-characters had some idea what they were getting involved with and had the time and means to prepare for it.

"I think I should enjoy trying your brew." Shiheel answered, "I take it that is what you are drinking?"

Eric was uncomfortable not knowing if the creature was looking at him or not, or looking at everything at once. "Yes, it is," Eric felt he was giving this dream too much serious thought, after all it had to be coming from somewhere in his own imagination, "It is similar to tea, brewed from ground coffee beans."

"That sounds interesting, I might even enjoy it." Shiheel seemed stiff to Eric, he did not gesture, no matter what he was talking about. The stranger was like a robot that also seemed to lack expression in his voice.

As Eric stood up grabbing his own plate and cup off the table, he automatically asked, "Would you like cream or sugar with that?" then realized before Shiheel answered, that the alien probably had no idea what he was talking about. Chuckling to himself, if it was a dream, this creature would know or not know anything he wanted it to, but he was having some doubts as to whether it was a dream.

Shiheel paused "Is that how you drink it?"

"Of course, you wouldn't know. Well, I'll serve it black and put cream and sugar on the table, with a spoon so you can mix it to your desired tastes." Eric thought this would also be an opportunity to see movement on Shiheel's part, letting him know that his conversation was not with a totally inanimate object.

"Thank you." Shiheel stated what seemed the appropriate social response.

Eric returned to the kitchen where he rinsed his plate and silverware before dropping them in the dishwasher, and then filled his cup and one for Shiheel. He brought everything back out to the dining room table, where the both of them were sitting. Eric was now ready to hear what Shiheel had to say. Shiheel sipped his coffee as Eric watched with intrigue, his smooth body movements seemingly designed for efficiency. Shiheel captivated Eric's attention, with his efficiency of motion as he sampled the cream and sugar and mixed the coffee to his taste. Then to Eric's surprise, he nodded his approval, a movement that seemed out of place and unnatural, "It is indeed a tasty brew. The sugar is a sweetener and the cream touches it off quite nicely, masking out some of the bitterness."

Eric's curiosity got the best of him, "How is it you speak without using your mouth?"

Shiheel chuckled "Oh wise and educated man, what is speaking but articulated sound. I make sound with other membranes, much like the membranes in your picture box or your music speaker box. It is with the facet in the center of my forehead that I make sound the same way I could produce any other form of energy. This is one of the abilities that causes those of the world I live in to call me magical. It is our outlet for the expression of energies. For example, here I can produce light." Shiheel went silent and a wide beam of light came forth from the center of his forehead and then stopped.

Eric's eyebrows lifted and he leaned back, "That is fantastic, that would be considered magical in this world, by most people, at least until

they dissected you to find out what made you tic." That did clarify the

lack of mouth movement, but it did not set Eric at ease with the rest of

Shiheel's lack of movement or gesturing. He kept feeling the urge to start

babbling, because he was nervous and was trying to guard against it. The

thought struck him though that might be why this Shiheel kept talking so

much, of course the rambling could be just to help Eric relax too.

Shiheel laughed "Yes, until your scientist studied our structure

and learned to understand how we are creatures of energy, and how we

function. As you well know science is considered magic by primitive

cultures who do not understand it. Likewise in the present world of Ethar,

that's where I am living, you could be considered a magical man because

of your great knowledge, and knowledge is power in this world and

thoughts carry the power of that knowledge. You will have to be careful

at first if you come with me." Even Shiheel did not know how prophetic

these words were, "You will have to study and work your knowledge

to see what kind of power you want to use. Be careful not to do things

that you don't want to do, think through the possible results of what you

introduce.

I will try to work closely with you and help you study the situation

at hand, and figure out what you can do. Unfortunately, I will not be

spending all my time with you, because I have much else to do. There is a

lot happening at this time, and though I see you as a key figure in helping

bring solutions to situations at hand, I also see that you need to be kept apart for a while, kept a secret. Your knowledge is great, but I must warn you, you may be affected by the passage between worlds in ways we don't yet understand. In passing through the portal, you will be passing through the barriers of time and dimension, and the energy fields that order the different universes. The only way for you to understand that power, is if you actually come with me and start studying how it works, and current events on Ethar. You might begin as a novice student to the ways on Ethar, not being familiar with the world around you and its ways, but I am sure it will take very little time for you to develop yourself into perfection. You are very apt at increasing your knowledge of new things and you work hard to keep building it. I'm sure you will have no problem building it a little further."

Eric sipped his coffee, he had always prided himself in his mental and physical development, his discipline, in working them to the best of his ability. He had a well fit body and a well fit mind. He had worked all the knowledge he could get his hands on and loved to work it. He had worked his body, he studied physical arts including the martial arts, and he was trained and disciplined. He had tried to master every weapon he could get instruction in. Knowledge was his soul purpose and pleasure in life.

Eric did not like the confidence this strange creature seemed to have, that he would return to this other strange world, a place that contradicted the line he knew between fantasy and reality. Eric like most people knew magic was not real, that fantasy was not truth. Fantasies were just games of the imagination, nothing of any real substance, a play performed in the minds of those who played it, sometimes shared with others. Fantasy was a game people played for fun escaping from reality. Now this, Shiheel, who was too fantastic to be real, was wanting him to go to a world where fantasy was reality, where reality was so different, he would have trouble accepting it as more than a game. His thoughts wandered. It was not so amazing that this creature would think he was willing to go, or that he was ready. That this creature suggested he lacked in knowledge or discipline offended him slightly, but he thought it wise not to say anything. Shiheel seemed to know a considerable amount about him and he knew very little about Shiheel personally, except it called itself an Eftite.

Then Shiheel spoke again almost like he was reading Eric's thoughts. "You may wonder why; I am so confident you are going to want to return with me. Well, that's a good question. I have looked at your life; I have been observing you for quite a while, during my development of the safe portal. You spend a large portion of your time developing and playing fantasy games in your world, getting others to play. You have made fantasy your way of life. You may find it intriguing to live out one of these fantasies. It is not as if it is not your choice, you will be able to return whenever you choose. I will give you an ankh that will open the portal to return you to your home at any time you wish. I warn you to be careful when you use it, that you don't do it at the wrong times. You don't need other things following you back or passing between worlds."

"Why should I want to go in the first place? What is there other than curiosity itself that would lure me to leave the comforts of my own world, to go into a world of uncertainty? Why should I even consider your proposition? How do I know I am not dreaming?" Eric asked, as he watched the way Shiheel's arm moved when he sipped the coffee, with wrapped intrigue. He wondered if this was a dream why he asked any of those questions, and why was his permission needed for his dream to take him to this new world.

Shiheel laughed again, this was amusing, as if curiosity were not enough. Shiheel knew Eric was simply trying to justify himself. Then he turned to Eric. "You like adventure. You'll want to live one, just think, when you are done, you can write a book, and nobody would believe it was true. It would be a springboard from which to write other stories. You could experience things to add to your games. It could become a source of personal profit. You will find ways to increase your wealth in your own world. I assure you that treasures you find are very real and you will be able to bring them back with you. They will be of great value. I am sure you will want to find out for yourself.

Haven't you wondered where the fantasies, legends and folktales of your world originated? There was a time when the pattern of movements of the two worlds overlapped in dimension and space. That is where much of the stories in your own world originated. There were changing passages between the two worlds, that some came upon by accident, and the results were fairy creatures passing into this world and men into Ethar. However, the natural passages no longer exist, and this snow storm is the result of the energy surges caused by establishing this portal. The energy surges were not anticipated and that problem has already been corrected. The storm will take care of itself with time, being passed off as a freak occurrence. You will be able to learn more of the history behind your own legends and fairy tales. You will be the first man in over fifteen hundred years to travel between worlds. I am sure you will find it quite thrilling, adventuresome, and want to go."

Eric found the idea, that fantasy and legend might have sound origin, quite intriguing. That they were not just concoctions of the imagination to explain the unknown was an amusing idea. He contemplated further debate for a few minutes, but he knew he would go. Indeed, he knew from the beginning his curiosity would dictate he go, that he wanted to know more. Curiosity was his real reason for wanting to go, the rest would just be added benefits. He was not ready to let Shiheel know his decision yet. He had to conceal his excitement. He also knew, if this was real and not a dream, his life would never be the same. He would never again be satisfied in his present limits, but he would not be limited again.

His thoughts went to Bonny. He thought about her finely chiseled lips and gentle caresses, and wondered what wise advice she would give him if she were here. He, Eric Marland, had met her shortly after his parents had died in an airplane crash, he had no ties to this world except for her. She was a very good friend. They both seemed to understand, that their relationship might never be more than it was now. If he was gone when she returned, which might take a while with this snow, she would worry about him. She would expect him to be back, she might have a problem if he never returned, but she would get through that. Besides he could come back whenever he wanted, and he would let her know what he was doing, maybe even ask her to join him. He would worry about that later though, there was no rush, she would have to make it home first. He thought about leaving that instant. He faced Shiheel and asked, "What would I need to take with me, if I did decide to go with you?"

"There may be many things you could wish to have with you, but I would suggest going first and then deciding what you want to retrieve afterward. There will be a warping of time, so you will be able to stay a month and return today if you like." Shiheel paused, "Why don't we go for a couple of days and let you see what it is you are getting involved with."

Eric knew he was going, but was struggling for a comfort level with the whole idea. "How can I know whether to trust you? How do I know you are not the evil force at work in this other world, causing whatever trouble might exist? The damage caused by your entrance into this world could just be evidence of your evil nature. You could be leading me into a trap, and I have no way of checking your credentials. If I should follow you blindly and you are doing this for evil purposes, then I would prove to be no less evil in my ignorance. What kind of assurance can you give me, that I am not stepping into an evil trap?" game or reality he was enjoying his part.

Shiheel sat there silently, lacking an answer, while Eric's

imagination went wild, envisioning this strange little alien reducing him to a little pile of ashes on his dining room floor. Eric's mind went through an endless series of possible scenarios of fictional disasters, before Shiheel answered. "I never considered that thought. The best I can do is just ask you to trust me." He paused before continuing, "If you don't, I will understand and leave you in peace."

Eric thought this is happening to fast, but he could not suppress the thrill of excitement and anticipation, "I will take a chance and work from the premise that you are not evil. Tell me though, what guarantees do I have that I am going to be able to get back?" In his mind Eric shook his head in disbelief of what he was saying and doing.

Shiheel handed him an ankh, gold on a gold chain and told him, "Hang this around your neck." Eric did so, then Shiheel added, "Picture your front door until you can see it in the ankh and rub the base of it."

Eric did as he was instructed, and found himself standing outside his front door, with the strange world at his back. He opened the door and came back in. Slightly dazed by the sudden displacement, but feeling pleased at the same time, he smiled at Shiheel. "Very well, I will go with you, at least to check it out, but tell me more about this portal. Does it stay open in your world, or can anyone see it and go through it?"

Shiheel looked directly at him, Eric could sense it and tell by the way he turned, facing him squarely with his entire body, "Yes, the portal will stay open, but not anyone will see it or be able to go through it. First you saw it because I was in it, now you see it because you have the ankh and it shows you. However virtually nobody else in your world will ever be able to see or know this end of the portal is here. When we get to Ethar, the ankh holds that end of the passage; no one else will know it is there, but you and I. Before we go there are a few things you will want. Do you have a good cowled cloak for weather protection and some of your weapons to carry? I will make you armor of chain mail and leather for protection. You are unfamiliar with our world and there are dangers you may encounter if you wander about."

Eric went and gathered the things that Shiheel had told him, to include a pile of trash, he said he would turn into armor by matter conversion. First Shiheel looked over the weapons and said, "These could use some improvement." A translucent blue beam spewed forth from the facet in the center of his forehead. He worked over the weapons for a few minutes, when he was done, they were all changed to a metallic appearance that matched Shiheel's natural body armor. Shiheel handed him back his sword and explained that it was now a composite, spun metal fiber, set with a frequency that was triggered by motion. It would aid in cutting and could now cut through stone. The only thing that could stop the edge was metal of the same sort. Shiheel went on to explain the effects on each of his implements.

Eric had selected his broad sword, a samurai sword, six daggers, six throwing stars, and a compound bow with eighteen arrows in a quiver, as the weapons he would take. Eric also chose a nine-millimeter pistol and six hundred rounds of ammo to go with it, but this weapon he had to explain to Shiheel. Shiheel made alterations on the pistol and ammo, before returning them. Then Shiheel went to work on the pile of trash and fitted Eric with harnessing for all his weaponry, a full coat of chain mail of the same strange metal substance, and leathers to completely cover the chain mail. Eric was quite impressed as he watched Shiheel work, with great speed and efficiency of motion.

Eric dressed fully and fitted his harnesses and weapons, with Shiheel's assistance. The only parts of his body that were not armor covered were his fingers, the bottoms of his feet and his face. He was amazed at how light and good everything felt. He felt totally unimpeded when he had it all on. He wrapped his cloak about the rest of it. His cloak was green with purple trim, his ancestral colors with his coat of arms on his right shoulder, a gold lion above crossed swords with a black background, over inscribed with the words 'Courage and Honor'. He looked in the full-length mirror they had in the hall and smiled at the image he saw.

He was anxious to begin. He was contemplating how he might be able to use his vast stores of knowledge and training, in this new world. He wondered how much of what he had developed in his computer games would apply in this strange world. He pondered Shiheel, a unique and intriguing character, one he was learning more about. A creature that spins metal the way a bee would spin a hive or a spider spin a web. The thought of how spinning metal could strengthen it was worth further consideration. The idea of setting frequencies to metal to make it more effective also had many possibilities. He wondered what effect these things would have on his bullets and gun, could they also go through steel and stone. Could frequency in metal help in medical fields like surgical tools? He needed to put his pondering on hold for now; he was on his way to start an adventure in another world.

They went to the door and Eric opened it, Shiheel passed through first, then Eric stepped through behind him. Going through the portal felt like passing through a wall of water that somehow flowed through Eric's body in waves, and left him with a quivering sensation. They stepped out into an unfamiliar and fantastic world. The energy from whatever they passed through felt like it was lingering and quivering within him, Eric figured it was just a residual after effect of the portal travel. Eric found himself walking on what appeared to be green lava rock, different from any rock he had ever seen before. He bent over and examined the rock for a few moments, concluding that it contained a large portion of copper and silver, oxidizing to give it color. He could not remember ever seeing green lava rock before, but the entire landscape around him seemed to be nothing but that. It was a very barren area, and the only sound he heard was from their fect on the porous rock, as he followed Shiheel, not knowing where he was going. This was Shiheel's world and the odd little guy led the way.

Shiheel knew that he was not affected by the transalteration portal, passing from one world to the other, but he did not know about Eric Marland. The barriers of time and dimension are very powerful and some believe they have their own intelligence. If it had not been for what Eric's knowledge could offer the south lands, he would not have even considered the risks of transalteration other than for himself. Eric would be able to help establish Talmorg's rule in many ways. Eric had a lot of knowledge, but what was more important was he could teach it. Eric had learned to apply his social, political and historical knowledge very extensively in his games and was versatile and adaptive in his application. He also understood warfare techniques that would help in the impending war that faced them from the north.

They walked down a small knoll, into a small hollow and entered a cave under an old lava flow, that Eric would have totally missed without his guide. Shiheel explained that the ankh also gave Eric the ability to see the entrance to this cave, no one else knew of its existence, nor could they see where it was if they were to walk right up to it. This was to be their secret also, and theirs alone. Eric wondered how many other secret caves Shiheel might have hidden around here. For the first time Eric wondered just who Shiheel was in the scheme of this world. He was still not even sure if he was good or evil. Eric did not believe he was evil or he might not have given him a way back. Shiheel was a mystery, peeking Eric's curiosity and keeping him on edge. Why had Shiheel gotten him so heavily armed and yet carried no arms himself, for that matter did not even wear clothes? Eric recognized that this creature did not really need anything and wondered what other powers might be held in that strange third facet in the middle of his head.

They passed through a small chamber and into a second that was like entering a huge laboratory. Shelves lined all the walls, filled with containers, books and tools, implements he recognized and those with no meaning to him. There were benches with various groupings of equipment set up on them, like something out of an old science fiction movie about a mad scientist. There seemed to be an endless maze of experiments strewn about a room the size of a couple of gymnasiums. Eric enjoyed the idea of puttering around in the likes of this laboratory, although to him everything seemed to be about six to eight inches low. Shiheel led him to the back, then passed a few doors and a couple of hallways to a room with a bed in it, with furs for blankets and pillows. Shiheel told him this was his room whenever he chose to stay here. Eric had no doubts that this was going to be an entirely different culture from his own.

Shiheel showed him to another room, "This is where I do most of my paper work, logging experiments and recording happenings. You may find the records kept here very interesting and amusing. The primary common language of this area is almost the same as your own. There are other languages in this world, you may or may not understand, some are of your world, some are not. I am amazed at how closely the languages have evolved, not all parallel worlds experience that. Here I keep all the records and writings that I have found throughout the lands.

My people have been here for less than five hundred years, so you will find little concerning us in the histories. This is also why we are not found in your own legends and fantasies; we have no common history.

This is the vastest library you will find in this world. I possess at least one copy of every known writing I have been able to discover, not that I have had a chance to read them all. Yet, I continue searching. There are still hidden histories and writings that are continuously discovered by adventurers who explore the remains of past cultures and civilizations. In many ways you will find this a primitive world and culture, yet there are things you will appreciate, such as chivalry, romance and honor, lost in many ways to your own society." Shiheel paused and turned to Eric, "What is mine is yours, the next room over is the kitchen. You will find all you need there. I know you probably have a lot of questions, but I am running late for an appointment. I must leave; I will be back in the morning. In the mean time you have free run of my home."

Eric was flabbergasted, and did not have time to recover before Shiheel had slipped past him and was gone. He felt somewhat ridiculous, standing now alone in this strange place. He now knew how Alice felt with that darned rabbit. He had a lot to think through and the portal left him feeling hungry. He was going to find out what he could, but he decided it would be more comfortable on a full stomach.

Why had he been brought here? Why was he fully armed if he was going to be in a safe domestic location? Why did Shiheel have to leave so suddenly? Food would help him think more clearly.

*   *   *   *   *   *   *

He yearned to prove himself. Mistav was a warrior by heart, but most Wonks were warriors. Wonks were their own race some said an evolutionary descendant from Elves, but both races would disclaim the relation. Their bodies naturally took on the colors and patterns from their backgrounds making them hard to see if you do not know they are there. They grew webbing from their arms and legs similar to flying squirrels that allowed them a decrease in falling speed and some gliding control. The webbing also allowed them to conceal any clear form when they laid flat on the ground.

As a people, Wonks tended to be very egotistical and quarrelsome making it hard for them to unite forming anything bigger than small tribes, constantly fighting amongst each other. Mistav wanted the position of leader of his tribe, and to get a bid at the position he was going to have to do something to prove his courage. He chose to enter into the Lost City of Death and his bravery would keep him alive and he would come back with proof and gain leadership of his tribe.

No one had ever returned form the city and the trail he followed was littered with the bones of those people and creatures who had entered too far in. The deadly gases seemed to have dissipated. As he got deeper into the city the remains seemed to still have more than just bones left behind. Mistav entered the building that seemed to the focus of the city. He could smell the remnants of the fumes of the poisonous gas.

The longer he was there the more he saw shadows moving out of the corners of his eyes and voices whispered in his mind. He pulled some items from the skeleton on the throne. He took a ring, a sword and an amulet, these would be the beginning of his journey to power. The voices told him he was unstoppable. He climbed his way back out of the city unknowingly leaving his sanity behind.

CHAPTER 02

Trouble to the North

The Walled City of Talmorg had stood for over fifteen hundred years, not that the Elves could ever boast of their stonework, next to the Dwarves. It had needed repairs many times and, on several occasions, the Dwarven folk had been kind enough to help, in exchange for favors the Elves had done for them. The city was named after the son of Bracken Elkinshane, Talmorg, who later became the father of Erron and Elron. The original building of the city was finished years before the last recorded contact with Earth. The population of the city grew and several groups moved farther to the east, to set up other centers of society. These Elven societies welcomed the peoples of other races to join them, and help in the growth and development of their cities. The Walled City of Talmorg maintained the status of being the greatest cultural center among the kingdoms and lordships of the south.

There was a period of time that passed, years of harsh weather, after which, skirmishes over land and borders started taking place. Years of wars and distrust followed, allies could not be trusted and Talmorg became the only city without the serious problems of racial schisms. The peoples of Talmorg were proud of their city, and the harmony of life they symbolized. Their city was the symbol of the unity of the races. It was during this period of time that the Eftites arrived. They earned their right to become a part of the society at Talmorg, by repairing the stonework to better condition than its original construction. The stonework of the Walled City of Talmorg became the envy of even the most skilled of Dwarves. The Eftites proved to be a great asset to the city in many other ways also. It became their new home.

The city of Talmorg became known for the Eftites and their magic, and their invincibility in battle. With the passage of time, the city of Talmorg became relied upon to settle skirmishes between other lordships, no matter what races were involved. Talmorg was looked upon as the arbitrator of conflicts, and made reference to as the high prince when such matters came up. Talmorg passed his rule on to his son, Erron, not long before his death. King Erron maintained a stable rule, peaceful and prosperous for his city. Eventually, Erron called for a counseling of all the lords of the southlands, to attempt to establish boundaries and spare lives, it became known as, the First Council of the Lords of the Southlands. It was at this council that Elron, Erron's younger brother and Malina Kelch, his wife, were granted some uninhabited lands, farther east, to start their own province. Some years later Erron had a son by his wife, Constance, who was named after his grandfather, Talmorg. Talmorg II was raised with the Eftites as a part of his society, they were his friends, and he grew with wisdom and became a great diplomat. He was famed throughout the south for being just and fair in judgment, and started to be called upon, like his grandfather, to arbitrate disputes, by other lordships.

The red-haired elf, in all of his proud five-foot two stature was pacing the stone floor. Talmorg was the Elven crowned prince, in line to his father's throne, the king, Erron Elkinshane, king of the western Elves. He had been given the responsibility of setting up the council meeting for the unified defense of the southlands. He had sent message of intent and invite to all the scattered kingdoms and lordships west of the Torak River. He also sent a message to the Dwarven city of Darkolon, far to the east, explaining what they were doing and suggesting they do the same, east of the Torak. Talmorg had been to the Dwarven city of Darkolon, a few times and discussed the future of the southlands with them, how their plans would benefit all the south. The messages he sent out, had been almost all answered within two weeks. The unified defense had multiple purposes. The most obvious at present was, protection from the northern tribes, Wonks, Nobs, Trolls, and Praks, primarily. The second purpose would be to protect the roads, between the kingdoms and lordships, from brigands and bandits, to allow safe travel and trade. The third and less supported purpose, would be to settle land disputes by council, rather than warfare, though these skirmishes had already been greatly reduced, by the establishment of political communication.

Dragoncove, the northern coastal city of men, was sending Hanser Schultzmann, the head of their defense council, with the binding authority of an ambassador. They were expected to come, it was to their advantage, they had been suffering the longest from raids by the Wonks, the nomad tribes of the deserts. The dwarves of Vorka had sent a message back, but the courier never made it. Prince Ashkin, himself, arrived yesterday though, Vorka also suffered from random encounters with tribal raiding parties. The flat land province of Harmosk sent Brask Scaller, second in command of their unified forces, which Talmorg was proud to have helped establish, to represent all six kingdoms of Darka, Zarco, Gorch, Tarsha, Prabish and Narcal. Gorch was a city of men, Narcal was gnomes, but the rest were elven. Talmorg remembered the forming of the province, he had played a strong part in its conception and birth, he was expecting their support and planned on using their success as support for the larger scale unification. The dwarves of Dargen and Morbin sent, Arnk, a scribe without any authority. They did not feel it was a matter of their serious concern, but did not want to miss out on what was going on. In part they felt slightly threatened by the idea and did not feel their men, should be used in battles that did not concern them directly. Berkin, the home of the stone giants, sent Keltook, chief warrior, who reported that the Dwarves of Darvin would not be there, but might send a token force for the unified defense, if it was established.

Azeel had come from Efra and reported that the crowned princess, Saphrine Barhallah, would be following later, to discuss other matters of state. Freebic Elkinshane, crowned prince of Elkinshire, Talmorg's cousin, had been intended as their ambassador, but had not yet arrived. The elves of the south land already looked at Talmorg as the high prince and would endorse his proposal on that traditional basis alone; in essence they have always been one Elven kingdom. The pixies of the Forest of Dreams had not responded, but that was expected, they had always stayed isolated from everyone. The council was supposed to meet tomorrow morning, but

Shiheel was supposed to meet with Talmorg at midday and he was already an hour late. They were going to review tomorrow's agenda and Shiheel had mentioned the possibility of a surprise that could be of great benefit to the unification. Talmorg trusted Shiheel and turned to him quite often for sound counsel. Shiheel also seemed to be able to find any information that Talmorg wanted and seemed to know whenever trouble was brewing anywhere in the kingdom and usually outside it also.

There was a knock at the study door. As he turned his aid, Gaib, an older Elf and longtime friend of the family, was standing at the door, "Prince Freebic has arrived, sire."

"See to his accommodations, he is family remember. I will go meet him. Maybe, Shiheel will arrive before I get back." He had hoped it was Shiheel, but it would be good to see his cousin again. Talmorg quickly checked his cloths to make sure they were in order. After adjusting his doublet and cape he headed out of the study.

Talmorg walked through the halls of the castle, the ceiling in the hallways were high enough to accommodate giants when they chose to visit giving them an expansive roomy feeling to most other races. The doors and side passages varied in size, some obviously not intended for anyone larger than an Elf. The great wooden double doors at the end of the hall were propped open to a landing and steps spilling down to the outer court. Passing by various groups standing or sitting in conversation around the garden of stone artwork he continued out the main entry way. These were the halls he was raised in, his home and place of learning.

Talmorg shared a lot of good memories with his cousin Freebic. The two of them had gone through training together, or at least Freebic went through training with Talmorg as his senior, though Talmorg was five years younger than his cousin. Five years was not considered much time to an Elf whose average life span was in the range of fifteen hundred years so by most Talmorg and Freebic were thought of as being the same age. Talmorg's cousin also spent six years as Erron's squire, though that did not seem to keep him out of mischief. Freebic was also irresponsible, always off on some adventure somewhere, instead of tending to affairs of state. Talmorg had gotten into trouble with Freebic on several occasions. Erron told him, Elron was the same way in his youth, that Freebic was a spitting image of his father. As Talmorg stepped out, Freebic rode up. Flaming red hair flying back, as he rode with a party of six Elven guards.

Talmorg started the formal greeting, "Welcome, Prince Freebic, to the house of Erron Elkinshane......"

"By the thunder of the mother, cousin, you've put on some build in the past five years." Freebic yelped, as he swung down off the saddle of his horse, before it had come to a full stop and was at Talmorg's side in a couple of springs. Freebic had a lot of respect for His cousin, Talmorg, but he did not like to show too much of it. He admired his diplomatic skill and respect for responsibility. "You've been training, protocol aside, we're family." he said, throwing his arm around Talmorg. "You'll have to take me to the training grounds, when we're done and show me what you've learned." he paused with a laugh, "I've been told this unified defense is your idea too. Good idea, I have to admit, but how'd ya think of it?" with a clap on Talmorg's shoulder he gestured toward the entrance, "How's Uncle Erron, cuz?"

He looked into his cousin's strong commanding face, characteristic of their family and the sea green eyes which belonged to all Elves. He noted how slight a change would be needed to make Freebic's mischievous smile to an outright evil one. Talmorg chose to answer the last question first, "Father does well, though he is starting to show signs of age and is turning more of his responsibility over to me. We will talk later however, I too, desire to know the welfare of Elron's clan. First though go and refresh yourself from your journey. I'll be in fathers' study; I am waiting for Shiheel."

"That little outlander, don't trust anything too small. Comes from knowing them blasted pixies down our way, can't trust them for anything, but pranks. I'll stop by the study shortly." With another healthy slap on the shoulder, Freebic took off one way and Talmorg headed back to the study, wondering how much the pixies had rubbed off on Freebic.

Shiheel was leaning over one of the tables examining some maps that were rolled out, when Talmorg stepped back into the study. Shiheel was wearing his usual dark brown, hooded robe and had his back to the door. His small stature always seemed to make his surroundings look larger or give the impression he was a child.

"Well, glad to see you could finally make it!" Relief was evident in his voice, as Talmorg stepped up next to the little alien, he had come to trust and think of as a friend, "We should have been finished hours ago," he exaggerated, "but no matter, what have we got?" Talmorg figured Shiheel must have come in through the window again, since he had not passed him in the hall and Gaib did not announce him. Shiheel had tried to explain to him once how he could weave light tight enough to walk on, but it was easiest to think of it as a form of magic. Shiheel always denied he knew magic when it was brought up, but to Talmorg like most, much of what the Eftite did, like using light to communicate was no less than a form of magic.

"It appears, that Mistav, has found a way of uniting the Wonk tribes. About three months ago, Mistav went into the ancient city of Tarf to prove his courage to his tribe. He came out again with a ring, a sword and an amulet. From the research I have done, I believe I know, what they are. All three are runes of great power, the Sword of Power, the Ring of Command, and the Shield of Darkness, forged in the fires of the death pits, about twenty-one hundred years ago, by Deassheema, himself."

"It has been inevitable, that the threat from the northern tribes would increase one way or another. I had suspicions that the tribes might unite," Talmorg interjected, knowing from experience that was almost the only way to get a word in, when Shiheel got going, "But Tarf is filled with the deadly gases of the Death Pits, which is what killed Deassheema. How could Mistav have survived?" As he finished, he placed the fingers of his right hand in the crook of his left elbow, as he placed his left index finger to his lips in thought.

"The tunnel connecting the Death Pits to the lowest dungeons in the city, apparently caved in and the gas has since cleared sufficiently. I would guess the cave-in happened about five years ago. The city is still not safe to inhabit, but a brief visit is survivable. The levels of toxic gas will not leave a visitor untainted though; low levels cause mental instability, possible insanity. Mistav is using the magic of the runes to unite the Wonks. He has control of about half the tribes and they are driving south at a slow, but steady pace. The increased raids of the south lands have been by the southern wonks, for provisions and weapons to fight Mistav. As you know, the Wonks are proud warriors, too proud to ask for the help they need it." Shiheel paused, "I would estimate we have about three weeks before Mistav reaches Dragoncove, and I doubt he will be satisfied with just the conquest of the Wonks."

"That would only give us three weeks to gather a defensive force." Talmorg jumped in, stepping over to examine the map spread out on the table. His agreement was evident in his voice; he knew from history; corrupt power was usually accompanied by an insatiable lust for more power. He had also come to trust Shiheel's perceptions and knew he was a totally reliable source of information, even though his father did not. "It is a week's march from here and other than Vorka. We are the closest significant help Dragoncove can hope for. How big an army will we be standing against when we get there?" He supported himself with his left hand as he leaned further over the table, studying the map with his right hand. He noted the limits of possible engagement areas along the

Feather River. The Pengona forests were quite thick and the landscape was extremely jagged in that region. It would be a good place to lay in wait for an enemy, not so good for a mobile attack force.

"Mistav will have a force of between thirty-five and fifty thousand, when he reaches Dragoncove. His army grows with each conquest. With that ring, he has no prisoners, just new recruits. Dragoncove has a standing defense of just over two thousand and maybe another three thousand that can be called to arms. Of course, if it comes down to the defense of the city itself, and the women and children stand in its defense..."

Again, Talmorg interrupted, turning to face Shiheel, "The best we could mobilize on time would be just over thirty-five hundred. Tomorrow we will find out who will stand with the unified defense. Are you sure you will not be able to make it, and counsel with us?"

"I will try to make it. There is much more at stake now than there appeared to be before. If I do, I will be bringing a stranger with me and he will be included in your council."

"Accepted." Talmorg stroked his chin with thought, wondering who this stranger might be and where Shiheel was bringing him from. "This could rearrange our agenda for tomorrow. It will have to take precedence over our political arrangements. We need to take care of the present defense of the south lands from a common threat. We can worry about political unity when we are secure again from any major common threat. One more thing, Shiheel, what is the surprise, you were going to tell me about. I hope the possible invasion, wasn't, what you were figuring would help with the unification of our defenses, not that it will hurt my

arguments any."

"Actually, the stranger I am bringing is the surprise. He has a

vast quantity of knowledge and understanding that will be quite useful

in helping you to establish your goals. Originally I was going to review

everything with him and give you his views on matters, but once I

discovered what the Wonks were up to, I thought it best to bring him in

person. I was going to bring him to you as an adviser in private, but events

preclude privacy."

"I take it that is why you will be bringing him with you tomorrow

than." Talmorg looked back to the map on the table, "I hope his,

knowledge, can work magic on this predicament we're facing now. If the

attacking force was only double ours, the dependability of the area would

work to our advantage, but these odds are unreasonable." He doubted

anyone could pull out a quick fix to this problem; even the hope of success

was rather dismal at the moment.

"I must go now, until tomorrow."

"Tomorrow."

Shiheel turned and was gone, leaving a trail of a vaporizing

rainbow behind him as he walked back out the window.

Talmorg stood in silence, watching his enigmatic friend walk

out on the path of woven light, cloaked in an intentional air of mystery,

concealing the friend he knew from the world around him. It still looked

like magic no matter what Shiheel said it was. He would have to tell the representatives and delegates, from the other lordships, the extent of the danger at tonight's banquet. He had been working long and hard on a peaceful uniting of the south land kingdoms, now he just hoped they were not too late in uniting their defenses.

"Where's the outlander runt?" Freebic entered the room with his unavoidable presence.

Talmorg turned and acknowledge Freebic's arrival. His insolence and blatant disregard for protocol irritated Talmorg, but Talmorg's diplomatic experience allowed him to overlook it. Freebic was family though and Talmorg realized he could be doing it just because it irritated him. "He is Gone already, though I would like you to come with me now, to audience with the king."

"Indeed cuz, I carry with me my father's greetings to uncle Erron. Tell me there, why the solemn mood. I'd think ya'd be joyous at the coming occasion, the unifying of defenses, even if all don't quite agree with ya." Freebic mocked, with all his respect for Talmorg, never could appreciate how he was always worried about something, even when nothing was wrong. "Ya just need ta loosen up a bit, cuz."

"I have received bad news and hope that the unification is not too late." Talmorg seemed slightly lost in thought.

"Here with, it can't be that bad now, little cuz."

Talmorg filled Freebic in as they work their way through the corridors, leaving the family area of the palace.

"Announce us." Talmorg told one of the royal guards at the door, and followed him into the throne room. After the formal greetings and Freebic's exchange of family information with Erron, Talmorg recited to his father the news he had received.

"Talmorg," Erron began, admiring his son's proud stature, with great compassion in his eyes, "This, is indeed ill-fated news. We have worked long and hard to establish peace, and so have the other lords of the south. I do not see that we can accomplish anything tonight, so this matter can wait until the council meeting tomorrow. We shall let the lords of the lands have this, one banquet, in peace."   Erron thought back, he remembered, battles fought like trivial feudal lords, fighting over areas of rock and dirt. He thought about all the treaties he had seen signed and the ones he had seen broken. He also saw the diminishing of the ability of the races in the south to use magic. It was as if the Ancients had deserted them, but he knew it was because they no longer lived near their Adomas. Their power was the power of the land, and that power was in the Adoma. It worried him some though, because magic was the best defense against magic, and Erron did not trust the learned magic as much as he would those that were by the nature of the race. He still had uneasy feelings, about the Eftites, and how Shiheel chose to be a self-appointed counselor to Talmorg. He had trouble trusting the strange outlander's guidance. He did not trust Shiheel's motives; he had no idea what they were. Yet the Eftites had proved themselves over and over, to be both honorable and honest, especially Shiheel, who seemed to always have the good of the kingdom in mind. He felt old; soon it would be time to pass his crown to

Talmorg, who could rule without having the misgivings and doubts of the past, to burden his decisions.

Talmorg was not exactly happy with his father's decision to keep what was happening silent until tomorrow. He felt it was not honest, yet he understood the wisdom behind it. Talmorg had a very sober expression as he and Freebic started down the hall.

"Perk up cuz, it's not as if your pet gerpin just died. Yes, the problems are serious, but they can rest until tomorrow. A peaceful dinner tonight, will be hard enough, to keep, without worrying about the shadows of tomorrow."

"Where do you get the idea you can give sound advice, after flippantly wasting your life until now?" Talmorg jeered Freebic.

"By the mother's thunder, listen to you, cuz, all pouty around the face. Here I make you smile and you go and accuse me of getting serious." Freebic chuckled and slapped an arm around Talmorg's shoulders, "We've got a bit a' time til dinner, let's go show me what you've learned, in the training fields and don't think that being an inch taller than me gives you any advantage."

"You couldn't handle me before, what makes you feel any tougher now, you been wrestling with some wacky bushes lately." Talmorg looked at Freebic with a smirk, "I have some smoke, to clear out of my thoughts anyway."

*   *   *   *   *   *   *

The Shadow Realms were out of reach from detection, but Darval could feel it when his keep was raised back up out of the mountains. If someone has the power to raise the keep, they can have it. He was passed having any claim to things on the world of Ethar. He brought the Dark Council here and they have their own world to play with. At best he owes his followers one return visit to offer them to come to the shadow realms.

Curiosity tug at him though, who would have the power to raise that keep. Even if they had the power, no one on Ethar should want to raise up his keep and what it symbolizes. He was the leader of the Dark Council who opposed the signing of the agreement that brought peace to the world of Ethar. The Ancients surrendered their authority to rule over to the people.

He could feel them walking the halls like three giant bugs. It did not matter who had the keep, he did not care. Ethar was no longer his home. The new world they were creating was their home now. They did not have to answer to the Old Ones for what they did or did not do. Darval could remember back when the Ancients treated the races as pawns in their games in the times before they knew, or understood the races they made were as living and sentient as they were. Ancients pit their work against each other causing wars and destruction all as competition in a game.

The day came when in a meeting of Ancients several members asked the question and it was quickly revealed that these games were wrong. Many realized the races were living beings with the potential of becoming as evolved as the Ancients themselves. Instead of making things better the wars got even worse as Ancients took a stand for their people. It got so bad that the Ancients and their off spring started dying in these wars.

The Old Ones stepped in and gathered the Ancients and their leader explained that they came to this world to set up a utopia without the violence of the world they came from. There had been dissension in their ranks and not all of them had been in agreement. They had presented the Ancients with a proposal to step back and take a less direct involvement in the affairs of the races. The idea was to see if the races could find ways of working things out themselves.

The Old Ones seemed on the verge of destroying everything and starting over, but the more powerful faction wanted to give the new races a chance to prove their worth. A third of the Old Ones departed the meeting to go and make their own worlds elsewhere convinced they could do a better job on their own. Darval secretly formed the Dark Council from among the dissenting Ancients, while Gaharias his brother and most powerful of the ancients worked with Drakalon the leader of the Old Ones to convince the rest to sign an agreement that could lead to a peaceful acceptance of the races ruling themselves with the guidance of the Ancients.

Darval wondered if the Dark Council was following the same path as the old ones did when they first came to Ethar. Even if they were, perhaps they could learn from the mistakes that had been made and it was their right to try. Unlike the Old Ones they were not starting a new world with the preconceived notion that they would be able to do better than the world they came from, just the hope that they would. Either way they were no longer interested in going back to the affairs of Ethar.

*   *   *   *   *   *   *

The great banquet hall was filled with the rumble of voices as he walked in. Talmorg smiled as he looked around. The Dwarves were the easiest delegations to locate, if he had not already known were everyone was to be seated. Dwarves and humans were almost the only ones who smoked, but the Dwarves by far smoked more than any other race. The smoke was like dark heavy clouds over where they were seated. The fragrance, however filled the air with the sweetness of the deep forest flowers, whose buds, leaves and petals, they smoked in their massive ornate pipes. Talmorg wondered if those pipes were why the Dwarves laughed so much. There were not a lot of Dwarves in the western parts of the south lands and though their loyalties were not as strong as Elven loyalties, they all traced their ancestry back to the Borken Mountain Dwarves, with great pride. The south land Dwarves also looked to the city of Darkalon, for guidance from the high Dwarven prince of the south. The city of Darkalon was named after the Old One, the dragon who showed favor to the Dwarves in the past. Those Dwarves that were here in the east rarely communicated with the city of Darkalon.

The next table to catch Talmorg's eye, was that of the stone giants, simply by their sheer size they stood out. Giants through legend and history, always communed well with Elves, being gentle lovers of the natural elements. They were also known for keeping to themselves as much as they could. There were many races of giants, from sea giants to storm giants, but the only ones here were stone giants. Talmorg knew that their loyalty was to their integrity and that of their tribe. Unlike humans who give their loyalty to causes, principles or anything else that will please their ego, giants do not care what others see or think of them. In actuality they went through meticulous care in dealings with others, to maintain their order of priority of integrity, their environment, their tribe, then others. Not all giants are good; however, the corrupt are exiled from their tribes.

Talmorg laughed to himself, with all the loyalties of traditions, he decided the best allies were probably, human. They may not have strong loyalties as a whole, but individually, their friendship can be stronger than their loyalties. A good human might break a bargain, with a friend, for what he thinks is a higher call to right, but still stand by you, in friendship. It is not that they are without the loyalties other races have, but free will holds a higher priority with humans. Humans would literally fight for the right to destroy their own lives with mistakes, rather than subject themselves outside the bounds of their own understanding of justice. There is no telling what other factors may come into play with human justice. Talmorg felt he learned a lot of his own temperance from dealing with humans.

Talmorg walked over and took his place, at the head table. He would be seated at the right side of his father, and his mother would be on his father's left. His mother, Constance Farber Elkinshane, had resigned most of her queenly duties over to her daughters; age was leaving its mark on her. Her presence still brought joy to any who were graced by her. She was still filled with the gentle magic of an Elven queen. He had barely enough time to sit, before his parents were announced and he had to stand again, with the rest of the assembly.

Upon reaching his place at the table, Erron lifted up his wine goblet, "I pose a toast, to unity and prosperity for the south lands, may we establish lasting bonds, and prove to all that the races can live together in harmony." After a returned bellow from his audience, everyone downed their drinks and sat down. The banquet had a festive atmosphere of anticipation and Talmorg did his best to be in good spirits, but stayed quiet for the most part, keeping his ill-fated news to himself, until the mornings meeting. He mused the evidence of secret communications between various groups in the assembly, after tomorrow's news, covert inner plans would lose their significance, at least for a time.

Freebic was seated across the table from Talmorg, he had found the afternoon bout with him quite exhilarating and chose to converse with him, to avoid thinking about tomorrow. "You gave me quite the run for it, 'cuz', I must be getting lazy for you to come that close to beating me at training games."

Freebic looked up with a vicious smirk, "And I thought a few small victories would take your mind off your work for a bit. Too bad I wasn't really giving an effort. You'd a lost a chip or two."

"Maybe, at table games in a pub. On second thought maybe I just got bored into sloppiness at your simplistic, slow tactics, but don't feel too bad, you did get one hit in, when you had to wake me up."

"Wake you up, you mean from your state of stunned shock at my display of speed and movement before we got started."

"Your right there, I was shockingly stunned that anyone that sloppy and slow would consider challenging me."

The banter went back and forth for a time, until, King Erron interrupted, "Tell me, young Freebic, how has the harvest been so far this year, in Elkinshire?"

"Thus far, sire, it has been better than usual, we might be actually trading some east. Rumor has it they are still suffering some shortages."

"They have not cultivated much of their land yet." Talmorg added in, "There is still a lot of feuding within the higher lordships Darbish, had three land disputes within their boundaries, in the past year." The Elven idea of cultivating the land was more to encourage greater natural production of what they needed and used from their environment, maintaining a balance of the land around them was more important than forcing it to produce volumes of preferred crops.

"Well, anything we can trade to them that can help relieve pressure or encourage peace, is good." King Erron went on, "It is good if we can build trade in any direction. Harmosk, has initiated trade with Prak rovers, apparently, they agree it is easier than scavenging the land. Harmosk is also gaining cultural insight from the exchange."

"Not to mention it has helped cut down on the Prak raids." Freebic snickered, "and from what I hear those rovers can't be trusted either. They will steal from you, whilst they got you looking at their trading goods."

"Be careful there, cousin Freebic," Talmorg interrupted, "don't let a few isolated incidents give you a bias against an entire people, group, or vocation."

"He is right you know, Freebic. We need to acknowledge the difference between individuals and groups. There are even among us those who do dark deeds, would you like to be judged according to their works?" Erron leaned back in his seat, "We would welcome any Prak that chose to move into our city, even help them find a job if need be. If a Prak tribe wanted to join a unified south, I should think we would welcome them, and count them among our peers."

"You are right sire, for the same reasons we should not let our personal bias effect how we think of them outlander runts either." Freebic stated after taking another swig from his goblet, knowing Erron didn't trust the Eftites any more than he did. "I shall strive to evaluate and reconsider my judgment of these things, my Lord."

At Freebic's answer, King Erron sank into thought, considering his own judgement of the Eftites. His son it seems honors the principles of the kingdom better than he has. Yes, soon he would pass on his crown.

CHAPTER 03

Sister City

Many years ago, Kent Barhallah left the Uklian on a journey with Talmorg Elkinshane, taking their wives and followers with them. They were moving to settle in a new land, no one remembers exactly why, but they went. They would fare well, the Elkinshanes had the magic of the power of the land and the Barhallahs had the magics of the elements and healing. Talmorg would be the ruler of their peoples, and Kent would be their high priest. The south lands at the time were uninhabited and the Elves spread themselves out in the various flat lands and forests building their homes and forming centers of social activities. At the time, they did not have to define their land and they welcomed any, who wanted to join in their new society. They would show the world the benefits of a society of mixed races and how they could work together, taking advantage of each other's abilities to compliment the functioning of their society. By taking advantage of the best skills of each race, they hoped to reap the benefits of each society also.

Kent established the center of worship, and called it Efra, or spirit of the Elves. With time Efra grew as a place of worship and other races started coming there to commune with their Ancients. As the needs of the people grew, Efra grew to become a city and center of other activities, and separate temples were built for the different Ancients. Efra became known as a place of peace and tranquility. With the growth of the city, the people of Efra turned to Kent for leadership, titling him as the lord of Efra, and laid at his feet the responsibilities befitting the title. During the times of trouble in the south lands, Efra by separation from the other Elven cities with all the feudal warring, became a kingdom unto itself yet remained a place of peace and tranquility. Efra was also a place where any could seek sanctuary and start a new life, as long as they abode by the laws, once they were there.

The peoples of Efra cultivated the land and sought trouble with no one. As a result of being a city of refuge, the kingdom of Efra experienced great growth during the times of turmoil and Kent's title of lord was changed again by the people to king. This was the first time in Elven history that a high priest held the title, king and it was accepted by Gaharias, the Ancient of the Elves. Gaharias gave a great day of celebration to all the Elves of the south lands, in the year thirty six, forty eight, when he crafted a crown for the lord of Efra. The Elves though separated later by boundaries, lordships and kingdoms, remained at heart, one kingdom. Even when Elron later set up the kingdom of Elkinshire, allegiance, even Elron's, as with Kent, continued to be with the city of Talmorg. That was just the way of the Elves, an unswerving loyalty. Efra being the spiritual center of the south land Elves and was exemplary in their loyalty, to Elven ways.

As time passed, Kent passed his crown on to his son, Berkas, who followed in his father's footsteps. His kingdom being at peace, prospered during its entire existence and developed, the greatest among its peers in the finer arts of healing, cultivating, painting, sculpting and other peaceful

endeavors. Their farm lands extended from the foothills to the coast, yet

they continued to share it with the animals of the land. The wildlife was

free to feed in the farmlands and when the Elves needed they fed on the

wildlife. They strove not just to be at peace with the rest of the peoples

of the south land, but with nature also. They also enjoyed controlled

harvesting from the ocean, to supplement their diets. Berkas took pride

in Efra and its peoples, only he never had a son by his wife Tamaria, but

rather had fifteen daughters. He was still proud of the daughters he did

have, and trained several of them, as though they had been sons, so that if

he needed to, he could name one his successor.

King Berkas looked out his study window, over the city of Efra.

Saphrine was doing a wonderful job with the responsibilities he had given

her and the people of Efra did not question the status, he had given her

as their next regent. The idea that the high priest would be succeeded by

a priestess, though never done before in known Elven history, seemed

to be taken also, without alarm. Gaharias had not let him know, one way

or the other, if she would be accepted. Some of the ways of the Ancients

had been lost to them, knowledge that had not been learned, yet, by Kent

when he left the Uklian. Berkas wondered if he had missed something

when he offered Saphrine, but in the past Gaharias had been patient with

them and let them know where they had lost knowledge. Was it possible

he had offended the ancient, by offering his eldest daughter, instead of his

brother's son? He had checked with them first, but none of them wanted the job, they lacked the background and training for it and preferred to take other positions in the responsibilities of the temple. To each of them Gaharias had shown his acceptance of the position they had taken, leaving Berkas only his daughters to choose from for a successor. It had crossed his mind that it was possible, Gaharias wanted him to split the priesthood from the lordship, but Gaharias seemed to be avoiding the subject. He knew Gaharias had not abandoned them, because they still communed on other matters.

Tomorrow Saphrine would be leaving for a period of time, to tend to her first official business outside of the kingdom. Berkas knew in actuality it was just an academic matter, and he hoped she was ready to attend to matters of negotiation. Regardless he knew it would be a good experience for her, to start to see how big the world around them really was. She had wanted to go to the council at Talmorg, but he could not allow that. He did not believe she was ready to deal with the lack of respect she would get as a female reagent. He also felt she needed to work her way up to negotiating under circumstances of such magnitude. Dinner tonight would be his last chance to give her any words of advice, the only difficulty with that was he felt fresh out of advice, and he was more worried about her role as a priestess, than that of a diplomat or reagent. He turned from the window, thinking to himself, *I still have a few things to tend to myself at the temple today before dinner time.*

Saphrine walked in to the family dining hall, and took her place on the right side of her father, King Berkas, across from her mother, Tamaria.

Her mother gave her a proud look as she took her seat. "Good evening mom and dad, what's for dinner. I'm starved."

"Sit down and mind your manners, sis." Narcia piped up with a smile. Narcia was the family's second daughter, and like the rest of the family proud of her older sister. "This may be the privacy of our family, but good manners are always in fashion, even when formality isn't"

"Who told you that rubbish, worm?" Saphrine laughed, taking her seat, intentionally bumping her sister.

"You did." Narcia fluttered her eyes innocently.

"That will be enough, girls. Let's have a civilized dinner this evening. I know this is your only time to cut loose and not worry about what you say or do, but it is also one of the chances we have to get together as a family." Berkas looked over his clan of blond-haired daughters with a smile.

"Yes dear, this is true and our oldest is going to be leaving us for a while, in the morning." Tamaria looked directly at Saphrine, "You have made your father and I very proud and our best wishes will be with you all the way."

"Oh mom, I have only done according as you guys have raised me. I am no more of a credit, then my sisters." Saphrine looked down the table at the rest of her sisters, involved in their own conversations. As she bit into the drumstick from the pheasant on her plate, she turned back, looking at her parents, "Besides, Narcia seems to take to the priesthood more naturally than I do and with Efra continuing to grow, I will need the help of all my sisters to keep order."

"This is true Saph, but you are the oldest and have the highest of responsibility. That reminds me, I would like to see you for a few minutes after dinner in the study." King Berkas told her, taking a swig of wine to wash down his last mouthful. Unlike Elven leaders where leadership was passed frequently to one of the younger sons, the head of priesthood by tradition was always passed to the eldest.

"Very well, dad, but you worry too much." she blew him a kiss, as she dipped her fingers in the finger bowl and wiped them off.

Tamaria shook her head slightly, with a deep sigh, "We only worry, because we love you, honey." She started to reach her hand gently across the table to her daughter as if to caress her check, but pulled it back not wanting to embarrass her. "Make sure you double check your personal things before you go to bed tonight. Dad said Narcia would be taking care of your domestic duties while you were gone."

"I am sure she will do the job just as well as I ever have, after all we do have the same parents and training." Saphrine smiled at Narcia, reaching over and roughing her hair a little. "She has also seen some of the mistakes I have made."

"I can try to make mistakes that are original." Narcia laughed, poking Saphrine in the ribs forcing her to pull her hand back. "I know we are all going to miss Saphrine while she's gone. By the way this pheasant is exceptionally good tonight; I must remember to compliment the cooks. Do the rest of you agree?"

"It is good, I at least agree." Saphrine nodded, cleaning her mouth with her napkin. "I understand that four of my traveling companions are new to the royal guard, is that wise?"

"If they hadn't proved themselves," Berkas said, sipping his wine, having finished eating, "They would not be Royal guard. Actually, being new they might be younger, and have better stamina, who knows," he said with a wink, "you might even find one you like."

"Oh Berky, the children are growing up fast enough on their own, you don't have to go trying to be a match maker too. They will all marry and start their own families too soon as it is." Tamaria said, as she backhanded him on the shoulder. "Saphrine, don't forget to ask Freebic how my sister, Malina is doing while you are there, and remember to give our highest regards to all the members of the Elkinshane family." She smiled thinking back to the day her sister Malina had married Elron and they had gone off with a small following and set up the community of Elkinshire. A lot of time has passed and Elkinshire had grown into a kingdom of its own.

"You know you carry our binding authority in all those kinds of social and political matters. You can overrule Azeel when you get there, but try to keep peace and work with him." King Berkas said, accenting his words with his fist on the table pointing to her. "He is our ambassador in the absents of family. He also knows us well enough, that most of what he does is in accordance with what we want. You two will probably be in agreement anyway, and he will function as an adviser for you once you get there.”

“Dad, I believe we have already covered all of that.” wanting to turn conversation to lighter subjects, she added, “Have you seen the new sculpture display at the art center yet. Some of the more intricate works are as good as history lessons, and they are done with such beautiful detail.”

“No, I haven’t, but I will make a point of doing so.” Berkas knew she was trying to change the subject and turn conversation back to more family related things. He understood and decided it was a good idea, to make this a more pleasant family meal. Conversation continued through the rest of the meal on more trivial matters of pleasantries, with laughing and smiles.

It was later in the evening, when Saphrine and Berkas walked into the family study together. “What’s up, Berk?” Saphrine asked, as her father shut the doors.

“You don’t want your mother to hear you call me that.” he chuckled.

“Come on, pops, I’ve never slipped up before. I would never let anyone know I call you, Pops or Berk, but it’s fun when no one else can hear it.” she faked coyness, taking his hand like a small child.

“Okay, I just wanted a little bit of time with my daughter, to make sure you were alright before you left.” Berkas said sitting down in a large reading chair at one side of the room, by the bookshelf. “Do you have any last-minute questions?”

Saphrine had a crafty smile as she hoped into her daddy's lap, "Well, now that you mention it, is this Talmorg fellow cute?"

"That's it you must be an imposter, Saphrine has never had an interest in males." he chuckled

"Oh, so true," she said dramatically throwing her head back, placing her hand to her head in mock shock, then added, sitting back up, "But I have never met males who were Royalty of the highest lineage, though, and a girl must have high ambitions in life." she posed a serious look, and then broke into laughter herself.

"I admit it, I am a foolish old Elf, who worries to much about his girls, but remember, I am here if anything comes up before you leave." he kissed her cheek, then almost dumped her on her seat on the floor when he stood up, "I'll reassure your mother for you." Their father daughter conversation continued for some time, wondering between insignificant matters and matters of state and temple.

Saphrine Barhallah woke up early, tomorrow Azeel would be at the council of Talmorg, but today she would start her twelve-day journey to the house of Elkinshane. This would be her first official business, with the Elkinshanes, as crowned princess, her first time to personally meet the high royal family and her first visit to the famed Walled City of Talmorg. She was finally crowned by her father, three years ago, when her father, king Berkas, gave up the idea of having a son, after the birth of her fourteenth sister. Now she was going to the Elkinshanes, to further negotiate trade arrangements, and she was thoroughly pleased with herself. She had gathered all the information she needed and had prepared the presentation herself, and then her father had approved it. She quickly dressed in her traveling clothes, everything was ready and packed. She would have breakfast, and then her and six royal guards would set out on an easy paced journey. The journey could be made in six days with a good horse, if an emergency called for it, but there was no urgency of time in her mission and she had every intention of enjoying the travel. It was still quite early and the castle was still quiet, as she flitted about, ate breakfast and went to the courtyard where the others waited. Farewells had been said the night before, and they did not want to bring any special attention to her departure, it seemed a little safer that way.

"Is everything set?" she asked, as she stepped out the side entrance, and swung up onto her mount.

"Indeed, my lady." one of the guards answered, and they headed for the gates out of the city.

"Have a pleasant journey, Lady Barhallah." one of the gate guards said as they passed by.

The morning passed in silence, and Saphrine thought about what her father had told her the night before, when she had asked again, about why he had not sent her earlier in place of Azeel. He had said, *"Sweet daughter, it would not have been fair to you. Your first time negotiating outside our kingdom, you should not have to deal with all the lords of the south at one time. I am sure you are able, but there is no need to rush you into the fullness of those pressures."* She still would have liked to have been there, but she knew he was a wise king. She had wondered though, about something Azeel had said a few days before he left, "*You are a female, and matters of military are considered by most to be best handled by males.*" She had wanted to rip him in little pieces when he said it, but realized he was speaking without regard to his own thoughts and probably had her best interest in mind. She thought that maybe there was more to what Azeel had said than her father was letting on, he had not been the only one to mention to her in the past, comments about females not being trusted with authority or important decisions. She had even noticed at different times that traders passing through did not consider their wives capable of handling business.

The people of Efra had quite readily accepted as reagent, but she knew that her father had not received confirmation from Gaharias concerning her appointment as high priestess. This troubled her mind some, but she did not think it was because she was female. Saphrine considered the old ways of the Elves, where matters of worship and state were kept separate, with the Barhallahs as lords of the temples and the Elkinshanes lords of the land. She thought that it might be time to make that separation in Efra. In her mind that explained why Narcia was so much more proficient in the temple than she was. Her thoughts were interrupted by a small trading caravan; they had expected a week earlier, delivering goods from Berkin and Darvin.

They only met very few travelers the road, before they broke for lunch. That afternoon she conversed with the guards as they road.

She already knew Kervin and Stead, but the other four, Kelt, Ander, Izac and Browman, were new to her. Browman was the youngest guard ever to make it into the Royal Guard; she was impressed at how fast he had moved through the ranks, but wondered if he had proved himself emotionally fit. She decided her father was probably right they would not be Royal Guard if they had not proven themselves, in all the ways that were required. She learned from them, not that she did not already know, that they had been recently promoted to Royal Guard.

"So, tell me," Saphrine spoke up, as they rode, "Have any of you ever been to the city of Talmorg before."

"Yes, my lady." Kelt answered, trying to show as much respect as he could as they rode. "Ander and I have escorted Azeel before and I was security on a couple of our armed trade escorts, before I was promoted to the Royal Guard."

Saphrine turned on her horse so she was riding backwards, to face him. "Is it really as nice as I have heard?" she asked with an eager smile.

"You can only know its splendor, my lady, if you have been there. The best that anyone could explain would be but slight insight to bits and pieces of what they beheld." Kelt answered smiling at her antics. Elves were proficient with horses and Saphrine had put a lot of effort into being one of the best. Her father said to her once, that she did not just live life, but preferred to play with it.

"As you probably know, I have never been outside the limits of Efra." Saphrine mocked a timid smile. "By the end of tomorrow, I will have gone farther than I have been before. I have only seen the mountains from a distance."

"I assure you, my Lady," Kelt responded with a slight bow, "you are in for a treat."

That evening they set camp along the side of the road and the guards rotated watch. By the end of the third day everything was set into a routine, and they entered the foothill pass of the Great Mother Mountains. These mountains got their name from the Dwarves that lived in them; they claimed they had survived long ago because these mountains had mothered them. The air had a fresh smell, in these beautiful, lazy, sunny, late summer days, as they traveled through the forest lands. As Saphrine bathed in the sun's warmth and the beauty of the lush forest, her thoughts drifted to the things she had heard about the Walled City of Talmorg, with walls of stone that glistened like fine jewels. She had heard that the Eftites had done masterful works of art in the face of the stone, portraying images of every creature that was known to Ethar. Azeel had told her once, that the Eftites had somehow bound the stone together so it had no seems and one torch gave the light of two or three because it reflected off the walls. The Walled City of Talmorg was also a planned city, having a proper place for everything and protected by a double fortress wall and a third inner wall. She had also been told that they now had the supplies and ability to withstand a siege up to three years if they had to.

The weather stayed nice through the fourth day. Sometime in the night it started to drizzle. It was a seemingly endless drizzle, that continued through the next day and night. On the morning of their sixth day of travel the drizzle let up when they broke camp. Shortly before midday when they were beginning to let their hopes build that the sky would clear, it suddenly started to pour, so bad they had to stop or loose each other in the rain.

It was late in the day, when the rain let up enough for them to resume riding. Saphrine had become solemn and irritable, with the rain, the warmth and beauty of the previous days faded to a distant memory. Her excitement and thrill were drowned in the murk of scattered and unpleasant thoughts, wishing she were home snuggled in the warmth of her bed, not soaked and trudging along like some poor peasant farmer. Her mood let up and her thoughts came back into focus with the rain as it started to clear, and she was even humming by the time they started watching for a place to camp, looking forward now only to a good night's sleep. Suddenly something lunged from the brush at the side of the road, knocking the two guards and their mounts to the ground, behind her, with bone crushing force. As her startled horse threw her, she heard one guard yell, "Ogre!" Impossible she thought, they do not come this far south, they do not even come as far south as Vorka. Ogres were rarely known to even leave their homeland, up north near Silver Lake. She saw the stone club smash one more guard before her head hit a rock as she fell. She saw stars and everything went blank.

The word 'Ogre', was bouncing around in her head, from somewhere, she did not quite know. A hazy light was reaching her brain from the middle of darkness, and she opened her eyes to a blurring of colors that made pretty trails of motion as she moved her eyes from side to side. Her vision started clearing and she began to feel her body at the same time. The sun felt good but the ropes were cutting into her a little. She was facing the ground over a large unlighted fire pit. Then she realized she was tied to a large wooden spit and there was a huge Ogre propped up against a nearby tree sleeping. A light breeze blew and she could feel she was hanging there totally naked, except for the ropes that held here up. Then her eyes caught sight of the remains of a horse next to the Ogre and she almost threw up. She started wriggling her hands and feet, she could hardly feel them. She had to free herself before that beast woke up.

She had no idea how long she struggled nor how many times she had passed out, before the Ogre awoke, but when the Ogre started stirring, her mind started whirling with panic. At first it seemed as though the Ogre did not notice her, as he moved around his camp, picking things up and doing other things. It was too much of a strain to keep a constant watch on him and she still kept passing out. She was awake when he headed towards the fire pit and she made herself stay quiet as the Ogre moved around, however when he reached down into a metal pot, pulled up some glowing embers, and started towards her, all she could do was scream, casting the thoughts of her mind to the ancient Gaharias in a plea for mercy. The beast seemed to ignore her screams taking its time as it sauntered towards her. In her mind she knew this was the end and she could do nothing about it, for that matter she could not even remember who she was or if it would make any difference. Then the Ogre squatted by the pit, he dropped the embers down among the kindle. She could no longer see anything, but those embers and flames slowly taking to life. Seeking the help of the ancients with every ounce of her being, her mind reached in despair for the high authority of the Father of the Old Ones. Mercifully she passed out unable to keep the darkness from engulfing her, hearing the oddest words as her thoughts slipped out of reach, "Good pheasant."

She saw things in the darkness, in shadow and in light. Saphrine found herself in the house of the Ancients, looking at reflections of things to come, knowing she would not remember this vision for years to come. Peacefully she slipped back into the darkness, knowing her time to leave the world of the living had not yet come, but a new age for the south lands was close at hand. She found in the darkness a new realm of light that could not be seen with the eyes, yet she knew she would learn to understand it and teach her first born how to use it. She trembled as even this light gave way to the enveloping darkness.

CHAPTER 04

Continuing Dream

Eric found all he needed, in the unique, in some ways primitive kitchen. Eric knew Shiheel had no functional use for a kitchen. This was one of the most phenomenal dreams, he had ever had, he only hoped he would remember it in the morning. He was having serious doubt now, that it was a dream, to many things were happening that should have woken him up, and it was lasting too long. Dreams had a funny way of warping time and events though too, so what is a dream memory may not have awoken him simply because it was never really a current event. What he was experiencing would all be a tremendous addition to the game, in the computer at the university even if it was just coming from his own mind.

He fixed a stew in the metal pot, hanging in the stone hearth over the fire. Shiheel had either been expecting other people to visit here, or he had set this kitchen up just for Eric. He did not know which, not only was it useless to the Eftite, but everything was built to the right height for Eric. Eric found the meal filling and quite satisfying, surprising he thought, for a dream. Normally when he ate in his dreams, he remained hungry until he woke up and really ate. He decided it was time to learn more about his surroundings. He noted the walls, of the caves and tunnels he was in, were carved out of stone, but the surface was slick, totally unrealistic. It was as if the walls were burned by intense heat, fussing the surface to glass. He decided his immediate surroundings, could wait, he wanted to know more about this strange world, Ethar that he had been brought to, so he headed for Shiheel's office, or library, whatever he called it.

Eric stepped in and took a good look around. The walls were covered, with shelves, filled with volumes and volumes of books and documents. There was a four-foot step ladder leaning up against one of them, though Eric could reach the top shelf with little difficulty. The storehouse of reading here was as big or bigger than that of the library at the University. Eric thought to himself, it could take a lifetime, to try, to read all that this room held. A second look around showed him a desk like area, with a small stool by it. Eric decided, this must be where Shiheel did most of his writing and sat down. Shiheel's most recent records were a good place to start investigating, so he started thumbing through the pages, neatly stack on the desk. To Eric's relief, though there were strange characters scattered through his notes, they were basically written in English. Eric presumed the odd characters were writing in Shiheel's native language. There was information about an Elven kingdom and plans to unite several south land kingdoms. Eventually he got to a page that grabbed his attention, *"Today, I discovered trouble approaching from the north. It looks like the Earthling, human, might even have more purpose here than I originally thought. Greperp told me, he was expected and I was supposed to bring him here anyway."* Eric leaned back and stroked his chin, and realized he had forgotten to bring a razor to shave in the morning.

The record went on to explain a race called the Wonks, were a chameleon like race, that blended into its background. Shiheel was as thorough in writing as he was in talking. These Wonks had common ancestry with the Elves, back in the legendary times of Ethar, only by necessity for survival they had been changed by their magic. These changes made them adaptable to flat open environments. Their feet formed like ostrich feet, and their arms and legs formed webbing to help them disappear when they laid flat in the deserts and grasslands. They were a fierce and warlike creature. Now a Wonk named Mistav, one of their leaders was uniting them by warfare and moving south. In about three weeks they would reach a south land city called Dragoncove, and Shiheel did not expect them to stop. Eric after reading the nature of the race's behavior, agreed with Shiheel.

Eric looked at some maps on Shiheel's desk, straightening out the few papers that were not neatly stacked, so as to see them better. He knew strategies and stratagems of war, from history and the games, and he wanted to study the situation and apply what he knew. It would be nice to have the computer to work things out on, he thought, and Shiheel had told him, he could go back at any time he wanted, to retrieve whatever he wanted. He sat for a moment longer, what else would he need or want.

He wanted his tent and ultra-light camping gear and he would need for the computer, his generator and fuel. He did not want to forget his traveling kit, so he could keep up his personal hygiene. He took the ankh in his hand, with only the slightest doubt as to whether it would work, visualized his front door in the loop and rubbed the bottom. With satisfaction he stepped in through his front door, and walked into his home. He realized that he did not experience the same sensations he had the first time.

The first thing that caught Eric's eye, when he walked back into his house, was that he had left the T.V. on. Then he noticed the clock, though hours had gone by on his watch, the clock only showed a few minutes, if that. His computer system was already set up on a rolling table, so he gathered the rest of the things he wanted and set them on the table, also. He took one last look around to be sure everything was in order and decided to add a medical kit to the pile on the table and headed back through the portal.

Eric was pleasantly surprised, to find the portal took him directly to Shiheel's office this time. It took him about half an hour to get everything set up, before he started punching keys and shuffling through Shiheel's notes. He took all the numbers and possible troop strengths he could decipher, from working Shiheel's notes. He figured the strengths and weaknesses of defensive and offensive battle formations according to terrain. He had no idea how long he worked, but when he was done, he picked up the stack of papers, printouts, charts, maps and graphs his computer had spit out and dropped them in his briefcase, then tidied Shiheel's desk. Though he felt the information he had was incomplete due to a lack of more precise input, he wondered how he might get this information to whoever would be leading this war.

He sat for a few moments, thinking something was still wrong, he felt it; maybe it was just the side effects of the odd portal he was still feeling. He had set forth and analyzed all the information he could, dealing with the coming battle. He had prepared a report and recommendations in everything, except one area, the area of magic. Eric had absolutely no idea what kinds of magic, would be employed by either side. He started through Shiheel's papers again, though he did not expect to gain any insight on any magics that were considered common to any particular race, he did hope to discover, at least some of the exceptional magics or any bits of unique information that could affect the results of what he had accomplished so far.

Eric got back to the information dealing with Mistav, the sword, the ring and the amulet had all been forged in the Death Pits. Giant tar pits boiling forth from deep within the ground, giving forth toxic fumes. The sword was made with a black blade and a crimson stone hilt, and the weapon spewed forth, streams of red fire. The ring, a solid black metal ring set with a crimson stone, was designed to make any who looked upon it obedient to the wearer. The amulet called the shield of darkness was a black oval, set in gold with crimson stones bordering it, with this devise, the wearer can generate a dense fog, impossible to see through to allow for escape. The amulet was strictly designed for defensive purposes, unlike the other two pieces in the set. The power of these devices, magical, draws itself directly from the pits, themselves. That power weakens the farther they are from the pits. The only two of these three devices that they needed to counter were the sword and the ring.

Eric leaned back and shut his eyes, oh, how he could use a cup of coffee hot with a little cream and sugar. Time to see what the computer has to say. He leaned forward and called up the right disk and file on the computer, with his hands passing over the keys. He tried, calling up dark swords of fire. Four different swords came up, none of them bore resemblance, to the sword that Mistav had found, two were destroyed by the fires they were forged in, one of them was thrown into the depths of the bottomless pit, and the other turned out to be mere trickery. He leaned back, picked up his coffee cup and drank down a few swallows. Nothing, nothing of any use, he set his cup down and leaned forward again, punching up defenses, against magical fire. The computer started feeding back to him, wall of ice, ice spells, dodging, dragon scale armor, magic shields, kill the bearer, etc. They were all possibilities, but what will work against this sword. The magic would be wonderful, if there was any that would be effective, but Eric had no idea what magic was available to stand against Mistav, for that matter he was not even sure what kind, or how much magic Mistav had. Kill the bearer had the most promise, but that meant getting close enough to risk looking into the ring and he also had no idea how close the ring had to be to work. Magical shields sounded good too, but Eric still had no idea what was available. It would be nice to have a book, or something, to find out what has been used against these weapons before.

Eric leaned back, picked up his coffee again and took another sip, before it registered, he was drinking coffee, where had it come from,

Shiheel had told him there was no coffee here. It must be some kind of trickery. If this was Shiheel's Idea of a joke, then Eric would like his sense of humor. Eric got up, stretched and walked over to one of the nearest bookshelves. He picked up the first book and opened the cover. "Deassheema has held me captive for seven years now." Eric knew immediately, this was the book he wanted. He returned to the chair and sat down, with anticipation and read it through.

Suan Perdone had been five years old when he was taken captive by the ambitious young Deassheema, sorcerer lord of Tarf, who slew his parents in front of him. Suan had to watch his parents slowly dipped in boiling oil, a memory he would never forget. That day he vowed his soul for vengeance. Suan's parents were court magicians of a long line of tricksters, who kept hidden theirs was not real magic.

The Perdone's lineage made the claim that their lineage always came to power at the age of twenty-three. Suan had learned only one of the family secrets, but it would be enough, paper that could burn through steel. At the age of twelve he started his diary and kept it hidden. He was allowed to wander freely the halls of Tarf, just not leave. He was six when they tunneled under the city of Tarf to the death pits and Deassheema forged by dark sorcery, a ring, a sword, and an amulet. He made everyone in the kingdom, come before him and look into the ring, after which he had absolute command, yet somehow its power could not touch Suan. Suan learned from talking to guards that the sword spewed forth fire and also used that fire to protect its bearer, not even an arrow or rock could get by it without exploding to ash. The amulet, was a simple cloak of fog, to call a retreat and rarely used.

At the age of eight, Suan was there when they sealed the tunnels, to prevent the toxic gas from escaping into the city, then he started planning his vengeance. At the age of twelve, while captives were being brought under the power of the ring, he overheard one telling Deassheema of some wizard, Starnook, who had found a way to destroy the power of his sword with a shield, he called it the shield of ice. That time Deassheema was gone for five and a half months, before he returned. Suan had started to hope him dead, but instead he returned with the shield, and used it for a back on his throne. Deassheema held a great feast gloating in his capture of the shield, as it turned out Starnook was led into an ambush, by the fog and was finished without ever trying the shield.

The years became darker and passed slowly, and Deassheema became drunk with power and announced that Suan would be beheaded in the throne room on his twenty third birthday. Finally the time had come the day before his birthday, Suan went down and wrapped the catches on the seals of the tunnel, with the paper that could burn through steel, in accordance with the time of his execution. He was brought before Deassheema. Suan faced the dark lord and said, "I have vowed my soul to avenge and now it shall be done, I give in curse, now you slay my soul, to the next world I shall cry, forever curse your hole, surely you shall die!" and his head was severed from his neck. He died having fulfilled his vow.

This book's ending really intrigued Eric, it had been finished by someone else. "I have finished this brave young man's tale and hidden this book for safe keeping under the chambers, at stone hedge, in my home world." Merlin Starnook. Eric fell asleep pondering this, dreaming it over and over in his sleep, watching it happen, in the screen of his computer.

*   *   *   *   *   *   *

Shiheel slipped out of the city and gave a shrill call, into the night, of a pitch higher than most could hear, and a shadow lowered in the night. He climbed upon the back of the giant Roc and flew off, headed back to the fire islands. It would take three hours to get there and Rousch would need a rest before the return trip. He was going to have to brief Eric quicker than he had planned, and hoped Eric could start putting ideas together. He flew through the night air, wondering how much he needed to tell Eric. Elven magics were primarily the magics of healing and life. When they used it in armor and weapons it was generally for the good and protection of the user, but some had learned to turn the life-giving magic around to make it life draining. Dwarven magics came from their mining needs and were used in their tools and weapons for accuracy and strength. The men and giants had no magic in particular, but studied magics were a totally unpredictable asset. He hoped that Eric would prove as valuable as Greperp had said he would.

The enemy was hard to see and the power held by Mistav was not specific. The traditional means of battle, has been the facing off of armies in honorable warfare. Eric would have to change that; these methods were deteriorating already and the Wonks do not fight that way. This would be a new and different kind of battle for the people of the south lands. He hoped they would accept Eric's ideas. He would not be able to tell Eric the extent of Wonk magics, he did not know himself, all he knew was they did have some. Shiheel's thoughts went on as he flew, until he reached his island. Shiheel had no idea how valuable Eric would prove to be to the world of Ethar, but he clung to the idea it would be enough to save the kingdoms of the south lands he had grown to love.

After landing, Shiheel gave Rousch food and water and went into the cave. Immediately a strange humming caught his attention. It was not a sound common to the volcanic islands and Shiheel followed it to his office, where he found Eric slumped forward, asleep on top of a book and a strange box with a handle he must have gotten from Earth. In front of Eric was a strange machine with writing glowing out of it. He could speculate on the tools Eric had collected, but did not have time. Shiheel figured Eric had gone home and returned in his absence.

They would have to leave the island in only a few hours and he still had to brief him. "Wake up Eric." Shiheel said, nudging him on the shoulder.

Eric jumped with a start, "Must a dosed off," he murmured, "Have to get the shield." Then coming more awake, he shook his head and turned to the Eftite standing next to him, "Oh, I'm still dreaming." Then he looked at his computer and remembered where he was. "Thanks for the coffee. I don't know how you did it but thanks." he said with a yawn rubbing the sleep out of his eyes.

"Come now, wake up. I don't know what you are talking about, but I have some important matters to discuss. You need to be briefed on what is happening and we have to leave in three hours, for the city of Talmorg. You will have to make sure you have everything together before we go."

"You might want to look at what I have been working on." Eric said, Shiheel's voice never expressed more than the slightest hints of emotion, but Eric did sense his urgency this time.

"Later, first I have to brief you for the council meeting of the lords of the south lands, and their war preparations, so you will have some idea what is happening when we get there."

"That's what I've been working on. I read all your notes and did some research." Eric answered, stretching a kink out of his neck as he opened his briefcase, "It's a good thing you have this diary of Suan Perdone, or we might not have a chance against that dark sword." he added as he pulled out his stack of printouts. "Do those Wonks have any other magic, other than blending into their background so you can't see them?"

"I see you already know more than the lords do. Who is this Suan Perdone, and what diary are you talking about?"

Eric picked up the book off the desk and handed it to Shiheel, saying, "This one, I thought it was probably one of the books you had read. It was on the shelf right there." Eric made a vague gesture in the general direction of the shelf he had gotten it from.

"I haven't read every book that I possess, but I know them, this

is not one of them. I don't know where it came from. You also said
something about coffee, like I said before we don't have any here." He
paused for a moment, Eric noticed for the first time a fluctuating of color
in Shiheel's third eye facet and interpreted it as the expression of emotion.
"How did you come upon the coffee, explain that and what happened
leading to the finding of this book."

"Well with the coffee, I was working away at the computer and I
wanted a cup of coffee." Eric turned his palms up and shrugged, "The next
thing I knew, I was drinking it. With the book, I couldn't come up with a
clear way to fight the magic sword of power. I wanted to find a book or
something, that would show me what had been tried before. I went to your
shelf and that was the first book I grabbed."

"Side effects, it must be side effects of the transalteration. It
has never been done before. I did not give much consideration to the
possibilities of side effects, due to the transition." Shiheel knew it might
have some effect on Eric, but never conceived the idea, that he would
be able to gain the ability to bring things into existence, a power that to
the best of Shiheel's knowledge was only held by the ancients. "It didn't
happen during the overlap, but there are additional distortion factors, in
effect of time and distance. You now enter the magical fields during the
transition unlike before. Instead of passing through openings in the barrier
you pass through the barrier itself. I would like you to try something if you
don't mind."

Eric shook his head at Shiheel's babble, "I suppose, I should not mind."

"Is there anything you did not bring that you would like to have, or might want to use?"

"Sure, infrared binoculars." he gave the Eftite a quizzical look.

"OK, get as clear an image as you can, in your mind and picture them on the desk here."

Eric did as Shiheel suggested and to his amazement, after a few moments his thoughts became reality, a set just like the ones he wanted appeared on the desk. To Eric this was more evidence he was dreaming. It was not uncommon for things to appear in a dream if you thought about them.

"We don't have time to work with this right now, but we should after tomorrow's meeting. You have gained magical ability, passing into this world. We only have about two hours left before we have to leave, we have other more pressing matters."

"That is fine with me. Let me show you now, what I have been working on, you might want to go over it." Eric handed Shiheel the stack of printouts, sat back down to wait for him to go through them and fell back to sleep.

Shiheel sat down and started through the material set before him, first examining the unique papers Eric used. It showed step by step the best ways to fight the battles, for both attacks and retreats. Eric had laid forth effective booby traps, and guerrilla warfare tactics, and the use of terrain for defense. It balanced force strength for limited engagement with the enemy, with alternate courses of action. Shiheel knew that this was the kind of power of knowledge that he had brought Eric here for in the first place. Eric had devised a series of alert systems to show the approach of the enemy. It was a better job than he could have done.

Shiheel took a little time to pack the things he wanted to take, then sat back down to read the diary of Suan Perdone, for himself. When he was done reading, he looked over the book itself, it showed no signs of age. It had been born of Eric's magic, not the original, but a perfect copy in original condition. Eric indeed had power, more than he had ever counted on. He wondered if this was the power that Greperp had been expecting. He was going to have to put Eric to a test, for the good of his own understanding of his new abilities. That will have to wait until after the meetings. He also felt that Greperp, knew a lot more than he had spoken of at their last meeting. Greperp, the Gerpin, was as close as Shiheel had gotten to being able to talk to any of the Ancients. At the very least Greperp was a messenger for the Ancients.

When Shiheel woke him up again, Eric was not sure if he was better off, or worse off for the little sleep he got. He realized he was dreaming when he had dosed off and concluded that the rest of what was happening could not be a dream, unless he was dreaming inside his dreams. As it settled into his mind what was happening, his senses seemed to be sharpening, and he started looking at everything around him as reality for the first time. Eric took a deep breath, and slowly exhaled it, he had come here thinking he was dreaming, now he sensed it was real, he decided to play it out anyway. He got up and fully suited himself, to include weapons and cloak. He drank down quickly the brew Shiheel gave him, hung his binoculars around his neck, grabbed his briefcase and the two of them headed out of the cave. Then Eric broke the silence, "How are we getting there in three hours?" he asked, when the fresh sea air chilled by the cool of the night, brought him fully awake.

"Flying, I have friends among the Rocs of screaming cliffs."

Eric knew what the giant birds of legend were and found the idea thrilling. The bird was monumental to Eric as it stepped out into the open. Shiheel quickly introduced them and showed Eric how to get on. They took to flight in the early morning air. As they flew Eric turned to Shiheel and asked, "What was that hot brew you fixed for me, it did wonders to wake me up?"

"It was dorack tea, with nutrition supplements to help keep your body chemistry in balance."

The crimsons and violets of the sunrise were a beautiful sight, cast against the mountains to the east, as the day began to break through the air, adding to the ecstasy and thrill Eric was enjoying on the wings of flight. It was followed by the spectacle of light casting itself across the land, when the city of Talmorg came into sight, the home of the Elkinshanes. They set down out of sight of the city to head the rest of the way in on foot.

CHAPTER 05

Shuffling the Deck

Talmorg was concerned, although this time he knew Shiheel would be late. The council meeting was already in progress and he had told them all he knew, which created a quandary at first. None doubted Talmorg's word, but they were all filled with questions. As the atmosphere settled and the assembly accepted the situation, the meeting had returned to order. There was a general acknowledgment of the need for unity and recognition of the magnitude of the situation. After regaining everyone's attention, Talmorg dove into the heart of the matter, petitioning those with the authority to give troop commitments, although it seemed as though only Talmorg and Vorka would be able to get to Dragoncove in time to help. Their hope was to slow the wonks down enough to give other support time to get there. With the armies of Talmorg, Vorka and Dragoncove combined, they would be outnumbered by three to one at best, with at least a week before any reinforcements arrived, after the enemy was engaged.

There was an atmosphere of gloom and defeat hanging over the council meeting. The assembly was solemn with Shiheel and his unknown stranger all they had to bring them some light of hope. King Erron was present, but he had given his son Talmorg full authority in the organization of this endeavor. Erron was also at a loss for advice to give his son. Talmorg was about to call for a recess, when Shiheel, in his brown cloak of mystery, marched in followed by a large figure wearing a cowled cloak.

The strangers face hidden in shadow, with a power and pride in his stature and his walk, that made Talmorg wonder if the stranger were a king from a distant land. The room went still with silence at the entrance of the newcomers. Shiheel led Eric straight to the lectern, were Talmorg stood waiting. Talmorg gave an abbreviated, formal introduction for Shiheel and discretely pulled a stool over for Shiheel to stand on, as he spoke, "Lords of the south lands it is my honor to introduce to you, Shiheel an Eftite of Esberk II, now a citizen of the city of Talmorg of the kingdom of Elkinshane."

Shiheel stepped up and onto the stool, "King Erron, Prince Talmorg, Lords of the south lands and their ambassadors. A few days back it was brought to my attention that the Wonks were at war with themselves, therefore I set about investigating the matter...." Shiheel went on to rehearse the entire threat to the south lands. The lords listened intently, as though this was the first they had heard of it, but paying special attention to details they had not previously noted. When he finished his meticulous recounting of all he knew, he asked if there were any questions.

The first question, was one he was expecting and it came from Freebic Elkinshane. "We, now know of the threat and have all given troop commitments, however this does little good, considering that by the time we can get word to our kingdoms, there will not be enough time for our troops to arrive before it is too late."

"If I eliminate the message time, will that help?" The volume of voices rose with doubtful affirmation. Shiheel raised a hand to silence the room. "I will personally see to the delivery of your messages, if you will write them and stamp them with your seals. Do not concern yourselves with how, but know that I shall have them delivered by midday tomorrow." A low murmur started rising again. "Tell your people, we meet in the fields east of Dragoncove as soon as possible. The sooner we are there, the better we can prepare for the enemies coming."

"What of provisions?" Brask Scaller stood up and asked.

"I believe that Dragoncove, Vorka and Talmorg will be ready to provide them, in order to expedite the arrival of your troops." Talmorg, Hanser and Prince Ashkin, each stood up and gave their commitment to that.

"What of this sword of power?" it was prince Ashkin that asked.

"My friend here will deal with that shortly." There was a pause, "With no more questions, I would like to introduce to you, Eric Marland of the United States of America of Earth." There was an astonished gasp from the assembly, followed by a wave of murmuring. Then someone asked how he got to Ethar from Earth. Shiheel answered that question before he stepped down, "a transalteration portal." The room went silent as Eric dropped his hood and stepped up to the lectern.

"Peoples of Ethar," Eric began, making a sweep look at the entire assembly, "It is an honor and privilege to speak before you. I have had some time to study and research your predicament and it is not as bleak as it appears...." Eric started by telling them about the Shield of Ice at Tarf and how that Shiheel would be able to retrieve it, which brought a cheer of relief, hope and enthusiasm. Then he proceeded through every page of his research, being sure to give enough detail that they could understand it, yet still keep as brief as he could.

The meeting lasted all day and into the night, breaking for lunch and dinner, before it reached a conclusion. During the course of the meeting, Eric learned from Azeel that his coat of arms was identical to the Royal Crest of Efra, only their background was green instead of black. When it was all over, the lords were to go to Dragoncove, Shiheel would meet them there in one week and Eric in two weeks. Shiheel was to deliver their messages and recover the shield, while Eric went through some special training exercises. The lords were responsible to memorize the documents Eric had provided and pass on the information to those who needed it. Eric realized the need for more copies of his document, and trying his newly discovered magic, he produced twelve more sets from his briefcase.

Eric and Shiheel left immediately after the meeting concluded. Eric had no idea what this training exercise was all about. He figured it was just a cover Shiheel used to get him out of there, so he could start working with this strange magic. It had been a long day with the council, Eric was pleased that he would get some solitude and some sleep. They were headed back to the cave in the fire islands.

*   *   *   *   *   *   *

King Erron Elkinshane sat in his chair facing out the open windows in his bed chamber, Constance his wife already lay sleeping.

Age was finally catching up with him. He mused to himself; it was high time to give the throne to Talmorg. Erron had been planning to give the throne to Talmorg when he got married, but he had been waiting fifty-one years ever since he came of age, for that and it had not happened yet. Talmorg had continued to pour his life into training and politics since he was twenty-five. Erron sighed my son is known and respected throughout the south lands. Erron knew he had accomplished great things with the first council of the south lands, over a hundred years before Talmorgs birth. He would go down in history as a wise king for ending the border wars, yet he felt his accomplishments small next to what Talmorg had already accomplished as his son and he was proud of Talmorg. By the time Talmorg was thirty-five he had established trade with Dragoncove, Vorka, Darvin and Efra. When Talmorg was fifty-two, he signed the trade agreement with Darkolon and all of the south lands were trading. As a result of the trading there was an increase in the mixing of peoples and racial fears subsided, roads became safer and patrol agreements were set up to help protect trade routes.

It was just over fifty years ago now that Talmorg went to the plains of Harmosk, when he was only eighty-three years old, to settle some trade friction that resulted from Prak tribes raiding grain fields. That resulted in the Unified Defense of Harmosk and later grew into the Province of Harmosk. Talmorg, the city, had become the central trade city of the west, and the dwarven mountain city was trying to do the same in the east. When Talmorg had come to him with the proposal for the Unified

Defense of the South lands, Erron decided that with the signing of the final agreements he would pass his crown on. Now with war imminent, that would all have to wait, as well as the signing of the final agreements. Erron knew, Eric was right, if they tried to fight this war by traditional means, army standing to face army, it would be a losing battle. The Wonks used their bodies for illusion and they were fierce warriors, who spent their entire lives fighting, anyone including each other. Hopefully the strange new ways of warfare that the Earth man brought would turn things in their favor.

Erron remembered his grandfather and his father telling stories of when Earth and Ethar still touched, of the crossing from one planet to the other. The kingdoms of Earth then were much the same as those of Ethar. With the deaths of those who lived during those times, the stories grew to legends of might and wonder. Erron's father and grandfather, had both told him the gap between the two worlds, had grown too big for even the greatest of magics to cross. Men got trapped on Ethar and people from Ethar got trapped on Earth, where their magics would vanish with time. Erron wondered if Eric was descended from an Elf trapped on Earth, if he were not so tall his facial features hinted at the possibility. How had this Eric passed from Earth to Ethar? Shiheel had something to do with it, he knew, but still how, if magic could not bridge the gap. Erron had never trusted the Eftites and as a result was uncertain how much to trust Eric.

The Eftites had arrived, after a five night long spectacle of lights in the sky, six hundred and thirty-seven of them. His father's last official act before passing the crown to Erron was to make the strangers to their world citizens of Talmorg. His father had told him that one day he would be thankful for having them as citizens. Six hundred of them enlisted immediately as foot soldiers, he had laughed at their size then, but to this day only two of them had died in battle, and they were good warriors. Thirty-five of them had become craftsmen, among the best in the city of Talmorg. Then there was Shiheel and Hesheil. Shiheel, became a self-appointed counselor, that spent most of his time away and Hesheil was almost never seen and when he was seen, he was always trading goods. Erron had long ago noted that Talmorg had always taken heed to Shiheel's counsel and given it merit in most decisions. Oh well, it looked like maybe his day for being thankful was coming soon. His men were headed to war and he would have to go with them, even though he was giving command to his son Talmorg.

Erron's other son Lacrane, had recently married Elisha Santine, last spring and they were spending their first year with her parents according to tradition. Elisha was one of the blond-haired Elves of Praka. The blond-haired Elves and the red-haired Elves were different, they had different magics and did not normally cross marry, because the children would have mixed magics and it was never known what the result would be. The magic of those with blond hair generally centered around healing, while that of the red-haired Elves was mostly for growing and preserving, both were life giving magic and the mix was rarely bad just unknown. Erron stood up and stretched, well tomorrow they headed for Dragoncove and he better get some sleep. He walked across the room and climbed into bed with his wife, Constance.

*   *   *   *   *   *   *

As far as anyone ever knew there have only ever been two gerpins. Greperp and his female companion Gerpep were separated when Earth and Ethar lost contact. Gerpep was trapped on Earth, Greperp waited patiently until a time would come when they would have a chance to be reunited again. Very few if any, really ever knew how these two fit into the scheme of things. Some said they were older than the ancients and may have been on Ethar before the Old Ones arrived.

Greperp knew everything he had seen through the ages. A gerpin does not get caught unless that is their intent. Greperp was preparing for changes he knew were coming and the coming storm would give him all the cover he would need. The new Earth man was the key to many things, not the least of importance rejoining him to Gerpep. A goddess from the future dressed in flames had told him her father would eventually grant them both the ability to travel between worlds. Her father's name was Eric.

Perhaps someday he would share this meeting, but they were not supposed to be able to travel through time. The closest ever done before that he knew about was Going to another dimension to meet someone at a time before they came to your own. The thing you could never seem to do was go to a prior time in the same dimension then the last time you were there. Time did not allow anyone to go backwards on their own time-line and many had tried.

This Eric was here now to save the south land kingdoms from being overrun by a mad man. He would test the heart and soul of this hero from Earth. Greperp had to test and follow through, even if he knew already Eric was the marker of change and the seed of a new future. Ethar was their world, home to the gerpin. The time was coming for them to start a family of gerpin.

CHAPTER 06

Beginnings

As they dismounted Eric could feel his lack of sleep creeping over him, yet he knew he would not sleep until Shiheel left to deliver the messages for the lords. They entered the caves and headed straight back to the office. Shiheel led Eric to the desk and pulled out a couple of maps, spreading them out where they could look at them. "You, Eric, have great skill and knowledge, also you have gained a very powerful form of magic in you passage to Ethar. I am sending you on an exercise to boost your confidence and knowledge of what you have gained coming to this world, to learn what you can do. It is quite unfortunate that I will not be able to work with you, and help you gain an understanding of what you can do, before we need to be at Dragoncove. You need to be in Dragoncove in two weeks and I won't be coming back here before then. Look at the map." Shiheel pointed as he spoke. "Here is where we are right now, there is Dragoncove. From here, there is a tunnel that leads to a hollow stump about here on the other side of Screaming Cliffs. If you continue down the hall we followed to get to this office, you will find the beginning of the tunnel. You will need these maps." he continued, rolling them up and handing them to Eric. Then he reached into a compartment under the desk and pulled out a simple looking apparatus. It was a small rod pointed at one end hanging by a string from a tripod, no more than four inches high. "This is a magnetic rod, here and through the area you will be traveling it will always point almost due north, close enough that you can use it for directions anyway." Shiheel set it on the desk to demonstrate. The pencil like metal rod of the primitive compass quickly settled into place. "I need to head out quickly if I am going to keep my word and get these messages delivered on time. You need to try your magic out and start learning what you can do, start small and try to get familiar with it as you travel." Shiheel started to turn and head for the door, but paused and turned back to Eric. "Do you have any questions?"

"Well a few. I know there is a difference in time here, but how is it measured?" Eric pointed to his watch, "My watch obviously does not match the passage of a day here."

"Alright," The question seemed irrelevant to Shiheel, but he would answer it. "One hour here is eighty of your Earth minutes, a day is sixteen hours. Eight days make up a week and forty a month, except the first fourth and eighth months have forty-one days. There are ten months or four hundred and three days in a year. The first month is spring when Ethar starts new life. The third month marks the beginning of summer. The sixth month marks the beginning of Ethar's sleep or what you would call, fall and winter. The years are measured from the last of the great wars, that left the world to start over. That was when the Elves first swore themselves to the protection and saving of life, though it was a hobby for many of them even before that. This is the second day of the sixth month of the year fifty-two hundred, six." he paused, "Oh yes, the first hour is the sunrise hour and this is the eleventh hour. Normally however time is just referred to as morning, midday, evening and midnight.”

“I wish I had a watch that gave the full digital read out of the time here.” Eric said with a yawn.

“Most people guess based on midday, sunrise and sunset.”

“So, I am to understand that I have sixteen days to get from here to Dragoncove. This is the challenge you offer me?”

“Oh, reasonably so. The point of the exercise is to use your new found abilities and learn what you can do. The catch is you must do it unseen, with the only exception being, if you should find someone in distress, you can be the noble hero, but I strongly doubt that will happen. There has been no trouble in this portion of the south lands for years.” Shiheel gave a hearty laugh, the one thing he did with expression. Eric sensed some comfort at knowing there would be no real danger, that this was more like a test in survival training and an exercise in learning what his new abilities were.

Eric laughed too, he must have looked worried and as it turned out it was just a game of hide and seek, where he was supposed to play with magic. He wondered what ‘magic’ he might have, or if this Shiheel even knew.

“Remember, the purpose of this little folly is to get you familiar with your newly developed talents, so don’t hesitate to practice. Is that all the questions you have?”

“I think so I will Inventory what I am taking and get some sleep before I go.” Eric replied, looking half asleep on his feet.

"Well, I have to take off then." Shiheel reached out his hand and they shook. The Eftite was much more powerful than he looked, Eric Thought. To an enemy the Eftite would easily be underestimated.

"See you in sixteen days."

Eric watched as Shiheel walked out, with the cape of his cloak brushing the floor, he appeared to be gliding more than walking. Eric chuckled to himself, the little guy he thought, still reminded him of a cross between an insect and a frog at the same time, and the virtually expressionless face was eerie and hard to trust. There was never a way to tell if he were lying or telling the truth, so far it had all been the truth.

Eric went to the sleeping chamber Shiheel had provided for him, sat down on the floor and started spreading his gear out in front of him. He had chosen his hip pack and his shoulder bags to take with him. The hip pack strapped around his waist and hung in the back, it was all nylon and red, part of a matching set with his shoulder bag. In the pack he had two space age thermal blankets, a nylon pup tent, a small mess kit that included a canteen and a five-day emergency supply of food rations. After he looked it all over, he took the one-pound bag of coffee, a small percolator and two plastic jars, one of cream and one of sugar, shoved them all on top and closed the pack. He knew what was in the medical kit, so he just shoved it in the shoulder pack, which only left a space two inches by four by eight, at the top and a small side pouch. In the side pouch he put his electronic ignition, butane fire-starter, "Starts even when wet.". He followed that with a pack of chewing gum, a flash light and a can of butane. Then he hooked his bath kit on the strap. It contained his razor, shaving cream, aftershave, toothbrush, toothpaste, soap and a roll of toilet paper. That left laying on the floor, a comb and a watch. He shoved the comb in his bath kit and picked up the watch. Eric stood up and looked at the watch, shock proof, five hundred meters, 12:06. He pushed the button on the side, 02:06:06. He knew at once what had happened, he had wished another thing into existence.

Eric lay down to sleep, but sleep did not come easy, he found himself staring at the ceiling. Everything was still going too fast, this stealthy hike would do him good, give him time to adjust to what was happening. His mind drifted back to their council meeting they had questioned everything. The Dwarven prince Ashkin had intensely studied and questioned the booby traps and collapsing bridges. They had all grilled him on the guerrilla warfare tactics, and Hanser Schultzmann was given the responsibility of taking care of the oil on the river. No one understood the purpose of strewing bits of sharp twisted metal all over the forest on the north side of the river, until Eric explained how the wonks would not be able to flatten out and crawl in it without getting sliced up, and that would reduce the effectiveness of their camouflaging bodies. They all approved of the hidden trenches and the techniques for engaging limited forces.

The wonks were used to flat open areas, the advantage would strongly go against them, fighting in the forests and Mistav would not know his losses, because he would not see them. The Elves already knew their forest signals, so they would immediately know when and where defense line breaches occurred, but the enemy would not. Mistav would not understand the shield, until it was too late and there was hope that the Eftite Lasers could get past the power of his sword. They hoped that as soon as the power of the ring was broken, the Wonks would quickly lose their organization and surrender.

The next debate, lasted to late afternoon and that was over troop distribution, their functions and objectives. He had given them the methods; they would have to take care of the execution and he lost track of what they were deciding. After that they went over estimated troop arrival times and reinforcements. While they were setting up, he would be sneaking his way to Dragoncove. First there was the tunnel, he would push that and make it in two days. The halfway point was marked by a chamber, but from that point it was all uphill, ending in a stairs that came up in a stump. His thoughts wondered for a while longer before he finally fell asleep.

He woke up early the next day, his new watch read 15:74, six minutes to the sunrise hour, he thought. Eric rolled out from under the furs and went to another chamber, Shiheel had told him about, that had a hot spring tub in it. He climbed in cleaning and soaking for about twenty minutes. It was relaxing and stimulating, the water came in one wall near the ceiling ran down the wall to a pool and then out the opposite wall. When he got out and dried with a couple of soft furs, he realized this was the only room in the green volcanic rock cave that was naturally formed, the rest all had slick glassy walls.

He returned to the bed chamber, and slipped back into his jeans and shirt. The chainmail slipped over his cloths like a sweater and a pair of knitted pants, overlapping and linking together at the waste. The leathers fit outside the chainmail in a similar fashion. He left the head gear on the bed for the moment, while he went and shaved. He had not shaved the day before and he enjoyed splashing on the aftershave and feeling clean again. He looked at the head gear, there was a supple leather hood that went on under the chain-mail and a hardened leather helmet that went on the outside. He slipped the head gear on, he felt good in the entire outfit and it was green with purple trim, his family colors. Next, he girded his weaponry starting with his belt, six knives alternating with six stars and his samurai sword on the left side. He strapped his broadsword across his back, so that the hilt, with his family crest and the top of the sheath stuck up slightly over his right shoulder. Across his back in the other direction, he strapped his quiver, with his compound bow clipped on to it forming an X on his back. Finally his hip pack and shoulder bag, covering everything with his cowled cloak. Standing six feet, one inch tall, he would have been an impressive sight to anyone who saw him, as he stood there fully equipped, with confidence in every ounce of his stature. He turned and headed down the hall.

When Eric reached the doors that marked the start of the tunnel, he pulled two torches out of a hollow in the wall, lit one and stepped through the doors. It was exactly the second hour of the day. Eric noted the walls, floor and ceiling were glass as though blasted by a laser, and the tunnel was perfectly round in appearance. He pushed forward holding the torch ahead of him, going downhill at a fairly steady pace. After about half an hour the tunnel leveled off and he noted that somewhere along the way the walls had turned to a dull grey, though maintaining the qualities of glass. It was not until he had been moving along for about three hours, that he started getting a crimp in his neck. He paused and realized he was ducking. The tunnel was six feet in diameter and he was six one. He had not noticed it at first because the duck was so slight, it had been automatic and without thought.

He sat down and grabbed a piece of jerky out of his pack, with all his getting ready to go he forgot to eat breakfast. Oh well, he had more than enough rations to get him through the tunnel. Sitting there he thought, as he bit off a piece of jerky, the tunnel would be the easiest part of his journey. Of course, with these walls he chuckled to himself, it would be a lot quicker on roller blades. He pictured in his mind what he would look like, dressed like this, with a pair of roller blades strapped to his feet, and laughed out loud. He stopped laughing though, when he felt a pair materialize strapped to his boots.

Eric stared at the rubber wheels for a minute, well why not, it would be faster. He got up and started zigzagging along the tunnel, picking up speed and working his way higher and higher on the walls. He felt like a kid playing in a culvert. He picked up speed and height on the walls until he worked up enough courage, to go up one wall across the ceiling and down the other. He came out of his acrobatic stunt and dropped into a racing squat. Before he knew it, he had reached the midway chamber and slid right past it before he could stop. He turned around and reentered the chamber checking his watch. It was not even the sixth hour yet. Just over four hours had passed and he was not ready to call it a day, but he did want to check the bed chamber out. The ceiling was higher, about eight feet, and there were six beds on the walls, three on either side. They were hollowed out of the stone and padded with leather, making them look quite comfortable. The walls were still like a dull gray glass. All only purpose for the chamber was a place to sleep, but Eric was not going to use it.

He turned with a quick fluid motion and continued down the tunnel. As Eric pushed forward, he became so busy enjoying himself, that the distance he was traveling just slipped right past, until he found himself going uphill. It did not take long for skating uphill to become work and he stopped to take the skates off. Sitting down he realized, he was worn out, hungry and winded. He looked at his watch, it read 07:46, the other end of the tunnel cannot be that far away he thought. He slipped off the skates and used the straps to fasten them to his carrying bag. Reaching around he pulled out the rest of the first day's rations. The pouch contained two nutrition bars, two fruit cakes and four more pieces of jerky. He ate the whole thing and stuffed the wrappings back in his pack.

When he started walking again, his legs felt a little rubbery, but after twenty minutes of walking, he seemed to walk it out. The tunnel went up at about the same slope as it had gone down and after a while the walls started changing colors, in a variety of Earth tones. It was the ninth hour, when he reached the bottom of the stairs that spiraled up. The steps looked like they had been melted from wax, multi colored in reds, greens, whites, browns and blacks, laced with bits of blue and purple. The climb seemed endless and he counted two hundred and thirty-six steps by the time he reached the top. He felt as though he had expended the last of his energy and he sat down on the landing at the top. He looked around the small room. It was round, about ten feet in diameter, extending up into darkness. It had taken him about sixty-five minutes to climb the stairs. He leaned his head back and was asleep almost immediately.

Eric Awoke the next morning to the muffled echoes of rain. Sometime in the night he had slid down the wall and sprawled out on the floor. He stretched and opened his eyes, to look up forty feet to a transparent roof, streaked with water from the rain, sheltering him from the release of the overcast skies above. How long had he slept? Looking at his watch, it was 1:06, almost eight hours, Ethar time, a long time considering the difference. He knew he was in the stump at the other end of the tunnel. He would step out into the lower foothills just north of Screaming Cliffs a day ahead of schedule. His plans were to go north and a little east to Keltser Gorge and follow it until he passed under the Keltser Gorge Bridge. Once he was out of sight of the road, he would go west until he rounded Fires Peak, a live Volcano. From there he would take Eliko Ravine, north out of the mountains and follow the west perimeter of the mountain foothills, to Silver Lake. He would cut across from there, using the road for guidance. The whole course should take fifteen days or less. He could not wait on the rain. He ate a breakfast consisting of a fruit cake, a stick of jerky and a few swigs of water. A more fulfilling meal was another good reason, not to stay in out of the rain.

He was ready to go, using his unusual compass and one of the maps, he calculated the direction he needed to go, then slipped them in his pack to stay dry. As he opened the door and stepped out, he was thankful Shiheel had instructed him to wear his weatherproof cowled cloak. He was going to have to count on his natural, keen sense of direction. With the drizzle and the heavy cloud cover, it was dark enough to leave everything in shadows, in the flashes of lightening. In the distance, slightly to the right and behind him, Eric could hear the shrill whining of the screaming cliffs, it would be for now his only point of reference. Any beauty of the forest, was lost in the shadows, and the dreary gloom of the day quickly started nipping at his mood as he set forth. He trudged along until a bit past midday without incident, the only changes being his jeans had soaked water up past his knees and his mood had turned foul. He stopped at the base of a tree, he guessed it to be a large tree from the size of the trunk, and cursed the weather as he sat down to eat his lunch. He had expected to be able to scrounge for lunch from the forest, but weather would not permit it. He quickly ate three pieces of jerky, stood back up and started moving on again, no sense dawdling in this kind of weather.

Eric had not gone on for more than half an hour, when he saw something that looked almost like a rabbit and his first though was dinner, but when he got closer and saw it struggling on the ground. He noticed its rear left leg was broken and pinned to the ground, by a freshly fallen branch. His heart went out to it. "Probably don't taste good anyway." he said to it with a slight snarl in his voice.

Eric felt tenderness, when the little fellow responded with a weak, "Gerp, Gerp." He knelt down and pulled out his medical kit, then scooped the drenched ball of fur up with one hand and lifted the branch with the other. He pulled a small pad from the kit and passed it briefly under the creature's nose. It would stay awake, but feel no pain. Eric waited to the count of three for it to take effect, then laid the fellow down, leaning forward to protect it from the rain and went to work treating and splinting its leg. The animal was a strange cross between a rabbit and a cat, but from its teeth it was a vegetarian. The head and back feet were those of a rabbit, while the front legs, feet body and tail were those of a cat, but its hind legs were a powerful cross between the two able to both hop and run effectively. When he was done, he put back the medical kit, wrapped his new companion in a thermo blanket and tucked it on top of his hip pack. Strangely Eric was in a much better mood again as he started moving on.

Musing Eric said, "I think I'll call you, Charlie."

Charlie seemed to approve, because he came back with a nice strong, "Gerrep."

Eric moved along now at a much better pace, the rain not bothering him anymore. Hours went by, before he started thinking how nice it would be to find a rock overhang to shelter them through the night. Then as he passed down a small gully, he practically walked right into a shelter, under a rock overhang. Eric examined the small sheltered area under the overhang, there was nothing under it except for a few dead branches. The space was about ten feet deep, six feet wide and just under six feet high. Quickly he dropped the bag from his shoulder with the medical kit and set it down in the back of his small cave. Charlie was sleeping on his waist pack, so he careful removed it so as not to wake him up. When he started a small fire near the edge of the shelter, it lit the entire inside, giving it a cozy glow. Then Eric leaned back against the stone, pulled out the fifth piece of jerky, the other nutrition bar and the fruit cake. He started eating, but as he took his first bite of the nutrition bar.

Charlie hobbled over. "Gerp, Gerep."

"Are you hungry, little guy." Eric reached down and pet the cuddly little thing.

"Gerp, Gerp gerep." The strange little animal expressed rubbing against Eric's hand.

"Here you go." Eric said, setting the fruit cake down where Charlie could get it.

"Gergerp." Charlie sat back on his hind legs, picked up the cake between his front paws and started eating.

When they were both done eating Eric stroked him gently. "Your leg will be better in no time." Then he picked him, spread one blanket out for him, grabbed the other blanket and they both wrapped up for the night. In no time the sounds of the rain lulled Eric to sleep.

The third morning, Eric was awakened Charlie's front feet pouncing playfully on his face, causing him to jump into the sitting position. Charlie was running in circles, pouncing and acting like an excited little puppy. "So, it's time to get up, is it? Your leg must be doing a lot better." he paused watching Charlie's charades. "Come here and let me check that dressing." To Eric's amazement, Charlie came over and laid down on his right side, as though he understood. He was even more amazed, however when he discovered the leg was completely healed. "You heal fast little guy."

"Gerp gerp, Gerp gerp gerp." Charlie jumped up stretched and took a few hops as if to make sure it worked right.

Eric got up and started a fresh fire and a pot of coffee using rain water running off the rocks. When the coffee was done, he poured himself a cup and mixed it with a little cream and sugar. He pulled out a day's rations and gave Charlie a fruit cake, sipped his coffee and ate a piece of jerky. Charlie stepped over and sniffed Eric's coffee once made a disgusted noise before sitting down and eating the fruit cake. The rain was still coming down in a steady drizzle and he and Charlie just sat there until Eric finished his second cup of coffee. Then with a deep sigh Eric stood up, rinsed out his cup and pot and repacked camp putting everything back in its proper place. Charlie scurried around watching his every move. When he was done, he strapped the pack back on and pulled the carrying bag back over his shoulder, before kicking out the fire.

Again, using the unique compass that Shiheel had given him, he checked his direction and stuck it back in his pack. He turned to Charlie to ask him if he was ready to go, but before he could ask, Charlie hoped up under his cloak and onto his waist pack. Eric turned in a north easterly direction and started hiking. The day was not any brighter than the day before, but with Charlie there to talk to, he did not let the weather bother him. He kept walking most of the day, not even stopping for lunch. They ate as he walked, Eric ate a few pieces of jerky and broke off a piece of fruit cake for Charlie. They reached Keltser Gorge just before evening and Eric pitched his tent in a flat area partway down the western wall. With the tent erected, he started a small fire and brewed another pot of coffee. Eric sat quietly with Charlie in the shelter of the tent, watching the fire while they ate their meager dinner from the day's rations.

Eric looked at the meager rations after taking a few bites. "I am supposed to play with this new magic I have. What do you think Charlie, I am hungry for something a little more filling and perhaps hot."

"Gerp, gerp." Charlie seemed to understand.

Eric pictured a steak dinner with green beans and a fruit salad. He watched it appear as he saw it in his mind. "I am not sure what you like Charlie." He pictured baskets of fresh fruit, grains and vegetables so Charlie could have a choice.

Charlie moved from bowl to bowl sampling everything.

Erics thoughts went to Bonny, he would be glad to see her again. He had not realized how much he had enjoyed her company and sharing his life with her. He looked down at Charlie, "She will never believe this, you know.”

Charlie just sat there and looked up at him, with his unblinking blue eyes, as though he were ready to listen to anything that Eric had to say. Eric did not say anything else though, instead they just sat there for a couple of more hours after the fire died, then curled up and slept.

Eric woke up early the following morning, there was a lull in the rain. Charlie was already up and looking out of the tent. Yawning Eric crawled over and stuck his head out of the tent. When he looked around, he saw the bridge no more than twenty-five feet from where they were camped. He saw the massive form of the bridge, silhouetted in the predawn twilight. He was supposed to make this trip unseen, yet if anyone crossed that bridge, they would surely see his bright red tent even in the rain. He immediately started packing everything as quickly as possible. In the process of packing, he gave Charlie another fruit cake and ate two sticks of jerky himself.

He was done packing in less than ten minutes and headed down into the gorge with Charlie now riding on his carrying bag, looking out the front of his cloak. They slipped down into the underbrush and headed for the bridge. No sooner had they reached the bridge, when Eric heard horses approaching, so he ducked into the shelter of the bridge supports. He listened carefully, it was a small party, sounded like a pair of horses followed by a second pair, then he was uncertain whether the third set was one or two horses in perfect synchrony and then a fourth and last pair. It was seven or eight horses that crossed the bridge over his head. He waited patiently, until he could no longer hear them in the distance galloping away, before he was ready to move on.

Eric Marland and his mascot Charlie traveled north through the gorge for about half a mile, before turning left and leaving the gorge in a westerly direction. With just a light mist falling, he had a small glimpse of some of the forest's beauty. The vast array of colors and sounds of forest birds were marred only slightly by the mornings weather. Eric stopped three times that morning to double check his directions and each time, he took a few moments to enjoy the wonders of the strange forest. Many of the plants he saw, he recognized, however there was also a large variety that were totally foreign, such as the trees he thought looked like ash trees except they bloomed with purple roses. Each time Eric stopped, Charlie would jump down and moving so fast that all Eric could see was a blur, gather nuts, berries and fruit, stuffing them into the top of the carrying bag and anywhere else they would stay.

"You must be really tired of those fruit cakes." Eric laughed, when he started walking again after the third stop.

Shortly before midday, the rain suddenly started to cascade so heavy, Eric had to feel his way as he pushed forward with an unyielding conviction to keep moving. He thought that it was only because he kept moving that his wet feet and legs were staying warm, so he did not stop for lunch, but ate while he walked. He offered Charlie a fruit cake and was a little surprised when Charlie stuffed it in the bag and offered him what looked like a peach. The strange fruit did not taste like a peach, although it was sweet and seemed to melt in his mouth. He quite thoroughly enjoyed the flavor, seeming to him to be a cross between cherries and apple. Eating the fruit effectively warmed him up and seemed to fill him with energy. Eric started wondering how smart Charlie might actually be. When he finished eating the fruit, the pit was like a pearl three quarters of an inch in diameter, so he slipped it into the side pocket of the carrying bag to examine more closely later. He did not know how much his progress was slowed down by the rain, but he wanted to reach Eliko Ravine before nightfall. As he continued to walk, he felt the air and maybe the ground around him was getting warmer. It was around the sixth hour the rain stopped and the sky cleared to allow the afternoon sun to shine through.

With the rain gone and the sun shining, Eric could see the ground had changed to predominantly rock covered with moss and the forest had given way to scattered brush. Looming up to his right and just ahead was Fires Peak, with smoke billowing out erratically. As he continued forward, small colorful geothermal pools appeared in mounds of mineral deposits. Every so often small geyser would spout up here and there, some of them out of the pools themselves. Eric realized how foolhardy he had been walking blindly in the rain and was glad it had stopped before he stepped in one of those scalding cauldrons of nature. He was walking around one of the pools that had a peculiar glow to it, when he noticed that each time he stepped, he caused a small cloud of colorful light to rise around his feet. He bent over and picked up a handful of the powdery rock dust from around his feet and looked at it. It was just a dull white powder, but wherever it dropped through the air, it filled it with a cloud of colored light that blew away on the breeze. Eric filled all the plastic bags from his previous meals with the powder and stuffed them back into his pack.

About an hour later, Eric was back in the woods, moving right along, when he crossed the obvious trail of some large creature, that walked on two feet and was heading north. It had left a foul odor in its wake and he had no desire to meet it whatever it was, so he quickly kept moving. It was approaching evening, when he reached the edge of Eliko Ravine, so he found a small clearing ideal for setting up camp. Stepping out he startled a few game birds into flight. He threw one of the knives from his belt, almost as a reflex, with great speed and precision, dropping the closest fowl from its flight. When he walked over and picked it up it looked like an exceptionally large grouse. Quickly he skinned and cleaned it. He started pulling his broadsword to use as a shovel to bury the skin and innards. He looked the blade and put it back in the scabbard and instead pictured a collapsible camp shovel and used it instead. Burying the remains would minimize the smell so as not to draw unwanted company in the night. After he got a fire started, he spit the bird and began cooking it while he set up camp.

Eric was amazed at the numbers and size of the antelope that passed within sight as he set up camp. They all shied back into the cover of the trees when they sensed him. When he was done setting up and his meal was finished, he sat back eating the first meal he had scrounged from the land and watched the sunset casting its golds and crimsons across the sky. It was a generous meal tender juicy meat, a variety of vegetation that he recognized and fruit and nuts that Charlie had gathered. The only part of the meal that Charlie did not share was the meat. Eric sat there, telling Charlie stories from his past, late into the night, while Charlie sat with his ears perked up listening to every word.

Shortly before they went to bed for the night, Charlie went over to the waist pack and pulled out the smallest bag of white powder and brought it over to Eric, setting it in front of him on the ground. Eric watched Charlie, as he held his paws in front of his mouth and blew across them. Charlie did this three times before Eric realized what he wanted. Eric took some of the powder and put it in his hand, about a teaspoon, then with a deep breath blew it into the air. A massive cloud of brilliant multicolored light burst forth in front of him, lighting the entire thicket. The cloud grew and dissipated as it drifted off on the breeze. Eric watched it go in wonderment, while Charlie ran in excited little circles, going, "Gerp, gerp gerp." until the cloud vanished in the night.

"You're a smart little guy." Eric mused as Charlie put the pouch back in the pack.

They slept well that night in the open under the stars. Charlie was still sleeping, when Eric woke up as the first rays of the sun cast themselves across his face. It was a beautiful morning, with the birds singing their morning songs. All about the forest and the fragrance of flowers filling the air all around them. Eric sat up and took several minutes to soak in the sights and smells around him. When he finally got up, his movement roused Charlie. They ate a quick, light breakfast of fruit and nuts and while Eric broke camp, Charlie tasted his coffee. Eric laughed, when he saw Charlie sip the coffee and spit it back out on the ground and accidentally kick his cup over. By the beginning of the second hour of the day, they were moving north through the ravine.

CHAPTER 07

What's for Dinner

They had traveled for less than an hour, when Eric heard the desperate screaming of a woman not far ahead. He ran forward, becoming increasingly cautious the closer he got to the screaming. Seeing a small clearing ahead, Eric ducked into the cover of the underbrush, working his way to its edge. He parted the branches in front of him and peered out. Stretched out face down, hanging from a huge wooden spit, was a gorgeous blond haired Elven woman. She was stretched, hands over her head, securely fastened, wearing nothing but the ropes that held her suspended above the unlit fire pit.   Perspiration of fear and effort glistened on her pallid skin, denying the cool morning breeze. Then he saw what she was looking at to the right, slowly approaching her, with hot brands of coal glowing in his hands, was the massive, ugly, giant form, that was basically that of a man, but Eric could guess to be none other than an Ogre. Eric circled around the clearing, so that he could come out behind the Ogre and drew his sword. The Ogre was kneeling, bent over the edge of the fire pit, when Eric charged into the clearing, sword raised high over his head in one hand and Charlie darting around in the open. The Ogre started turning and Eric's first stroke severed off its left arm, but Eric looped the blade around and took off the Ogres head, before it could get to its feet. The head fell off first and the body crashed down on top of it in the edge of the fire pit, smothering the fire. Eric wiped the putrid smelling blood off his sword on the Ogres loin fur and returned it to its sheath.

Eric went over to the Elven girl; she had passed out. He cut the bindings holding her up with one hand, catching her with the other. She had a beautiful body, with fine sharply defined features. She was about five feet two inches tall and thirty pounds lighter than she looked. Eric could not help himself, but to admire the beauty of her smooth skin and fine form, for a few brief moments, before wrapping her in his cloak. Carefully he carried her to the edge of the clearing farthest from the Ogres camp and laid her on some soft grass in the shade. He looked her over for injuries. She had a nasty knot on the back of her head, that had scabbed over. There were scattered scrapes and bruises and the bindings had cut into her wrists, waist and ankles. He treated her head first, cleaned it, put some medical ointments on it and wrapped it with gauze, securing it around her head, keeping as much hair as possible away from the wound. He treated her wrists and ankles in a similar fashion and used tape on the gauze bandages where he treated the cuts just above her hips at her waist line. He cleaned the other scrapes he found, but deemed they did not need covering. When he was done, he wrapped her back up in his cloak, covered her with one blanket and tucked the other under her head for a pillow. All the while he worked on her, Charlie just sat quietly and watched.

"That must have terrified her." Eric said looking at Charlie, "She is quite beautiful, you know." He paused, turning to put everything away, "She took a bad blow to the back of her head, but I think she'll be alright, given a little time."

Eric started a small fire and using water from his canteen began making a pot of coffee. "She is going to need some rest and I can't leave her out here alone, so it looks like we'll have a new traveling companion for a while at least."

"Charlie gave him what seemed to be an understanding look, then with a gerp, headed off into the woods. Eric was sitting in thought watching the young Elven girl when he returned. Eric turned and let his thoughts sink into the flames of his small fire as he sipped his coffee.

Darkness swirled about her overwhelming her with the bittersweet taste of fear, burning away at an unreal sensation of sanity slipping out of her reach. In the distance she heard a faint buzz, she reached for it running towards it, trying to contain her mounting fear. Moving closer to the buzzing it changed to a shrill whine and a distant point of light started to appear. She threw herself forward faster, afraid to yield to total and blind fear. The point of light grew as though she were moving through a tunnel carrying a silent scream with her. Suddenly the light surrounded her and she could feel her lungs fill with air.

Saphrine came conscious with a scream, vaulting to a seated position. Her eyes were blurred and she saw the form of a man turn towards her, seated a few feet away, before dizziness forced her to lay back down. The Ogre, she thought, she should be dead, cooked alive. She screamed again. He was cooking her and she was hallucinating. Her mind reeled and her head was pounding. She screamed without control. Her thinking was sporadic, she could not be dead, it hurt too much. She felt someone cover her back up, she was not burning over a fire, but how. Someone lifted her head and was holding something to her lips, she drank as the liquid entered her mouth. It felt good on her parched mouth and sore throat.

"The medicine should ease the pain shortly." the smooth soothing male baritone voice resonated in her ears. He kissed her forehead, somehow comforting her, she let her eyes open again. It was a man, with a strong, but gentle face framed with hints of dusty blond hair sticking out from around the edges of his leather helmet, hinting at concealing a chain-mail hung metal helmet underneath. His eyes were blue, but she sensed somehow, they could change colors. He had a powerful jaw and a strong line to his face, but the gentle, soft look of great compassion in his eyes vanquished all her fear. He smiled at her. She gave what she knew was a feeble attempt at smiling back. She noticed that her pain was subsiding and her head was clearing. The man had an insignia on his breast, a lion sitting over two crossed swords on a black background. It was somehow familiar, but she could not quite place it.

Eric looked down, into her sharp, yet soft Elven features, she was petite, her fine eyebrows sloping upward accenting her sea-green eyes. Her soft thin lips, had just tried a weak smile that made his heart throb. She started to sit up and he helped her, holding his cloak and blanket around her shoulders. "Take it easy, you'll be alright. Just relax and don't try to talk until you get your bearings. My name is Eric. I slew the Ogre that had you and not at all too soon."

Saphrine sat up, fear shot briefly through her as she remembered the Ogre. She was thankful for this stranger's help. His said his name was Eric and he had a strange accent she could not recognize. When the ground stopped moving, she realized she was naked and wrapped in the stranger's cloak, it had his emblem on the shoulder. He had seen her naked, the thought embarrassed her, but she knew he could not have helped that, the Ogre had stripped her. She thought this was a typical story for children, where the handsome prince comes and saves the lady in despair. He was handsome and looked like a man of might in his armor, of leather and chain-mail. He could be a prince, but he was a human. Did that matter, she could not remember. His weapons were unique, different from any she had seen before, and she had seen a lot back home in..... Where was she from? She could not remember. She had to.... She was important she though, after all she was.... She could not remember who she was. Maybe she was a nobody, after all she had nothing to indicate otherwise. Maybe this man who saved her knew who she was, though maybe not, since he introduced himself. What could she remember? She remembered an Ogre, it was going to cook her and eat her, an awful memory. Before that she remembered falling...., her head.... She remembered language and could recognize things, but not her life, her parents, who she was or where she was from. She was afraid again and she wanted a hug, needed a hug.

Eric fixed some coffee and repacked everything except the cup and pot. He mixed it with cream and sugar, figuring she had never had it before and it was an acquired taste, black. Charlie had disappeared, but showed up in time to slip a couple more leaves into the coffee. "Gerp gerp, gerp gerp." sounding a little urgent Charlie looked at the girl and back to the cup. Eric knew he could trust the little one and left the leaves in the cup of coffee, as he brought it over to the Elven woman.

"Here drink this. It might help you feel a little better." Eric saw the fear in her eyes. She was afraid, but not of him. He handed her the coffee. "It is alright you are not in danger now. I will protect you. I won't hurt you."

Saphrine took the coffee. "Thank you," she spoke with the same strange inflections as the other Elves he had heard in Talmorg. She sipped the drink, it was warm and felt good, helping her to relax slightly, yet it seemed to be giving her strength. "Hug me." She looked up at Eric, tears welling up as their eyes met.

Eric knelt down and gently embraced her. She was shaking. "Hows your head feel?" his voice rolled with tenderness.

"It hurts," she sobbed, "and I don't know who I am. I don't remember anything. I am scared. Who am I?"

"It sounds like you may have amnesia." Eric leaned back, holding her by her shoulders and looking into her face. "I am new to this world and I am sorry to say, I do not know who you are. It is probably the blow you took to the head that stole your memory. I am sure it will return in time. Do you remember anything at all?"

"The Ogre, just the Ogre, and waking up to see you." her eyes rested on the ground between them. She had to trust him she had nothing else and he saved her life.

"I don't know you. I would guess you are from either Efra or Talmorg, those are the nearest Elven cities, but I could be wrong. Can you remember anything, rooms, flags, emblems, faces?" He watched her eyes, but they gave no sign of anything coming to mind.

"No, nothing." she said pausing between her words.

"Well, I am going to search the Ogre's camp, to see if there is anything that might help you remember. In the meantime, you need something to wear other than my cloak, alone it doesn't offer much comfort or protection." He thought about the magic Shiheel had told him he had. The only thing he had used it on was a pair of roller skates and a meal since he left, and part of the reason he was out here was to learn to use it. He paused, because Charlie hopped into his lap.

"A gerpin." the Elven girl said with stunned excitement, they were creatures of legend to her. "They were magical creatures of luck, that saved the very existence of the Elves, back in the beginning of legend."

Eric looked at her, she remembered something, though it seemed odd to him that his companion was a creature only known in legends on Ethar. He looked at Charlie and then back at the young Elf girl. "This is a gerpin?" He couldn't quite hit the way she pronounced her vowels, "I found him with a broken leg, under a fallen branch."

"If legend is right, he feels he owes you his life and will stay with you, bringing you luck, at least until he feels his debt is repaid, maybe longer." she paused, reached over and pet the gerpin with some reverence,

"I also am in your debt, you saved my life, too. I do not know who I am or if I can repay you."

"Don't worry about it, I do not expect payment for doing what is right. Let me give you some cloths, so you will be able to get up and move around. Take it slowly though I don't think you should try too much, too fast." Then with a big friendly smile he added, "As for your memory, you remembered the legend of the gerpin, I am sure you will remember everything with time." Eric turned slightly and looked at the ground next to her. He pictured a pair of designer jeans, a blue T-shirt, panties, a bra, a pair of socks, a sweatshirt, a pair of moccasin boots and a cloak much like his own. As he pictured each item it appeared on the ground where he looked. Saphrine watched the clothing form in a nice neat stack, in stunned silence. "Here you go, put these on. I am going over to the Ogre's camp now and I will be right back. Charlie, the 'gerpin' will keep you company, until I return."

Eric stood up and walked across the clearing, to where he encountered the Ogre. He searched all around the Ogres camp. He did not find a shred of her cloths. All he found was a half-eaten horse, a stone club he could not pick up and the Ogre. On the Ogre's rope belt, was tied a hefty leather pouch, which Eric quickly cut off. He opened the bag, to examine its contents. There were precious stones, a variety of jewels, coins and jewelry inside. He pulled the draw strings closing the bag, threw it over his shoulder and carried it back with him.

While Eric was gone, Saphrine worked on getting dressed in the strange clothes. They were all of strange materials, but she had no trouble figuring out the socks, shirts, pants and boots, but she did not understand the laced pieces of material. The one looked like it may have been for support, but the fastenings were not familiar so she left them laying on the blanket. When she was dressed, she walked over and picked up the odd-looking pot next to the fire refilling her cup. The liquid was darker than the cup he had brought her and had a terrible taste, but she remembered seeing him mix the white powders from another container on the ground, in her first cup. She opened the container and used the spoon to scoop it out, as she had seen him do, then stirred it in. It tasted much better, she decided after sipping it again. The stranger who saved her was a warrior, a healer and a wizard, a very strange combination indeed, she thought. For some reason it was especially strange because he was human, but she could not remember why that would be stranger than anyone else. She wondered where he was from, he had said he was new to this world, but that could simply mean he had walked across the continent to get here or this was the first time he has been outside his home city. She wanted to know him better, she already felt like she could trust him. He would help her remember if he could. What if he could not, after all he did not know her either. The names of the cities he had mentioned sounded familiar, but she could not place them in her mind. What was he doing here in the middle of nowhere, what was she doing here, alone?

Walking back over Eric noticed she had put the clothing on he had left for her. "How do they fit, are they comfortable?"

Saphrine stood up, turning front and back to show him the cloths, "They fit fine, except, I don't know what those are for or how they work." She gestured back to the bra and panties, left on the blanket.

"These are to protect your more tender skin, from the roughness of your trousers." Eric said picking up the panties first and indicating the groin area. Then he picked up the bra, trying to demonstrate its use on his own body. "This is for support and protection of your breasts. You put it on similar to a shirt, putting your arms through these straps, and hooking it together in the front. You may find it more comfortable traveling with this on. I presume you will be traveling with me." He paused looking in a northerly direction, then back to her, "I am heading to a war, north at Dragoncove."

"I don't know where else to go!" she said emphatically stomping one foot in frustration, and quickly regaining her composure.

"Well, I could detour, to the Walled City of Talmorg. You could stay there and someone might recognize you. If you go with me to Dragoncove armies from all the cities in the south lands will be there and there is a good chance someone might know you there too. Those garments go under your other cloths." Eric added seeing her starting to slide the bra over her shirt sleeve. "Do you remember if you were on horseback?"

She paused for a few moments, remembering she was falling, "I was falling," She said as she dropped the cloak to the ground and pulled her shirts off, not being ashamed of upper body nudity, which was not considered indecent on Ethar, "I think there were horses. Would you show me how this works?" She held the bra out to him and he felt himself starting to blush, as he took it and helped her put it on, hooking it together in front feeling her warmth. "And others. Yes, there were others too, someone else yelled 'Ogre', I heard them." She enjoyed the feel of his hands against her, but tried not to show it.

Eric stepped back and while she put the shirts back on again, he said, "Well, that's a start, if you don't mind, I will need a name to call you by. Do you have a preference for now?"

Bending over and picking the cloak back up off the ground, she answered, "Tamaria, is a name I remember from somewhere, I don't think it's mine, but it will work for now."

"I found this bag in the Ogre's possession," Eric said dragging the bag over to where his cloak still lay spread out on the ground and squatting down. Saphrine sat on the ground next to him. "We'll look through the contents and see if there is anything familiar."

"Eric dumped the contents of the bag on his cloak and spread it out. They both started looking through them, the coins caught his attention. There were a lot of them and they had different impressions on them. He picked one out that seemed to have his crest on it. He guessed the coin came from Efra. Turning the gold coin over, on the opposite side it had the impression of a phoenix. He dropped that coin back in the pile and picked up a silver coin that had the crest of Talmorg on it. The crest was a scepter crossed over a sword, dominated by an oak tree and wreathed with garland. The opposite side was a dragon with wings spread, with an Elf riding on its back.

While Eric was looking through the coins, Saphrine, looked through the rings and found one that felt familiar. It was a gold ring, inlaid with an emerald, that had an impression in it, matching Erics insignia, wreathed in roses, formed from sapphires. It fit perfectly on her index finger, where she tried it first. She showed it to Eric. "This ring seems very familiar."

"That looks like an insignia ring from Efra, except I do not understand what the roses would be for." Eric said pausing, something was nagging in the back of his mind but he could not place what it was, so he let it go.

"It fits perfectly on my index finger and that is where I felt it belonged. Maybe it will help me remember." Her stomach growled while she spoke, cause her face to go a light shade of pink with embarrassment.

"Sounds like it's time for lunch." Eric laughed, standing back up. "After we eat though, I think we should try and put some distance between us and this clearing, if you're up to it. I don't think we want to smell it if the wind changes directions."

"No," Saphrine agreed, "I have smelled all the Ogre I ever want to smell." Then she started returning the small treasure to the bag.

Eric pulled his mess kit out of his pack and divided the meat he had from the night before into two of the pans, threw in some of the nuts and fruit that Charlie had continued to gather and grabbed his canteen of water. He carried them back over, sitting down he placed them on his cloak that Saphrine had just cleared. "It is not much, but it is what I have, without hunting for more."

"It looks fine and I am hungry now, thank you." She took the pan closest to her and started eating, with Charlie sleeping next to her.

While they ate, Eric Told her how he had come to Ethar and the things that had happened since he had arrived. Then he told her how he had found the gerpin Charlie. She was surprised, when he told her he did not have any magic before he left Earth, but understood his journey was on a schedule. Eric did not know what to say, when she commented that if this journey was to teach him to understand the magic he had, he should use it more, not just when he needed it. He had to smile and agree though, when she laughed at the expression on his face. He gave her more medicine with the meal to help keep the pain in her head subdued. When they finished the meal, Saphrine helped him clean and repack, then insisted on at least carrying the shoulder bag, as they headed down the ravine.

While they walked, Saphrine and Eric talked about the things they saw and she quickly learned he knew very little about the plants and animals of Ethar. So, she spent most of the afternoon teaching him as they walked. Several times they saw wild herds of varied animals, and she named them all, telling him their habits and stories about their significance in history. She also told him which ones tasted better on the dinner table. As evening approached, she gathered a wide variety of vegetation,

Charlie kept gathering fruit and nuts and Eric took down a large game bird, according to what Saphrine had told him would taste the best. She called the bird a carmigan and cleaned it while Eric set up camp in a small clearing. They had been out of the mountains for the last hour of their travel and followed along the bottom of the foothills. They stopped when they came to a small clearing, that had, at its edge, a steam with a pool at the bottom of a waterfall. Saphrine fixed their dinner and the three of them sat down to a small feast. She proved to be an excellent cook and among the vegetation she had picked, were seasonings, that really set off the flavor of the meat. Charlie stuck to fruit, nuts and vegetables, then curled up in front of the tent and went to sleep when he was finished eating.

"Do you have any idea who you are, yet?" Eric asked, as they sat together by the fire, staring into its flames.

"No, though I don't think I am poor. I was not impressed by that bag of trinkets. If I was poor, I would have been." She answered, referring to the bag he had gotten from the Ogre. "I am however a very fortunate Elf to be saved by you." She poked a stick in the fire, causing a cloud of sparks to rise up. It reminded Eric of the powder he had in his pack, but he did not bring it up.

"Maybe you are royalty?" Eric suggested, looking at the quarter moon lowering in the east.

"That would not make sense, though it is a nice dream." She smiled at him with genuine affection, "If I were a princess, I would have been traveling with protection sufficient to protect me from such hazards, and I would have been traveling by roads, not through the forest in an area where an Ogre might be found. Your friend, Shiheel knew it would not be dangerous for you, because you have your magic to protect you, yet he also made sure your weapons were sufficient to slay even a giant rock marmot."

"How about an adventurer, you know quite a lot about the plants and animals. Do you know how to fight?" Eric looked at her thoughtfully, considering the possibilities, "You could be a soldier."

"Possibly, except I have no previous scars, from training or battle. I can fight, I think. I feel like I have been trained in fighting, I think it was formal training." Saphrine's eyes sparkled at the thought of sparring with Eric.

"It would seem that we will not figure out who you are tonight," Eric stood up, "I am going to clean these dishes in the steam, would you like to keep me company?"

"I can do that," Saphrine said scrambling to her feet, "and you can keep me company."

Eric wondered where custom stood in this land, if it was a matter crossing over expected roles of gender. "If I were still alone, I would have to wash them myself." Eric ventured, testing the subject.

"It would not be proper, for me to allow that, as long as I am here." Saphrine answered his unasked question.

"Very well, but the least I can do is help." Eric replied, and the two of them carried the utensils from their meal over to the edge of the water.

The dishes were cleaned quickly in the tepid water of the stream and Eric turned to Saphrine. "I'm going to take a bath in that little pool up there."

Saphrine looked back at him with a mischievous smile. "It's dark, I think I will too." She turned to carry her arm load of pans over to the tent, then looking over her shoulder added, "We really need to wash our clothes also, unless you object." Smiling she continued back to the tent. Eric followed her up with the rest of the utensils, he had no objections.

Eric was surprised when he first saw the second moon rising, while he was rinsing the soap off Saphrine's shoulders. She had come to him and washed his back first. Now the light of the moons, was glistening off the silky skin of her shoulders as he gently rubbed them. They had been laughing and playing in the water for over an hour, now Eric leaned forward and gently kissed her on the shoulder. Saphrine leaned her head away from his kiss exposing her neck. He pulled her willing form closer through the water, embracing her and caressing her form in his hands. Gently kissing he inched his lips along the curve of her shoulder, up her neck, to find their way to her earlobe and softly nibbled. Her breath heaved heavy in her chest, as the warmth of his breath passed over her ear. No longer able to resist his luring warmth, Saphrine turned in his embrace to wrap her own arms around him, running her fingers down his back until they came to rest on his back under the water. As she gently squeezed him closer, he responded caressing the back of her head with one hand and letting the other drift down in the water, back, he coddled her lips with his own. They became entwined in their passions losing the world around them for a period of time. Eventually they noticed gain the starts that filled the skies and the light of the two moons. Saphrine and Eric moved to rest their shoulders near the edge of the pool, where they resorted to tickling, laughing and gentle petting, before rising up out of the water. They stood at the edge of the pool embraced in a long-held kiss, then hung their cloths from tree branches, before crawling into the small tent together.

Eric could not resist the call of her soft, warm, suppleness lying next to his. His desires for her met hers in playful antics. She whispered in his ear "Again, you need a small harem to take care of your needs." Eric smile as they indulged time passed seemingly forever and too fast all at once. Their passions crested and calmed. They held each other tight for a few moments, before they both relaxed and collapsed, falling to sleep in each other's arms. It was a night that neither would ever forget.

<h1 style="text-align:center">CHAPTER 08</h1>

Pathways North

The individual units moved out joining the larger formation of the army outside the gates. Each Unit comprised of four rows of eight soldiers and one unit commander. Three units formed up side by side making up a group with a group commander and a messenger. The next group formed up behind the one in front of it. The thirty-five groups made an impressive army as they set into motion. Approximately a third of the active army was staying behind to defend the city and reserves were being activated.

Talmorg rode at his father's side, as they marched out from the city with the lords of the south lands, leading thirty-five hundred active troops from the city of Talmorg. It had only taken half of a day to have all the main force, of the active military ready to march. The commander of the royal guard and all the captains, had been informed right after the council meeting the night before and started mobilizing the troops. The mobilized force though of mixed races, was primarily Elven, since the greater part of the population was Elf. The minimal training any soldier in an Elven army had, was the basics of being a swordsman and an archer. Additional training was dependent on the individuals desire and abilities. Those who stood out in ability and proved to have the right character for it were inducted into the Royal Guard. To be in the royal guard the individual had to first prove an unswerving loyalty to the royal family and secondly, they must prove to be skillful in combat with no less than ten different weapons. Generally speaking, an individual who was inducted into the royal guard had already earned a nickname among his or her peers. At present the Royal Guard made up about eight hundred of the thirty-five hundred, that followed the lords out of the city of Talmorg.

Talmorg contemplated the make up of their army. The city of Talmorg had the most females of any known army, they strove to deal with gender prejudices at the same time they dealt with the racial ones. Other lordships in the past had told them it would weaken them in battle, but Talmorg had learned from experience that at times the female warrior could be even more savage than the male, his mother had said it was because they had stronger emotions, which made them much fiercer at times. He had also learned from his own sparing experience, their movements are subtly different, along with some of their techniques. Talmorg remembered the first time he had ever sparred with a female trainee. His instructor overheard a comment he made about females in battle, he could not even remember what he had said. He was pitted against a girl two levels of training behind him and lost the first match, that is when he started learning how to counter their differences. Talmorg later learned how fierce they could be, when after he had beat girl at his own level of training, she got mad and swung full force with her wooden practice sword. It broke against his when he blocked the swing, but the piece hit him in the head, dazing him and she won that match with his sword, after that they started wearing hardened leather helmets in training.

For the two thousand on horseback and fifteen hundred on foot, marching behind him training would soon be mixed with experience. Only the Royal Guard would remain on horseback in battle. The official bowmen would take up positions behind the foot soldiers. Though all of them carried bows, once swords were engaged, the official archers would continue to reduce the enemy from a distance, stepping up as replacements with their own swords as needed.

Talmorg turned to his father, "The armies of Vorka could arrive at Dragoncove ahead of us, if Shiheel gets the messages delivered on time."

"By the Ancients, he better." King Erron looked at Talmorg with concern, "Our success depends on his getting those messages through."

"Father, I am sure he will. I was not thinking about that, it just seemed a waste, if the soldiers of Vorka had to wait a day or so for us before they could do anything."

"You needn't worry bout that." Prince Ashkin reined his horse closer to the conversation, "They'll get the message today, but by the time they verify it's real and get organized, another two days will pass. Then as you know we, don't like riding animals. We like to keep our feet to the ground. They will press their march, but they will not get there ahead of us."

"In that case, I've worried for nothing." Talmorg smiled, "We will have a lot of work to do, when we get there and sufficient but limited time to do it in. Lord Ashkin, do you think it possible, there might be spies belonging to Mistav in the area?"

"Doubtful, Wonks are good warriors, but simple thinkers. Mistav probably doesn't even think much beyond his next conquest." A fret passed across his face, "He probably is not thinking past his next conquest. I would guess that uniting the wonks is already a lot for him to think about. He probably hasn't gotten to thinking of it as anything more than a big tribe, though tribe rules would fall way short in keeping a kingdom together."

"We must never underestimate our enemy," King Erron added, "even the simple can be cunning. If his thoughts are as simple as you say, isn't it possible he is having simple thoughts of world conquest, not understanding what it means?"

"That is possible." Prince Ashkin agreed, "But I would say, spies are out of the question, it would still be too complicated an operation. The closest thing he might try to that would be a raiding party. Besides they don't trust other races, and one of them among us would be easy to see."

"Actually, these are matters we should be discussing with all the lords, maybe around dinner tonight." Talmorg looked at the sun low in the eastern sky, "We need to think about stopping for the night."

"Not really too much to think about here in the open flat lands." Prince Ashkin snickered, "I'm sure your troops are practiced at it, the only decision you have to make is when you want to stop."

"Your good friend here, isn't going to let you worry," King Erron smiled borderline on laughing, "at least not about nonsense, son." The three of them laughed.

When they stopped, the troops broke into companies of one

hundred to set up camp. While camp was being set up Talmorg spoke to his father, "You know father, you did not have to come to this war. The ride is showing your age."

"I know son," Erron answered, rubbing an ache out of his back and wincing as he straightened it out, "but I am still king, even though you were elected to command the combined army. I still have a responsibility to my subjects."

"True father, but you could fill that responsibility, by sending me. Your subjects, know the years of devotion you have given them and they are not ignorant of your age or health. They would respect you no less, if you took some care of your health, and delegated some of your responsibility."

"The kings and high lords of the other kingdoms and lordships will be there for the same reason I will." Erron leaned against his horse and rolled a kink out of his neck, "I will be fine, Talmorg, don't worry so for me. You have enough to fill your thoughts, without needless worry."

Talmorg signaled Calbork, who came immediately in response, while Talmorg said to his father, "Very true father, but you tell me if you need anything."

"Yes, my lord." Calbork said as he stopped a few feet from Talmorg, in response to his signal.

"I wish a meeting of the lords in the main tent. We will need our meal delivered; would you be so kind as to attend to the arrangements." Talmorg stated, looking into the hard lined face of the sandy haired warrior.

"Yes, my lord." Calbork said simply with a bow, then turned and walked away, not needing an official dismissal. Calbork was an average height, sandy haired Elf, about one hundred and twenty years older than Talmorg, and his right arm. He had a scarred and battle-hardened face, the scar running from the corner of his right eye, diagonally to the corner of his mouth gave him a cruel hardness and the small scar giving him a cleft chin gave him an almost comical seriousness. He was the only Elf Talmorg could not consistently beat in any sparring match, he was also Talmorg's instructor. Calbork was four foot eleven inches of ideal Royal Guard.

The evenings meeting went well. Calbork even managed fresh Eliko meat for their meal. They reviewed several pages of Eric's documents discussing point and counter point and practical application. They also decided each of them would study a section during the days ride and collectively work their way through them at dinner meetings each night. The pattern was set, and it had become routine by the third evening meeting. By the time they gained sight of Dragoncove, the documents Eric had given them became an integral part of the thinking of the lords of the south lands.

Talmorg led the way until they were within a half hour of the gates of Dragoncove, shortly before midday. Hanser Schultzmann went ahead into the city, while the others worked on details of a command camp and base camp from which to operate in the open fields east of the Dragoncove. Calbork organized the armies of Talmorg in the area allotted them, leaving a handful of Royal Guard to set up the command tents.

"So, tomorrow morning, seventeen score of my horsemen will pair off with yours of equal number and cross the river with traps and alert signals." Hanser continued his conversation with Talmorg.

"Yes," Talmorg returned, "they will each have at least fifteen traps and four alert trip signals to place."

"I expect my people to arrive, tomorrow." Prince Ashkin put in, "They will be able to start working on front line preparations, as soon as I can explain to them, what we have planned. I must say though, I thank the mother mountains this Eric is on our side."

They all gave a chuckle, and Hanser added, "Aye, and I pray whatever gods are out there, that our success might be quick."

The council of Dragoncove gave them the use of the second floor in the city council building to use as a command center. The first floor of the building was built from the basalt rock found along the coast, while the second floor was built of timber taken from the Pengona forest. The structure was typical of those found in Dragoncove, including the fortress wall that surrounded the city. Talmorg concluded that the city would not withstand a major war, but it never needed to before. The wall was more for night time security and kept the animals out.

The council building would serve during the weeks of preparation and they would move their command center to the field when the conflict began. The dwarves of Vorka actually arrived two days later, when the major trenching, bulwark construction and front-line preparation began.

The dwarves engineered and built the collapsing bridges and pit traps they would retreat across and release. The horsemen of Dragoncove set barrels of oil upstream for torching the river. By the end of the first week major progress had been made and troops from other south land cities started arriving.

"What are ya fretting about now cuz?" Freebic asked from where he was seated looking over the maps spread out on the table.

Talmorg paused in his pacing, glancing at his cousin, realizing his pacing was at best just irritating those around him. He stepped over and sat down next to Freebic. "I'll stop pacing. Everything seems to be running according to schedule. Efra is a day late in arriving, but we know they are on their way. Shiheel is late and that worries me. I know he has been late before, but that has only been by an hour or so, not a day or so. Also, even though Eric was not supposed to arrive for another week I was expecting him with Shiheel." Talmorg leaned his head back and stretched his neck, closing his eyes briefly, "On top of what's happening here, the Princess Saphrine Barhallah, should have arrived at my home court about a week ago and nobody knows where she is, six Royal Guards vanished with her."

"That is the only thing you have mentioned worth worrying about." Freebic shook his head, "But there is nothing you can do about it from here, so either concentrate on what is happening or get some sleep so you can."

Just as he finished, Calbork stepped up, "The commitment from Dargen and Morbin has arrived, sire, and another five hundred volunteers from Tarsha of the Province of Harmosk. Their arrangements have been seen to, my Lord."

"Thank you, Calbork." Talmorg smiled and turned to Freebic again, "You see 'cuz' my people are so efficient that I have nothing to do but fill my time with needless worry." Turning back to Calbork he added, "I will be having dinner in the field this evening, gather the officers I want to be sure they have been reviewing our new tactics."

"Yes, My Lord." He made a curt bow before turning to leave.

*   *   *   *   *   *   *

Shiheel left Eric and took off on the giant Roc. He hoped that the massive bird would be able to hold up long enough to deliver the messages, then he got another idea and whispered in his winged friend's ear. No ordinary creature, other than the birds could handle the screaming sound that came from the rock cliffs in the most subtle of breezes. Then Eftites were not ordinary. Quickly others gathered around, at the summoning of Shiheel's mount. In a few brief moments one by one the birds took flight each carrying a message to a different destination. '*That's half the mission.*' Shiheel thought to himself, '*Now on to Tarf.*' He gently stroked the back of the white feathered head, understanding the signal, the great female, queen of her brood, took to flight. Shiheel estimated it would take him five days to get back to Dragoncove.

It was afternoon, when they reached a small jetty about half a day's travel south of the death pits. Shiheel knew Eerka had pushed herself to fly this far without rest, and did not want to endanger her by bringing her any closer. The gases would not reach this far and she would be safe resting in the rocks here. The Eftite focused his attention on a small pile of rocks dematerializing them and then re-materializing the energy in the form of food for Eerka. After communicating his appreciation for all she had done, Shiheel walked a couple hours up the coast.

Finding a discrete place in the rock shoreline, Shiheel started burning a tunnel, using a portion of the matter he was tunneling through to convert to the energy beam, he projected to form the glass walled tunnel. He was the most powerful of his kind on Ethar and as a result could tunnel faster, but it would still take him at least two days to reach his destination. It had taken him years to develop his skills to the proficiency he now had. He remembered his hatching day, burning rock came by instinct, but several of his siblings did not survive their first attempt. By the time they were hatch-lings, their parents had passed on to them the majority of what they knew, just as he and Hesheil were doing with their egg-lings. Learning had been a dangerous thing during the first years of their lives.

As he tunneled, he reminisced in his mind, his hatch-ling years on Esberk II. The first week as with all hatch-lings, their heavy gold eggshell was what they ate for sustenance. It took a couple of years to learn to convert matter during which time their parents provided for them through energy matter conversion. Shiheel and Hesheil had been selected for parenting long before their hatching and received the special preparations needed to serve their destinies. The two of them developed much faster than the rest of their nest, their purpose was to be the leaders of their hatch.

Unfortunately, before they reached full maturity the Esberkian star system was attacked by the vicious Scaldorians. Having depleted the resources of their own neighboring system, the Scaldorians sought to conquer the Esberkian system. The powers released in the resulting war set their sun into an imbalance, and their parents' generation sent out life capsules to all parts of the universe, in hopes of preserving as much as they could of their home worlds. Shiheel and all his siblings were among those who escaped before the sun went supernova, taking the Scaldorians with it.

It was three days later when Shiheel surfaced again in Tarf and stepped out of his glass walled tunnel. It was a ghost city, barren of life for centuries, since the handy work of Suan Perdone. He had been here before, on one of his quests for knowledge and the writings of Ethar. Shiheel had acquired several shelves worth of books from here, but he knew the book Eric had read was not one of them and wondered where the original might be hidden. Now that he was back in the city, Shiheel also wondered how Merlin Starnook had managed to retrieve and complete the document, especially since he was supposedly already dead at the time. Merlin was now an enigma that Shiheel planned to dedicate some time to when this whole mess was over.

Merlin Starnook had been considered a great wizard, as great if not greater than Deassheema at the time. He had vanished after his battle with the evil warlock, presumed dead, but his signature in the book Eric had replicated into existence proved otherwise. Shiheel wondered why the old lord of magics had never shown his face again and if he still might be alive somewhere. Shiheel laughed to himself thinking of Hesheil, '*Well brother hatch-ling, this is a mystery you too will want to solve.*', then turned back to the task at hand.

The first thing he wanted to do was reopen the tunnel to the death pits. Deassheema had created and acquired too many runes of darkness and Tarf just oozed with dark magic. The deadly gases would once again seal the city off from the world of the living, though the gas would not affect him, being a none breathing creature. He had come up in one of the outer merchant markets near the Palace. He moved through the ancient crumbling city with precise knowledge of where he was going and what he was doing. He entered the palace knowing its pitfalls and secret passages, he made his way quickly, to the bottom level of the dark dungeons, six floors below the surface of the ground. The double doors leading to the deadly pits stood wide open, but just beyond then Shiheel could see the obstruction that allowed no more gas to pass, lift the forbidding seal from the city. The top of the tunnel had given way, filled the passage and no longer allowed the slightest wisp through. Shiheel remembered the first time he had seen the tunnel; he was sure then it had outlasted its expectation. There had been minimal wood bracing as if it had only been built to serve a temporary purpose. Now he knew why, Deassheema had only needed it to forge his implements of power.

In solitude he set to work carving out a new tunnel. Shiheel used the material as he cut it away, converting it and forming structure to his new tunnel that would last indefinitely. If he had thought to raze the city, he might have done that instead, but he wanted to ensure that no one would ever use anything forged by the power of Deassheema again. A day and a half passed while he worked, during which time he gave thought to what he knew about the powers of the Ancients.

In another place the Ancients might be referred to as gods, and those that were most familiar as lesser gods. They were in fact the immortal origins of the races of Ethar. Having grown into the power they now possess; they had been given a choice by their creators. The command they received was simple; either set laws restricting the use of their power so that the lesser races could learn and grow in their own ways, or laws would be made for them. These powerful beings no longer had authority to control the course of history in the making, though they still had a strong influence and retained the right to help and guide their people. They formed an entirely different realm of existence within which they now dwelt, from which they could exercise their influence in the affairs of Ethar, while still leaving the future of Ethar in the hands of the peoples of the world. Tarf and history both proved that the freedoms given them were not always used for good.

In many of the books Shiheel had gotten from Tarf, there were references to the Dark Council of the Shadow World. He had never been able to figure out exactly what they were, nor did he have any real proof of his suspicions. There were some things that the Ancients and the peoples of Ethar never wrote about and kept as well guarded secrets, but he had theories and believed that not all of the Ancients, or should be Ancients abode by the rule or even lived in the world of the Ancients. In one of his writings Deassheema made reference to having found favor with the Lord of the Shadow World and gaining secrets to steal back the world from the disgrace of the self-proclaimed Ancients. There were strong indicators in some of the writings of Deassheema that he was having hallucinations and a loss of his reasoning faculties too. This diminished the credibility of anything he wrote. Still Shiheel found that the history of the Ancients was well guarded if even known.

Shiheel climbed up from the depths of rock and dirt, casting his mind back to the matters at hand, the salvation of the south lands. He headed for the recovery of the shield. He wondered why he had not noticed the shield on a previous exploration of the throne room, however when he got to the throne this time, he realized that in fact the back of the throne was a shield.

The remarkable shield formed by white magic had not been damaged, but it took some time to separate if from its fastenings and remove all the extra trimmings. When he was done, he held a shield that was about six foot tall, oval,two foot wide at its widest point and rather plain looking. The back of it was completely covered with elaborate characters of the old language of the Elves. The front side of the shield looked like nothing more than polished steel. Shiheel took the shield in one arm and started the long journey back to Dragoncove.

CHAPTER 09

Remember

Eric woke up early the next morning, the sky just barely beginning to glow. He looked into the beautiful face of the Elf snuggled close and wrapped in his arms. Something was nagging at the back of his mind. Eric felt as though he should know more about who she was, but could not figure out why he felt that way. Then something Azeel had told him came to mind and he saw a possibility he should have seen right away. She could be and probably was the crowned princess Saphrine, who had been on the road from Efra to Talmorg. Even the ring she had selected from the Ogre's treasure should have told him, that ring could very well be her royal signet ring. She also found it natural to wear the ring on her ruling finger, a mark of authority, and it had fit perfectly, matching the mark in her finger where she had previously worn a ring. She was still asleep as Eric started whispering, "Saphrine, Saphrine, wake up."

She rolled over slightly and murmured, then suddenly opened her eyes, "My name, you said my name." She pressed against him giving him a tight hug and a kiss of pure delight.

Eric returned a somewhat weak smile, not knowing how he should properly behave, only that he had not been wise to bed the royal princess. "Then you are the crowned princess of Efra and you were on your way from Efra to Talmorg."

She looked into Eric's eyes with a touch of uncertainty in her own, she had to considered the ramification of their actions if this were true. She sat up next to him not bothering to conceal herself, though much more conscious of her nudity with the thought of being a princess, and took a deep contemplative breath, "I do not know about all of what you have said, but that is my name. What has brought you to all these conclusions?"

Eric lifted himself up on his elbows and began, "Six days ago, I was at a council meeting in the city of Talmorg for the first time, where I met Azeel an Ambassador from Efra. I learned from him that the crowned princess Saphrine would be on her way there to discuss trade agreements." He paused shifting his weight, "The timing would be right for you to be on the road not too far from where I found you. Then there is the ring you are wearing, it bares the insignia of the royal family of Efra circled in roses. It very well could be what makes it your signet ring." Eric watched her expression as what he said soaked in.

She looked down at her knees feeling a sense of shame for her own behavior. "If this is true than I have compromised the royal house of, what's my last name?" she asked looking back to Eric for an answer.

"Barhallah." He stated after a pause remembering what Azeel had said and noticed the recognition in her somber face.

Silence held them both for a time before she spoke again, "I am still in your debt for saving my life, what is mine is yours, and" she added, "we cannot change what has already been done. I don't think I would want to change it anyway." She smiled and Eric could see in her eyes that she had surrendered her heart to him. It was a wonderful pat on his ego, yet at the same time, though he found her attractive and had passion for her, he was saddened for her, knowing that neither could he be hers, nor had his own heart surrendered its love to her.

Eric suddenly felt embarrassed, but managed not too blush down playing his thoughts, "I still need to keep heading to Dragoncove. I only have nine more days to get there."

There was almost no conversation through breakfast, both of them being absorbed in sorting through their own thoughts. Charlie however seemed to make up for their lack of conversation, running around gerping all morning. When they started walking again, Saphrine, changing the subject of their morning thoughts, started asking more questions about Eric's life. At first, she had been shocked when she learned he was from Earth. His strange accent and mannerisms helped her passed the difficulty she had believing it. Their hearts lightened as she asked questions and he tried to describe a world as alien to her as Ethar was to him.

They stopped for lunch, eating what meat was left over from the previous night's carmigan and some of the nuts and fruit that Charlie had gathered. When they were through eating Eric decided to check her injuries and change the dressings. They were both surprised when they discovered she was completely healed, with no marks to indicate she had ever been hurt.

"You heal remarkably well." Eric had started, but Saphrine laughed.

"You have very powerful magic, for not knowing what you have."

she commented between laughing.

"You think I am responsible for your quick healing, too?" he asked in surprise.

"Of course," she stopped laughing, pulling her composure back together, "I have no other explanation for it, and you told me how well the Gerpin healed. At first, I thought he might just be a fast healer, but me too?" she left the question hanging, in answer to itself.

"Maybe Charlie here is responsible." Eric stated not yet ready to accept a new aspect of the power he had gained coming to Ethar.

Saphrine smiled finding his denial amusing, "Then wouldn't legend have mentioned the healing powers of the Gerpin? Wait and see, I'm sure you will be able to find out soon enough." Their eyes met and both of them went silent. She knew somewhere in her depths, that Eric would return to his world and she was a crowned princess, with responsibility here, unable to return with him if she could. She did not want to accept it, but she also knew that she would. He had told her that he believed what she felt for him was a result of his rescuing her and doctoring her wounds. He said she would probably find true love somewhere else. When he was telling her about Bonny, she could see it in his eyes that his heart was already taken, though he did not know it yet, himself. He knew he missed her and Saphrine was convinced that the next time he saw Bonny he would know why.

The private thoughts of their passionate stare were broken when Charlie let out an alarming, "Gerp, gerp, gerp!"

Charlie was staring into the woods in the direction of the mountains. Eric looked but could not see anything. Carefully he lifted his binoculars and set them on infrared. He scanned the forest and stopped when he found a hot spot. What he saw appeared to be about two hundred feet away. Eric Interpreted what he saw as a four-legged animal about fifteen feet long, stalking its way back and forth in their direction. The forest sounds went silent around them and Saphrine let out a small gasp. Eric dropped his binoculars and slipped his bow from under his cloak, notching an arrow in the same motion, not letting his eyes shift as the giant Saber-tooth cat appeared through the trees. Its fur was green in color and blotched with varying shades making it more difficult to see in the forest. Its eyes fixed on Eric and a deep rumble started deep in its throat that seemed to shake the ground they stood on. Eric drew the arrow back, but stayed his shot. The large cat was dragging one of its back legs, the right one, and two cubs were following behind it. He did not really want to shoot a wounded mother.

"Charlie, can you talk to cats?" Eric asked, trying to flippantly shed a little stress, so he could figure a way out of their dilemma.

"Gerp." to his surprise Charlie stepped forward.

"Well, if you can, tell her I can fix her leg." Eric thought it was absurd, but he hoped somehow Charlie understood him and would relay the information to the lethal looking cat now stopped about twelve feet in front of him. He realized the massive beast had come to a stop and knew there had to be a way out of this, other than kill or be killed.

Charlie moved up to the cat, seeming to communicate with it in silence. Then Charlie held forward his own left rear leg, that Eric had worked on some days earlier, and the giant cat leaned its head down and sniffed at it. Eric chanced a look at Saphrine over his shoulder. She was staring in shock, mouth hung open and shaking like a leaf. As he turned back to the cat, he thought he might have to treat her for shock when he was done. The great cat was now following Charlie with its head lowered. Eric lowered his weapon and set it on the ground when the cat laid down in front of him.

When the giant cat exposed her injuries Eric saw the leg more clearly, and had to hold down tears of compassion, that were welling up inside. Her hip had been crushed and the flesh tattered. Now Eric hoped Saphrine was right and there was healing magic in his touch, and that it would be enough to take care of the job now before him. As he approached the cat, he could sense more than hear her quiet whimpering from the pain. He held his hand in front of her nose to help her become familiar with his scent. He called Saphrine over to get his medical kit from her and she move mechanically not taking her eyes off the cat. Eric slipped the medical kit from Saphrine's shoulder and removed two pads like the one he had used on Charlie. He held them in front of the cat's nose until he saw the pain in her eyes relax. Then to his surprise she fell quickly to sleep.

"She probably hasn't slept since she was hurt," he observed aloud, "the pain must be incredible, and two babies to feed."

"Gerp gergerp." Charlie expressed his own compassion.

Eric moved around to the injured leg, "Saphrine, snap out of it, and come over here and help." He pulled his mess kit out of his hip pack.

Saphrine broke from her trance and obeyed his voice, "It's a Dark Moor cat," she said with almost reverence, "and that Ogre, there must be something terribly wrong to the north."

"Start a fire, fill these pots with water and start them boiling. Charlie I need some disinfectant herbs and make it quick." he turned and started physically removing debris from the injury.

Both Charlie and Saphrine did as they were told. The two cubs were suckling on their mothers breasts. Eric meticulously removed gravel, crushed pieces of bone and anything foreign to the leg from the injury. Then he thoroughly cleaned the wounded area with water and herb tea made from the leaves and roots Charlie had gathered. When he was satisfied with its cleanliness, he held the lower portion of the leg in position with Saphrine's help. Eric gave a small prayer to God, closed his eyes and pictured a stainless-steel core, nylon hip and leg bone, replacing what was missing. A wave of relief went up through him, when he opened his eyes and it had worked. He then turned to one side and visualized the things he needed to put the rest of the leg back together, then proceeded to realign tissue stitching it together where necessary, thinking to himself that Bonny being a doctor would have been more proficient at finishing the job. He finished by stitching the skin and fur back in place as best he could and thoroughly covering the area with gauze securing it in place.

Eric pulled out one of his blankets, which barely covered the injured area, to keep it warm. He stepped back and looked at the beautiful cat, its colors were mostly dark greens and she was still sleeping.

"We have to get her some food; she will be hungry when she wakes up." Eric said stretching his aching muscles, "Charlie when she does wake up, let her know she needs to be careful with that leg until it is healed. Saphrine, if you want you can set up camp, we won't be going any further today. I don't think anything will come near camp with the scent of this cat here. I'll be back shortly."

Saphrine looked at Eric with Almost reverence in her eyes. "You have the gifts of the Ancients." was all she said before turning to the task of making camp.

Eric had seen an Eliko buck earlier, not to far back and picked up his bow and headed after it. He found its tracks quite easily just west of their camp. He was not gone thirty minutes when he caught up with the buck, grazing in a small thicket. It was a small animal, having barely earned the spike antlers it proudly wore on its head. He dropped a shaft into place and drew back the string, in one clean shot the animal jumped once and fell to the ground. Eric skinned and dressed the Eliko quickly were it lay, wrapping the innards in the skin. The animal was small enough he had no difficulty packing the whole thing back to camp, where he left everything, but the skin in front of the cat. Saphrine wanted the skin to tan it for other uses.

When he was finished with his task, Eric sat down near Saphrine and took a sip of the coffee she had fixed for him. He pursed his lips, he would have to teach her how to make coffee, this was way too strong. She had relaxed some, but still kept a tentative eye on their new companion. Eric looked at the cat himself, "Now what was that you started to say, this is a Dark Moor Cat? If I recall my maps correctly that is several weeks north of here through the mountains."

"Yes, they are a fearless cat of the Dark Moor and have always lived there. They have never been seen anywhere else, that is until now. The oddest part of it is Ogres have never traveled this far south either. My conclusion is, there must be some kind of real trouble that far north."

"I have no clue of what might be happening around Dark Moor, but we have plenty of trouble coming to Dragoncove, that threatens the sanctity of the entire south lands. Trouble is the reason I am here and the reason I am headed for Dragoncove. Most of the armies of the south lands will be gathered there by the time we reach it. Then we can present to them what has happened here." Eric looked thoughtfully at the cat, she had awakened and was eating the Eliko he had set before her. "I hope she heals as fast as the rest of you. I am supposed to be there in less than ten more days, but it looks as though I might be a little late. I cannot leave her until she can at least walk again." He said gesturing to the Moor cat, "She has cubs to care for."

"I don't think you will exactly leave her then." Saphrine turned from watching the cat to look at Eric, with wonder in her eyes, "They are not ignorant wild animals. I think she may choose to stay with you, just like Charlie, as you call him. Like the gerpin she will hold an unbreakable loyalty to you. With her though it will be strictly of gratitude as a friend, not of debt."

Eric lifted his eyebrows in mild surprise, "Are you suggesting, that the Moor cats are of a higher social order than most animals."

"Oh yes, they have their own government and society in the Dark Moor. They have no less intelligence than we do." Saphrine looked at the cat, then back to Eric. "It is very strange that she is not with her mate. It is possible that whatever hurt her, killed her mate." Then she smiled an impish smile, "Are you going to name her, too?"

Eric was glad to see Saphrine's attitude returning to normal, or at least what he had become used to, "Does she already have a name?"

Saphrine laughed, "I am sure she does, but neither of us could say it?"

Eric stood up taking Saphrine by the hand and she followed his lead. They walked over to where Charlie sat by the resting cat, "I am Eric Marland, this is Saphrine Barhallah and this is Charlie the Gerpin." he said pointing to each as he named them. "May I call you, Lady Moor." The great cat rubbed her head against Eric's leg, almost knocking him over and gave a deep rumble within her chest, as if in approval. Eric had no way of knowing how close to the truth he was with the title he gave the great cat. He had no way of knowing this was the sister to the Lord of the Moor Cats, sent in hope of finding help.

Eric gave serious thought to Saphrine's early thoughts, "What danger could be so great, as to send Moor Cats and Ogres fleeing south."

Saphrine shook her head and a twinge of worry crossed her brow, "I don't know, but I am sure she would tell us if we could understand her. I have heard that at least at one time there were people who could understand them, maybe someone at Dragoncove..." she trailed off at the end.

"Even if someone could understand the Gerpin language, then Charlie could translate." Eric added

Saphrine smiled when she caught Eric's eyes, "My memory has been returning, by the way."

"I suspected as much." Eric interjected.

"My father is Berkas, King of Efra. If the armies of the south lands are gathering, he will be there. He trained all of his daughters with the use of weapons. I am as good as any from Efra. When I saw your weapons, I thought them strange, now I remember why I was familiar with weapons. I feel almost naked, now without them now."

"Nice thought, but you don't look that way to me." Eric smirked, "But if you would like I could supply you with something to wear."

Saphrine returned a fake coy smile, "I would like." she said in a thick seductive voice.

Eric thought for a moment, if she wanted weapons, he wanted to be sure they were the best he could give her. He remembered a bow from his computer game, the magic Bow of Nester, it needed no arrows. He also selected the Sword of Sapphire and the Twin Daggers of Elisha from his game. He turned around and pictured them on the ground. He picked the bow up first and handed it to her. She looked it over admiring it. It was a gold bow with a gold string and fancy carving all over it to include the symbols of the elements and dragons.

"Alright now, see that stump over there, draw the string and aim it, think wood and loose the string."

Saphrine was a little bewildered but did as she was instructed. A wooden arrow flew from the bow and hit the stump dead center. Saphrine almost dropped the bow in surprise. "It makes its own arrows?!"

"That's not the half of it, do it again only think ice." Eric smiled feeling a little proud himself in her amazement.

Saphrine repeated the process, only this time thinking ice. The second arrow split the first and the stump was instantly frosted over. "And what else can it do?" she asked, knowing he wasn't finished.

"My compliments to your accuracy and skill. You are right, the bow also works with fire, lightening, rock and steel, and may have interesting effects with a few other things. " Eric gave a triumphant wink.

Saphrine looked like a little girl receiving birthday presents. "It's wonderful, no need to carry arrows, it makes its own."

As Eric picked up the Sword of Sapphire, he thought about how much power he was giving her and the implications of how much power he had. He drew the sword from its sheath and handed it to her. She examined the highly polished blade and razor-sharp edge, then moved to the jewel studded gold hilt, created around a two-inch sapphire. "Point the blade at the stump over there," Eric instructed, indicating the same stump she had shot the arrows into, "then squeeze the handle."

As Saphrine did as she was instructed a blue flame leaped from the blade leaving the stump in ashes. She slid the blade back in its sheath and looked up to Eric, "This is too much." she replied, feeling undeserving of such wonderful gifts.

"When it is used as an ordinary sword, it also delivers the power of its magic." He did not tell her it would cut as well as the one Shiheel had given him. Eric picked up the two daggers by the blades, handing the pearl handles to Saphrine. "These are perfectly balanced for throwing and you will find the blades to be of the highest quality."

Saphrine gave him a big hug and he thought he saw tears at the corners of her eyes as she said, "Thank you. You have given me, now both life and treasure. I envy Bonny your love."

Eric was taken aback for a moment, by what she said, then for the first time in his life he realized it was true, he really loved Bonny. There was not much more conversation between them the rest of the afternoon and evening. They went to bed early, snuggling close against the cool evening air. Saphrine, ruled by her heart and the moment stripped her clothes off completely and pressed Eric to enjoy the pleasures of their shared passion one last time. They both found pleasure, though it lacked the innocent wonder and enjoyment of the first time. Saphrine's mind was back to being the crowned princess and Eric's mind was on Bonny. Even with their minds occupied with their private thoughts they both found comfort in having the other there to hold, and slept easily.

The next morning, they woke up early to a nipping chill in the air. They were slow in separating from the warmth and comfort of each other's arms and the blanket. Eric finally got up first, leaving her with a kiss on the tip of her nose, he went out and started a fire. Lady Moor lifted her head and with a lazy motion turned to watch. Charlie who was cuddled between her cubs stretched with an obvious yawn and strutted over to join Eric by the fire. Saphrine was out and sitting with them a few moments later, as they watched the sunrise light the skies over the mountains, in a spectacle of colors forming ribbons of gold, crimsons and violets. They sat in peaceful silence a little while longer, then Eric decided it was time to have a hearty American breakfast. He held his hands out, palms up and pictured two plates, with a steaming hot breakfast on each. He looked at them with satisfaction, ham and cheese omelets, hash browns toast and bacon, with a glass of orange juice and a glass of milk balanced on the edge of each.

"Hungry this morning?" He smiled and winked as he handed Saphrine a plate, and settled next to her to eat his own.

She smiled back at him, with a twitch of the ear to return his wink, "It smells delicious, but does this mean you don't like my cooking?" her face filled with gleeful mischief.

"No, no, your cooking is fine, I mean good." Eric stumbled over his words, "Just thought this would be quick and easy, and a tasty change of pace." he felt himself blush a little when he looked at her and realized she was jeering him. It reminded him of how Bonny bantered him. He shook off the thought, "How do you like it."

"Well, I'm not exactly sure what everything is, but it doesn't taste bad." Saphrine said after tasting it.

"Oh, I forgot, you're not used to eating with us commoners." Eric bowed his head slightly; it was his turn to be mischievous.

"That's not true," She started in annoyance, then seeing his expression, "you ergnob!"

"What's an ergnob?" He knew it was an insult, but he didn't know what it meant.

"Tch, tch, shame you don't know," She teased, as she poured them both a cup of herb tea, she had made in his coffee pot. The banter went back and forth through breakfast, with Saphrine getting the better of Eric and stopped when he set down his plate and stood up.

"Better check Lady Moors dressing, see how she is healing up." He turned to the cat that was licking clean a front paw.

Saphrine and Charlie followed Eric over to the big cat and watched as he removed the wrappings. He was very careful, especially when he got down to the scabbed wrappings. When he was done however, he stepped back staring at a leg that might never have suffered even a scratch from its outward appearance.

"Amazing, but how? I'm not even a doctor." Eric turned, slightly bewildered to Saphrine, who looked back and only smiled at him, with admiration and respect in her eyes. She answered his question without saying a word. He turned to Charlie, "Tell her to get up carefully and try it out."

"Gerp gerep." Charlie leaped in front of the cat and moments later, Lady Moor was on her feet walking around camp, then running and pouncing. Satisfied finally, she walked up to Eric and rubbed him with the side of her head, knocking him off balance. It was an obvious affection of appreciation and Eric laughed as he stood back up, reached around the scruffy mane and gave a gentle squeeze.

"I guess that means we can move on. Charlie, would you burn those wrappings while we break camp?" Eric and Saphrine set about cleaning and packing camp. Charlie snagged the pieces of bandaging from Lady Moors injury one at a time and dragged them over, pushing them into the fire. The cubs were playfully wrestling and Lady Moor decided to help Charlie. When everything was packed Eric pulled out his unique compass and a map, while Saphrine kicked out the fire and buried it. Eric thought to himself as he looked at the map, he was supposed to be in Dragoncove in nine days. He figured the distance he had left would take significantly longer even if he were traveling alone. They had moved much slower through the woods than he had figured and he had lost more time being a healer. He also realized looking at the map now he had miss judged the distance of the route he had chosen.

Saphrine saw Erics frustration and sat down next to him. Brushing her long blond hair back over her shoulders she asked, "What's wrong, can I help?"

"I don't know. You see the map, we are here, still a day's travel from Lone Peak. I can't see how we can make it to Dragoncove in less than fourteen days and I'm supposed to be there in nine. "

Saphrine sat there for a minute, then looked over at the giant Moor Cat, "Well maybe we can ride Lady Moor, she can move much faster than we can, and she has the strength to carry us."

"This is true, but how will we keep from being wiped out by the branches of the forest, riding on her back." Eric too, was also looking thoughtfully at the Moor Cat.

"Well less than a day's travel north of Lone Peak, the forest ends and there are open grasslands until well north of the Arbron River." she pointed to the map as she spoke.

"That will save us some time and maybe we can save a day or so, cutting across south and west of Silver Lake. We'll give it a try." He said putting the map and compass away as he stood up and looked at the sky.

It was still morning as the six of them set forth in greeting to a beautiful day. It was warm, but not hot and Eric noticed that some of the leaves had started changing colors, giving hints of autumns lovely array. Charlie continued scurrying off, gathering a variety of things and stuffing them any place he could find room. He collected roots, nuts, berries and various green leafy plants, some of which they ate as they traveled.

Several times that day Lady Moor wandered off and came back, leaving her cubs in their trust while she was gone. They did not stop for lunch being satisfied by the fruit and nuts they munched as they walked. It was shortly after midday when they started getting glimpses of lone peak, and by evening the solitary pinnacle was on their left.

Lady Moor vanished again as they started to set camp, returning just as Eric finished building the fire. Lady Moor returned carrying a large eliko from her jaws, which she held out in offering to Eric. He cut off two very generous steaks and Lady Moor dragged the rest over to her cubs, where the three felines started eating. Saphrine insisted on doing the majority of their dinner preparations, however she allowed Eric to help and showed him a variety of plants, explaining what she used them for in her cooking. When dinner was ready, Eric, Saphrine and Charlie sat down together by the campfire. Saphrine told stories of Elven history while they ate, with Eric throwing in questions now and then. Charlie just listened and curled up between them when he was finished eating.

After dinner Saphrine told Eric, she wanted to save the fur. He helped her salvage it from the remains of the moor cat's dinner, then she scraped it and wrapped it around the other she had been carrying. While Saphrine was cleaning the fur, Eric cleaned their dishes and stoked the fire. They sat appreciating the fire for a short time before conceding to their weariness and going to bed. They slipped under their blanket using their shared warmth to gain comfort against the cool of the night and went quickly to sleep.

The following day went by much the same, until late afternoon. As the afternoon passed the forest thinned out, the trees becoming sparser, but fuller and the forest floor gave way to underbrush. The underbrush slowed them down, but it too quickly gave way to open grassland and rolling hills. Eric used his bow to drop a carmigan they had startled out of some of the underbrush. Saphrine again coached Eric on local herbs as she prepared dinner. They continued casual conversation through dinner.

As she finished her meal, Saphrine set down her plate and looked up at the grassland expanse in the twilight and asked, "Did you know that there are small farm communities of Talmorg spread throughout the grasslands? The closest one would be less than a half of a day's travel away."

Eric looked out across the rolling hills himself, "Really, no I didn't know Talmorg was that expansive. I do however know that, that was your destination before you got waylaid."

"Yes, that is true." she said, turning to see his reaction she continued, "Now I am going with you to Dragoncove."

Eric raised an eyebrow and returned her gaze. "Wouldn't it be safer, if you stayed at Talmorg, away from the battle?"

"The people I was sent to speak with are now at Dragoncove, my people are going to war and I am their future leader. I should stand with them."

"But you were on a peacetime mission, and your..." Eric stammered a little.

"I am what?" Irritation was evident in her voice, "A female, and therefore weak? Would you dare to challenge my skill?"

"Well, that was not what I was going to say, but it is true you are female, I was considering other things...." Eric stuttered again, stunned a little by her anger.

Saphrine cut off his words in anger, "Match my skill if you can. Use your Magic and make some training swords, I will prove my skill. You will not think of me as a feeble female when we finish."

Eric was now more than a little irritated at her for presuming to know his thoughts. He produced a pair of plastic swords and tossed her one. She caught the sword in the air and attacked immediately. He parried and struck, she parried. They went back and forth for several minutes, when Eric jumped forward and to the side, barely catching her left arm with the tip of his sword.

"A nick!" she snapped, as they continued their engagement. This time she parried and rolled, the tip of her sword just catching the back of his left hand as he pivoted to follow her movement. Again, it would have been no more than a nick. They continued their parlay for about an hour, both of them pacing themselves and neither wanting to seriously hurt the other. Then Eric had an idea, he reached around with his left hand and grabbed a small handful of his volcanic white powder. Jumping back, he threw the powder in the air, then rolled forward to get behind her, thinking to end their little match. Saphrine recognizing the cloud of color from legend stepped into it disappearing knowing she could see him from within it. Then before he could see her as the cloud dissipated, he felt the tip of her plastic sword under his chin.

Charlie was rolling around gerping in such a manner that Eric knew he was being laughed at.

"You shouldn't play with things you don't yet understand." Saphrine smirked as she started to rematerialized in front of him. "I recognized that powder from stories, as soon as you threw it in the air." She drew him towards her with the tip of her sword and kissed him before lowering it. "It is very rare though, thought to no longer exist. How did you come upon it? As you could see anything that passes into the cloud becomes briefly invisible. Elven wizards used to use it, but they would put it in rings that would render the wearer invisible. It is also quite valuable; you could have almost bought a kingdom with the handful you just wasted."

Eric was intrigued by what she said and wanted to know everything he could about the powder, but decided to put it off for the moment. "First I would like to apologize, for any foolishness I may have indulged in, and more than that I am happy to have you with me." He sighed and shook his head, "Next time though let me finish before you get mad, I was considering your Royalty not your Femininity, being able to get a safer escort, if you went to Talmorg. Enough of that though it is your choice." He paused his mind going back to the powder, "I found that stuff near Fires Peak, quite by accident actually."

"The luck of a Gerpin!" Saphrine quoted a cliche, then blushed remembering and looking at Charlie. She quickly turned back to Eric, "How much do you have?"

Eric lowered his waste pack to the ground and showed her. He had about half a cubic foot in little plastic bags. Saphrine's eyes opened a little wider and her mouth dropped open slightly as he pulled it out and said, "This is all I picked up."

Excitement danced in her eyes as they came back into focus, "That's all?!! That is worth more than all the treasures of the south lands, all put together. I will tell no one of it, neither should you. You could get killed for it." Her face sobered, and the sparkle subdued, "All you picked up, there was more than."

Eric was surprised at her enthusiasm and conviction to keep it secret. It took Eric very little consideration to realize the potential value and danger of the wrong people knowing of its existence or gaining possession of it. He realized that danger increased with the thought of taking any back to Earth. "Yes." he nodded "I guess it would be wise to keep this stuff a secret."

"To be honest this is actually the first time I have ever seen the magic powder. It is said that the last source of it was lost when we became separated from Earth. I have heard many stories though. In one story the powder was formed as a result of the great wars over five thousand years ago." She smiled at Eric, "Stories sometimes come from the truth, but they can't always be relied upon."

Eric gained a thoughtful look, "If it still exists here, and it came up out of the ground, then it seems it could come up anywhere."

"Maybe, but I still wouldn't tell anyone about it, no one." she said as she stood up, "Let me see your sword and some of that powder over by the fire.”

 Eric handed her his sword and a small pouch of the powder, and followed her to the fire after picking the rest up and replacing it in the pack. He watched as she took a piece of damp cloth and diligently rubbed the blade of his sword down with the powder, leaving it completely coated with a thin film. Then Saphrine handed the sword back to Eric.

“Reach the blade forward and touch the tip to the fire.”

Eric did as she instructed and as soon as a lick of flame from the fire touched the tip of the sword, it flashed a brilliant white, encompassing the entire blade. When his vision cleared from the flash, he could no longer see the blade of his sword. It looked to him as though he was holding a useless hilt, but from the weight and balance in his hand Eric knew the blade of his sword was still there. Eric tested the movement and balance before sheathing the weapon, then asked. “Why did you choose my sword instead of your own?”

With a chuckle she answered, “Because the mixing of magic can be dangerous, and I would not want to risk damaging a gift I received from you.” She smiled a broad self-satisfied smile, then pursed her lips at him kissing the air in his direction.

“Your ways are befitting your appearance; both are lovely and able to melt the heart of any man.”   He smiled back at her with a wink. “It is late and we have another long day ahead of us tomorrow. Shall we?” He gestured toward the tent. His desire for her rising deep within his body.

Saphrine melted into his smile again and did not resist. With an arm around his waist, she followed his gentle guidance. She was his as long as he wanted, she tried to justify herself with thoughts of owing him that much, but knew in reality she simply wanted him too.

Saphrine had breakfast ready before Eric woke up the next morning and was humming some tune Eric had never heard before, as she walked back from waking him. He got up quickly, dressed and shaved before eating. She fixed some steaming hot fruit wrapped in delicate green leaves and some tea to go with it. The meal was delicious and they shared it with Charlie who thoroughly enjoyed it once it cooled enough for him to eat it. Eric and Saphrine laughed a few times, watching Charlie's antics, until he tucked his tail between his legs, laid his ears flat and hid his face under his paws in exaggerated shame and embarrassment.

When they were done Eric told Charlie to ask Lady Moor if she was ready to give them a ride this morning, he had gotten what he thought was permission the day before. Then he and Saphrine picked up camp together exchanging smiles and kisses in silence. Lady Moor strolled up with her two cubs on her heels and Charlie riding on top of her head, just as Eric finished kicking out the fire. The great moor cat lowered her front quarters and Eric helped Saphrine up, then climbed on behind her.

"Tell her to go straight north." Eric said to Charlie who had been watching them climb on.

"Gerp gergerep gerp." The gerpin said quietly to one of the large moor cat's ears.

They started moving forward in an easy fluid motion, about three times faster than they could have on foot, yet a speed that did not give the cubs any difficulty keeping up. The grasslands sped by under the powerful strides of the moor cat, slapping Erics cloak in the air behind him. The two small people gave no significant hindrance to Lady Moors movement, as she swept forward all morning and on another hour past midday. It was then that they startled a herd of tiger deer, that looked like antlered zebra. Before Eric even gave it a thought Saphrine had dropped one with a single arrow and they stopped. Eric skinned the animal and removed the antlers, keeping a small piece of the bone to hold them together. Saphrine quickly scraped the skin clean, wrapped it around the other two she had been carrying and then tied the antlers to the bundle. After taking aside meat for dinner and eating a light lunch of fruit and nuts, they rested for the rest of an hour while the cats ate and played. Charlie teased the cubs, by jumping on their tails, then moving just too fast for them to catch.

"After this I'm going to find riding horses boring." Saphrine smiled, running a finger along Erics chin.

"I think I will miss all of this just as much as I miss my home right now." Eric sighed as he took her hand and kissed it gently.

"Do you have to go back?" Genuine sadness showed in her eyes as she asked.

"Yes, but I will return from time to time. You will probably be married when I return, how will you explain me and how will you face me then?" Eric asked with a touch of sadness shading his own face.

A smile crossed her face, "You will be a hero, and I'll sneak off to you in your chambers when you are alone." Then her eyes filled with mischief, "I might be married then, but I am sure you will be, and then it will be our dark secret." She laughed, throwing herself at him with an embrace, flattening the grass where they rolled.

They both got up laughing, and it was time to move on. Lady Moor carried them the rest of the day until evening. This time they did not set up camp or start a fire, not wanting to draw attention in the open grasslands. They gave the meat they had from the tiger deer to Lady Moor and ate fruit, nuts and raw vegetables, then curled up with Charlie and the cubs in Lady Moors protection under the stars.

It was the suckling of the cubs that stirred everyone awake the next morning, just before sun up. Eric used his magic again to produce an inviting breakfast and decided to try hot chocolate instead of coffee, for a change of pace. Saphrine liked it much better and spared no time in telling him so. He decided to keep that in mind as he looked at the plates they had left when they finished eating.

"I need to start using the plates we already have when I make breakfast like this. We don't need the extra weight." He said as he started to pick them up.

"Why don't you use your magic to get rid of them?" Saphrine gave him a curious look.

Eric wondered if he could, and why he had not thought of trying that himself. "I don't know. I never tried before." He looked at the dishes wondering for a moment what to do with them, then visualized them changing into the substance of the barrier from which he drew his power. To both their surprise, the dishes turned into white powder, just like that Eric had put into the plastic bags back at fires peak. It did not take him a lot of thought to figure out that was how the substance of the barrier manifested itself when brought into the world.

In no time they were off again, speeding across the open plains of the grasslands. They startled three herds of grassland grazers before midday, each herd numbering in the thousands, sounding like thunder as they stampeded away from Lady Moor. Eric dropped one from the last herd just before midday and they stopped for lunch. The beast looked like a bison with the horns of a Texas longhorn spanning seven feet from tip to tip. Saphrine cleaned and added the fur and horns to her growing collection. This time they saved some of the meat for dinner, wrapping it in a small piece of scraped fur. Lady Moor and her cubs ate the rest. Charlie had stopped his gathering as they traveled across the grasslands, except when they were stopped for the night. Even then what he did gather was more meager and he was starting to put a dent in his supplies.

Eric and Saphrine continued their playful antics, flirting and bantering to pass the time. The afternoon went by quickly and they only startled two more herds, one of them from a drinking hole. They stopped by the water hole to refill their own supply, while Lady Moor seemed to want to drink it all. Then they rode until evening when they finally reached the Arbron River, setting up camp on its southern bank. Eric looked out across the river; it was a good quarter of a mile wide as it flowed lazily through the flatlands. He would have to wait until morning to guess its depth.

They started a small cook fire to fix dinner, and when they sat down to eat, Saphrine asked, "How do you plan to cross the river?"

Eric looked at her slightly surprised by her question, "We can look for a place to ford, or maybe swim across."

She gave a slight snicker, dismissing his answer. "The current underneath is very strong, Lady Moor would even have trouble making it alone." She looked at him with a smile shaking her head doubtfully, "Fording is out too, it is too deep unless we go up in the mountains almost to Vorka. We could go to the edge of the forest and make a raft to cross."

Eric looked at her thoughtfully for a moment, "It can wait until morning. I'll sleep on it there isn't anything we could do now anyway." When his eyes came back to focus on hers, his expression went soft. "I think we should call it a day, what about you?"

Saphrine smiled back and leaned forward, planting a kiss on his lips as she stood up. "I'm going to bath first." she said and turned toward the river's edge.

Eric thought that was a good idea, "May I join you?"

"Of course, I have nothing to hide from you." she gave him a smug sneer, "I might even make you a part of my royal harem, then you couldn't get married and leave me." She laughed and started undressing under the light of the stars.

Eric watched as she undressed with her back towards him. Her tanned skin was pale in the night light, and the definition of her features was slightly washed. It did not detract from the beauty of her firm rounded features though, and he filled his eyes as he started removing his own garments. Her movements had grace and poise as she walked up and tested the water with her foot. It was all he could do to keep his body under control and not run after her.

She walked out about twenty feet and the water reached her waste, before she slipped under the water and came back up another ten feet down stream. As Eric was entering the water, Saphrine turned around now glistening with moisture, resting just above the surface of the river, shoulder rising up and then standing out beckoning to him. Eric walked out to his waist and they both dove towards each other, meeting about half way, embracing and kissing as they bobbed to the surface. They both caught a breath and slipped back under the water, kissing each other and getting lost again in passions pleasures until both of them were trembling with anticipation. They danced in the current at the edge indulging in their forbidden pleasures. They stayed in the water about another hour, never leaving each other's reach. Finally climbing out of the water they carried their things back to the tent with them. They were quickly under the covers and asleep in each other's arms.

CHAPTER 10

Dragoncove

Morning found Eric up pacing the edge of the water. Even if they went up stream, they would have to build a raft big enough for Lady Moor, or loose four days in the mountains. In addition to which, a raft would not be easy to steer across these waters without moving substantially downstream, especially with a cat fifteen feet long, not counting its tail. If only he had a yacht or a paddle boat. He could try he thought, but this was bigger than anything he had ever tried to this point. He sat down, shut his eyes and pictured a forty-foot motorized boat like one he had seen before, anchored just off shore. When he opened his eyes, it was there, but he noticed he was sweating and very hungry. He got up and turned back to camp, Saphrine was up and had already finished fixing breakfast. Strange he thought, she was not up when he had walked down to the shore and he had not heard her.

"Are you alright?" a look of concern was on her face.

"Yes, I think so. Why?" he answered slightly bewildered.

"Well, your sweating, you were pacing down there for quite a while and you did not answer me when I called down to you letting you know breakfast was done about a half hour ago." She had a note of irritation in her voice.

"Half an hour?" he said in surprise. "I only sat long enough to bring us that boat, although I did pace for a while before I decided what to try." The magic may have cost he thought. Maybe, nothing else had been big enough for him to feel it. Interesting, hungry, sweating and lost track of time yet he did not feel drained or anything.

"Sorry about being angry, but I did expect an answer." Saphrine paused, "Sit down and have something to eat. I'd be more careful next time, I didn't know your magic exacted anything from you, although most magic does, because the power passes through the user."

"That must be it that is the first time I have done anything that big or complicated." He looked at her and smiled appreciatively, "I am hungry."

"Well, your color is coming back at least." her relief was evident in her smile and her voice, "I prepared too much, so eat what you can. You look like you could use it."

Eric sat down, and smiled up at Saphrine as she handed him a plate piled high with a sweet mash she had made from a variety of fruit, nuts and grains. "Thank you. I am hungry after making that boat."

"Just curious," Saphrine looked at the boat, "but why didn't you just summon one instead of creating one, it may have taken less energy?"

"I had not thought of that." Eric looked slightly troubled at the thought. "Wouldn't that be like stealing. I mean to summon something means you are calling it from another location, so summoning something that is not mine would be stealing it."

Saphrine laughed, "I never thought of it like that."

"You know," he started, and paused before continuing, "I have been thinking. We are heading towards a war zone, and you are going to need armor before we happen upon any enemies. Though, I am sure I am being needlessly concerned, undoubtedly you can be suited when we get to Dragoncove. Besides that, you will probably be kept out of the fighting, at least at first."

Saphrine laughed, with a touch of irritation, "I am a princess, first heir to my father's throne. If my people are at war I fight." She looked at him where he sat eating. "It may take a few days, but I will be suited in full armor." Then a touch of sadness crossed her face, "There are going to have to be a few changes by the time we reach Dragoncove. I am a princess after all, I will have to start acting like one. Promise me you will never mention our affair. Even if we were to get married to each other, my behavior has not been exactly acceptable for a princess."

Eric felt a sense of loss, though they had not yet reached Dragoncove, "I promise." was all he said.

"What we did while my memory was gone, will be accepted and forgiven, but once we knew, I should have stopped. What we did, even in ignorance, will be considered payment in full for saving my life." Eric saw the hurt in her eyes, "My family cannot be held bound to the debt."

Eric felt a slight sense of shame, "There never was a debt, it is only right to help those who need it." He stood up, "Anyway, enough said, we need to continue before we waste half the day." As he looked around, he found Charlie packing food into the top of the carrying bag. "Charlie, get Lady Moor please, we are going boating."

Charlie flashed off across the grass. Eric shook his head at the speed he moved with. Then he turned back with Saphrine and they broke camp together, packing everything for travel.

When they were all down on the shore, Eric gave a few instructions, including, asking Lady Moor to stay near the middle of the boat when they got on board. Then they all started wading out to the boat. Eric and Saphrine carried the packs out over their heads and Charlie moved so fast he had no trouble walking on the surface of the water. Charlie was the first on deck and sat there watching the others approach. Eric helped Saphrine up the ladder then tossed his pack up to her before climbing on board himself. Lady Moor set her cubs on board, then climbed aboard, on the opposite side from the anchor.

Once the large cat was situated, Eric started the engines and hoisted the anchor. Eric was not very familiar with the controls so the boat lurched to a start. It was a short smooth ride until they reached the other side of the river. Eric did not know when to slow down and wound up beaching the craft. Charlie embarrassed Eric by running circles around him and obviously laughing at him again.

They all climbed down from the boat, nobody was hurt. Lady Moor was glad to have her feet back on solid ground and had no problem when they remounted. It was only about an hour later when they had to dismount, having reached the edge of the Pengona Forest. The leaves here had started falling and lightly covered the ground with color. Charlie quickly resumed his habit of gathering, and had the packs overstuffed before he stopped and jumped up on the carrying bag.

Progress on foot seemed slow after the previous days riding. They also found themselves moving steadily uphill. Charlie helped the time pass faster, by clowning in the leaves and seeing how many he could get in the air at one time. Game animals were still plentiful, but not in large herds like in the grasslands.

Shortly before midday Lady moor started rumbling deep in her throat and sniffing at the air, and Charlie became suddenly more attentive. Eric and Saphrine also hushed their conversation. After a little while Charlie and Lady Moor made it obvious, which direction they sensed trouble coming from, ahead and to the right. Charlie started gerping in low tones, as if muttering to himself. Eric and Saphrine started smelling a foul odor, then they came upon the trail.

It looked to Eric to be the same kind of trail the Ogre had left, only more like two or three of them. Their trail seemed to be heading southwest. Eric realized the Ogres would be cornered in the fork of the river and probably back track to the mountains, finding their trail. Moor cats and Ogres were natural enemies. Lady Moors rumble had grown to a steady growl and her hair was standing on end. They continued on in silence the rest of the day, all of them on edge and thoroughly worn out by worry when evening came. Eric calmed Saphrine by agreeing to trade watch with her, but fell asleep before waking her up, trusting the cat's instincts to wake him if danger approached.

Eric woke up early the next day, slightly cramped from sleeping against a tree. He got up stretched, then noticed Lady Moor alertly watching the direction they had come from and rumbling again. He lifted up his binoculars and looked that way himself. They picked up a heat source a little over a mile away, that was moving. Not willing to take unnecessary chances he got Saphrine up and they pressed forward without their normal breakfast, being thankful for Charlie's fruit and nuts as they went.

They had been traveling for an hour already at sunrise, and did not take the time to enjoy it. Eric knew he had caught his first Ogre by surprise, when he rescued Saphrine, but did not want to face two or three of them head on. He suspected that it might have been one of their massive stone clubs that had been used on Lady Moor also. Moor cats and Ogres were creatures matched for size and strength.

Morning changed to midday and still they pressed on pausing only long enough for Eric to locate their closing pursuers, with his infrared view. The distance between them had been cut in half. As evening approached, they heard the sounds of Silver Falls ahead and pressed on under the starlight.

An hour after sunset they reached the cliffs of Canyon River and the air filled with the roar of Silver Falls echoing through the canyon. It was forty feet to the other side of the half mile deep cut in the ground made by the river several hundred feet below. Before Eric had time to wonder how they would cross, Lady Moor picked up one of her cubs and leaped the gap with ease. One by one she carried them all across. They finally sat down to rest behind some brush on the other side.

Eric quickly slipped into an exhausted doze, until Charlie pounced on his stomach. He came awake jumping to his feet so fast, Charlie stumbled onto the ground. He heard a tremendous crash as a tree fell across the gap of the canyon. Peering out through the brush, he saw three Ogres on the other side, using their clubs and strength to uproot trees and lay them down bridging the canyon.

He told Charlie to go and wake up Saphrine, then stepped out from the brush drawing his now invisible sword. Lady Moor was crouched just out of their sight in the brush waiting. Eric started yelling and jumping to draw their attention. Immediately all three started across their tree bridge. With one stroke he cut the first tree sending one Ogre screaming into the darkness having lost its balance when the tree fell from under its one foot.

The other two paused only for a moment in their approach. A second tree fell into the water below, the Ogres were now half way across. Lady Moor leaped across the chasm and immediately turned around and started knocking the trees off the other side. The last Ogre was almost across and suddenly the tops of the trees burst into flames. The trees fell taking with them the last attacker in a spire of flame that lit the canyon below. Saphrine stepped out of the brush smiling, with her bow in her hand, and Lady Moor leaped back across. Eric sheathed his sword and gave them both hugs. They all slept well the rest of that night sprawled out on the ground. Eric and Saphrine both slept late into the next day.

The sun had been up for a couple of hours the next day, when

Saphrine finally got up and fixed breakfast. When it was all prepared, she went over to wake up Eric. He looked so peaceful sleeping there that she hesitated then bent down and woke him up with a kiss. "Good morning sleepy."

Eric opened his eyes and took a moment to remember where he was, seeing Saphrine's face was all he needed to wake up with a smile, "Morning." He sat up smiling at her.

Saphrine looked to the north, then back at Eric, "I think we should detour to Silver Lake, and clean a little before continuing." she gave him a radiant smile, "or they will smell us at Dragoncove before they see us."

"Gerp, Gerp." Charlie seemed to agree.

"Very well, I could use a bath and some clean cloths. The smell of those Ogres does seem to have gotten to us." He smiled back at Saphrine and got to his feet.

Saphrine had prepared a salad of cut roots, greens and fruit and they sat together to eat, Charlie sharing the meal with them.

"We are almost there," Eric said, a look of triumph reflecting in his eyes, "three more days of travel."

"Then everything begins." she could not help laughing at his small sense of triumph.

They headed north after breakfast and made it to the lake by midday. The lake was a magnificent sight, the bottom was actually silver. They decided, with Saphrine's persuasion, that they needed a day of rest and chose to spend the rest of the day and night on the shore of Silver

Lake. No sooner had they made their decision and they were stripped and in the lake. Even Lady Moor, her cubs and Charlie all cleaned in the lake. The water of the lake was warm, its source was deep in the ground and the silver was carried up in the water.

Eric and Saphrine used the time to enjoy the pleasure of each other's company, in the water and on the shore. They used the time as lovers who knew this would be the last chance, they would have to enjoy their time together. They were totally uninhibited in their feelings toward each other for the entire afternoon. As evening approached, Eric used his magic for towels and a change of clothes for both of them. They dried off but did not get dressed. They fixed dinner, ate and went back into the water. When they finally grew tired, they lay on the shore, embraced and slept.

The next day they woke up early. Sometime in the night, Charlie had covered them with a blanket and curled up nearby. They got up and dressed in their new clothes, Eric putting his armor on over his. Then they gathered up their scattered belongings and repacked getting ready for their continued journey. Before they started under way, Eric turned to Saphrine, "It is time you had some armor. The best I can offer is ethereal, a mythical chain mail having no weight, yet ten times harder to penetrate than ordinary armor." Saphrine's eyes went wide, just as Eric closed his. He opened them back up and Saphrine was rubbing the chain mail, now on her body, in disbelief, with tears in her eyes again. "Do you like it." He asked with a smile.

Saphrine stammered over her words, "Ethereal chain mail is the armor of legends. It belonged to Armacus, the greatest wizard to ever live, back before wizards could not wear armor of metal." She blinked at him in amazement, "I can never repay you for the gifts you have given me."

"There is no debt, now, let's get going before you get too mushy on me here, and I have to take advantage of your body again." He laughed, forcing Saphrine to smile and then laugh in return.

They turned again towards Dragoncove and headed off through the woods. Their morning travel went without incident, until about midday when they approached a road. They heard troops moving on the road as they approached and had to remain hidden for over an hour before an opening availed itself big enough for them to cross. They used increased caution to avoid being discovered, to include no more fires or hot meals. They traveled until evening and camped down in some underbrush. The following day went without incident. The next day they almost came out on a road again and had to readjust there direction slightly.

At midday they found themselves in open fields south of Dragoncove, and through the brush they could see Dragoncove in the distance. Eric had a plan to get to the gates almost unseen. He pulled out a medium pouch of powder and they got on the back of Lady Moor, with the cubs traveling directly behind her. Then he changed his mind, he did not want to chance losing the cubs.

He pulled out his tent rope and tied it to Lady Moors tail, then put an end in each of the cubs' mouths, to lead them with. He got on Lady

Moors back blew a cloud of dust and walked through. He repeated it each time he started to see any of them. They came within a hundred yards of the gates before anyone noticed one of the bursts of light. When they stood before the open gates, he quickly slipped the bag back into his pack, before they could be seen again. Charlie jumped on top of Erics pack, hiding under the cover of his cloak.

CHAPTER 11

Gathering Forces

Talmorg was surprised and disturbed, when he got the message that a man, an Elven lady and a Dark Moor cat with two cubs, had appeared in the gateway to Dragoncove asking for him. He was expecting Eric Marland, Shiheel or both, but they were traveling alone and from the wrong direction to arrive with a Moor cat, especially a Dark Moor cat. He also figured that those he was expecting, would probably wind up in his office chambers undetected.

Talmorg had never believed that Dark Moor cats were really more than stories of the imagination. There was no one in all the south lands that he had ever heard of that had actually seen or met a Dark Moor cat. They were just stories passed on to the next generation at bedtime or around campfires.

Talmorg and his personal guard left the banquet hall, mounted their horses and headed for the gates. As he approached, he slowed down and dismounted, for indeed it was a Dark Moor Cat, stretched out facing the gates, casually licking its paws. It was Eric on its back, with an Elven girl wearing his colors. There were two cubs, snuggled up to the great cat looking about, nervously flicking their tails. Talmorg raised his hand signaling the archers to lower their bows. Eric got down and greeted him with a handshake.

"Howdy, Talmorg, allow me to introduce Saphrine Barhallah and

Lady Moor." Eric indicated each with his hand as he introduced them.

Saphrine stepped up, "Greetings Prince Talmorg, son of King Erron Elkinshane of the Walled City of Talmorg, it is an honor to be in your company." She bowed her head and curtsied. Then returned to her most regal posture.

Lady Moor assumed a more regal posture, gave a low growl and a nod of her head in greeting.

Talmorg was caught by surprise, but returned the formal greeting, "Greetings Eric, greetings Lady Moor and greetings Princess Saphrine Barhallah, crowned daughter of the King Berkas Barhallah of Efra. It is a greater pleasure to meet you, than to just hear of you. Your father has been mourning the loss of you, thinking you were dead. Word reached us two days ago, that your party was ambushed by an Ogre, that all were killed and you were taken. Ah, but by the luck of a gerpin, you're here."

"Gerp."

"Come follow me, your stomach sounds hungry. Shiheel has not arrived yet, Eric, have you any idea what has delayed him?" Talmorg asked as he started leading them down the street.

"No, we had to go separate directions, but I do have a story to tell." Eric could tell by the way Talmorg looked at Saphrine and Lady Moor, he wanted to hear it.

They were all given royal treatment and thoroughly refreshed. Eric left most of his belongings in his room and changed the attire he was wearing. Charlie stayed hidden under his cloak. Even the Dark Moor Cat and her cubs were given thorough care and attention.

They gathered in the dining hall. Over dinner Eric relayed his excursion to Talmorg, discretely leaving out certain details, such as the magic powder and those necessary for Saphrine's sake. When he was done, Talmorg sat and stared at him in silent thought and amazement for several minutes. He still did not know about Charlie, when the gerpin chose that moment to come out of hiding and jump on the table in front of Eric. Eric then had to fill in those details of his adventure, how he could communicate to Lady Moor, but not the other way around and how Charlie had traveled almost all the way with him. When he was done, Talmorg was beyond the point of being amazed and though he had seen two creatures of legend and the return of a dead Princess in one day, now managed to maintain himself.

"I am sorry to say there is no one here who can understand the Dark Moor Cat, though if Shiheel ever gets here he might, and likewise with the gerpin here. So, they will have to wait. We will give Shiheel until midday tomorrow and then we will have to review our readiness without him. Until then, I would suggest rest, but you are free to do as you wish. Lady Saphrine, your father desires to give you audience and we must first have your proper insignia on your garments, so, if you would be so kind, allow me to escort you when we are done here."

As they finished eating conversation bounced from one thing to another, until they were all done and they parted ways. Talmorg had given Eric the protection of his personal guard, who escorted him where he wished, which at that time was his room. He was going to go through the portal, back to his home and he wanted to do it in secrecy.

Saphrine was on her way to see her father, she was now properly dressed with the exception of her armor and weapons. Eric had omitted them from his story to Talmorg, and the guards were a little distressed when she refused to exchange them for those bearing the royal insignia of Efra. She would have to explain it to King Barhallah, so they told her, but she only smiled and said don't worry. She knew he would be worried, and maybe even still mourning his loss of her, and she hoped he would be too filled with joy at first to notice.

The first thing he would do would be to look at her birth mark, then probably ask a few questions, to confirm she was not an impostor. They approached the stone building that the men of Dragoncove had provided for him. Dragoncove had no royalty of their own, they were governed by a council, but did their best to provide for the visiting kings. Her escort of six Efrian Royal Guards stopped outside, and she was admitted entry, with the proper exchange of salutes and words. Saphrine grew a little nervous as they got to her father's chambers. She would have to tell him things she really did not want to, knowing he would accept them, but he would not really be pleased. There were two guards on either side as she entered, and her father was seated in a large wooden chair waiting for her. His eyes lit up as he saw her.

"Greetings, Father, King Berkas Barhallah of Efra, I am honored to be given audience." She stammered slightly over the greeting and went down on one knee with a bow; formality had to be given for the sake of the guards, who under different circumstances would not be there.

"Rise Daughter and come forward. You know I must first see your birth mark and ask you a few questions to prove your identity, before I can dismiss the guards."

She got up, then lifted her chain mail and undid her leather tunic to expose the underside of her right breast. She showed him her birthmark. It was a four-pointed crown, which no one knew of except her parents and now Eric. Then quickly she covered back up.

"What do you normally call me in private?"

"Pops," she smiled, "or Berk."

He smiled back, "What did I give you in secret the day I crowned you Princess?"

"My grandmother's pendent, with the insignia of Parschakin, which is still in my jewelry box in my room."

"Guards, you can go, there is no doubt this is my daughter."

The guards bowed deeply and went out the door, shutting it behind them. King Berkas looked over his daughter then got up and gave her a hug, "At least you are safe and unhurt. Now tell me what happened."

"As you have heard Father, we were ambushed by an Ogre on the road south of Eliko Ravine. I was knocked off my horse, hit my head on a stone in the road or something and knocked unconscious. When I regained consciousness, that Ogre was preparing to cook me. Again, I passed out, this time when I came around, I had been rescued by Eric. I was wrapped in his cloak and blanket." She paused and swallowed, how would he take this next part, "I had no memory of who I was. I was overwhelmed with passion for my hero and savior, that night I gave him my body, with more than gratitude. If I had my full memory we would not have acted so rashly. Eric found a bag with jewels and coins on the Ogre and had me go through it. My signet ring was in there and I was drawn to it, but at the time it did not help us figure out who I was. The next day my injuries were completely healed by Eric's treatment, but not my memory. Somehow, later Eric figured out who I was. It wasn't until after that my memory came back with Eric's help. Then I was ashamed of how I wantonly threw myself at him."

"How did he do that?"

"By asking me about history and anything else I knew," She looked into her father's eyes, "and telling me things he knew." She was surprised there was no anger in his eyes, only love and sympathy.

"Can we keep this matter of what you did a secret?"

"Eric promised not to speak of it, but," she rubbed her stomach. "I fear it will not remain an easy secret though, I have given him a part of my heart," she smiled slightly, "and he has given me a part of himself."

"Does he know, you carry his seed?"

"No."

"Do not tell him. We shall reward him for saving you, for the sake of public image." King Berkas noticed her weapons for the first time, "You have not received any Royal arms yet?"

"I will take the blame for that. These," she indicated the weapons she carried, "are magic and a gift from Eric. He was concerned for me and gave them for my protection." She had tears welling up and could not hide them. "He is a good man."

Berkas could see his daughter's love for Eric and knew she would always have it, though with time she would learn to control it. "Show me his gifts."

Saphrine began to show the gifts to her father. First, she brought attention to the sheathed sword. The sheath was gold, smooth, and simple. The hilt of the sword was also gold, also simple in design, but as she drew it the blade was translucent blue. "This is the Sapphire Sword, it will cut stone with little effort and it shoots a blue flame, which I shouldn't demonstrate in here." Her father stayed silent and she pulled the bow from her shoulder. "This," she said picking up the gold bow, "is a magic bow, the 'Bow of Nester'. It does not need arrows, it makes its own out of what I desire: fire, wood, ice, and more." She pulled two daggers from her waist. "These he called the Twin Daggers of Elisha." holding them in her palms, "They are well balanced for throwing, and the nicest daggers I ever had." She paused, "Lastly, the greatest of what he gave me, is ethereal chain mail." She displayed her translucent armor from under her cloak, sliding her hand across the hauberk and indicating the chain leggings and went silent.

King Barhallah looked at his daughter and at the gifts she had received from the visitor to their world. He did not trust the stranger, his gifts or any human for that matter. He did not trust anything, or anyone that was not Elven. His daughter's judgment had always proven good in the past, but she was in love with this stranger, and love clouds good judgment. All the same, the future of their world was resting in the hands of this stranger. By his works he was proving to be a good man. She had good reason for her gratitude to this man and Berkas himself was very thankful for what Eric had done. "It is too bad he is only visiting. You may wear his gifts in place of the royal arms they will give you better protection by far. We can adorn them with the Emblem of our House later." He hoped he was right allowing her to wear the gifts instead of the royal armor. He felt very tired and old now, breathing a deep sigh, but glad he had her back. He said to his daughter, "It is good to have you here, but we shall talk tomorrow. Now it is time to get some good rest." They embraced and both called it a night.

*   *   *   *   *   *   *

Eric entered the room, that had been provided for him. He was being housed with the royalty of Talmorg and treated with the same respect. He sat down on the edge of his bed. He knew he needed the privacy, because he was going to go back to his own world for something. But now he could not remember what or why. As he sat there an ache within him told him what it was. He missed Bonny.

Eric knew even if he did go back, she would not be there, with the time distortion it would still be the same day as when he left. He could leave a message for her, but she would never believe this. How could he explain what was happening to anyone? Of course, he could leave her a message that said nothing more than he would be back in a few days, or he could try calling her on the phone.

He rubbed the bottom of his ankh, without thinking about the fact he was sitting down. Suddenly the bed was gone from underneath him, and he landed on the seat of his pants looking at his front door. There was no one there to see it, but Eric felt himself turn red with embarrassment. Charlie landed next to Eric and started his gerpin version of laughing. Eric looked at him a little confused, not realizing he had somehow transported the gerpin with him. Eric did not know Charlie had his own reasons for going to Earth.

Eric got to his feet. He reached for his pocket to get the keys, but remembered it was not locked and opened the door. Charlie slipped in ahead of him and started exploring the house, while Eric went into the living room. The TV was still on, with another news broadcast. The wall clock told Eric it was six thirty in the evening, as he sat down next to the telephone and picked it up. The line was dead, probably knocked out as a result of the storm. Eric sat watching Charlie exploring and studying his house, which was as strange to the gerpin as Ethar was to Eric.

Grabbing the pen and pad by the telephone, Eric started writing. He took about twenty minutes, before he was satisfied, with what he wrote. He tried to explain the arrival of Shiheel and the portal to Ethar, and the gist of what he was doing. He said he should be back in a few days and signed it, Love Eric.

When he was done, he called Charlie, who came quickly from some other room in the house, hopped up on Eric's shoulder and they headed for the door. As Eric was expecting they returned to the room within seconds of when they had left.

Eric was about to and lie down when a knock came to the door. It was still late evening and Eric wondered who it could be. "Hello, who's there?" He asked as he stepped over to the door and opened it.

"Lord Marland," one of his guards started, "a messenger from King Barhallah." then stepped back allowing an Efrian guard to step forward.

"King Barhallah asks that you allow him to give you audience, Lord Marland." The Efrian guard said with a slight bow of his head. "What answer shall I return with, my Lord?"

Eric wondered what Saphrine had told her father as he answered, "It will be my honor to oblige the good King Barhallah." The messenger turned and departed, with Eric and his guard escort not far behind him. It was a long meeting with King Barhallah. Eric told him the story of his rescue of Saphrine and answered a variety of questions, not all related to their situation.

Eric felt as though he was being tested and though he answered everything with honesty, he was not completely comfortable with the way King Barhallah seemed to consider him. Then Charlie decided to show his face and the King's attitude changed to one of a little more respect and less apprehension. Just over three hours had passed when Eric finally returned to his bed and got some sleep.

The next morning Eric was awakened by a knock at the door. It was still early, Eric noted, it was still dark outside and his lamps had burned out. "Yeah?" He grumbled and then, "Who's there?" he called from his bed.

"Shiheel requests admittance, Lord Marland." One of the guards outside the door replied.

"Send him in." Eric answered sitting up, swinging his legs over the edge of the bed.

 Shiheel entered carrying a lighted torch, which he placed in a wall bracket. Tucked under his other arm, was a silver shield, about six feet long and two feet at its widest portion which was the majority of the length. That must be the Shield of Ice Eric thought.

"You're a little behind schedule." Eric chided.

"Had to tunnel back, it's a little slower than flying you know." Shiheel laid the shield on the foot of the bed. "So, you ran into much more than I expected, at least from the wild stories I hear of your grand entrance. You must introduce me to the Dark Moor Cat and tell what else, other than the Princess of Efra, that you ran into."

Charlie stuck his head out from under the covers, "Gerp, Gerp."

Shiheel looked at the gerpin and nodded, "I see that rumors do not carry all that has happened. What else, but a gerpin to charm your way here."

"Only Ogres," Eric smiled, "Nothing significant."

"And you are unharmed. Believe me I would not have sent you, if I had known there was anything that dangerous in your path."

"Ah, but if you hadn't, the lovely Princess Saphrine Barhallah would have been lunch for one of those big louts." Eric turned to the gerpin, "and Charlie here would have been a sitting duck to anything that might have come along, and Lady Moor would still be dragging around a pulverized leg." Eric was twiddling the ankh in his hand as he spoke.

"I will need to speak with the Dark Moor Cat. I guess that is 'Lady Moor' as you so eloquently put it." Shiheel went on. "There may be more happening then just Wonks approaching to drive Ogres this far south and dark moor cats out of their homeland."

* * * * * * *

Jamis had shoveled the way clear to the door and Bonny slipped her key into the lock. It was already unlocked. She opened the door wondering why Eric had not shoveled the sidewalk. She walked in with Jamis right behind her.

"I wonder if he has come up with anything new in the game, for my character Hans to face." Jamis said, anxious to see what Eric's imagination might have dreamed up on the computer.

"Hello, Eric, I'm home. Hello?" she paused for a moment, listening. "Strange, I don't hear the shower, he's got the TV on so he must be around here somewhere. Besides, how could he leave without clearing a path somewhere?"

They looked around the house with no luck, though she did notice his main computer was missing from the office. They finished the search quickly, then Bonny found the note and started reading it.

"Horse pucky! Look at this rubbish Jamis. I hope he doesn't expect me to believe it." She handed the pad to Jamis who started snickering as he read it.

"He must have taken off at the beginning of the storm. He's probably out socializing with the neighbor." Jamis laughed.

"Let's find out!" They headed for the still open door.

"Watch out for strange portals now." Jamis mocked.

Bonny shot him a look of disgust. "Right!" She snapped and grabbed the doorknob stepping out behind him, shutting the door at the same time. A strange rippling sensation passed through them, coupled with a momentary suspension of time and space. Suddenly they found themselves walking towards a wall in a strange stone room, lit by a torch in a carved stone sconce.

"Interesting," Shiheel commented looking at the unexpected arrivals.

"Now how did he do that?" Jamis asked with a look of amazement and delight. Eric fumbled the ankh and it dropped to his chest.

"It's not funny, Eric, where the hell are you?" Bonny raged, "This is totally absurd! Where are we?"

"On Ethar." Eric said from behind them, looking at the ankh he had been twiddling between his fingers.

"Eric! What kind of crap is this?" Bonny's eyes were flaming as she spun around. Jamis also turned, but looked instead at Shiheel as excited anticipation filled his face. Bonny continued her anger, only slightly tempered by apprehension, "What the blazes is going on here?"

"Interesting," Shiheel commented again in his matter-of-fact way, still looking at the unexpected arrivals.

"What type of character is that?" Jamis asked, pointing at Shiheel, "Is it friend or foe?"

"Bonny, did you read my note?" Eric looked up from the ankh, thinking she looked ravishing when she was angry.

Jamis looked at himself, "You can't bring me into the game out of character, where's my armor and weapons? I'm supposed to be Hans Spardic, The Ebony Warrior."

Eric looked at Jamis, "This isn't a game, if you read the note, I explained what's happened." He turned to Shiheel, "How did they wind up coming through the portal?"

"It is simple you were toying with the ankh. You must have opened the portal and they just happened to step through." Shiheel answered.

"Bonny, Jamis, this is Shiheel an Eftite from Esberk II," He looked at Jamis, "a friend."

"This is all a bunch of hogwash!" Bonny interjected emphatically. "I don't want to play any games right now; I've been up all day and I want some rest. It's nine in the evening, Eric." Bonny was enraged.

"I'll play, but I need to get in character, you know what I need."

Jamis was all but bouncing off the walls with excitement.

Just then, one of the Elven guards opened the door and looked in, with surprise and alarm on his face.

Eric waved him off and quickly said, "It's alright, don't let anyone else come in for a while."

Jamis looked at the Elf and smiled broadly, unable to contain his excitement. "Come on Eric, you're the Game Master, let me have my equipment, and I'll get into character. I see you have royal guards."

"Here, Bonny, sit down on the edge of the bed next to me. I've missed you. I've been here, what seems like forever, not just two weeks." Totally flustered, Bonny conceded to Eric's request.

Shiheel stood up, "I am going to go talk to Lady Moor, I think you can better handle this alone, or at least without me here." He headed out the door.

Eric nodded acknowledging Shiheel's departure. Then turned back to his friends from Earth. "Bonny, I apologize for getting you involved, but why don't you stay for a little while as long as you are here," he paused briefly. "A month or so goes by here before a day goes by back on Earth, so..."

"Eric," she interrupted, in a hushed voice, her anger giving way to weary frustration, "this isn't real, I'm not here, and I need some real rest."

"Oh, come on Bonny," Jamis broke in, "you told me you didn't need to get up until almost noon and you don't have to work tomorrow. Stick around for a little while and just enjoy the game." He turned his attention back to Eric, a little more self-composed than before. "Eric you're going to have to show me the programming and equipment you used for this one. You'll never have to work another day of your life with a game like this. Will you allow me to bring Hans Spardic in, or do I have to start from scratch?"

Eric looked at Jamis. Hans Spardic the Ebony Warrior was a character Jamis played in the computer game at the college. A ninth level warrior, one of four characters Jamis played, but it was his favorite. "Look, Jamis, this is not a game and I don't make the rules. This is Ethar a parallel world..."   Eric started to explain, but stopped when he felt a tingling sensation in the room around him and Jamis' appearance started changing.

The items of the Ebony Warrior started appearing on Jamis' person one at a time; first the black ethereal plate mail, his magic Sword of Cutting, a Laser Staff, then a Boomerang of Striking, with its special gauntlet for catching it, and lastly, two sets of collapsing nun chucks. Eric sat there with his mouth open, stunned and would have kept staring, but the sensation in the room had not let up and Bonny's outfit also started changing.

He watched as light leathers formed around her, accentuating her beauty. The outfit had several pockets carrying a variety of implements, a belt with what he could only describe as a medicine bag, a sword of elegant appearance and fine craftsmanship and a variety of other closed pouches. Next to her on the bed a long staff and a rather large satchel, then the last thing to appear was a large chest on the floor in front of her. Almost as in the same instant the chest appeared the odd sensation left the room. The sensation had been similar to the portal, yet slight differences. Eric was no less than astonished as he sat there in open mouthed silence.

"I knew it wasn't real, but, oh horse piss, I'll play, but only for a little while." Bonny was calming down and her and Jamis seemed to be taking what was happening better than Eric.

Eric wondered if the portal had done this and how else it might have affected them. Shiheel had mentioned something about the barrier through which it passed having an intelligence of its own and great power. Jaffro Jamis was his full name, though he went by Jamis, because he did not like his first name and he liked to think of it as a mistake. Jamis had not necessarily been change in the same ways Eric had. By the looks of her new wardrobe, Bonny probably had her own set of alterations. It was about this time that Eric noticed their insignias and loyalty emblems. Bonny over her right breast had a medical emblem, much like those worn by the Elves, with the exception that it was circled in gold indicating royalty and her loyalty emblem on her right shoulder was Eric's coat of arms. Jamis on the other hand, had a sword and crown centered on his chest, the emblem of royal guard and he also wore Eric's coat of arms on his right shoulder.

Eric wondered if she might have gained a similar magic to his, so he asked Bonny, "Would you try something for me? It may sound silly, but please try. Hold your hands in front of you and picture you are holding a cup."

"That is silly, why would I try something like that. Oh, never mind, here I go." Bonny held out her hands and nothing happened, "Alright, so what."

Eric said apologetically, "You guys have been magically altered coming here, so I am curious as to how, but I guess only time will tell."

Jamis, admiring himself as Hans Spardic, looking at the way the black armor set against his dark skin, was still not paying too much attention, "What is our adventure and where are we headed, to some dark dungeon maybe?"

"Eric started with Shiheel's arrival at their house after the snowstorm, and started telling them what had been happening, discretely leaving out certain details. They talked for over an hour, with him answering a lot of questions. Bonny would not stop denying any of it was real and Jamis could not get it out of his head that it was all just part of a game. When at last a guard knocked on the door and poked his head in.

"Lord Marland, breakfast is ready and they await your presence in the great hall." he paused and looked at Jamis and Bonny, "Will it be three my Lord?"

"Yes, thank you, we will be right there." Eric stood up, strapped on his equipment and threw on his cape. Then he turned to Bonny and held out his arm, "My Lady, may I have the honor of giving you a proper escort." She took his arm and he led them from the room. Jamis paused and picked up the shield from the foot of the bed before following. Four guards escorted them to the dining hall, where the Elkinshanes were seated.

King Erron was seated at the head of a very large table, on his left was Talmorg and what must have been his brother, Lacrane, followed by their advisors. On the Kings right were three empty chairs waiting for them, and then Shiheel followed by other lords of Talmorg, most of which were wearing military garb. As soon as they were seated, breakfast was served,and Eric quietly introduced Jamis and Bonny, to King Erron and Prince Talmorg, who in turn introduced Lacrane. Lacrane complimented Eric on his battle plans and was interested in learning more of his strategies. When all the Platters were served, King Erron Elkinshane, formally introduced his three guests, Bonny Harrison the healer, Hans Spardic the Ebony Warrior and the Lord Eric Marland to be considered second in command under Talmorg in the coming battle. A cheer filled the room. When they were reseated, everyone began to eat and conversation filled the air.

"My Lord King," Everyone at the end of the table turned and looked at Shiheel, "I have talked with the Dark Moor Cat this morning and there is a greater danger than this present battle that we will have to face. It comes from the once abandoned Darval Keep on shadow peak east of the Dark Moor. Some force is uniting the Ogres and Millmorgs of the mountains and the Rackenwolf, and forming a mighty army. These are not the most intelligent of creatures, but the power behind them is. Whatever they are, they have driven the Dark Moor Cats out of Dark Moor, with a demon leading united force. The Moor Cats are returning to Black River, just west of the Great Mother Mountains, to reform their army against this dark power, in about three weeks, if possible. She will help us here, if she can and inquires if she might get our help when she returns. I tell you; I believe it will be wise to help now, or we might find ourselves crushed later." as he finished a wave of silence finished filling the room.

"Bring this up at the council this afternoon, but I don't know how long this battle will last, nor what our strengths will be when we are done," King Elkinshane answered, "but if what you say is true, then indeed it would be wise to help before such an evil enemy became too powerful."

Conversation began around the room again at a much lower volume. During their breakfast conversation, among other things, Bonny agreed to visit the local hospital facilities. She also noticed during the meal, that King Erron Elkinshane was suffering from arthritis and offered to give him some minor treatment for it later to help ease his discomfort. When they were getting up, she told Eric what she would like to do for him, but she did not know whether she would be able to find what she needed in this primitive culture.

"Why don't you check what's in the chest and satchel back in the room." Eric suggested.
She laughed and then commented, "I keep forgetting you are the game master and none of this is real." Then she took off in the escort of two guards, telling the King she would return to treat him in private. Eric

and Hans Spardic (Jamis), went with Talmorg, to review their military readiness and Shiheel went to spend more time with Lady Moor.

CHAPTER 12

Players to the Game

Mistav was relishing in his endless victory, he now ruled over all the Wonks and three Nob tribes, all of which he had conquered. The last seven Wonk tribes had freely surrendered, so he killed their chiefs for their cowardice and to display the power of his sword before his subjects. He was going to rule the lands to the south next, and eventually all the known world. No one could stand in his way, with the power he possessed with his sword.

To think he had this great power, because Stavic had questioned his right to rule and challenged him to prove his courage as leader of their tribe. If he had not gone into Tarf, he would have had to fight Stavic or lose his position in line to be chieftain. He killed Stavic when he returned anyway, of course in a fair fight, each of them used their own swords. Now the world would be his and he enjoyed killing for it, to feel the power rush through him when he used the undefeated sword.

Since he began his campaign of conquest, he felt a growing bond with the sword, they were both made for the same destiny. It is true originally, he had only planned on uniting the Wonks, but now that was no longer enough. Now he wanted it all, nothing would get in his way, or he would destroy it.

His armies were in the Pengona Forest now. Wonks had raided south land villages before, but they would never expect an army, especially one this size, they would fall quickly and then join him, by the power of his wonderful ring. His army was now fifty-seven thousand strong, give or take a few. They had just reached the end of the old road to Dragoncove. It wasn't much, but it was easier traveling than the dense forest.

His plan was to leave the road about half a day's travel north of the Feather River and then seize Dragoncove under the cover of the darkness of the night. Their survivors would replace his losses or better, he gloated in his next victory as he moved southward with his troops to meet it. He laughed to himself, he had only one hundred soldiers ahead of him, he planned on being in the thick of the battle, he was the key to his own success. Suddenly a part of the road up ahead collapsed and twenty-three soldiers disappeared, where flames spurted up out of the ground, followed by a cloud of dense green smoke that rose into the air.

"Damned! The old road is worse than I thought, keep a hundred Nobs in the front, they're more expendable." He was obeyed without question and they continued their march. They were only two days from the river, this was no time to start losing his good soldiers to accidents. Still, when they left the road, he could not send the Nobs in first, their inferior lack of natural camouflage would give away their approach. They marched until night fall and then laid in camp.

They set out again the next morning and had only marched about an hour when another section of road collapsed, taking with it fifty-one Nobs, to a flaming death and sending up a cloud of red smoke. Mistav called a halt. They were supposed to reach the river by evening, where they would rest a day and attack the following night, but the road was not as safe as he had expected, so he decided to leave the road now. "Spread out and reform, we are marching through the forest." They turned off the road and continued moving, an hour later there was a sudden rain of about two hundred arrows, forty-three hit their mark. It must be a counter raid against other raiding parties, Mistav thought. He sent his first infantry, about five hundred Wonks in to flush them out, and they headed in the direction in which the arrows had come from. Death screams came back through the forest to Mistav's ears and he smiled. He was confident they were the screams of men his wonks were skewering. They had been caught and Dragoncove would not be forewarned of his attack, or so he thought. Yet as they road on there were scattered random screams through the woods around him and nobody had returned with a report. When he finally did get a report there were two thousand thirty-six dead, all Wonk and Nob. He went to the head of the progressing lines and pulled out his sword. He walked ahead twenty feet and a spiked branch swung around at him, fire leaped from his blade and it was gone.

"Damned and double damned, booby traps." He looked around, "They are probably to stop scattered raids, it would work too, but not against us. Form columns, twenty across and follow me, we will spread out again when we reach the river. " He led the way, holding his sword forward, burning the assaulting booby traps that came at him, but he still lost another nine hundred and twenty-one soldiers before they reached the river and laid in for the night. They would keep watch and rest through the next day. Mistav was angry and was considering attacking without delay, he had lost almost three thousand men just getting here, to the road and then those damned traps.

*　　*　　*　　*　　*　　*　　*

After she had treated King Elkinshane, Bonny could see the relief and gratitude in his eyes. He was so thankful he personally escorted her to the hospital, it was on his way to the council halls. Now she was at the hospital. When she first walked in, she thought it was no more than a crude first aid station, using very primitive methods.

After a thorough tour, she realized they depended heavily on Elven magics, but had little or no actual operating equipment. They also had a vast knowledge of herbs and natural medicines, which they used in their healing process. As she walked through, she gave a lot of advice, she seemed to know exactly what was wrong with each patient she touched. *'It's like a dream'* she thought to herself.

She could not leave after finishing her tour and asked if she could help. She washed in an herb bath they used for sterilizing. When she was finished cleaning, she went on rounds with a couple of their healers, sharing with them bits and pieces of her knowledge where it would help, and observing their methods. Somehow, she had gained a certain amount of knowledge of their methods and of the herbs they used, she passed it off during the tour, as just a piece of knowledge from something she read or studied a long time ago.

It was an experience that captivated her interest, though she felt somewhat crippled by the lack of hospital equipment she was used to and realized her own dependency on higher technology. Bonny did not know how, but she had somehow gained a vast knowledge of healing magic and the use of herbs she had never seen or heard of before, a knowledge she did not have before coming to this strange world. In her mind she was combining the two totally different skills and started realizing the potential advantages of that combined knowledge. She could no longer pass the knowledge off as small tidbits she had picked up here or there, it was too much.

These people did very little operating and that was restricted to putting together what had been torn apart before they got there. Yet with their skills a lot of operating was unnecessary. Many things Bonny would have normally operated on to cure, they used herbs and magic, often getting better results. Bonny also noticed that there were some things they cured without even knowing what was really wrong. There was one man who was brought in with what they called a stomach fire, which from all the symptoms was a ruptured appendix. They used magic to stop the infectious spread and herbs to heal, actually liquid extracts in this case. They would never consider removing something that was a part of the body, believing it all has some purpose. It was a concept that seemed so fitting to the strange world that surrounded her.

*   *   *   *   *   *   *

Talmorg led Eric and Hans Spardic (Jamis) down the main road to the governmental hall at the center of the small city. The majority of the buildings were made of stone and mortar, and were stout one-story buildings. Those that did have a second story, used wood for the second floor and all the buildings had wooden roofs. As he looked at the buildings, Eric remembered the outside walls of the city were made the same way, the base level stone and the upper portion from wood.

Dragoncove was quite different from the stonework at Talmorg, it was not the highly skilled work of the Dwarves, or the artistically fused stone of the Eftites, just simple stone and mortar. Finally, they reached the city hall, it was a fairly large building with a second floor. They entered passing two security guards as they went through the front doors. The timbers inside were all hewed by hand, the floor was wooden planks and the ceiling had large beams supporting the floor upstairs.

Talmorg gestured to a stairway on their right, leading up, "We will be meeting down here in the main hall later, but for now all our plans and preparations are made out upstairs."

They climbed the stairs and Hans had to lean forward, so the shield he now carried strapped to his back would not catch on a cross beam. When they reached the top of the stairs, they entered a large room filled with rows of tables. Most of the Lords were there and the chief officers of their armies. They were looking over maps and briefing themselves on the plans and strategies, Eric had provided.

Talmorg started at the end of the first table, introducing the Lords and their officers as he went along briefing Eric and Hans on what was happening, "Everything has been set up according to your plans, with a few minor deviations, where the actual terrain doesn't match the maps and the maps have been updated to show this. The north side of the river has been thoroughly booby trapped and a signaling system has been set up to indicate their approach."

Just then an Elven woodsman bounded from the top of the stairs, "Lord Talmorg," he panted catching his breath, "the first indicator has been triggered, they are two days north of the river, on the road. We saw the green cloud rise this morning, about an hour after sunrise."

"Spread the word among the lords, we meet at midday, we can discuss the matter then." He turned to Eric, "We have little time, they were not supposed to be here for at least another four days. If you wish we can continue to review our set up."

"It is all done according to plan, correct?"

"Yes, the worst problem I had, was getting the different armies to mix troops, to best use their strengths. They still have traditional distrusts for one another, but necessity has dictated and they have conceded."

"Jamis, I mean Hans Spardic, you go ahead and review the operation, if you have anything you can add tell Lord Talmorg." Eric turned back to Talmorg, "You don't need to lead him through it all, just set him in the right direction. I need to go see how Bonny is doing. I will be back for the meeting. I will leave my escort here you can make better use of them as messengers with the field units."

"After the meeting, there is going to be a banquet, bring Bonny to that, or have her meet us there."

"Very well, I will tell her. Now, how do I find the hospital."

"It is on this same street, just turn left when you go out the front door, after you leave here, you'll see it. There is a green flag, the color of life, on a staff at its front door." Talmorg face intensified, "Stay on the main road, there are rogues and vagabonds in the alleys."

"See you at the meeting." Eric turned, went down the stairs and out the front door. He turned left down the walkway next to the street. The roads were paved with cobblestones and had well-groomed trees along either side, that separated it from walkways along the fronts of the buildings. The city was an attractive and well-kept city and Eric was enjoying its quaint clean attractiveness as he move down the cobble walkway.

Before he had a chance to get lost in thought, something caught his attention out of a dark sheltered alley to his left. He turned and looked, back in the shadows there were the forms of two bearded men hunched over someone struggling on the ground. '*Stay on the main roads.*' Talmorg had warned, but it was a woman on the ground and he could not just leave her to the mercy of the two rogues. "What's going on here?" he called down the alley.

One of the men turned, "None of your business pretty boy." The man was drunk and armed with a sword. The drunk lifted his sword in Eric direction, "We heard we're doomed and we're just making a little sport before we go. You just go about your own, before you get hurt."

"You worthless louts, leave that woman alone and go back to your own misery." He started toward them, drawing his own sword.

The other rogue, backhanded the woman across the side of her head and she lay still. He too stood up and drew his own sword, "You can't take the two of us, your sword is even missing its blade, fool."

They couldn't see the blade, but Eric knew it was there, "Be gone with you and no harm shall come, you are drunk and don't know what you are dealing with."

The two were no more than five paces away, when they leaped towards him. Eric stepped to one side, deflecting the sword of the nearest rogue, knocking him off balance into the other fellow and they both fell to the ground. With a quick stroke Eric cut the lacing of the cloths of the one, leaving a fine red line in his skin underneath, as his garments spread open. They stood up again, the first falling quickly down again, tripping over his own fallen trousers, causing the other to fall on top of him. This time Eric slit the back of the others coat and shirt open, causing him to jump up and run disappearing in the darkness. The first rogue also followed after him, crawling on his hands and knees, leaving his sword behind on the ground.

Eric stepped over to the lady lying there, her clothes were half ripped off and blood was dampening her hair. He picked her up after sheathing his sword and carried her back out of the alley. When he got her back out in the light, he noticed she was still breathing and seemed to be basically alright. She was a dark-haired lady, with very strong features. She had an exaggerated, but attractive build and wore clothes, Eric could only relate to those he had seen in movies with magical gypsy attire or perhaps part of a circus act, though he had heard about nothing of that sort since he had been on Ethar. He loosened the bindings on her hands and removed the gag on he rmouth, then continued carrying her, as he went to the hospital. Just ahead he could see the green flag as she started to regain consciousness. He looked at her face and she opened her dark brown, almost black eyes. He looked quickly away, to the hospital door, "I am Eric, I am taking you into the hospital."

"No, you can't." there was fear wavering in her, enchanting voice, "I am Stralina, a Jinn and we are not trusted outside our own land, I must stay hidden." Eric noticed a look of puzzled shock on her face, as he pushed through the doors, "You didn't recognize I was a Jinn, who are you. If you missed my silver nails, you should have seen it in my eyes, yet you insist on helping."

"It's a Jinn, it's trouble." the lady in admitting said staring at them making no attempt to hide her disgust and animosity.

"I told you." a shiver went through the woman he was carrying.

"Quiet." Eric whispered, then turning to the lady that spoke to them, "This is a hospital and she needs help, where is Bonny?"

"But, sir, Jinn cannot be trusted, they are thieves with magics of a cunning sort!"

"Bonny?!" he faced her with anger.

"Yes, sir." She said, quickly turning and going through a door into the back.

Eric laid Stralina down on the counter, "Please don't be afraid, but tell me, if you can't be seen in public out of fear, where are you from and why are you here?"

She looked up at him, she had to trust someone, "Three strange out-worlders, they came some time ago out of the sky and into the mountains. For a long time, they stayed to themselves, but for several years now they have been building a dark empire and we have not the power to keep them from our land. We are not a united people, but a free people and we are being driven from our homes. Unfortunately, our history is not so favorable with the rest of the peoples of this world and we have no place we can go openly. We once served Darval, a dark time for us. Then there are those of our people who are as that lady said 'thieves with magics of a cunning sort'."

"Eric." Bonny walked in. Then seeing the hurt lady on the counter, she came over and examined the injury on her head, "Are you hurt anywhere else, besides your head?"

"My pride and bruises." Stralina answered, amazed to find another person who did not despise or fear her.

"Bonny, this is Stralina, Stralina, Bonny."

"Bring her back here, Eric."

He picked her up again and followed Bonny, then placed her carefully on a padded table in the small hospital room. Bonny quickly went to work cleaning and fixing Stralina's head, "You know, Eric, I could sure use a fully equipped operating room to help these people here."

"Did you ever open that chest or satchel back in the room?" Eric asked, then added, "It might contain everything you need."

They sent a couple of runners back to the room to fetch the chest and satchel. When they brought it back and set the chest on the floor. Bonny opened it up and found everything she needed, including a small generator to run the equipment that operated on electricity. When she finally looked up, she blinked and shook her head and then looked at Eric, "I keep forgetting this is your game."

"It isn't a game. Anyway, I will be picking you up for dinner later after the war council meeting."

"You can sit up now, Stralina. Why not lunch now."

"That's an excellent idea, but this evening we will be at an official banquet." Eric smiled and gave her a slight bow.

"There is a saloon across the street, let's go there for lunch. Would you like to go with us, Stralina. I wouldn't mind keeping an eye on you for a couple of hours just to be sure you're alright?"

"If it's not a burden, I would enjoy some friendly company for a change." She stood up and with a wave of her hand in front of her person she was in a clean new outfit. She smiled at both Bonny and Eric and her eyes now had a red flame in them, giving them an appearance similar to cat eyes, except they flickered. "That first blow they gave me temporarily disrupted my power; it seems to be back now."

Eric held out his arms and escorted both of them out and across the street. They walked under a large sign, that read, Armigan's Saloon, and through the open doors. The place was rather full of people. They chose a table two away from the doors and sat down. An attendant came over to them, a young man, maybe fifteen years of age.

"Can I help you; our lunch special is barbecue eliko sandwiches and fried bourga root."

Stralina answered first, "That will be fine for me and a glass of dragons breath."

Bonny looked at Eric and nodded. Eric told the attendant, "We will have the special also, and ale, thank you." and the attendant turned and left.

"How was your morning," Bonny asked, "Mine was quite busy."

"Well, it was interesting to say the least," Eric said looking at Stralina, then back to Bonny, "War is two days away, or less here, and there is darker trouble farther to the north."

"Your war here is nothing by comparison. The empire of Scaldor, as they call themselves is a growing awesome force, with magics of a strange sort. We are not a weak people, our magic is powerful, I was caught by surprise by those two back there, while I slept."

The attendant came back carrying everything on a tray. He started setting things on the table, when he lost balance of the tray.

"Bonny, look out." Eric yelped urgently. Bonny lifted her arm protectively and a blue shield of light appeared, stopping the food from hitting her, as it slid off onto the floor. Eric nodded his head with his mouth hanging a little open, "Remarkable."

Stralina looked at Eric, "I thought you two knew each other."

"I'm sorry." the attendant apologized.

"We do, we're from Earth and coming here changed us." Eric stopped, catching what he was saying.

The attendant was embarrassed and nervously trying to clean up, "My boss, will pay for your meal. I hope I don't lose my job, I'm sorry."

Bonny turned to him and said, "It's okay you didn't hit anyone, just relax."

He hurriedly picked everything off the floor and departed to the back again.

"Bonny, you generated a shield," Eric grabbed her hand, "didn't you see it."

"Don't be silly he just missed me, at least he gave us our drinks first." Bonny said, taking a sip of her ale.

"You saw it didn't you, Stralina?"

"Yes, you said you were changed, how." Stralina asked with acute curiosity.

"Magic, I don't know. You said they caught you asleep," Eric wanted to change the subject, "were you sleeping in that ally?"

"Well, I'm not really welcomed to this city. Men are afraid of our magics and the stories of Jinn being dark tricksters in the past." She looked at Eric, "That little accident, will probably be blamed on me because I'm a Jinn. I could have, but I didn't cause him to drop that. The only good thing about it is that boy probably won't lose his job, if his boss blames me.”

“Our fantasies never held Jinn or genies as tricksters in that way, maybe, gremlins, goblins, leprechauns or gnomes, even pixies, fairies and brownies are given that kind of credits, if you could call them that.” Eric gave her a curious look.

“I’ve heard of all of them, but most don’t live on this continent.” Stralina stated curiosity still in her expression, “Here if anything goes wrong, it’s the Jinn, Pixies or Fairies that are blamed. If one of us is around any accident is blamed on us.”

Bonny gave Eric an odd look, “I thought you knew all this, if you’re running the game, Eric, or is this for my benefit?”

Stralina looked at both of them oddly her interest increasing as Eric answered, “Bonny, like I’ve said before, this is not a game, I repeat, not a game.” Eric looked at Bonny, “I do not know everything here, I do not run it either. Don’t you think you would have known if I was designing something this elaborate.”

Stralina directed her attention to Bonny, “Can I help you this afternoon, in the hospital.” she looked down at her plate, “Maybe I can show at least someone, that we can use our magic for the good of others.”

“Ah, sure, I think so. It’s not my hospital, but I think, I can get you in.” Bonny said smiling now at Stralina.

The attendant came back after some delay, with fresh food and another round of drinks. They ate their meal conversing more lightly. The owner did buy their meal, but Eric produced a piece of gold for the attendant anyway, worth about a lot more than the price of their meal and left it on the table. When they were finished, Eric walked Bonny and Stralina back to the hospital and returned to the city hall.

Eric entered the council meeting a few minutes late and they had already started. They were still going through formalities and Eric took his seat between Shiheel and Talmorg. Hans Spardic was on the other side of Shiheel and looking quite at home.

"Lords and Ladies" Talmorg was saying. "With the Wonks only two days from the river this morning, we'll be in the midst of battle quicker than expected. Tomorrow we will have to take our field positions. Remember let them on the bridges, before we move. Eric will be facing off Mistav with the Shield of Ice. Hans Spardic, will fight at his side, to cover his back, everyone else is to avoid Mistav. Our battle strategies are all laid out and we have already covered them several times. Now Shiheel has some new business to bring up while we are together."

"Kings, Lords and Ladies, as you are all aware, a Dark Moor Cat has been in our presence lately. I have been talking with her at length, to find out what has brought her this far south. There is an evil kingdom rising from Shadow Peak and the old abandoned Darval Keep. The Milmorgs and Ogres are being united under a dark force, that we don't know as yet. Ogres that are not joining are fleeing south and the Dark Moor Cats are being driven out. Now the Dark Moor Cats have spread themselves out across the continent seeking help and Lady Moor, as Eric appropriately named her, has come to us. She volunteers to help us in exchange for us sending help back with her, to fight an enemy we will have to fight sooner or later anyway, especially if we don't send help now. We need to give her an answer at the end of this meeting."

A rumble started rising in the room, as Shiheel sat back down, but it hushed when Eric stood up. Talmorg acknowledged him and he began, "The Jinn are also being driven out of their homes. The Jinn I spoke with informed me that many years ago three beings, descended from the skies, and several years ago they started the rise of their empire. They call themselves the Empire of Scaldor."

"No, it can't be!" Shiheel stood up, showing more emotion than anyone had ever seen in an Eftite before.

"It is true, brother Shiheel," another Eftite seemed to materialize out of nowhere at Shiheel's side. The other Eftite wore a dark blue robe with silver stars glistening all over it and a tall pointed wizards' hat in the same colors and pattern, "I have discovered Scaldorian magic being used in the mountains to the north and its web is reaching out further each day. I believe they have already engaged the Elves of the Uklian and some of the races in the Rackenwolf." The two brothers faced each other and a beam of light passed between them for a brief moment, then broke off.

Shiheel turned to the council, "The Scaldorians are a race born of dark sorcery on a planet in the neighboring star system to our home world. Hesheil is the only master of Esberkian sorcery we have. They use the same type of Magic, but have a different source than our own. If there is a way, we need to stop this little war here before it starts. Then, maybe even march north as a united force, but not under Mistav." a rumble started rising again.

"How do you suppose we can stop this war without fighting or surrendering?" Brask Scaller piped up.

"We would have to get rid of Mistav, he won't give up you know." Hanser Schultzman added.

Eric missed part of the small volley of exchanges that followed. He sank into thought, concluding with the idea of sending a champion.

"Wait," Eric looked around the room and everyone went silent, "There is a way. A champion, we call for a champion. It has been done in the past. You choose a champion from each side, and the two fight each other, which ever champion wins, wins the war saving bloodshed and preventing extended battle. We need to lure Mistav into fighting the Shield of Ice."

"And what if our champion loses?" Prince Ashkin asked

"Then you have a choice, honor the champion battle, or fight." Eric said, "besides Mistav will be his own Champion, he believes he's invincible with his sword. As soon as he tries to use his sword against the shield, it will destroy him. I will go against him, with the shield and his own sword shall do him in. This is the only way to separate him out. Without Mistav, the Wonks will be without leadership again and no longer under the spell of his foul ring. They might unite with us then."

Azeel spoke up from where he was seated next to King Berkas Barhallah of Efra. It sounds practical. The worst that could happen is if you lose, we have to fight anyway. If you win, we may still have a war, but against a divided enemy or they will surrender as separate groups if they see their imminent loss."

"So, is it agreed?" Talmorg asked, not completely pleased with the idea of Eric going against Mistav. The hall was filled with voices giving their agreement.

"Then we send a runner to speak with Mistav when he reaches the river, but we still prepare for battle and proceed as planned, if he should decline our offer. Now who should be our runner? Do we have a volunteer?"

Hans Spardic stood up, "I will do it."

"No," Shiheel spoke, "You can stay near, but Eric should voice the challenge openly in front of both armies. He should bring the shield with him then, if Mistav responds he will do it then, or he might try to use the sword or ring against the messenger." Shiheel turned to Eric, "You need to challenge his honor and pride. I think his ego won't let him turn you down."

Then Talmorg addressed him, "Eric, do you accept this arrangement."

"Yes." Eric said with confidence.

"Then that settles it." Talmorg finished the topic, "The next order of business is our readiness for battle." They spent the next couple hours reviewing their battle readiness. There were twenty-nine thousand troops already present, three thousand should arrive in the next few days and another Eleven thousand before the next two weeks passed. They went over positions and attack, counter attack and retreat plans. They would be defending against a force of almost double their size, but they had the advantage of surprise, they knew the enemy's movement, but the enemy didn't know theirs. They were laying in cover and the enemy had to pass through the open at the river. They established who would take charge of which positions, their backups and coordination exchanges. They reviewed communication codes and signals. Supply points were reestablished and inventories reviewed.

When they were done discussing their battle plans, they moved on to matters to the north. All agreed to go in hopes of thwarting a later threat to their homeland, it was better to fight to protect their homes on land elsewhere. They also agreed to sending a message to Darkolon and the council of the east south lands, to give them all the information that they could. It was at times a very heated discussion, some thought it would be wiser to build defenses in the south and prepare for a future attack, but in the end all agreed. It was Hesheil's knowledge of their magic and potential that finally convinced them. When they were done, it was decided to wait an hour before their banquet, to give everyone a chance to refresh.

CHAPTER 13

Preparations

Eric walked in the front doors of the hospital, nodded to the woman receptionist and continued back to the room where Bonny was working. Stralina was back there with her, helping. Talmorg had asked Eric to invite her to the banquet also. The two women evidently had some free time, because when Eric walked in, they were both laid back on the table, chatting.

"How was your day?" Eric asked, as they sat up.

"Busy, but a lot smoother with the right equipment." Bonny smiled and hopped down from the edge of the table, stepped forward and kissed him.

Eric kissed her back and then turned to Stralina, "Stralina, Talmorg would like me to extend his invitation to tonight's banquet to you. We all need to be there in about fifty minutes." He looked back and forth between the women, "Looks like you'll both need to change and freshen up, is there any place here you can do that?"

"Sure, there is another room in the back." She turned and they all headed for the door, "Stralina has been a great help, she learns remarkably fast."

As they walked down the hall, Stralina asked, "Why was I invited?"

"Out of appreciation for your information on matters to the north,

I think." he smiled, "It seems as though you are both in need of a change of clothes, something befitting a royal banquet. I magically summoned clothes before, maybe I can do it again."

"That won't be necessary, I can change these hospital gowns into whatever we need." Stralina gestured to some hospital outfits hanging in the back room as they walked in.

"She is a Jinn, honey, with some magic of her own." Bonny hugged Eric and gave him a kiss.

"I hadn't thought about that really." Eric said, returning her kiss and embrace, "I'll just wait for you two out in the hall." Then with a long look in her eyes he added, "I love you, Bonny." With one more kiss Eric left the room to wait in the hall.

It was about twenty minutes later, when the two ladies stepped back out into the hall, laughing at something that happened before they walked out. Eric looked them both over from head to foot. Stralina looked like she was wearing something that a Jinn would wear to a formal or regal function. What bonny was wearing looked appropriate, it was a beautiful green leather outfit, with all the trimmings, but it still bore all her proper markings and insignias. Bonny's medicine bag, belt, pouches and sword were all in their proper places, only the leather work was dressed up elaborately. When he was done looking them over, he said, "I am privileged to escort two of the most, no, the two most beautiful women known, to this royal banquet."

"Don't let it go to your head, big boy." Stralina laughed.

Bonny chuckled and then said, "It might just be fun to experience a little more of this strange world. I never thought it could be this much fun!"

They walked out into the street talking and laughing as they walked. Bonny suddenly got a chill; something was wrong and turned to look across the street. Just then a small boy tripped and fell down the steps in front of the building she was looking at. She ran across the street to help and the others followed. the boy was just scraped and bruised, so they had him fixed up in no time. When they turned and started back on their way, Eric looked at Bonny and asked, "You knew something was about to happen before it actually did, didn't you?"

"It was just a feeling, nothing really." Bonny looked in his face, he was right she thought, "Female intuition." she tried to play it down. They walked the rest of the way in silence, each in their own world of thought. When they reached the doors of the city hall, they were greeted by an escort, who led them to the head table. The tables were all large round tables and the serving platters were placed in a large lazy-Susan, putting them in easy reach as it was rotated around the table.

Seated around the table they were brought to starting from Eric's left were; Hans Spardic, King Erron Elkinshane, Prince Talmorg Elkinshane, Princess Saphrine Barhallah, Lacrane Elkinshane, King Elron Elkinshane, Prince Freebic Elkinshane, King Berkas Barhallah, Shiheel, Stralina, Bonny Harrison and back to Eric. When they sat down, Saphrine was looking at Eric with a longing sadness in her eyes and Eric caught it, before she caught herself and smiled to Bonny before averting her attention elsewhere. Eric turned to Bonny wondering who else might have seen it. After introductions had been made and they started eating, everyone conversed freely, jesting and enjoying the fellowship of each other's company.

Part way through the meal, King Berkas Barhallah turned to Eric, "I must thank you publicly for saving my daughter's life, Eric. Saphrine is very important to me and I can only show you a token of my appreciation, but that will be later."

Saphrine blushed crimson, but managed a smile through her embarrassment, "It is true, Bonny, he saved my life and quite valiantly. I envy you his love, yet I am sure it is best for all."

Bonny looked at her confused for a moment, but quickly figured out that the Elven princess loved Eric. She looked at Eric, he stared at his plate and fiddled with his food for the briefest moment, then looked up into her eyes. She at once saw that he indeed loved her and had come to realize it himself. She leaned towards him and gave him a long kiss.

"Eric is a valiant man of honor and has done much for all of us." Talmorg stated, as he looked at Saphrine with passion showing in his eyes and she returned a gentle smile.

Eric gave a quick look at Stralina, and saw that she seemed to know exactly what was going on. "You are very kind, King Barhallah, but I assure you in keeping with true honor, I cannot accept a gift for what I have done. If you must give something, offer my reward as a grant it to the people of your own kingdom that have need."

"Truly noble." King Erron said.

"Yes, but at least take a token." Barhallah seemed to ponder a moment, "I shall give to you a medallion, bearing my own seal, it shall open any door in Efra." Nodding his head, he pulled the medallion from around his neck and handed it to Eric, "Take it, it is but a small token."

Saphrine had a shocked look on her face, she knew its meaning, but obviously Eric didn't. "Father?" It gave him equal authority to the king in Efra. She knew he would never accept it if he knew.

Eric hesitated, when he saw her reaction, but it was too late, King Barhallah gave him a stern look and insisted, leaving Eric no choice. He placed the gold chain and medallion around his neck and dropped the medallion under his armor. He did not recognize it as anything more than a medallion to honor him, except for the expression on Saphrines face.

"How appropriate, Lord Barhallah," King Erron said, "He stands now in the protection of both our houses. His honor is our honor and through him our honor is made one, amending any breaches between our houses. Speaking of which," He continued now looking at Talmorg and Saphrine, "I think our houses seat well together. What do you think?"

"I agree fully." Barhallah said smiling a silent victory. Saphrine nodded to her father in silent consent.

Eric knew some political arrangements were just made and suspected it was the marriage of Talmorg to Saphrine, which would unit their kingdoms. Though unofficially Efra served the Elkinshanes anyway.

The meal went on with varied light conversation and when they were done eating everyone wondered the room in a social mixer, getting to know each other just a little better. Eric noticed Stralina seemed to attach herself to Freebic and he seemed to enjoy escorting her. By the time the dance area was cleared and music began to play, Eric was sure that he and Bonny had been introduced to everyone at least once.

Drinking dancing and laughter cap of the night, taking all their minds, briefly away from the coming battles. Eric and Bonny enjoyed themselves for a while, then bid their farewells for the evening and headed back to Eric's chambers. The streets were well lighted and they took their time as they strolled along, looking up at the stars and the two crescent moons lighting the night.

They were greeted at the doors by the guards, who opened and shut them as they entered. Once inside they went straight to Eric's room. As he shut the door Charlie who had remained hidden under his cloak all day, hopped out and ran around the room. "Gerp, Gerp."

"He looks excited to be able to stretch his legs out a little, doesn't he Bonny?" Eric said as he laid his cloak across the bottom of the bed.

"What is he?" she asked watching his furious run around the room.

"He is a gerpin, I call him Charlie." Eric pulled out a bottle of wine and two glasses he had brought back with him from the banquet, placing them on the small table by the bed. "I have missed you. There is a time warp between here and Earth and although I have only been gone less than a day, I have been here for almost a month. Don't worry about your work,

I will have you back and well rested before Monday." He hugged her as they sat down together on the edge of the bed.

They already had an ongoing affair living together, with breaks now and then, when one of them thought they were serious about someone else. In the past though, when one of them started acting serious about the other, they would break things off for a couple of weeks. Bonny hugged him back, she knew he was serious now, but this time she wanted a serious relationship with him too. She had realized that at dinner when she had felt angry, because she could tell he had slept with Saphrine. Though she couldn't blame him, Saphrine was beautiful and Bonny knew she had given him no reason not to. She had felt better about it, when Saphrine told her Eric loved her in front of everyone. "I love you, too."

"I think it is time we got married." Eric said, pulling from the pouch hanging form his belt a blue diamond ring he had gotten earlier.

Bonny looked at it as she let him put it on her finger. It must have been a two-karat blue diamond, set in a ring of sapphires and emeralds. "It's beautiful," She whispered, then looked up into his eyes, "Yes, I accept, I will be glad to marry you." They embraced and kissed each other.

"Bonny, I never knew how much you meant to me before, well before Saphrine showed me." he was stumbling over words.

Bonny interrupted with a vicious delight in her eyes, "Was she good?"

"Well, ah," Eric knew he had gone completely red.

"You could always tell me before." she gave him an innocent smile and fluttered her eyelashes.

 Frustrated he almost blurted, "Okay, yes, she was."

"She loves you. You know that, don't you?" Bonny paused, "You don't know, she is keeping a secret from you, something to do with you and her father knows also."

"Why would you say that?"

"It is just a feeling I had at dinner." Bonny looked at Eric's face, "What would you do if she was pregnant?"

Eric looked back at Bonny with a stunned look on his face. What would he do, "I hadn't ever given that a thought, I don't think she would hide that," he paused "I don't know?"

"Never mind, I'm just making wild guesses now. Let's forget about that now, we're ruining the mood of the evening."

Eric sat there for a few moments, then lifted the wine bottle, "A glass of wine, dear." eager not to think about Saphrine for now. As he poured the wine a thought struck him. "A political marriage is being arranged, between her and Talmorg, she can't be pregnant." They both laughed.

Eric stood up and removed his armor, laying it on a bench at the foot of the bed and sat back down again. He looked at Bonny, her long wavy red hair, flowing in its natural locks over her shoulders. As he looked at her, he thought she was the most attractive, understanding and loving woman he had ever met, or would ever meet in his life. They toasted each other and passionately cuddled until the wine was gone. Then undressing with other pleasurable plans in mind they crawled under the covers. Before they could follow their intentions through, the weariness of the long day and the drinking overtook them and they fell asleep in each other's arms.

Morning came early and Eric and Bonny where awaken by a knock at the door. From under their covers Eric called, "Who's there?"

"Breakfast is ready and waiting, sir." one of the guards answered.

"Very well, we will be out shortly." he answered.

Eric got out of bed and found a pile of fresh cloths that had been provided for them on a stand by the door and carried them over to the bed. Bonny got up too, and they both cleaned in the wash basin that had also been provided, before they quickly dressed. Eric wore leathers that had been provided under his armor and Bonny dressed in a leather outfit that had been died Eric's colors. With a big embrace and a long kiss, they headed for the door. Charlie took his normal shelter under Eric's cloak. When they reached the dining hall, the others there were already eating, but paused to make formal greetings.

"Sleep well last night?" Talmorg called, "Come, have a seat and eat before it gets cold."

They seated themselves where Talmorg had indicated a couple of empty chairs. Breakfast was set before them; some cut fruit, a small piece of meat, and a small warm cake covered with hot berries. To drink with the meal, they had some blended herbal tea, which seemed to be a favorite in Dragoncove.

"It looks like an excellent meal." Eric said.

"It is." returned Hans Spardic, from across the table.

"Are you ready for today?" Talmorg asked, "You'll start carrying that shield after breakfast."

Eric looked at Talmorg over his fork and raised an eyebrow, "Are you trying to ruin a perfectly good meal?" then with a smirk, he added "I'm as ready as I'll ever be."

"And you," Talmorg turned his attention to her, "Bonny, will you stay and help at the hospital, we will need healers if a battle starts?"

Bonny looked back and forth, between Eric and Talmorg for a moment, then answered, "I am sure I will." then returned to eating.

"We will be forming up and ready to go in about an hour." Talmorg said rising from the table, "I have much to do, see you at the gates." he turned and left.

"Jamis, you're really enjoying this a lot, aren't you?" Bonny asked looking straight at Hans Spardic.

"Please, I am known here as Hans Spardic and yes I am having a blast. If I, could I would never leave." He looked at Eric, "I tried to talk Talmorg into letting me be the champion, but he trusts Shiheels judgment explicitly, saying if it doesn't work, you'll need me to protect your back."

Bonny looked at Eric a little irritated, "You're not going to try to take on the enemies best alone, are you?"

"It is a unique situation, honey, I'll be alright." He smiled at her, realizing she was starting to take things seriously, "The idea with the shield is not to actually fight, but to lure him into taking a swing at the shield and it will do the rest."

"Hog slobber, you fool, whatever made me agree to stay here?" Bonny spouted, then regained her composure, and a slight look of evil mischief in her eye, "Excuse me, I keep forgetting it's your game."

This time Eric did not correct her, and tell her it was not a game. They finished the meal, listening to Hans Spardic telling them of the battle practice he had been doing, with the other soldiers. When they were all done eating, they headed for the city gates, this time Eric was carrying the Shield of Ice. They were embraced and saying their farewells at the gates, when Bonny turned from Eric in alarm. Eric looked up just in time to see a lit torch falling from a stanchion, towards a baby basket. Bonny screamed, "No!" and stretched out her hand. The torch struck a blue shield of light, that formed over the baby, and slid safely to the ground. The baby turned out to be the son of one of the city councilmen. He and his wife could not restrain, expressing their thanks to Bonny, who was not even sure what she had done.

Hans Spardic and Eric ran out of time and had to head to the lead of the small group, that marched out to lead the battle. They mounted their horses and headed out with a final salute. As they left the city, almost immediately they started splitting in different directions, to man their respective positions. A couple hours later, Eric, Hans and Talmorg met Shiheel and Lady Moor in some underbrush, overlooking the river, just west of the road, where it turned north.

"Any signs yet?" Talmorg asked.

"Nothing since the red cloud this morning, but they should arrive sometime this evening." an Elven officer standing there answered. Archers filled the brush, all along the top of the riverbank. Several feet behind them, pikemen and swordsmen, were quietly relaxing, leaning back on trees or stretched out on the ground, waiting out their time. Eric lifted his binoculars and scanned the area, nothing, they were still out of range, at least fifteen miles away and it was approaching midday. He looked again at the soldiers he could see and among the archers he saw Saphrine, holding the bow he had given her. She smiled at him when he saw her, but quickly looked away.

"They are still at least three to four hours away." Eric told Talmorg, "I can see about fifteen miles with these and right now, there is no sign of them." They waited in silence, or whispered conversation, Eric using his infrared to keep Talmorg updated on the progress of the approaching army. As evening set in, they watched Mistav set camp on the other side of the river. Hans, Eric and Talmorg rotated watch, while Shiheel stayed awake at all times through the night. In the morning Mistav still did not make a move. Talmorg concluded that he planned a night attack and sent Eric back to get a horse and a spear with a truce flag attached, from deeper in the woods. He was to ride forth and call for Mistav at midday. The morning passed and at the appointed time Eric road down to the water's edge and stopped at the end of one of the bridges. He held up the flag of truce, stopped, stabbed the spear in the ground and dismounted.

At first nothing happened, though Eric knew they watched him from the other side of the river. Finally he lifted his voice over the river and called out through the trees, "Mistav, Mistav, I call you under a flag of truce. We have watched you approach for weeks and know you are there."

"Who calls for me." came a voice from the other side of the river, "Why should I take a truce and not a surrender!"

"You are facing the combined forces of the south lands, a force larger than you are prepared to reckon with. Yet I offer you an opportunity to rule both forces, yours and ours, or loose both, depending on the outcome of one man fighting you. First we must talk under the flag of truce."

Eric recognized the pendant and sword, as Mistav stepped out of the woods and approached the bridge with an arrogance Eric had expected. "You and I shall speak in the middle of the bridge." Mistav stated plainly.

"Very well." he answered. They both walked forward, Eric holding the Shield of Ice on his left arm and keeping his other hand clear of his sword. Mistav on the other hand, carried no shield, but kept his right hand on the hilt of his sword.

"This is close enough." Mistav rasped, "What is it you propose?"

"I propose that you combat one of our warriors, one on one, which ever wins, their side wins the war without battle, saving thousands of lives and giving you an opportunity to rule half the south lands by this one small combat."

"How do I know that you speak the truth, that there is a combined force waiting for me here today."

"I wear the seal of Efra, my spear is of the royal Elkinshanes, my horses harnessing is of the Harmosk calvary and you have never seen my royal house before."

"Convincing enough, I will meet your great warrior here in one hour!" Mistav started to turn, then stopped, "What do you have to gain by this."

"There is a greater enemy to the north, and allies that need our help, this way will take less time, than defeating you in all-out battle."

"You mock me." Mistav drew his sword, turned and walked off the bridge.

Eric walked back to the spear with the flag of truce, drew his sword and cut it in half, signaling back the challenge had been accepted. Then he slapped his horse, sending it back, sat down facing the bridge and waited. Mistav had tried to lure him into looking at the ring while they talked, but failed. Mistav was a trickster, what else might he try. Eric tried to prepare himself for anything.

It was about an hour later when Mistav returned to the bridge, "Where is your champion, or are you the chosen one to die?"

"Your ignorance makes you foolish, Mistav." Eric said standing up, "I know who you are and what I face, you go to battle as a fool not knowing your adversary."

"You are bold in words, are you as bold to face your death?" Mistav asked drawing his sword and stepping out on the bridge.

Eric walked forward holding his shield in guard, but did not draw his own sword. "Your courage is in your sword and not your own, so I will defeat you without even drawing my own sword."

Mistav's anger flared, "Die then fool." He pointed his sword at Eric and a red flame leaped from the blade. Eric braced himself, received the impacting power into the shield and the powers of the magics locked. Terror ran across Mistav's face, when he realized he could not break off his attack, nor could he escape the power of the blade himself. In a scream of anguish and pain, he fell to his knees, just before the sword blew up from the overload of power.

The blast took out the bridge and blew Eric back off the end of it, flat on his back on the ground. Mistav was no more, leaving the massive wonk and Nob army without leadership, and confused, fractured memories since looking into the ring on Mistav's hand. Lost, their tribes mixed and bewildered, the Wonks were thankful for their liberation from Mistav and eager to cooperate with the south land forces. Leaders were picked among them and a portion were sent home to take care of their tribes. Eric returned to Dragoncove with the south land leaders and the new leaders of the Wonks. The fierce warriors and traditional enemies, were now thankful for their deliverance from the repressive darkness which was all they could remember of their service under Mistav.

They reached Dragoncove by nightfall and Eric went straight to the hospital to meet Bonny. Stralina was still working with her and had become, apparently, accepted by the rest of the staff. They were both busy, when Eric walked in and he was asked to wait in the entry room. The woman that was there praised Bonny's healing magic, telling Eric, that everyone she had touched the day before was totally healed. Eric immediately recognized the healing, as something similar to his experience with Charlie, who was still his secret passenger, then with both Saphrine and Lady Moor. He wondered if Jamis, Hans Spardic, also had a healing ability.

Eric waited almost an hour, sitting down, getting up, pacing the floor, and conversing on and off with the receptionist. Finally, Bonny came out and gave him a weary smile and they embraced. Stralina was right behind her and also showed signs of an exhausting day. She walked past them and out into the night. Eric decided, he and Bonny needed a good night sleep and some time together.

"Bonny, we are invited to another banquet, but I would rather have a quiet dinner with you and turn in for the evening."

"Oh please." She kissed him. He took her by the arm and escorted her out.

Talmorg was thankful Hanser Schultzmann had volunteered to see to the accommodations for the new Wonk leaders. He was consulting with his father and Shiheel while they prepared for the banquet. "Father, I don't think it is a good idea for you to head any farther north with us. You are no longer as fit as you once were."

"Don't worry for me so, Bonny's medicine has worked wonders, I haven't felt better in years. " Erron Elkinshane looked at his son, "Besides you are the chosen commander of the combined forces, so you will need me to lead our own forces."

"Lacrane can handle that."

"No Lacrane is going to guard the home front in our absence. You also know I cannot put both of you in peril for your lives at the same time. You are my heirs and if something should happen to one, the other must be there to avenge him."

"What about Eric?" Talmorg was searching for a way to keep his father from going.

Shiheel interrupted, "Enough, Eric is going on a different mission. He has to penetrate Shadow Peak and cut the source off the Scaldorian power or we won't stand a chance of winning this war."

Both looked at Shiheel with surprise, but stopped their personal debate, "Does he know this?" Talmorg asked.

"Not yet."

"Aren't we going to use his battle strategies?" inquired Erron.

"You have enough to work with in the notes he gave us. All you need to do is take the methods he has laid forth and apply them to a different situation. It will be enough of a task implementing what you have." Shiheel stepped to the window, "You also have the Wonks on your side now. Remember You're also just a small part of this war. The Borken Dwarves are already experiencing border battles in the Rackenwolf and you will be fighting at the side of the Elven people of the Uklian, your ancestral kin. The Scaldorians are fighting in every direction."

"Very well." Talmorg spoke, "Is Eric to go alone, or are we taking volunteers?"

"I recommend, Lady Moor and Stralina the Jinn, they know the area, Hans Spardic, no warrior can match his skill and five volunteers, one from each of the races. We will, or I should say, I will be responsible for Lady Moors cubs in her absence, until we meet with the other Moor cats."

"Well, let us head to the banquet, we shall assemble the party there and you can go over the details with them in the morning." King Erron went to the door and opened it. The three of them continued their conversation as they walked to the banquet hall.

A messenger informed them, Eric and Bonny would not be there, when they arrived. Acknowledging the message, they seated themselves at the head table and the banquet began. With all the leaders at the head table, Talmorg brought up the subject of the special expedition and it was discussed at length. Finally the members were established. Shiheel's recommendations of Lady Moor, Stralina and Hans Spardic were quickly agreed upon and they were all ready to go. Garth Kor, a Wonk, volunteered, who boasted of being the best tracker alive. He was five foot five and a half inches tall, sandy haired and brown eyed Wonk, carrying a curved Wonk sword, a dagger and a pouch on his belt, who claimed he needed nothing else. Kole Boort a Nob hunter who volunteered, knew a large portion of the area they would have to travel through, being one of the most respected merchants among the Nobs. Kole was one of the more experienced Nobs in combat, but he knew his way around the land as a merchant. He had black hair, dark brown eyes, stood about four foot tall and was a little less stocky than a Dwarf. He carried a short bow, an axe and a large dagger. He was ready to take any provisions they were willing to give him. Of the Dwarven volunteers, Kedd Darset was chosen, he was also an experienced tracker and a scout. His arsenal consisted of a couple dozen knives and a battle hammer, he also carried a hundred feet of rope attached to a grappling hook. Kesker a particularly rough looking stone giant volunteered, with a smile reflecting his love for adventure. None challenged his right to claim a place in the expedition. Choosing their Elven companion seemed more difficult at first. The number of volunteers was overwhelming. Hesheil settled the difficulty, by volunteering his best student of Esberkian magic, Brent Kelch, saying he was the best suited to recognize and deal with the Scaldorian's wizardry, and though without complete trust, everyone agreed.

Those of the party who were there, were instructed to meet with Shiheel and Hesheil, the second hour of the morning, for breakfast at the inn across from the hospital. Shiheel agreed to talk to Eric. Then everyone retired for the evening, to meet again in counsel at midday the following day.

CHAPTER 14

Prepare

Eric had serious doubts about using his magic, after the loss of time he had experienced creating the boat. He still did not know what or even if there was a price to pay for its use. The boat had taken time and he saw no other effects later, so he decided it was worth the risk now, to do something nice for Bonny. Eric produced an oriental spread, then he and Bonny sat down to eat by candle light. Bonny was thrilled by the romantic setting he had prepared and tingled all over with anticipation. She looked at Erics handsome features, mischievously enhanced in the flickering candle light, yet maintaining their distinguished strength and confidence.

Charlie had silently slipped out the window and was wandering off in the night, a habit he had all along that had gone unnoticed, because he usually left after Eric was asleep and came back before he awoke. Eric was thankful to have some time alone with Bonny, his love filling him with a trembling thrill and excitement. He was filled with an overwhelming desire to give her something, as his mind filled with visions of marrying her. It felt like a new romance with the nervousness, anticipation and giddy feelings that go with young romance. He stared into the fine features of her face, with an unbreakable smile and expression of love.

"I love you, too." her voice broke through his thoughts, bringing him to the realization that he had spoken.

He wanted to give her something and in his mind, he saw a blue diamond pendant and earrings that matched the ring he had already given her. "Dear Bonny, you're marrying me will make me the happiest man in two worlds." He leaned forward, fastening the pendant he envisioned around her neck and then handed her the earrings.

Bonny's eyes lit up, as she drew a deep breath in amazement. Looking at the flaming blue diamonds he produced, "You are wonderful." she said unable to keep the quivering out of her voice. Bonny looked at the earrings for a long moment before putting them on.

Eric saw the flickering tears of joy in her eyes and leaned over embracing her. They embraced and poured the passions of their hearts out on one another with kisses for several minutes. Then though they had barely touched their food, they rose up and moved to the bed, tangled in each other's arms and dropping cloths as they went, conversing without words, primal passion pouring through their blood, lading their breathing. They fell together onto the bed, the last of their garments falling to the floor, uncontrollably caressing and fondling each other's passion with their own. Their bodies driven by desire to give themselves wholly to each other, with senses heightened and pleasantly distorted by their love.   They held back until their bodies could take no more, then they gave themselves fully to each other. Nothing else existed to them, as they moved in pulsing rhythmic waves, transcending together as one, enveloped in physical sensation. If fireworks could break it was filled by their sharing so intense, so wonderful, as it ripped through every part of their bodies, leaving after shocks, forcing them to gradually slow down, until they collapsed into the bed, in an intertwined mass, holding close to each other's warmth. They laid there for unmeasured time at total peace, with bliss, losing time and somewhere passing into sleep.

Somewhere in the night they awoke enough from the chill air, to get under the covers, but not enough to remember covering up. Their sleep was undisturbed and nurtured their strength, preparing them for whatever might lay ahead. They had joined together this night in more ways than they knew and became a part of this strange world and Ethar became a part of them, they would never fully understand, nor would they fully grasp the extent of the power they had gained.

Eric woke up well before the dawn, to the smell of a hot breakfast and sat up feeling fully rested and ready to take on the world.

"I took the privilege of ordering room service. I hope you don't mind." Bonny smiled from the wash basin, and then lit the second torch in the room.

"Oh, not at all, love." he stretched, stood up and wrapped in one of the fur blankets. "You look exceptionally radiant and beautiful this morning."

"Thank you, you don't look half bad yourself, though you looked better without the fur." She laughed, walking up to him with a hug and a kiss, "Shiheel stopped by when he learned I was up. The council wants you to head a special expedition to Shadow Peak. They are gathering at the inn across from the hospital for special instruction. I am invited there with you, but not on the expedition. I'm supposed to travel with the main force to Black River, as a part of the medical team.”

Eric looked into her eyes for a moment, “You’ve accepted the reality of this world, and what is happening, when?”

“I’m not sure, I am not sure I have really accepted it either.” her face was puzzled for a moment, then she continued. “But if Stralina is right, then you are the greatest of wizards, that ancient legend and lures spoke of when they looked ahead. A man who would come with the combined power of the original fairy lords, tapped into the heart of Ethar itself. Jamis is your warrior, who cannot be defeated, I mean ‘Hans Spardic’. She referred to him as the warrior with the power of the shadows and the sun in his hands, whatever that means.” Bonny gave him an inquiring look.

“I don’t know, at least not yet,” Eric shrugged, “but let’s eat, it smells good.”

They sat down and started sampling their meal. It was made up of some strange berry muffins, a sweetened hot cereal and seasoned meat patties, not too different from sausage back home. “We better eat while we can.”

“It’s quite tasty.” Eric commented. “Did she happen to have any reference for you in these prophecies?”

“Mmm humm.” Bonny returned through a mouthful. Holding a finger up indicating she had an answer. Then swallowed what was in her mouth. “Something about the light of protection and healing in the other hand from the warrior, I didn’t get the references she made with that.”

"We will have to make our wedding plans, when we get back. I am sure it will be good news to 'mom'. Not to mention a surprise to a lot of people."

"I'm sure. Everyone is convinced we are going to be perpetual roommates, destined to never find the right partners." She laughed and took another mouthful of cereal. They finished breakfast, laughing and talking about how everyone would react to their announcement. When they finished, they got dressed and decided to walk around town and enjoy the sunrise together.

*   *   *   *   *   *   *

Hans Spardic had made fast friends with Prince Freebic Elkinshane. Freebic was an untamable adventurer, who shared and exchanged stories with Hans, who shared stories of his game adventures as if they were real. Freebic had offered him a bunk in his quarters and he had accepted. After the dinner banquet, Freebic had thought to make Hans take the expedition more serious, by sparring with him a little. Freebic had rarely been beat in sparring matches and then it had only been one out of three in a match. After ten bouts with Hans, using different weapons, Freebic conceded Hans was unbeatable. The two of them had a few drinks of ale and spent a couple of hours in storytelling before they crashed for the night.

Hans lay there for a little while thinking about Freebic's legend of a castle that mysteriously sank in the Rackenwolf, filled with riches and treasure. He and Freebic were going to find it after this war was done with.

Freebic had gathered all the information he could and was already making plans before the Wonk threat had been made and they had been called to arms. Now it would have to wait even longer. Finally dosed off only to be awakened all too soon to get ready for the morning meeting.

"Get up you sleeping bum," Freebic roared, "or should I have the early morning prowlers polish your steel with sticky fingers."

Hans sat up with a halfhearted yawn, "Let the games begin." and threw a small ball of fire from his fingertips, lighting the only unlit torch in the room. "Getting a little better control of it." he mumbled.

"Sorcery crap, you're a fighter not a court magician." Freebic shook his head with a snicker, "We need to hurry and get you over to that inn. I sure wish I was going with you, but the armies need leaders too.... Oh well, next time maybe."

Hans decided this was a good time to check out his 'lightning speed' spell and used it to get ready.

"Hot dragons' teeth, you're as fast as an angry Gerpin, when you want. You were just gaming when you spanked my horse."

"What's a Gerpin, Prince?"

"Just a creature of legend, saved the Elves once early on. They bring luck, which is how the first Elves escaped the 'Lost Tunnels'. I'll give the pigs squeal of it sometime over a brew. Let's head out."

Freebic showed Hans the way to the inn, before they parted company and Hans went in. Everyone was there except Eric, but it was still early. When Hans sat down, he was served breakfast. The rest were already eating, so he dug in.

*   *   *   *   *   *   *

During their morning walk, Charlie joined them and hopped up under Erics cloak. He was well hidden when they walked into the inn. Seeing Bonny was with him, the men all stood until she was seated, then went back to eating. Eric and Bonny having already eaten, requested tea only.

The Dwarf Kedd Darset spoke up, "Ya better et, yer go'na need it."

"We already ate a couple of hours ago, thank you though." Bonny said smiling at his concern.

"Git up early eh, good." Kedd said with a scrutinizing look, then went back to eating.

"Well, we are all here," Hesheil began, sounding no less like a monotone recording than Shiheel normally did, "Your purpose is to knock out the Scaldorians power translator. It is being kept in the heart of Darval Keep somewhere. It gives them unlimited, continuous use of their magic. It translates the power from an alternate dimension and saves the power generating time for the users. If they can use it, when they come out to face our troops, our armies will not have a chance. Kole Boort knows the territory halfway there, Lady Moor knows the area near the keep and Stralina was a captive and escaped, she knows the keep and the tunnels in and out under the keep. The translator is inter-dimensional and Brent Kelch knows how it works. You have two trackers that should be able to cover the distance and keep you from getting lost. We know they have unified armies of Ogres and Millmorgs that you will have to get past, either through or around. With your combined skills and knowledge, I believe you have the best chance of success, you are also diverse enough you should be able to at least understand the gist of any language you might happen to overhear. We need to get you supplied out today, so you can leave tonight."

There was a long pause, then Kole Boort the Nob, spoke up, "This is suicide!"

Kesker grunted his agreement, but gave a vicious smile.

From that point they proceeded to cover every detail that any of them knew and what they would need to deal with it. They were going to try to pass as unnoticed as possible, hopefully all the way. After the plans were fully laid out, everyone had a flagon of brew.

After their first toast, Stralina spouted, "I don't see how we can make it. The only reason I am willing to go is because, I believe Eric is the Wizard Master of Legend."

"Master Hesheil," Brent Kelch, spoke distracted by his own thoughts, "You know I am not yet of the power to match the Scaldorians."

Shiheel answered, "You have more power traveling with you than you know."

"Maybe, but to pull this off we will need the luck of a Gerpin." Garth Kor, the fearless wonk, spoke this time. He would go for the honor of his name, even if it meant certain death.

To Erics surprise, Charlie chose that time to show himself and there was a stunned silence around the table, with open mouthed stares, followed by whispered ascents to the success of their mission.

"Gerp, gerp, gerep."

Hans was unsure, but concluded that the strange creature before him, must be a gerpin.

"Everyone, meet Charlie, a friend of mine I met on the way here." Eric said, then turning to Hesheil he asked, "Hesheil, can you bond volcanic ash with gold to make rings, for each member of this party?"

"Yes, but that would be a waste of time."

"Not this ash." Eric produced one small bag and took a small pinch, dropping it over Charlie, who, after a burst of color disappeared for a few moments. "Do you recognize it?"

"Yes, I have searched for it for years, ever since I first heard of it in the legends and stories of this land. I should be happy to accommodate you, in exchange for whatever is left in that bag when I have finished." Hesheil had an anxious tone as he spoke.

Eric tossed him the bag and said, "Done.". Everyone else followed the bag with their eyes as Hesheil caught it with his tail and slipped it in under his cloak. They too recognized it, though they had never seen it before, they had been raised with the stories from early childhood and knew the bag Eric just tossed To Hesheil, could buy a small kingdom.

"Spewing forth the water brings,

Volcanic dust he'll use in rings,

With the charm of a gerpin,

His comrades are made certain. " Kesker quoted a verse from the Never Ending Poem and laughed, looking at Hesheil.

"What is that from?" Eric asked.

Brent Kelch answered, with a slightly smug attitude, "It is a verse from the Never Ending Poem, which prophesied the coming history of Ethar to the Ancients. Master Hesheil fancied himself to be the wizard spoken of in the poem, but it seems it might just be you."

"There are references to the great wizard that spans a length of time that exceeds fifteen hundred years." Shiheel laughed, "Eftites are the only race whose life expectancy exceeds the necessary time. It was a logical conclusion."

Everyone was silent for a few moments, each for their own reasons, some with respect for the poem, some surprised at Brent open reference to the Ancients in front of humans, some giving serious consideration to what was being said, then Eric asked, "What else does this poem say of the wizard?"

Kesker began again,

In times gone by and magic past,

What lies ahead was seen and caste,

Times of peace and times of war,

Magic becomes the thing of lore.

Race and powers from worlds away,

Will make a show and have their day,

The wizard master shall in the south appear,

He shall bring a warrior who knows no fear.

With the powers of shadow and sun in his hands,

He shall travel undefeated through the lands,

With shadow skin, and armor black to play the game,

For adventure and challenge he can't be tame.

The greatest wizard shall be his master,

To save Ethar from real disaster,

Tapped to the heart, the wizard gives with nothing taken,

Magics move and stir, in the peoples reawaken.

The master and partner Ethar's protector,

From water, air and land every sector,

He will bring the races together,

But come and go like the weather.

He is the greatest wizard who knew no spells,

His knowledge is power in hidden wells,

Doing deeds not for themselves,

Rule shall be given to the Elves.

Shadow weaver your mother is queen,

Elven beauty with eyes of green,

But you have received the blood of him,

For whom Ethar gives upon a whim."

Kesker stopped and everyone was silent for several moments, as if expecting more.

"It is called the Never Ending Poem," Shiheel broke the silence, "I have collected over a thousand verses to it, but no one is sure of the order or the total number of verses. Nor do they know for certain its origin."

"It is rather ambiguous than and each verse could refer to someone entirely different and you don't know." Bonny had an expression of some displeasure as she turned and looked at Eric, "It could have absolutely nothing to do with you Eric. Maybe you are even an unforeseen change, who really knows."

"Ah be a sport, Bonny nothing will get to Eric, without first having to go through the Ebony Warrior." Hans laughed, "When do we start, I am anxious to see what lies ahead."

"Don't git in a foolish rush, boy," Kedd gave him a stern look, shaking his head, "no sense in dying of foolhardiness."

"Courage and honor need wisdom to survive." Garth Kor added, doing a great job of mocking wisdom by trying to emulate it, giving an opulent bow and an extravagant waving of hands.

Eric looked around the table, nine of them were going on this quest, ten counting Charlie. Shiheel originally wanted fifteen volunteers, but a party that big would have drawn too much attention. The only ones there that were not going were Hesheil, Shiheel and Bonny. They would be going with the armies later to some great rendezvous to the north. They were the oddest-looking group. Garth Kor was a Wonk, he was five foot five and a half inches tall with sandy hair, brown eyes and a hint of Elven features in the face. He wore a minimum of clothing so as not to inhibit his use of those strange muscular membranes that Wonks had. His legs ended in what Eric could only describe as ostrich feet. In Erics opinion Wonks were basically very ugly and evil looking. Whatever Wonks might lack, they made up for it in arrogance, ego and fighting ability.

Then there was Kole Boort, four-foot tall, dark brown eyes and black hair pulled back and tied behind his head. He looked like a Dwarf, except for the sick green color to his skin and the fact like most Nobs he was not quite as heavy set as most Dwarves. Brent Kelch was an Elf, but all details were obscured by his hooded wizards cowl, except for the cold and mischievous look in his eyes. Kedd Darset the Dwarf, was five foot tall, very stocky, with gray eyes and black hair. His face was as hard as stone, with a scar running from the left corner of his mouth to his temple. Kesker the stone giant was a forbidding character, who could have very well been made from stone. Stralina in with this group, seemed like nothing but more trouble to Eric, while Lady Moor and Charlie were the most comforting. Even Hans Spardic looked as fierce and dangerous as the rest. Eric wondered if he was going with heroes, or a bunch of cutthroats and thieves. Eric guessed it would take at least a month to lead this group to their destination and then he would have to lead them back when they were done.

Shiheel broke the group up into pairs, to gather their supplies. Garth left with Brent, Kole went with Kedd, Kesker went with Hans and Shiheel teamed Stralina with Eric, before taking off with Lady Moor. The rest took off leaving Eric standing there with Bonny and Stralina.

"This is the strangest world I have ever heard of." Bonny commented, "I wish we could stay together, but I guess this is necessary."

They walked Bonny to the hospital first, where she gave them some medical supplies, which Eric added to the medical kit he was already carrying. After a long tender embrace, Eric left Bonny and continued down the street with Stralina.

"We'll go where ever you want first," Eric said, "but the last stop will be Hesheils shop so he can have time to make those rings." Eric did not really have any other stops to make, he figured he could use his magic for anything he really needed and they only had half a day left anyway.

"Okay," She kissed the air in his direction, "We'll get spices and herbs first than."

The afternoon went by quickly, with little incident, though Eric noted that Stralina managed to make everything she got disappear into her loose-fitting garments. He guessed that most of what she got, had to do with her magic and even recognized some of the supplies she picked up. When they stopped for a lunch break, she only ate a salad and Eric enjoyed a fresh fish sandwich. As it got later in the day, they finally went to Hesheil's shop.

"Ah, there you are." Hesheil said as they walked in, "Come have a seat." He indicated a couple of chairs at a small wooden table.

"Are they ready yet?" Eric asked.

"Of course." He answered sitting on a stool across from them. The small table was obviously built for his comfort as he set a small wooden box on the table and held a ring out to each of them. "These are yours, put them on."

Stralina and Eric put on the rings they were handed. They looked like simple gold bands, which seemed to have the same fibrous shimmer to them as Shiheel's handiwork. All the way around the rings, Eric could see strong, clear, black lettering, in symbols that were totally senseless to him. The rings fit perfectly, but nothing happened.

"How do they work?" Stralina asked, in a manner that suggested she only asked because she was expected to.

"It is actually quite simple. If you look closely, the middle of the band is a separate ring, just turn it to vanish and turn it back to reappear." Hesheil gave them a simple answer, not giving them the wordy explanation, they might have received from his brother Shiheel.

The two of them followed his instructions, proving the rings worked both ways.

"Here are the rest." Hesheil said, pushing the wooden box across the table to Eric. "They all work the same way and I even made one for the Gerpin, though when he is riding on your backpack, he won't need to use it." Charlie slipped out from under Eric's cloak and he put the smallest ring on one of his front paws.

"How did you get all of our sizes?" Eric asked out of curiosity.

"Simple observation, when we were around the table this morning. Please look around and see if there is anything else you would like. I will consider the powder you have already given me as sufficient payment for whatever you want."

"Do you have the items I requested?" Stralina asked as they stood up and Eric started looking around the shop, more out of being curious than desiring anything.

"Yes, Stralina, they are in that bag on the counter." He said pointing at a cloth bag with his tail. "The devise you will be looking for when you reach Darval Keep, will look like a giant metal ball. It will have many tubes coming out of it, one will be much larger than the rest, seeming to lead to nowhere, that is the one that needs to be disrupted. Though if you can find a way, destroy the entire thing before you are done."

"How come you and Shiheel don't go and do it?" Eric asked.

"The Scaldorians do not yet know we, Eftites, are here, or they would have directed their full focus against us first. However, if one of us got that close, they would be alerted and we would not have a chance. We need to try to stay out of their range until that source of their power has been destroyed."

"Why won't it be heavily protected?"

"Eric, they will not expect anyone of this planet, to know what it is, or how to deal with it, so they have no fear of its discovery, unless they were to draw attention to it, by over protecting it."

"It is true," Stralina interjected, "When I was a prisoner, I think I saw it, they call it, the toy."

"You see, even without it, their only threat to the best of their knowledge, would be an Eftite anyway. Of course, they don't know of you, Eric and they don't believe the Ancients are real. The device is a dimensional portal of sorts, not all that different from how you got here. We will need to figure a way to plug it after the war, so it doesn't leave a permanent leak in the dimensional barriers."

"And how can we do that?"

"I am not sure, Eric." Hesheil shook his head, "Shiheel and I will have to work on it, or it might be in you power, your magic does draw itself directly from one of the barriers."

Eric was a bit surprised; it was true he didn't really know what his magic was, or how it worked. He wondered where science began and magic ended, or is it where magic ends and science begins. What he did know was he had undergone some permanent changes, he didn't understand.

Stralina had gathered up a few other things she had found and Hesheil was writing them down, on an account sheet.

"What did you want the extra powder for anyway, Hesheil?" Eric inquired.

"It has many legendary uses, but I also wanted to examine it, to see if I could reproduce it."

"Can you?"

"No." He shifted, almost uncomfortably, "At least not yet. When I try to study it, it seems to be there and not to be there at the same time. It is like a material with no real substance, made of an energy that doesn't exist. Even with the use of Esberkian magic, which has similar properties, it is the same way. I made a ring for my pet falcon and while he was disappeared, I could not detect him, even with my magic, while I was holding him. Whatever it is, it is not from either dimension I work with."

As Eric talked with Hesheil, he could not help, but notice, how Hesheil was constantly working with both hands and his tail in everything he did. "I notice you use your tail more than Shiheel."

"He avoids using his, to make the people around him more comfortable. I figure they can get used to it. It would be like you not using one hand, because you were among people who only had one arm. Try it sometime." They both laughed, Eric could understand the analogy and it somehow made him a little more comfortable around the Eftite.

"The Scaldorians make materials a lot like yours, if it weren't for the stupidity of the Millmorgs, I would never have escaped their prison. I have seen Eftites at the forge work with, ah, that, eye, I guess. How do the Scaldorians do it?" Stralina asked.

"Their hands, or if you prefer, split tentacles have multiple facets, like the suckers on an octopus. Many of their abilities are generated through these with contact."

"Oh."

"You guys had better head to the main gate, or the rest will be waiting for you."

"Gerp gerp." Charlie had been wandering around the shop and quickly hopped up to his favorite hiding place.

"Well, thank you." Eric said, as he and Stralina headed out the door. Eric wondered why Hesheil was seemingly mistrusted by most. Of course, Talmorg had told him, the magical Eftite was a mystery, that kept mostly to himself. Though Eric thought to himself, he seems to have a shop in almost every town, from what others had said, even if they were normally run by his apprentices. Eric sank into thought and Stralina, amused, guided him by the elbow as they walked.

CHAPTER 15

Imminent War

Talmorg looked anxiously up the street when someone said Eric
was coming. He had a table set up with baked pheasant, fruit and salad,
so the members of the special expedition could eat, before they left. A
mounted escort would lead them as far as the source of Feather River and
east to the North Arbron, before sending them on their own. Talmorg had
already had a long day. He was making preparations to lead a combined
army, of ninety-four thousand strong, on a long march north. He was
thankful that Shiheel volunteered to take care of arrangements for the
small party, but felt he should be here to see them off. Garth and Brent
were the last two, arriving just after Eric and Stralina and they all sat down
to eat.

There was very little conversation, while they ate and everyone
finished quickly, anxious to get started. Everyone that is except Eric, he
was still deep in thought. Stralina was the first to become real concerned,
because he had been that way, since his talk with Hesheil and she brought
it to Talmorg's attention. It did not take too long before everyone noticed
and Talmorg became uneasy about it, after all Eric was supposed to lead
this party and if he remained withdrawn and to himself, he would not do to
well. Finally, when they were all set to go, Talmorg drew Eric to one side,
before the party mounted up.

"Are you alright, Eric?"

"Ah, yes," He paused to look at Talmorg, "why, is something wrong?"

"Only that you seem to be almost totally oblivious to what is going on around you." Eric could see the concern in Talmorg's face.

"Sorry about that, I've been contemplating several things, I learned from Hesheil."

"Well, you can't very well lead these people, if you're not with them." Talmorg said, trying to sound stern and reprimanding.

"Kedd can lead us till we reach the North Arbron." Eric said, as if not noticing Talmorg's attempt at reproving him. "I'll be fine and may have solved a few riddles by then."

"Very well, but you had better mix in with your fellow travelers a little more, by then."

Eric grinned at Talmorg, "You worry too much. I will set forth my intentions to them than and we will be off." They walked back to the rest of the party, "Fellow companions, may I have your attention?" They all turned to face him, "As you know, we have been provided mounts and an escort to the North Arbron, where we will continue on foot. It will take us four or five days to get to that point and after that, we will be dependent on each other for survival. I suggest we take full advantage of this first leg of our journey, to prepare our minds and senses for the rest of the journey. I am designating Kedd Darset from Vorka to lead us to that point, he is already familiar with the area and is best suited to pick the more ideal resting stops along that route. Kedd when you are ready, we will begin."

"Den let's git goin, and be done wid these blasted horses."
Everyone knew, Dwarves hated riding horses and Kedd was no exception.

Talmorg stood next to Shiheel for a few minutes, as they watched the mixed party of strangers riding away from the gates of Dragoncove.

"Now we must get on with our business." Shiheel said, placing a hand on Talmorg's shoulder, "We ride north in the morning."

"Do you think they will succeed?" Talmorg asked watching the dust settle.

"If they don't, neither will we." Shiheel answered as they turned and headed back into town, "What do the prophesies of your own legends say?"

"Can we know which prophesy we are filling, before it is filled?"

*   *   *   *   *   *   *

Bonny said her farewells to Eric and watched him leave the hospital with Stralina, before she turned from the receiving room and went back into the work areas to help with the preparations. Today there would be very little patient care, fortunately there were very few patients. They were packing more than half the facilities resources in horse carts, to travel north behind the great army. Bonny worked close with Elisha and Darset, the heads of the medical staff and found she was really enjoying herself, even though many of their methods seemed to range, in her eyes, from primitive witch doctor techniques to medieval. Elisha was a lighthearted and fun-loving Elf, who could cheer anyone up and Darset was a woman of stern and strict character, who kept everything in order and though at first she seemed very hard-nosed. Bonny now found her softhearted and a very good friend.

Bonny, had given up worrying about how she would get back to work on time and gave in to enjoying herself while she was in this strange world. She would hold Eric responsible for getting her back home when the time came. If she was late for work, she would take her anger out on him, but there were plenty of other hospitals that would be glad to have her if she lost her job. Bonny also wondered if she would bring any of this magical world back with her, or retain any of the knowledge of herbs and strange remedies she had mysteriously gained when she returned. She also still pondered the thought this was all a dream anyway. She gave up on the idea that it was a game Eric designed, no computer could support this much detail, or such a full submersion.

The day wore on long and hard, making it well after dark before they were done and Darset could send a messenger to report to Talmorg they were ready. With the messenger sent, they were done for the day and Elisha invited them to join her for dinner at the inn. The three of them went across the street, to relax, sit down and eat dinner together.

"During the south land border wars, we were always protected," Elisha continued, as they picked at their fruits and salads, "The medical wagons were considered off limits to battle, but this time I don't know. From what I hear the enemy seems to be quite different and less civilized, as if war can be civilized."

"We are staying back from the battle." Darset said, "What I want to know is how we are expected to handle all those injured soldiers. I am not an Elf you know, I am not old enough to remember the border wars. Glad of it to!"

"Field working conditions are always bad, in any war." Bonny said.

"What are wars like on Earth?" Elisha asked.

"War is war, the weapons are different, but lots of people are injured and lots die."

"How do you handle the injured there?" Darset asked this time.

"They get field treatments; first priority is trying to keep them alive. Those that can be fixed enough to send back into battle are, while others are flown back to hospitals or home." Bonny smiled and took a sip of wine, trying to conceal what she was feeling, at the thought of war.

"Flown back? Do you have alliances with Rocs?" Darset asked in amazement.

"No, we don't have any birds that large." Bonny laughed, "We have airplanes and helicopters. They are flying machines, like I said our weapons are different, we fight wars totally different. Our world has developed weapons that kill more and faster, there is no glory in death."

"Have you worked with war injured?" Elisha asked.

"No, not under actual war conditions." There was a long pause, of silence, "War isn't the only thing we developed though. We have developed many things for peaceful societies too. Although some of that was developed because of wars too."

*   *   *   *   *   *   *

Talmorg walked back with Shiheel. They walked in silence all of the way to the city hall building. Shiheel finally spoke breaking the silence, "You need not worry about Eric, I am sure Hesheil must have given him significant information concerning their mission. He was probably just sorting through the implications and possibilities. Look at what he has done so far, I am sure he will succeed." Shiheel spoke boldly, but he too had doubts, but chose to keep them to himself, at least for now.

"I guess you are right. I should listen to the advice I gave him, I can't lead the combined forces, if I spend my time worrying about Eric." Talmorg shifted the burden of his thoughts as they went inside. The building was crowded, all the active leaders of the south lands were there, with their executive officers, working over final details and double-checking readiness status for mobilizing in the morning. The air was filled with the tension of a lightning storm. Talmorg acknowledged the greetings of the guards as he scanned the room and turned right, heading up the stairs with Shiheel. Upstairs was only a little more subdued, here was the heart of the leadership of the main forces. They walked around the perimeter, exchanging comments with the other war counsels, on their way to Talmorg's main counsel table, the very heart of the whole organization.

Talmorg's father, King Erron Elkinshane, was seated at the head of the table, when they arrived. "Greetings my son, Talmorg, all is in readiness the final messenger just left."

"Thank you, father. Did everyone agree with the division of forces once we reach the Wonk desert and with the rendezvous at the fork of the Black River."

"Yes, Hanser Schultzmann and Brask Scaller will lead their forces, of Dragoncove and Harmosk, across to the Black River and follow it north. Prince Ashkin and Keltook will lead the forces of Vorka, Berkin, Darvin, Dargen and Morbin along the edge of the foothills and you will head the forces of Talmorg, Efra and Elkinshire. The Wonks have divided themselves to balance the size of the three commands of the combined army. All have conceded that we will be able to get much more of our provisions from the land this way and messenger relay points have been established."

"There is one more thing ya might want ta know about, dear cousin." Freebic said walking up to where they were standing, "We've had fifty-seven more Jinn appear out of nowhere and volunteer to fight at our side."

Talmorg looked across the table at Freebic's smile, "Handle it, they are not a trusted people by most, but they are fighting for their homeland. Have them joined to the central body; it is safest for all concerned to keep them with the Elven armies."

"That makes it simple than, they will ride with me." Freebic's eyes sparkled with the thrill of adventure. Freebic had wanted to head the scout party that would ride ahead of the central force, but conceded to taking his responsible position at the head of his father's armies. Azeel was chosen for the scouting party, since Saphrine insisted on leading the troops of Efra in her father's stead.

"Borak," Talmorg turned to his acting messenger, one of his personal guards, "Inform the conference heads, to finish up as quickly as possible, we move at sunrise. There is nothing more to accomplish tonight, except rest."

"Yes, My Lord." Borak turned and started making his rounds to the other counsel tables.

"Our work is done for the day, let's get some sleep." Talmorg said to those at the table and they headed back out.

CHAPTER 16

Found Friendships

Five nights had gone by since they had left the shelter of Dragoncove. Eric had been the first one up, every afternoon. He had decided to experiment with his magic during the first night and spent the first hour or so, when he got up each day, playing with it. The first day when he got up, he did not know exactly where to start and Charlie insisted on staying with him, when he separated himself from the rest of the group. He had sat there doing nothing for about fifteen minutes, with Charlie quietly watching. His eyes came to rest and he thought aloud, as if conversing with himself, '*Where do I start, what am I capable of doing? So far, I can produce things with thought, but what else and what good is it against the unknown magic, how does it work and what is its source of power. I could make better and more weapons, but that could corrupt the balance of the world. Why do I keep carrying all this volcanic ash around, how will this all come together?*'

Another thought came into his mind, not his own, '*Wake up, your power is direct from the source.*'

Eric responded, still staring at Charlie, though not really seeing him, '*The barrier?*'

'*Yes.*' again a thought as if from someone else entered his mind.

'*I'm talking to myself.*' Eric shook his head trying to clear it.

'*No.*' at the same time the thought entered his head, Charlie got his attention, "Gerp gerp."

"Is it you?" Eric looked at Charlie unable to believe he could communicate with the little creature.

"Gerp." Charlie tugged at Eric's hand.

'*Was or am I talking to you?*' Eric thought as he lifted Charlie into his lap.

'*Yes.*' Charlie nodded his head at the same time, '*I have been waiting for this. I don't know why you have not heard me before; except I think you had to open up the line of communication first.*'

'*Can you answer any of my questions?*'

'*Your thoughts are power. Your mind can tap into the barriers between our dimensions, maybe more. Shiheel didn't know exactly what he was doing, he doesn't really know who you are and bungled across the power of your mind and used it for a focal point to work from when he set up the portal. Though he doesn't know or understand the power you have I told him it was in your mind, he assumed it was what you knew.*'

'*Well, what can I do with it?*' Eric asked not feeling any of his questions had actually been answered yet.

'*A lot.*' Charlie stated simply.

'*How can I learn to use it?*' Eric tried a different angle.

'*Experiment,*' Charlie hopped down, '*It's time to get back to camp.*'

That had been the first day and since then he and Charlie had gone off every day and had practice sessions. Most of Charlie's answers seemed to be indirect or even cryptic, but Eric did find some understanding. It was the third day when Charlie asked him where everyone was, that he found he could reach out with his new power and see and feel things outside himself. It was then too that he learned that Hans Spardic, his friend, Jaffro Jamis, worked out every day when he got up and then again before going to bed, but out of sight of camp. It was the fourth day Eric found he could communicate with the moor cat too, though they had to rely more on visual images.

Now they were camped by the Arbron. Everything had been re-packed and readied for the escort to return to Dragoncove and the rest of them to head north, all after a good day's sleep. Dinner had been prepared by their escort for the last time, a duty that they would have to share in from now on. They had gotten used to eating around the campfire, occupying their time with small talk, about their backgrounds. Lady Moor never ate with them, but always sat around the fire and listened, taking in their tales. Since he had conversed with her, Eric picked up on little comments and images that Lady Moor thought during their tale telling.

"We were all awakened by the sounds of the sand shifting." Garth Kor continued his Wonk tale, of the desert drum sands west of Tarf. "Peering out across the moonlit sands with swords drawn, seeing nothing, when suddenly the ground thrust upward in a burst. No more than twenty feet away the massive creature rose up like sudden death in the night. Even the light of the moon passed partway through its skin, giving it a ghostly appearance. We all knew this would be our final battle to glory, as the beast rose forty feet straight up. Then to our surprise, it arched away from us and plunged down again into the sand, as a fish might jump in the water, leaving us standing there like fools chasing our own shadows, as the night returned to its still silence." Garth looked into the fire, his face becoming distant, but alive with the flames of memory and a mild smile. "Death was joking with us!"

There were a few moments of silence as everyone stared at the flames. Then in a mesmerized tone, Brent Kelch spoke, "I never used to believe the tales of the drum sand worms until Hesheil told me he was studying their ways of life." All eyes were now on Brent.

"What kine ah things does he say?" Kedd asked, suspicion etching his eyes and doubt echoing in his voice.

"He said they are a little more than giant earthworms, overall and of their own equivalent intelligence, but they never leave the drum sands."

'*He doesn't understand them.*' Charlie shifted against Eric's leg, '*Shiheel could have told you more, he's the scientist.*'

"I'm git'en some sleep." Kole Boort got up and walked over to his bed roll, "The sun is comin up."

Lady Moor yawned and stretched, while Hans scratched her shoulder, "I agree, evening will come, before you know it and we'll be on foot from now on."

They all murmured in agreement and turned in.

It was early afternoon, when Eric woke up, fully rested. As it was, a habit in the forming, he separated himself from the encampment unnoticed by the sentry on watch. Charlie was right there when he sat down in a nearby clearing. *'Good morning, Charlie.'*

'Good morning, Eric.', "Gerp." The gerpin sat next to him, looking up at his face, *'What will you try today.'*

'Oh, I don't know, any suggestions.'

'It's more fun watching you bungle along.' Charlie snickered.

'Thanks, a heap, now I feel like your personal circus freak show.'

'A what?'

'Never mind,' Eric looked around him and spotted a small green crystal on a rock, reached over and picked it up, brushing off the dirt and lichen. He carefully separated the green crystal from the rest of the rock, as best he could with his hands, *'Looks like an emerald chip, it would be a treasure if it were any bigger than a chip of dust.'*

'Make them grow.', "Gerp gerp." Charlie did what Eric interpreted as another laugh.

'Very well. If you think I can do it, I'll give it a shot.' The more Eric used his new power, the more he felt it was a part and an extension of himself, though sometimes he wondered if he was not just an extension of it. Now he reached his thoughts into the depths, feeling the flow of energy from within himself, passing to the small crystal he had placed in front of him. Eric could feel the energy now, almost see it within himself and as he moved it. He pictured the crystal in his mind growing as though it had taken on life, then he stopped and opened his eyes. In front of him, to his amazement, sat a perfect crystal, half the size of a man.

'Surprise, surprise.' Charlie broke into his amazement, *'You can*

make useless rocks grow.'

'*Not useless,*' Eric answered, '*with crystals like this you could build a laser, that could cut this planet in half.'* He got up and grabbed the crystal, '*Watch.*' Turning the massive green gem, so it caught the sun just right and a stream of light came out scorching the ground.

'*Yeah, cutting the world in half would be useful'* Charlie did what Eric learned to understand as laughing again.

'*Hans is getting up now, I can feel his movement. Stralina is awake, too.*'

'*You're doing well, I can tell you, now, no one knows your abilities, or their limits. I don't even know if there are limits.*'

'*That's wonderful, I could spend a life learning and never knowing, what I could or couldn't do.*' Eric shrugged, '*You seem to know a lot about what I can do, why don't you teach me.*'

'*I don't know what you can do until you do it, though I doubt you could surprise me. I also have to let you learn on your own, we all live under rules, even ancients and their heirs.*'

Stralina heard Hans get up and watched him disappear into the woods. She had noticed a few days earlier, that Eric and Hans were always up before the rest and spent time away from the encampment, until after everyone else was up. Her curiosity could not be ebbed this time, so she quickly dressed under her covers and followed after the direction she had seen Hans go. She had not gone far, when she saw him in a small field through the underbrush. Stopping she watched as Hans worked out, going through a ritual of motion, to keep his body in shape and rehearse the movements of battle. Stralina was entranced by the grace and flow of his movements and lost track of time herself, until he was finished. She watched as he sat down and decided to accidentally walked up on him. getting up she casually stepped out into the field.

"Oh, excuse me, Hans. I didn't know you were here. What brings you out so early."

Hans looked up and smiled, "You've been watching me for half an hour, I think you know what I have been doing. I don't mind, a beautiful woman like you, can watch anytime you like."

Stralina blushed, "How did you know?"

"I heard you, part of a good defense, is knowing what is coming, hearing can be a vital part of that." Hans answered from where he was seated on the ground.

"That's amazing, I thought I was pretty quiet and I was still quite a distance away" Stralina said, a little nervously glancing back at where she had been hidden.

"A lot of it is trained instincts, and I wouldn't be the best, if I didn't stay sharp." He gave a lighthearted chuckle as he got to his feet.

"I have to admit, your motion is like a master piece of art. I have noticed that before." She said, taking a couple more steps in his direction.

"What brought you out here, anyway?" Hans asked, trying to read what she wasn't saying, from her expressions and movement.

"Curiosity, I have to admit." She glanced around the field again, "I wanted to know what you and Eric did before everyone else got up, but I guess you both do different things." Her eyes returned to meet his.

"I don't know what he does either, but he isn't really a fighter, though he can hold his own. He is a game master, so there is no telling what he might be doing. It is not my concern though, if he wants to tell me something he will." Hans glanced off in the distance, he was curious about Eric, himself.

"Well, I will find out, but for now I am with you. I have never met a human whose skin held such a dark tan. I think it is very nice. Are there many like you?" Stralina asked as she worked her way closer to him.

Hans laughed, "Oh yes, a large number on Earth. We are called African's, Negros, blacks and by a few other names, not all respectable. I am glad you like my skin, but I should hope your likes don't stop there."

While Hans spoke, Stralina brushed her sleeve, secretly releasing the pollen from one of her special flowers, so he would breathe it in. "How long have you been a warrior?"

"As Hans Spardic, I have trained since I was a child and I am a master of weapons. That is a lovely scent you are wearing." he said giving her a dreamy smile as he felt his passions being stimulated on a different level.

"Oh, thank you." She smiled and moved in, close to him, looking into the depths of his eyes. Hans was a little surprised, as he felt his urges rising up within himself and found his eyes admiring her well-endowed body, wrapped in its scant Jinn clothing. Overcome by the intoxicating sensations, he found himself in an embrace with Stralina, kissing her and rolling in the grass. Stralina giggled softly, relishing the moment, taking pleasure in the animal drives, she had brought to the surface. Hans felt wonderful in her arms and his embrace was both strong and gentle. They dropped their clothes randomly, as they rolled through the grass. Hans touched her body with great skill, bringing Stralina to uncontrollable desire and they came together as one, thrusting in frenzied need to quench their fiery desires, passion burning in every breath. It was an experience of physical pleasure, beyond any Hans had experienced before. They came together in unrestrained lustful desire, then with an explosion of sensations, they reached a dance of passion that was almost unbreakable, suspending time between them. Feeling the waves of artificially created passion, several more times, they collapsed, completely relaxed, side by side on the ground, rolling apart and stared up at the sky.

After a long pause of silence, Hans asked, "What brought that on?"

Stralina answered, as she turned her head to look at him, "I felt like it." Jinn had a bad reputation, in part because they have no bounds to sharing themselves compared to most cultures.

Hans pulled his eyes from the late afternoon sky to look at hers, "And you always do that, when you feel like it?"

"Well, normally, are you angry?" genuine concern, was evident in her eyes.

"No. It was wonderful. I'm just a little bewildered." He said looking back at the sky and then sitting up.

"You're good." Stralina giggled openly.

"You're not half bad yourself." He smiled at the giggling Jinn.

"We better get dressed and head back to camp." Stralina said standing up and stretching in front of him and turning to gather her cloths.

Hans looked at her body, as she deliberately showed him its entirety. It was a body he had only dreamed of ever seeing and he stared at her, without restraint. He was still feeling some of the after effects, but he could tell she was enjoying the lust he watched her with. She was intentionally showing him, everything his eyes desired to fill themselves with, even as she dressed and brought him his clothes and belongings.

"Come get up and dress, we don't want everyone to come looking for us." She smiled with a look that could have lured him into doing almost anything. Stralina gave him a kiss as she handed him his clothes and as he dressed. Hans felt like a child who emptied the candy dish, while his parents were sleeping.

Brent Kelch was the first one of them with cooking duty and he was busy working around the campfire, when Eric walked back into their midst.

"Eric, have a cup of tea." Brent said gesturing towards a pot and cups.

"Thanks, Brent. I see everyone is up." Eric looked around, everyone had camp almost completely broken down. He took the cup Brent offered.

"Yes, Hans hasn't gotten back yet. Stralina is also off somewhere today." Brent stated, stirring a pot full of food.

Eric took whiff and he started rolling his bedding and picking up his belongings. "She is with Hans, this afternoon, they'll be back shortly."

"Guess ya gotta git up early, ta know where everyone is." Kedd said as he walked up with a leather bucket of water, for washing.

"Ah'l roll their beddin, save time." Kole said, having his own belongings ready to go.

Brent stirred the contents of one pan and then another, "Breakfast will be ready in about five minutes." Hans and Stralina, walked up as Brent spoke.

"Have a rejuvenating afternoon, Hans?" Eric asked, winking at Stralina, who blushed, "Getting up early, has its advantages."

Hans looked at Eric, "Ah, yes, as a matter of fact, it is always nice to be awake, before breakfast." He played it off and gave Eric a plea for silence, with his eyes.

Kargin, the captain of the escort, walked up to Eric, "Sir our detail is ready to leave, have you any further requests?"

"No, but thank you, Captain Kargin, for your help and have a safe return." Eric shook the Elf"'s hand, and they all watched the detail depart.

"Well, looks like we're on our own now, no more babysitters." Garth Kor said, in a matter-of-fact tone, "It was a considerate gesture on Talmorg's part to send them."

"We gotta take time ta forage, each day, now. Supplies we carry are small." Kole threw in.

Eric pulled out a map, "How much farther north have you been, Kedd?" He asked spreading the map out on the ground.

"Oh, a couple a day' I guess, pass that fork there." He said, pointing to the map.

"Very well, you and Kole will take turns scouting ahead. You with Garth and Kole with Brent. We'll see how that goes for a few days." Eric looked at the dusky sky. "We'll start sending a scout team, once we cross the fork. In the meantime, we'll head out when everyone is done eating." He finished, picking up the map and returning it to his back pack.

Conversation ebbed, as they started out following the river bank north. Kedd and Garth took the lead positions, traveling two abreast, with Kesker and Kole directly behind them. Stralina, took a position beside Hans, Eric and Brent traveled last and Lady Moor traveled as she pleased. Charlie zipped in and out, filling any space he found in their backpacks with various fruits and vegetation as they traveled.

Stralina now gave thought to Hans' comment, about Eric being the game master, she wondered what it meant. She knew it was more than a presiding tournament lord, but she also wondered what Hans meant when he kept referring to games with everything. These two men were both a curiosity to her, either one could bring great treasure and wealth, by their own means, a dragon's treasure in riches, but neither placed much value in that.

"What are these games, you keep referring to, Hans?" she finally asked.

"The games of magic, swords and adventure, that we play on Earth." He paused, "I'm at a loss to explain it any better, but what is real here would be considered fantasy there." He looked over at her and saw a puzzled expression and knew he had not really answered her question. Perhaps he made it even more confusing than it already was for her. It was all he could do not to laugh.

"Esberkian magic is the most powerful of what I have learned." Brent was saying to Eric, "I have never seen any other that can compare. It has more precise control than others."

"How does it work?" Eric asked, listening and watching the night, while conversing with Brent.

"A lot of it is mental focus, like any other magic, but Hesheil gave me a sphere to tap into the source of Esberkian magic, instead of the less stable energies of our other magics." Brent said, stroking his own ego, with his knowledge of magic.

"So, it is similar to other magics, only with a different power base." Eric observed.

"That could be one way of putting it, I guess." Brent smirked, uncertain he like the simplification.

"Why do you maintain such, an air of mystery, even though it draws distrust."

"It allows me to use the mental focus of others, when I need it for help. If I didn't believe you to be the master wizard, I would not so freely share with you. Besides, look at the mystery you carry with your magic. I would not mind studying with you also.”

“I don’t know if I could teach it.” Glancing ahead, Eric said, “We better catch up with the rest, something is ahead, can you feel it?”

“I haven’t learned that yet.” they had to jog to catch up.

Kedd interrupted what Garth was telling him, “Look at the brush o’er there, some ah the leafs are turned on a side.”

“You are correct. It is large, whatever it is, let’s see if there are tracks. It could have been Lady Moor.” They both stopped and scanned the ground.

“These are definitely not from a cat.” Kedd said kneeling, scraping some clear slime off of a twig, “Slugs trail like this.”

“I don’t know what it is either.” observing other trail marks.

The rest of the party caught up with the scouts, “What is it, Kedd?”

“Do’en know, Eric.”

Stralina stepped up and knelt next to Kedd. Eric watched her and saw her pale a shade. “What is it?”

As she and Kedd stood up, Stralina answered, looking into Eric’s eyes, with a very serious tone in her voice, “Looks like the trail of a Dark Moor Lizard.”

Kesker was visibly shaken, it was unnerving to the rest to see the massive stone giant shaken by her words, “We cannot let it see us, one of them killed my brother, like a fly.”

Eric took his words with great gravity, Kesker almost never spoke and was always like a stone pillar of strength. After a moment’s thought,

Eric said, "We'll use our rings, but first run a rope back in file, so we don't get separated."

They resumed their order, each holding a loop in the rope that joined them together, then one at a time they turned their rings, Kedd first and Eric last. As he turned his ring, Eric noted a strange wavering sensation, that stayed with him. He had felt it before, but it took a few minutes to place where it has been. Then he realized it was during the transalteration, that brought him to Ethar, to begin with. Curious he thought. He brushed aside the ideas formulating in his mind for now, as they moved forward in total silence. Progress was slowed greatly by their having to coordinate their movement. They had only gone about forty yards, when they heard a commotion to their left. They stopped and Eric turned, just in time, to see a leaping Eliko snagged out of the air, by the forked tongue of a giant lizard. The lizard swallowed the animal in the same motion. The giant lizard stopped and fanned the ground with the tip of its tongue, right where they had been less than five minutes earlier. It was smelling their trail and turned in their direction.

Eric focused on the beast and pictured it shrinking in his mind, directing the energy from within. The lizard was suddenly encompassed, in a multicolored sparkling cloud and began shrinking. Eric continued until the lizard was harmlessly no bigger than the smaller ones he had seen before on Earth, then stopped. When he was done, he turned the ring on his finger and became visible again. The wavering sensation left. "I think he is harmless now." The rest of the party reappeared next to him.

"The magic of the ancient masters!" Brent was stunned.

"Good job!" Hans said.

"Shall we continue, while we still have the light of both moons." Eric smiled. He saw however, that they were all dazed, so he called a halt as they rounded a bend in the river.

"Let's sit down and rest. Hans would you start a fire and make some tea. We'll take a break and give everyone a chance to recover."

"How did you do that, you did it didn't you?" Stralina asked.

"Yes, I did it." He paused, "I can't explain how yet, but it has to do with directing energy or power from its source."

"Glad it worked, don't wan'na see more," Kedd said, "less'n I gotta."

Hans had water boiling in no time, he had used his magic fire ball spell, to start the fire, but nobody noticed. He preferred it that way. By the time the tea was ready, they had all started to relax and come to themselves.

Kedd sipped his tea and turned to Eric, "The river fork's jus' up there, kin almost see from here."

"Could cross a'fer mornin ya know." Kole added, "a rope bridge, a hundred foot from the mouth."

"When everybody is rested, we'll cross." Eric stood up, "What kind of snacks has Charlie provided?" He reached into his own backpack and pulled out a round red fruit, that was about the size of his fist. He took a bite and to his surprise, it tasted like a giant blueberry. '*Mighty good,*

Charlie.'

'Thanks.'

'Do you think their ready to move on?'

'Yes, it would be a wise choice,' Charlie looked east, *'we have a storm coming in.'*

Eric followed Charlie's look to the east, he could feel it too, now that he thought about it. "Alright, let's get across that bridge."

They all got up and started along the riverbank again, only in better spirits this time. After about a half mile of walking, they rounded a small bend and came to the mouth of the river fork. Within sight there was a rope bridge crossing the west fork of the Arbron. Charlie jumped up on Eric's hip pack, when they reached it and they crossed in single file. Lady Moor leaped across below them and met them on the other side, with a mouth full of fish, that she dropped in the sand at their feet. Eric thanked her and dropped his shoulder pack to the ground.

"Set up the tarps, it is going to rain today. Secure them well it might be quite a storm." They looked at him with strange expressions, but did as he instructed them. "I'll get these fish ready and fix dinner."

First, he cleaned the fish at the water's edge and hung them on a branch, keeping them out of the sand. Then gathering drift wood, washed up from the river, he started a fire on the beach. He took their largest pot and turned another pan upside down inside it to get a dutch oven effect, so he could bake the fish. He laid the fish on top of the inverted pan, poured about a half a cup of water in the bottom of the pot, to keep the fish from drying and hung the pot from a tripod over the fire. Next Eric filled a smaller pot halfway with water, dropping into it roots and tubers, Charlie had gathered and dropped in their packs. Eric set the second pot on the fire, then watched as Charlie added various leaves and seeds to both pots.

'*Got to keep everyone healthy.*' Charlie's thoughts answered the question in Eric's mind.

'*Vitamins and minerals?*' Eric's thoughts questioned.

'*Seasonings too for flavor and a few medicinal herbs.*' "Gerp." Charlie answered and then continued, '*I'll teach you of our flora sometime.* '

'*That could be quite useful.*'

'*By the way, nice shrink job you did on that lizard. Amazing what you can do when you put your mind to it.*' Eric could almost hear the laugh in Charlie's thought.

'*Thanks, but I could have just shot it and not taken an unknown risk.*' Eric thought shaking his head.

'*Shooting it could have been risky too, but what you did was better than killing it. All it was doing was fighting for survival, the only way its simple mind knew how.*'

'*I guess you are right, now it can live on insects, which are plentiful here by the water.*'

"May I taste?" Stralina asked walking up.

"Certainly." Eric smiled to her.

She took a small stick and stabbed a root, about bite size and tasted it, "Delicious, maybe you should cook all the time." She winked at Eric.

"Charlie seasoned it." Eric responded a bit defensively.

"Oh really?" She looked at the gerpin, "You can season my food anytime." She said, petting him between the ears.

'Sexy creature, isn't she?' Charlie snickered in Eric's mind.

'Charlie, please.'

"That was an amazing display of power earlier. It definitely surprised me." she paused, then asked, "How do you know it is going to storm, the sky is clear and calm?"

"Charlie told me, then Lady Moor confirmed it, when she dropped off the fish." Eric glanced up at her from stirring the pot of food.

"Oh, I didn't know you could understand them." Stralina looked puzzled.

"Sure, Charlie thinks your sexy." This time Eric threw a mental snicker at Charlie.

"Now you're teasing me." Stralina said, brushing her body against his, as she squatted down next to him.

"Careful now you're the only woman with seven men here. If you start something you may have to take care of all of them." Eric tried cautioning her.

"Sounds like fun, but unfortunately it doesn't fit well with all their customs and cultures." She gave Eric a saddened smile.

"And it does fit with your customs and culture or that of the Jinn?" he said with slight surprise.

"Of course, a Jinn lives to serve, please and build treasure, sex is one way of giving pleasure and service, sometimes even building treasure." She batted her eyes at him with a playful smile as she stood up.

"What of things like love and marriage?"

"Our ways are different." she said in a faraway voice.

"Probably why your people aren't trusted."

"What's cooking, chief?" Hans asked, walking up as everyone started gathering and the morning sky started brightening.

"It should be done." Eric announced and everyone dished up and sat around the fire.

"Time fer tales." Kedd said taking a seat in the sand, "Kesker, tell us 'ow ya got yer scars."

"Which ones?" Kesker asked with a vicious smile and then laughed his ground shaking rumble. Then he stopped laughing and began his tale, "It happened when me and my brother went out on our journey of manhood. It is a part of our custom, taking a one-year journey within five years of manhood. We decided to go to the great northern glacier...." Kesker rambled on, but Eric was distracted, there were two strangers approaching from the woods. They stopped out of sight and were watching. Charlie's ears perked up and Lady Moor was sniffing the air. Eric sensed the strangers were not hostile, but rather very much afraid. The rest of the party was entranced in Kesker's story and Eric slipped almost unnoticed from the fire. Hans noticed, but was good about not intruding, maybe he would leave well enough alone and stay with the others.

As Eric walked into the tarp, he turned his ring, now invisible he slipped the rest of the way up the sand to the forest edge. Quietly he moved around behind the intruders, close enough that he could see them. They were both about four feet tall and from what he could see, they had very wide short heads, with eight inch pointed ears. They had powerful stocky builds, with long hands, both carried swords and short bows. they were just standing there watching camp. Finally, the one spoke to the other, "If we can't find company in a mixed group like that, Jahar, how would we ever find refuge in the south lands?"

"Calhan, that bunch could be bandits, rovers and thieves. I mean look, they have a Jinn in their company. Besides why would they be so far from any community, unless they were fugitives or bandits?"

"I don't know, but we cannot go back, I'll go mad if we don't find more company and reason of some kind to go on, a hope of escaping from those evil scaldo's"

They both turned back to watching the camp, as if trying to build their courage. Eric moved around in front of them to see their faces, but was not prepared for what he saw. They had extremely large eyes, that slanted up from a knobby nose and large mouths, that somehow managed to look cute. He was about five feet away from them, just out of their swords reach.

"Be at peace." Eric said in as comforting a tone as possible and watched fear fill their eyes, "Do not be afraid." Terror ripped at their faces as he continued, "I am going to appear in front of you."

"We're dead." the one named Jahar said.

"No, you're not." Eric almost laughed, turning his ring and appearing in front of them. "Come forward, my name is Eric and I am the leader of the expedition you are spying on." The two strangers just stood there in terror. "Look if I wanted to kill you, I would not have let you see me." That appealed somehow to their logic, it worked and Eric could see them visibly relax a little, though they did not drop their guard completely. "Now, Jahar and Calhan, come forward and partake of our meal."

They came forward, still a little shaken and followed Eric back toward the fire. The rest of the small company turned and watched their approach. Eric heard his fugitives whispering behind him and noted the looks of distrust coming from his circle of companions. Eric was about to speak, when Kesker suddenly came to his feet, "Jahar,,,Calhan, look at you. I thought I would never see you again."

"Kesker?" both spoke with doubt in their voices.

"I was just telling these good people about my journey to the glacier. You look like you've been through hell, sit down and eat something." Kesker turned back to the fire, "These two and their family, gave me and my brother hospitality, while I recovered from my fight with the ice beast."

CHAPTER 17

A Little Rain

Dragoncove was awakening, stirring well before sunrise. By the time the suns first rays had broken the horizon, a force of ninety-four thousand, was in motion, with a medical support team of eighteen thousand following. Talmorg was leading the largest force ever assembled in the south lands, riding with his family banner waving high in the hands of his banner bearer. The march had begun and the awesome war machine was in motion. The Elkinshane banner, a sword pointing down, with a wreath of healing herbs coming out of its hilt, had been passed down from the very first ruling family of the Elves, to which Talmorg was heir. They were a proud family, who had always stood for the protection of all people and their lands, a heart for peace and healing. The great army now marching under that banner, moved in six columns, headed from left to right by Hanser Schultzmann, Brask Scaller, Saphrine Barhallah, Erron Elkinshane, Prince Ashkin and Derkle Darset of Darvin, followed by their own banner bearers. The formation would split in three when it reached the wonk desert, in four days and each pair of columns would close ranks at that time to four abreast.

The day went without incident, the military forces held perfect formation and the medical support, followed in three groups. The first group was attached to and would follow the left flank when they split. The second group was led by Bonny, Elisha and Darset, they would follow the middle two columns and the third group would be attached to the right flanks.

Evening came and they broke into camps to eat and sleep. They carried three months' supply of regular rations and a two-month supply of iron rations. Talmorg was not going to risk strength and morale to a lack of supplies. Progress was slow, but scheduled, to preserve their strength for their final destination, yet not allow the troops to get soft. The Elven troops and the men were all on horseback, while the giants and Dwarves chose to stay on foot. The Wonks and Nobs, traveled according to the group to which they were attached and though the Eftites were attached to the Elves, being from the city of Talmorg, they remained on foot. For every hundred there were two wagons, a weapons wagon and another for other supplies, including; food, armor repair equipment, minor medical supplies, rope and a mixture of other supplies according to the skills of each group.

Time passed steadily and everyone moved with somber purpose, all knowing there had not been a war of this scale fought, since before any of their lives had begun. There was such a variety of feelings going through each of their minds, by the time they reached the Wonk deserts, that the division of the forces was serving another purpose, to ease the building tension between the races. Talmorg found a lifting of pressure in his own mind, once the division was complete. All the planning and preparation had been finished and over rehearsed. The remainder of their march he would be able to direct his attention primarily in the area of morale and mixing with the troops. He would start at the rear, with the medical support group and Saphrine had chosen to assist him.

*   *   *   *   *   *   *   *

It was early morning when Elisha woke Bonny up, today they would march. They met Darset for a quick breakfast, followed by a brief meeting with the other medical support group leaders. Each support group consisted of about six thousand and was broken into three charges of about two thousand. Elisha, Bonny and Darset each had a charge, consisting of five hundred medically trained personnel in each charge. The balance were carriers, food servers, supply staff and a variety of other needed support. Bonny was impressed by the medieval preparations. She couldn't help thinking as she saw various details, she had never read about this in any books. As Bonny, Elisha and Darset were making preparations. Darset spoke, "Glad the meetings are over, but I sure hope you have tough butts. Horseback is worse, but these wagons are none too comfortable."

Elisha shook her head, "I see you are going to be the fun of the ride; you've got us laughing and looking forward to it already."

"Elisha, how do you live so long and keep the child alive inside?" Darset asked.

"That is how I live so long." she answered with a giggle.

"Does that work for men too?" Bonny asked as their cart started moving forward, leading their section of the medical caravan, "Eric is never going to grow out of his child hood." and they all laughed.

Just then Freebic road up alongside them, "I know where I'm

riding, where I can feast my eyes."

"You're not going to be riding here!" Darset said, giving him a mock scowl.

"Oh, but it was you who caught my eye and stole my heart." He mocked a look of pleading sadness back to her.

"You animal, you better get back where you're supposed to be." She tried not to show her pleasure in his flattery.

As he turned and rode off, Elisha commented, "He is the cutest,"

"For a lizard." Darset retorted.

"Are you two always at it, or is this a new sport of banter?" Bonny smiled, they both looked at her and raised their eyebrows, "Besides, it was me he looked at." She baited with a laugh.

"You're spoken for." Darset stated.

"I can still steal hearts." Bonny winked.

"You wouldn't?" Elisha acted taken aback.

"Who knows?" Bonny primped.

"Children, you all act like children." Darset shook her head and waved her finger, as if to scold them, "Men don't want children you know, they want mothers. They only want to play with children."

Elisha put on her most innocent face, "I like to play, mom. Can I play?" and they all broke out in laughter again.

After the first day's ride, Bonny was the only one, who was not stiff and sore. Elisha had been prepared for it though and had already prescribe a muscle relaxing herb tea, for everyone who was not used to riding and it helped. It was not until the third day, that they concluded, Bonny's healing magic was protecting her from the stiffness common to everyone else.

The day after the split of forces, Talmorg and Saphrine rode back into their group for breakfast.

"Good morning ladies, is everyone surviving the ride?" Talmorg greeted them.

"I died, three days ago." Darset complained.

"Now see, that's one less person to worry about." Bonny smiled at Darset, "We'll be alright, your highness." she added directing her attention to Talmorg, "Thank you for the courtesy of a visit, it should be uplifting to the general morale."

"We are planning on spending a day with each group," Saphrine stated, "And probably start over again when we finish."

"That's wonderful, I'll send a message to our cooks." Elisha started.

"No. We will eat whatever everyone is normally eating. We ride together, I need to be aware of the effects of our journey on everyone, to include their diet." Talmorg stated as he and Saphrine dismounted, "Tonight we should have fresh meat though. I let Freebic go ahead with a hunting party, to appease his zeal for reckless adventure."

"It was either that, or put up with his ceaseless pleading and generally growing irritability." Saphrine added shaking her head in disapproval of Freebic's behavior, "He'll be in his glory on the battle field.”

“Let's not be hard lined about this, he is the best we have ever seen in battle.” Talmorg stated, “Even if he does put adventure in priority over responsibility. He would just as soon somebody else were to rule in his stead.” He shook his head with thoughtful disapproval, “Enough of that though, I'm hungry and we should eat before we start marching again. My father will have us moving on schedule.”

“Well sire, this way to the breakfast line.” Darset said, turned and started toward the food supply wagon.

“The cooks have been setting up and preparing our food from the back of the wagon.” Elisha added.

Saphrine turned to Bonny as they walked, “Have we had anyone fall back from the ranks, for your aid yet.”

“Not yet, not even a scratch.” Bonny smiled, her normal pleasant smile.

“After this is all over, are you and Eric going to be at our wedding. I mean, me and Talmorg. You are invited.” Saphrine looked at Bonny as if measuring her response.

“I hope so, but Eric will have to determine that, probably according to when it is. I don't know how the transalteration works.” She paused a moment, then added, “It would be a pleasure and an honor, though. I thank you. Will that also join your kingdoms together?”

“Yes, it will, that is a part of the reason. Our fathers have requested it. We have also accepted because it will be best for our people.” Saphrine lifted her head with a little pride, "Freebic will probably freely concede his thrown to us also. Talmorg wants to unite all of the south lands. We believe the time has come and he will succeed."

"I'm sure he will. I know Eric wants him to." This time Bonny was watching Saphrine's reaction and thought she saw her breath deepen, with a subtle flinch in her expression, when she mentioned Eric's name. "I think he will probably help. Eric has always been quite the man. He also likes to play the part of a hero."

This time Saphrine got a distant look in her eyes, which told Bonny what she was looking for, "Yes he is." Saphrine said unconsciously caressing herself with one arm, unaware of her reaction, "You are fortunate."

"He likes you, too." she placed her hand on Saphrine's wrist, bringing her attention back and returning her posture to a more regal manner. "He and I have become too much a part of each other to separate now. You two I am sure will know that bond, you have taken on the responsibility of a kingdom and you and Talmorg do make a lovely couple."

Saphrine now had a look of shocked amazement, at Bonny's candor and was at a loss for words.

"Don't misunderstand me, we love each other, just like you and Talmorg will love each other. He is a good 'man', too."

A silent bond formed between them, as they talked, one they both knew would last. They chatted through breakfast and wound up spending the whole day together, until everyone went to bed.

 Sometime in the night it had started raining. At first it came in gentle waves that were comforting and soothing. Then the main storm hit, with a flaming burst of light and roaring explosion, as if the heart of the planet had been ripped out and all forces of hell let loose. Bonny like the rest of the encampment, was jolted awake in a panic. The lightning struck camp, somewhere the winds ripped through the air, beating the rain against the tent in every direction. Elisha and Darset were standing next to her now and the continuous roaring of the thunder, made it hard to think.

"It's the thunder of the mother." Darset said, "The mountains are the Great Mother and this is her anger."

Bonny saw a flickering of flames outside in the wind, then there was a great gush of water and they were gone. "We better see if anyone is hurt." she said, heading for the door.

"No! This storm will take you away!" Elisha protested, but it was too late, Bonny stepped out.

 As she stepped out, Bonny was hit by an onslaught of rain that burned her face. Instinctively she raised her arm to protect her face, as she did, a strange blue light encompassed her about and shielded her from the storm. It was just like the one that had formed, when she had reached protectively for the child in Dragoncove. Nothing of the storm touched her, as she stood there looking out over the devastating effects of the storm.

The flood waters were forming quickly, carving at the ground, like a hot knife in butter. There were tents down and wagons overturned. The horses were bucking and wrenching at their fetters. She decided to head that way first, walking past a wagon that had been blasted to splinters and burned by the lightening. As she neared the horses, she reached out protectively, wanting to calm the horses and her blue dome of light extended itself, to include the horses in her private calm against the storm. The horses stunned by the sudden calm, became deathly still and their recent panic was still reflected in their eyes.

Bonny looked at the horses and suddenly felt foolish. She had not brought anything with her to sedate them and here she was, sheltering horses, when people's lives were at stake. She looked about, wondering what to do, if she abandoned the horses they would frenzy again and probably break loose. Then her thoughts progressed, maybe she could protect them and go about other business, she did not know her ability, maybe she could shelter the whole encampment. Immediately she started waving her arms protectively over larger and larger portions of the encampment, watching the blue light dome expand.

Talmorg ran up to her, "How long can you keep that up?"

"I don't know, I didn't even know I could do that." She stated, diverting as little thought as she possibly could to his question, but noted that it had not affected the shield, at least not this time.

"I will send a messenger back to you." Talmorg spoke quickly, "If you feel you are losing control of what you are doing, send him in warning."

"Okay." She could tell there was a lot of activity going on around her, but refused to look. Bonny held her mind tightly, she knew that she alone, separated their encampment from further destruction.

*   *   *   *   *   *   *   *

Kesker finished his story, praising Jahar and Calhan, to the small company, while they ate. Then Jahar and Calhan began telling of their escape from 'Scally' rule, when it started to rain. They moved up to the shelter of their tent and everyone decided, sleep was more important, they could talk when they got up. Kesker volunteered to stand the first watch. He wanted to catch up a little, with Jahar and Calhan, for old times' sake.

Eric crawled down into his sleeping bag. The steady drone of the rain was soothing and the distant rumble of thunder, lulled him off to sleep.

"Pigs snouts and chicken lips," Eric woke up to Kedd spouting off, "How kin he sleep in this. Are ya sure he's still alive?"

"Yep, he's movin." Kole said.

Eric pushed his head out of his bag and was instantly drenched by a blast of wind. He turned to see everyone huddled in the far side of the tarp lean to, holding the side flap down trying to stay dry. He shook his head and shut his eyes. He felt the wind stop hitting him and heard the rain hitting the outside of the walls and roof, then the crackle of a fireplace in the corner. He was sure he was just dreaming when he opened his eyes. It was just as he had pictured it, with the tarp shelter inside the dirt floored cabin and a fire burning in the corner fireplace. Charlie was the only one moving, he was hopping around, checking the place out. The rest were still huddled, holding down the flap of the tarp, with peculiar expressions on their faces. "Go back to sleep." Eric said with a chuckle and pulled his sleeping bag back over his head.

He woke up again after midday some time. The winds had died and the rain let up to a slow, but steady drizzle. Walking to a window he looked out at the rain. The waters had risen, moving the river beach up, swallowing their firepit from the night before. It was dreary and the oppressiveness of the drizzle almost overwhelmed Eric. He was ready to go back in and catch a couple extra hours of sleep, then he noticed the fierce turbulence of the river was eating away at the sand, cutting closer to their shelter.

Quickly Eric woke everyone, "Wake up! Wake up!" he shouted, "Get everything packed, we have to move quickly. Get up!"

Everyone stirred awake, startled and looking at Eric through blinking eyes, murmuring obscure, but obviously disturbed muttering.

"What's wrong?" Hans asked sitting up.

"The river has risen from the rain, a little longer and it will wash the cabin away."

Immediately everyone started moving significantly faster. Their murmuring turned to a mixture of silence and intermittent grumbling.

Three days of drizzle were wearing steadily at the team's morale and Eric could see it. He was supposed to be their leader, but his own temper was growing short, even if he had not shown it. Eric knew he would have to do something when he called them for a lunch stop. Lady

Moor and Charlie were the only two, that seemed totally unaffected by the rain. Lady Moor kept them in fresh meat and Charlie found an endless supply and variety of vegetation.

"Blasted foul weather." Kedd spat as he dropped his pack to the ground.

Brent sniffled, he was showing signs of a cold, "Walking around soaked like this will be our ruin. Those Scaldorians won't need to worry about us."

"It'll stop a'fer long." Kole said.

Garth had started a fire and set up a cooking tripod. Eric noticed Stralina was shivering when she came up to help him with the food preparation. He had given her his cloak to wear, when they left the cabin, but it was proving to be insufficient. Hans had withdrawn, into himself and become as quiet as Kesker. Jahar and Calhan, even though they had become a part of the small company by unanimous decision, were still unsure of where they stood and stayed mostly to themselves.

What should he do, he was responsible to keep this small party going? Eric knew he had to do something, or they would start fighting amongst themselves. No one had slept well, he thought, not since everything had been soaked. Eric decided they all needed a full day of good sleep and rest.

"Here you are, Stralina. Why don't you keep it stirred?" Eric said, hanging the pot of stew they had just put together, from the tripod over the fire, "I believe you could use a little of the fires warmth." She did not answer, only nodded her head and Eric turned away, looking over the area where they stopped.

Kole walked up to him and spoke quietly, "Can I have a word with ya, in private?"

"Sure." Eric said and they moved away from the rest of the group, "You seem the least affected by the weather, what is on your mind?"

"I take it ya mean wud I wanna ask ya." Kole started, giving Eric an odd look, "Well, I hunt these parts a time er so. En there's a cave not far. It's gotta hot springs in it. Little off course, but could make um a bit friendlier." Kole pointed to the group with his thumb.

"That's an excellent idea, Kole." Eric was thankful for a way to ease their discomfort, "You can lead, after we eat."

"Yep." Kole turned and started back to the rest. They all ate quickly, when they finally got their food. Then Eric told them Kole would guide their way for a little while and they headed off. They walked for less than an hour, when Kole led them to the caves entrance.

"We are going to take shelter in these caves for a day." Eric said, "Kole told me he knew they were here, and was willing to lead the way."

They all looked at the entrance, it was neatly cut with four columns forming a square in the entry way. There was a strange lettering engraved in the flat area at the top of the entry.

"That's ancient Dwarven lettering." Kedd stated, pointing at the lettering.

"Can you read it?" Eric asked.

"Some maybe." he stepped up, "It's a warnin' somethin about an endless puzzle or riddle."

"Maze maybe." Brent interjected.

"Yep, could be." Kedd said.

"If this is a trap, Kole, I'll give you an Esberkian melt down." Brent said, "Is this an entrance, to the Endless Cave of Mazes?"

Charlie thought to Eric, *'They are the caves Brent refers to, but it is safe. Kole doesn't know it his ancestors built the caves with magic and his blood line cannot get lost in them, plus you've got me and I know them. Nobs separated from the Dwarven lineage, because they used magics to tunnel and the dwarves used tools. That is part of why they evolved to a lighter physical build.'*

'Thanks, Charlie.' Eric then said, "It's okay Brent, calm down. These are the Endless Cave of Mazes, but Kole can't get lost in them and we do have Charlie."

"How kin that be?" Kole spoke up, "If so, how come Kole don't git lost?"

"He doesn't know it, but he is descended from its builders and therefore an heir to their magic. He can't get lost." Eric shrugged.

Kole looked at Eric suspiciously, "How kin you know more 'bout me than I do?"

"Nobody has found these caves for thousands of years." Brent proclaimed, then looked at Kole, "How did you know where they were?"

"I would presume that their magic, being kin to him, lured him here when he got close enough." Eric said.

"But I ain't got no magic." Kole blurted in frustration.

"Let's get out of the rain," Eric said, "If you don't trust him, trust me, if not me trust the gerpin, but let's go in."

Charlie hopped off Eric's pack and led the way in. Reluctantly the rest followed. Once inside, the caves were warm and dry and they all set down the loads they were carrying.

"There's a good ole hot tub in here." Kole said, turning and walked through a wall and disappeared.

"How'd he do that?" Kedd asked baffled, "He walked through the wall."

'The magic illusions of the caves don't affect him.', "Gerp."

"Kedd, tie an end of your rope to one of the columns outside the door. We will follow Kole, using the rope to mark our way back." Eric said.

"We're supposed to walk through the wall?" Brent asked in a ridiculing voice.

"Now, Brent, I'm surprised, with your knowledge of magic, you can't detect an illusion generated by ancient magic." Stralina laughed, then blew something from her hand at the wall. The place where Kole had walked through the wall, now glowed. "There's where Kole walked through, a magically concealed door." and she walked through the wall too.

Lady Moor grabbed the rope in her mouth, Kedd just let her have it and they all followed the cat through. From the other side the rope also looked like it went right through a wall, they could not see the door from either side. Eric turned and looked over the room, it was large, about thirty feet in diameter, with a twenty clearing to the ceiling. The majority of the room was filled by a large pool of hot water, bubbling up from the bottom through the rocks.

Both Kole and Stralina had stripped and were laid back in the pool. The light was very dim however and he could just barely make them out. The rest of the small party stripped and climbed in. The water was hot, but comfortable and they all relaxed for about an hour. The large hot tub had the desired effect, everyone relaxed and the feeling of comradeship started returning. Eric found it so relaxing, he laid back at the edge and fell asleep.

Eric was awakened by someone stroking his hair. When he opened his eyes, it was Stralina. She was dressed and leaning over him at the edge of the pool.

"The others all went to sleep a little while back. They're in the other section of the cave." She smiled at him. He had an overwhelming sensation of intoxication and somehow knew she had slipped him an aphrodisiac or something to bend his will and desires. "How are you feeling, sweety," she continued, "a little light headed, maybe. I promise it won't hurt." She said with a sensual smile, as she dropped her cloths, slipped in next to him and kissed his ear, pressing her body against his.

"Why?" Eric asked, not complaining.

"Because, I like your body and you, so I give you the service of my pleasure. Besides it will help you relieve tension that has been building on this journey."

Eric could not help but yield himself in to her mercy, as she led him and lured him into playful games of lust and pleasure. He smiled, "One of the many reasons Jinn are not trusted."

*   *   *   *   *   *   *   *

Talmorg was coordinating the salvaging of the rest of the encampment, from the medical camp. They had been at it for a couple of hours and they were almost done, but he was concerned for Bonny's sake. The day before no one had needed any medical attention, now the medical staff were up and busy in the middle of the night. The last messenger finally reported in, all was secured. There were about seven hundred injuries, fortunately almost all were minor, considering the lightning struck in the middle of camp. Talmorg wondered how the other two commands were fairing the storm, or if they were even affected by it. He looked up, the lightning had stopped above the blue dome, but he couldn't tell how much the rain had let up. How long could she keep it up he wondered. He decided he better not find out; he had no idea what it was doing to her.

"Saphrine, I'm going to tell Bonny, she can drop the shield, it looks like it's only raining now." He said turning to face her in the tent, "Can you handle everything here?"

"I'm sure, but you might want to bring a couple of rain hoods with you." she snickered, tossing a couple from the pile.

Talmorg blew her a kiss and stepped out of their temporary command tent. He is a good Elf, Saphrine thought to herself. It would be so much easier, if I already loved him, but how can I make myself do that. She sighed and sat down on a pillow. She knew she would have to find ways to enjoy her time with him, without thinking about Eric. She just needed to stop thinking of Eric so much. No, she needed to start thinking of Talmorg more, then her thoughts of Eric would diminish.

Talmorg headed straight toward Bonny, but his thoughts did not leave Saphrine. Their fathers had arranged their marriage, yet he found the more time he spent with her, the more he liked it. She was the most wonderful she Elf he had ever met. It was going to be wonderful ruling, with her at his side, all they had to do was survive this terrible war.

"Bonny you can stop." Talmorg said putting the rain hood over her, "We can handle rain, it looks like the lightening and winds have calmed down."

Relief showed in Bonny's face, as she broke off her concentration, "Thank you." She started, but then realized, the blue shield she had produced, had not vanished. The three of them, Bonny, Talmorg and the messenger, who had been assigned to her, stood there staring up for several moments, before Bonny continued, "I don't understand. I know I was forming the shield, why didn't it collapse when I stopped focusing on it?"

"Maybe it takes time for it to wear off," the messenger elf volunteered, "I have read some magic is like that."

"That is true, Bonny and you have put a lot into it too." Talmorg added. Looking at her in the dim light he could see she was tired. "Come, don't worry about it. You need some sleep; besides it will keep the rain off and it will probably be gone by morning." He smiled at her, dismissed the messenger and escorted Bonny to her tent. Talmorg then returned to the temporary command tent, where he and Saphrine turned in for the night.

When Bonny stepped into the tent Darset and Elisha were already asleep. She climbed into her own sleeping roll and lay awake several minutes. Bonny wondered about the magic she possessed, how it worked and what it was. She also wondered how Eric and Jamis were doing, wherever they were. Then she faded into a less than peaceful sleep. When Darset woke her up in the morning, she knew she had dreamed about Eric, but she could only remember bits and pieces. A giant lizard, a cabin washing into a river, eyes in a cave and wings overhead were all she could remember.

When she stepped out of the tent to go eat breakfast, Bonny noticed it was still overcast and looked up. The blue dome was still there. Would it be permanent, she wondered? Talmorg and Saphrine had already moved on to the next group. She was sorry she had missed their departure, as she sat down with Elisha to eat. Bonny stayed quiet, most of the time, she was still tired and Elisha respected her silence. It was not until they were getting in the wagon that the subject came up.

Elisha asked, "How long will that shield last?"

"I don't know." Bonny said, looking up, shaking her head and trying to conceal any real concern she had.

"Will it follow us?" Elisha asked with naive innocence.

"I don't know that either, but I don't think so. I don't know what it is or how I do it. Maybe someone can explain it to me sometime." Bonny laughed and shrugged.

Darset climbed up, "You look exhausted, Bonny. Why don't you climb in the back and lay down? I am sure we can handle anything that might come up today."

Bonny did not hesitate, she climbed over the back of the seat and laid on top of the pile of blankets. "Thank...." before she could finish her expression of appreciation, she was asleep. This time she slept well, without interruption and without dreams.

Talmorg was apprehensive as the large force set in motion, forming their columns and heading north. They had lost three wagons and suffered a large number of minor injuries. The redistribution of the wagon cargo had been easy and Darset had assured him the injuries were all minor and would heal in a few days. Talmorg was still uneasy though, morale would be lower and the continuing overcast weather would not help.

Saphrine rode up to Talmorg, "Are you still sending out messengers as scheduled?"

"It is necessary, we need to give the others reassurance and learn how they are faring." He looked ahead with an expression of deep concern. "We are going to be late for our rendezvous with their messengers." Talmorg turned to Calbork, chief of his royal guard. He was the best Elven Warrior from the Walled City of Talmorg and proved his loyalty to Talmorg many times over the past eleven years, never being far from his side. "Calbork, have Freebic organize a special hunting party to go ahead. They can also rendezvous with the messengers, from Hanser Schultzmann and Prince Ashkin."

"Yes sire." Calbork responded and turned quickly to his errand.

Talmorg watched him for a few moments, with a silent respect and appreciation, that Saphrine could see in his eyes.

"He is one you have come to count on for loyalty and dependability." Saphrine said softly.

"Yes, he is also the only one in my service, whose skill in combat exceeds that of some of the Eftites." He smiled and turned back to Saphrine, "The columns are ready. It is time to lead them out of this protective dome."

They turned their horses and took their positions in the front, Talmorg raised his arm and signaled the march. A little over a hundred yards ahead of them was the edge of the dome and they would be exposed once again to the rain that was still drizzling down. They moved forward at a modest steady pace. The question in the front of Talmorg's mind, would the shield move with them, faded with each step they took, until they were about ten feet from its perimeter. Then their sheltering protection started to move with them. A hush swept back, followed by a whispering murmur and then a wave of cheering.

Turning to Saphrine, Talmorg smiled, "Something good for

morale."

CHAPTER 18

Marching On

He had forgotten to tell them of the sand worms. With all his careful planning and strategy, if he did not make it on time now the south lands could loose a full third of their forces, because he overlooked the great worms of the drum sands

Shiheel had left the day after Eric had, from Dragoncove, taking the cubs to the safety of Hesheil's keep in Hesheilville. Then seeing to their safe keeping, for they were the future lords of the moor cats, he returned to his secret caves on Fire Islands. At the caves he prepared an electromagnetic tensor disc, so he could operate above the battle field with Hesheil, when it came time to face off the Scaldorian slime. But it was not until he was at the screaming cliffs, dispensing a summon to the creatures from every corner of the continent for the great day of battle, that he realized he had forgotten to tell Hanser Schultzmann and Brask Scaller about the sand worms. If only Merlin Starnook, the last of the ancient wizards, had not fallen to Deassheema, he would have been of great help. At last, he was gone, Shiheel and his brother Hesheil were trying to serve this world in his place.

    *   *   *   *   *   *   *   *

When they had started across the drum sands, their movement set of deafening echoes across the desert. It was not too long before it bothered everyone and set them on edge. It was already night fall so they set camp just inside the border of the drum sand desert and they all laughed about the legendary sand worms, rehearsing stories they had heard over dinner. Nobody slept well that night, though silence prevailed at breakfast and clear through the mornings march.

At about midday the horses became increasingly nervous and fidgety. Then they all heard the sound of scraping, shifting sands and the legends of quick death from the sand worms filled their minds. There was a moment of heart stopping silence and fear, but what happened next turned their bones to mush.

The sands of the desert rose up and cascaded down from a hundred feet in the air. Then with a thunderous roar the worms dropped their heads to the sands, facing the armies left flank, mouths gaping open like twenty-foot-high entrances to bottomless caves and stopped. Hanser Schultzmann picked himself up from the ground, where his horse had dumped him. Still stunned he saw that not one of his men had managed to keep their mount. They were picking up their bows and weapons, but there was no chance they could win a fight with the worms. "Hold you're fire!" he yelled at the top of his lungs, but he was too late, the arrows flew. A sudden burst of fire filled the air with a crackle, followed by a loud scream of terror and everything went silent again.

The shrill scream of a large bird descending from above, caught everyone's attention. A Large white bird carrying Shiheel, landed on the sand, between the army and the worms, dropped off the Eftite and left. Shiheel seemed to be communicating with the worms for several minutes, before he turned and headed towards Hanser Schultzmann and Brask Scaller. The two men managed to pull themselves together and issue orders to break into camp groups and wait, before Shiheel reached them.

"Forgive me this oversight." Shiheel started as he approached, "They are intelligent and have no desire to hurt intelligent life."

"That's nice, anything else you forgot to tell us?" Hanser asked with cold sarcasm, subduing the violent urge to strangle Shiheel with his bare hands. Brask just grunted.

"The drum sands are the home of the sand worms. They don't care if you pass through, as long as their home is left for them unharmed. I told them you were just passing through, and of the battle ahead. They said they would like to help, but they cannot leave the drumsands."

"It will take us a couple of days to recover our horses now." Brask Scaller snapped, "and that will put us well behind schedule."

"I will recover your horses." Shiheel turned to face Brask, "and I am sure the worms can carry you across the desert in a day, if you will accept the ride."

"That would save us two days, Brask." Hanser said, his mind back on their mission, having regained his composure.

"It is not our decision alone; we may not be able to convince the rest of the men." Brask quickly followed Hanser in regaining a professional attitude. They were soldiers first and learned to set their feelings aside a long time ago. "I think we should do it." Then turning back to Shiheel, "Seriously, Shiheel, is there anything else you forgot to tell us that you know about?"

"Nothing that I can think of. I will talk to the worms and you talk to your men." Shiheel started turning, "We must hurry, I still have too much to do elsewhere."

With the plan set, the worms agreed and for the rest of the day and half of the night, the worms carried the men and their horses across the desert of the drum sands to drop them off at the closest edge to the black river.

*   *   *   *   *   *   *   *

Eric woke up he knew it was early morning, he knew because he could feel the time. The rest were all asleep. Their camaraderie had grown strong, even more so since they had started to travel through the tunnels. Eric looked around at his sleeping companions. Kole Boort the Nob, a brave little guy, who would go out of his way to help anyone, yet he tried to leave the impression he would cut you up as to look at you. He was the only one who could not see, or be deceived by the illusion of the caves. Charlie had said it was because he was descended from its Dwarven makers. Next to him slept Garth Kor the Wonk, he still protested walking through walls, even though he was getting used to it. He was still too wrapped up in his traditional Wonk pride, to admit he liked someone and he let everyone know he did what he did, only for the sake of honor. Kesker the stone giant, his big tough exterior protected a soft and gentile heart, though even knowing that he was still intimidating. Then there was Brent Kelch the intellectual Elf, the mind is more important than the body. He was almost constantly at odds with Kedd Darset, the dwarf who thought everything should be done by physical ability and 'natural thinkin', or common sense. Jamis, Hans Spardic, was finally having some doubts as to whether this was just a game, especially since the second day in the tunnels when he tried to walk through the wrong wall.

Jahar and Calhan, the Milmorgs, had become quite at home with the small party and fit in so well, everyone seemed to forget they were not there from the beginning. Lady Moors mind pictures had shown Eric that the cats were by no means primitive or lacking in intelligence. Finally, there was Stralina the Jinn, and she was definitely a Jinn. Her moral standards were different, she had found ways to serve her body to every one of them in secret. The only reason Eric knew was because he could see without being there and he never told her.

Looking at her now, brought his mind back to the first day in the hot spring. She was good and he had to admit to himself that he had made no attempt to resist. He should feel guilty, he thought, but he did not. That bothered him a little at first, after all he was going to marry Bonny, they were engaged. A couple of days later Eric gave up worrying about it completely and started taking serious note of the situation he was in.

That day had been a very uncomfortable day. Eric had awakened, as usual ahead of everyone else. When he sat up and looked around, it was as if he realized for the first time, he was not dreaming. What was happening around him was real, as real as the college, his job, Bonny.... the rest of his life, maybe even more so. Eric felt as though he were on the edge of hysterical laughter. His pulse picked up and his senses sharpened and he felt crystal clarity to his thoughts. Some primordial instinct for survival had set him on full alert. For the first time, he knew his life was hanging on the edge. Then he thought of Bonny and Jamis, in his fumbling he had set their lives in constant danger also. It was foolish of him; they had not even been given a choice like he had and Bonny had not even wanted to stay.

The whole day he had been very irritable, as they traveled through the heart of the 'lost caves of no return'. Even Charlie gave him space, room to deal with himself. There were a few things about that he realized as he thought about it now, that he would have enjoyed. His instincts were so heightened; he could feel the eyes in the cave watching him. He did not miss one insect, rodent or reptile as they passed. That could have been fun if he had not been so paranoid and irritable. The sensation that every part of his body had been over charged with energy, that and the sensation that everything around him was moving in slow motion gave him the feeling of awesome power. Eric was definitely glad it was over though. The fear left as quickly as it had come. It had been like a light switch, that had been turned off as soon as deep within himself he gave in to a quiet acceptance, then click, as he sat there eating dinner, suddenly everything was alright.

Eric smiled as he thought back, it was then Charlie went, "Gerp, gerp.", '*Welcome back.*', he knew what was going on.

Eric scooped Charlie up with one hand, as he stood up and walked across the room, or cave chamber they were sleeping in.

"Gerp", 'What's up?'

'We are all creatures of the day, how long till we can surface again?' Eric asked as he stepped into an adjoining chamber.

'We can be out in three days, if we go through the caves of the catlings, but they are wild and could be dangerous.'

'What are the catlings?'

'They are in appearance, half cat and half one of you two leg walkers. They are the result of a curse of one of the Ancient ones.'

'Sort of werecats?' Eric sat down.

'You could say that, but not really they don't change form.' Charlie curled in his lap.

'How dangerous are they?'

'Nothing you couldn't handle, as long as you knew when they were there, just be vigilant for them.'

'Jamis is up, he's coming this way for his morning workout.'

'You can feel with the power of the barrier, that is how you know. Some of the ancient wizards learned to see with the barrier. Some used water solutions others used crystals and yet others used mirrors. Some of them learned to control drug induced trances to focus their minds through the barrier and see past, present and future events. That is how we got portions of the Never Ending Poem. Merlin Starnook knew how to physically enter the barrier. It is still hard for me to believe Deassheema overtook him by surprise. He traveled both our worlds. It was the last time I saw him; I learned my mate still lived and waited for me in your *world.'* Charlie, Greperp his real name, was careful not to introduce any information he had learned from the future goddess and daughter of Eric, knowing that knowledge of the future can result in changing what happens.

Hans Spardic stepped in, "Good morning, Jamis, Hans I mean."

"Good morning. You don't mind if I do my routine here, do you?"

"Not at all, Hans, you have a very impressive routine."

"I guess the game master would know that. Sometimes I forget that this is your game. Everything seems so real." Hans said, looking around, shaking his head and acting obviously impressed by his surroundings.

"Jamis, it is real. There is no computer on Earth, yet, that could generate an illusion of this finite degree. Don't you know things you didn't know before, a program can't simply plant information in your brain. Besides, how would I ever come up with a program like this on my own." Eric stated with an exasperated sigh.

Hans took a deep breath and started expressing the puzzled frustration that shadowed his face, "Eric, I know you got me here and I know you outfitted me. I know you have a damned lot of power in this world and I know the things you did or do in any fantasy game, where you are the master, but you know, I think I believe you didn't create this world. I am at the edge of grasping the possibility that this might really be an alternate reality. The problem is that I don't understand then how I was changed to an image, that only I actually held in my mind, unless this is a dream. Too much has happened for me to except that this is all just a dream, I will need to come to terms with this in my own way." Hans Spardic turned and walked to the center of the darkened chamber of the caves and took a deep breath. He had become an artist of motion.

"Gerp" '*He was transformed, even as you were, by going through the barrier. Anything that goes through the barrier can be changed the first time.*' Charlie barely stirred in Erics lap.

'*Yeah, and so was Bonny and so was I, but we were all changed in different ways as though totally by random.*'

'*Not by random, Eric, but drawn from within each of you…. think about it.*'

For quite a while they just sat there in silence. Eric watched Hans for a brief period of time before closing his eyes and focusing within. He reached out with his mind, '*feeling with the barrier*' was how Charlie had put it. Expanding and filling the chamber he was in he could see and feel Hans Spardic working out. Then the next chamber where the others slept. Lady Moor was awake, patiently resting, while waiting for the others to wake up. Stralina the Jinn and Brent Kelch, Elf and student of Esberkian magic would be awake shortly. This was not why he was reaching out though, he wanted to reach ahead and so he did. The caves were a seemingly endless maze, constantly splitting off in every direction and circling back on themselves. A normal person would get lost down here, even without the illusions set up ages ago, back when the caves were first dug by the Dwarven ancestors of Kole Boort the Nob, heir to the caves. Kole could not get lost here. Reaching out in his mind, Eric found some adjoining caves, that were dug after a different manner, rising upward towards the surface. He followed them up past a couple of chambers, until he came to a large chamber. Eric sensed there was something living there. He counted twenty-three of the strange creatures sleeping in the rock ledges around the chamber. Bringing them into better focus, he realized they were the catlings. This was the closest route to the surface and they would take it. It would be a couple of days before they got that far. Stralina woke up in the next chamber and Eric came back to himself.

'*Charlie, the others are waking up.*'

"Gerp gerp." Eric stood up holding Charlie and returned to their sleeping chamber.

Lady Moor rumbled a familiar deep, yet quiet growl, that Eric took as a "Good morning."

"Good morning, Lady Moor, Stralina." Eric said softly, "Breakfast of fruit and nuts again. We will be out in the daylight in a few days."

"Good morning, Eric." Stralina said yawning and stretching her voluptuous, well-endowed body before his admiring eyes. She walked over to Eric, where he was setting out breakfast for everyone, lifted up on her toes and kissed his cheek, "Can I help."

"That's all there is to it, right there, but by all means enjoy your breakfast, while I indulge my eyes." Eric winked and smiled as he spoke.

Stralina smiled, lowering the front of her blouse teasingly, "That could be dangerous, I might cast you under another spell first."

Eric chuckled, but decided not to continue the banter. He did not really want to lead her on into another scene of seduction. He shook that thought out of his head too, he had made a commitment to Bonny and should try to honor it even if they were not married yet.

*   *   *   *   *   *   *   *

No sooner had Bonny gone to sleep in the wagon, when Freebic Elkinshane road up with Browman, the only survivor from Saphrine's Royal escort who managed to make his way to the city of Talmorg after Saphrine was discovered to be alive. Browman with King Elron's consent, had joined himself to Freebic for training to sharpen his battle skills as they traveled.

"Well Elisha, looks like the rat has crawled out of the wood work with company now." Darset started, "Who's the villainous scoundrel you have dragged along with you Freebic?"

"Good day to you also, sweet Darset." Freebic smirked, "Meet Browman, of Efra's Royal guard. He's now in training with me. You know learning to master his skills from the best."

"Rouge training...." Darset began, when Elisha interrupted.

"Browman!" Elisha exclaimed, "I haven't seen you since I left to start training at Dragoncove over two years ago."

"Heard you two had something steamy going on before." Freebic laughed.

Elisha blushed and looking at her with mild surprise, Darset said, "Be nice now Freebic, or go back to your vulgar lot."

Browman now riding along where he could see Elisha, flashing a smile and a wink said, "My dear Elisha, you still have the finest Elven features in all the land."

"Apparently not fine enough." She came back at him "Or you would have at least sent a message to me some time in the past two years."

"So, this is the rat you couldn't stop talking about, when you first arrived at Dragoncove." Darset said giving Browman a scowl.

"Give me a chance to explain." Browman pleaded.

"This should be a good one girl. Maybe we should sit back and give it an ear." Darset said with a lofty look. Elisha gave a mild nod of agreement and looked at Browman with suppressed yearning in her eyes.

"This should be good." Freebic said looking at Browman with blatant doubt, "I didn't know you were ever involved in any serious relationships."

"Well, it has been two years," Browman started, "When you first left, I was in the elite cadet training and..."

"Freebic!" Calbork interrupted as he rode up. They all turned towards him. "Prince Talmorg requests a special hunting and scouting party to ride ahead. You will be getting game for dinner, selecting the best route for advancement and meeting the other messengers at the rendezvous point."

"Browman, you are going with me. I still want to hear this explanation when we get back."

"We will need a route for at least the next two days." Calbork added.

"Consider it done." Freebic answered, "Let's go Browman." The three of them turned their mounts and headed forward, leaving Darset and Elisha to watch them go.

"I don't trust him." Darset said to Elisha.

"He was ready to explain." She objected.

"I still don't trust him."

"You don't trust any men."

"You probably have that right, but this is different. Two years and even Freebic doubts he can explain it."

"But Darset, that's because Freebic has never been serious enough about anyone, to be able to have a loyalty that would last two years of separation. Browman has always been very valiant."

"Two years without a word, maybe there is a remote chance Elisha, but I have a feeling you are going to be hurt by him. Seems to me a Royal Guard could have gotten at least a message out."

Silence fell between them, as they continued to ride, Darset handling the reigns to guide the horses and Elisha daydreaming.

*　　*　　*　　*　　*　　*　　*　　*

When Talmorg turned and faced her, Saphrine got lost in his eyes for a long moment. He was handsome and his eyes had a strong magnetism to them. For the first time, she let herself feel her heart throb as she looked at him and smiled a smile of genuine caring back. Then breaking off their gaze, she said, "Yes, it will be good for morale and a lot more pleasant not getting wet, but how long will it last?" She stared at the shield, but her mind was on Talmorg. Neither of them seemed to notice at first, as their horses marched from the damp firm ground, that had been protected from the rain, to the slop that had received the full impact of the steady down pour.

The rolling terrain in this desert area actually looks rather nice in clear weather and there are usually a lot of small game animals, that live in the sage brush. "We will reach the southern most parts of the Uklian by evening." Talmorg rambled, looking for conversation. "I have been in these parts once before. Have you ever been this far north?"

"No, I haven't. I haven't even traveled all of the south lands before. This was supposed to be my first trip to your home city." Saphrine wanted conversation also, but just then Freebic and the lead of the hunting party caught up with them.

"See ya in a couple of days cuz." Freebic hailed to Talmorg, "We'll have a supply of meat readied." Freebic did not even slow down, nor had Talmorg expected him to, though Talmorg was relieved to see, that Freebic and his men that were still filing by, passed easily through the strange barrier without difficulty.

"I wonder what the nature of this shield is anyway. I don't recall having ever heard of anything quite like it before, neither in history nor any of the old legends." Talmorg said returning his attention to Saphrine again.

"It is new to me too." She admitted, "I am glad to stay dry, but I'll be even more comfortable when both the rain and the protection are gone."

"Do you think they'll be able to get back in?" he asked, thinking about the implications for the first time.

"I hadn't thought about that. We just sent out a hunting party of about five hundred, if or when we can get back together." Saphrine was starting to get lost in Talmorg's eyes again, "I don't think you need to worry..." she added sounding as if she had dropped off in the middle of her sentence.

"Why shouldn't we take concern for it, this could become a real problem." Talmorg said admiring her cute gentle smile.

"Yes," Saphrine said hoping she might be able to lift some of the burden of worry off of his shoulders, "but it also could be gone before we need to worry about it and it may not even be a problem to begin with. So, for now save yourself some peace of mind."

The day went by with idle chatter as they rode, the blue dome pressing its way ahead of them. It was about midday when Talmorg called a halt so they could take a break from marching and eat some lunch.

"Saphrine, let's go back and see how Bonny is dealing with what is happening."

As they rode back through the ranks, they made conversation, checking the attitudes of the troops as they went. This is when they first noticed that the ground was quite wet and the more trodden it was the deeper the mud was. When they got back to the medical support team, the ground was over a foot deep, with sloppy mud.

"Hail Prince Talmorg and Lady Saphrine." Darset greeted, as they approached, "It's nice staying relatively dry in this sloppy weather, isn't it?"

"Yes, it is Darset." Saphrine said with a radiant smile, "How is Bonny doing."

"She woke up when we stopped, so you can ask her yourself, when she comes back out." Darset answered, "Personally, my butt is calloused, so I'm doing well now." She volunteered as if she had been asked.

"Greetings, thank you, your highness." Elisha acknowledged the daughter of her king, "I have decided to return home after we get back."

"That will be wonderful, Elisha, we could use your skill in Efra." Saphrine smiled appreciatively.

"Good morning." Bonny said, still groggy, sticking her head out of the wagon. Everyone there laughed a little.

"It's a little late, Lady Bonny, for good morning, it is already midday." Talmorg explained, "But fair greetings to you also and how are you feeling now that you've had a little rest."

"I'm feeling fine, I think, at least once I wake up and eat something."

"Very well than we shall dine together." Saphrine quickly said and Talmorg nodded his ascent.

"I see you're doing better...." Bonny smiled at Saphrine, who smiled and nodded back.

"Yes, we are." Talmorg answered. "Thanks to the wonderful protection you provided from the rain."

"Thanks for your praise, but I don't know how long it will last." Bonny glanced up.

"Yes, and I wonder what other effects it might have." Saphrine added with a pondering expression, as she looked up, "It has brought a strange quiet over the land.... of course, maybe the birds and animals still know that it is raining."

"Or maybe an army this size has simply scared them off." Talmorg laughed. Saphrine blushed a little and laughed also.

"We better eat," Elisha interjected, "We will have to start moving all too soon." They all walked together over to the food wagon, where a cooking area had been set up.

After lunch Talmorg and Saphrine went back to leading their mighty army. Bonny rode in the front of the lead medical wagon with Elisha and Darset. Bonny remained silent however, for her mind had become occupied with Eric. She really missed him now, everything that was happening around her was like the stories he would tell her when he was first designing his computer games. She could remember being next to him in bed, as his enthusiasm poured out while he explained how different characters interacted, with the latest software and programing he had locked into the computer system.

She thought back to one of the picnics they had been on, and how he had taken words and transformed the forest around them into a magical fairyland. His weaving of tales was so fascinating it had seemed at the time to even grab the attention of the forest itself. Bonny remembered how his eyes seemed to sparkle and how the intensity of his voice could command her feelings. Her thoughts kept wondering until she found herself thinking about the last lecture he gave at the university. Eric's lectures were always packed, he had a way of making the most boring details seem like an adventure. That lecture had been paid for by a computer manufacturer he did side work for. The subject had been the automated home. It was funny Bonny thought, the only computer they had at home was the one he had hooked up to his different business terminals including a link with the university.

"Bonny! You with us?" Darset broke through her thoughts, as they slowed to a stop. "Ya miss him, huh?" she smiled.

"Yeah." Bonny answered, she found comfort in Darset's company. She was another human in a land of creatures she had only read about. "I miss my home world too, I think, but it would be better if I was at least with Eric."

"Seeing Browman again has brought back memories of Efra." Elisha put in, "Now I'm feeling a bit homesick too."

"At least you're in the right world." Darset gave Elisha a cool look, "I have always wondered what it would be like to be on Earth. All I know of it is what has been passed down through my family. My ancestors supposed to have come from some place called York." She looked at Bonny as if she had asked a question.

"I have never been there it is thousands of miles and across an ocean from my home." Bonny shrugged, "I am sure it is quite different from when they left it."

"Well, we'd best set up for the night before dark." Darset slipped into the back of the wagon. The three of them set to work, setting up their part of the traveling tent city.

Talmorg called a halt in a large, relatively flat, open clearing. They still were not in the dense forest of the Uklian. There would not be any large clearings after that. After they dismounted, Talmorg, Saphrine and Erron took time to examine the maps. They should meet up with Freebic and the hunting party around midday the following day at Berges rock. They were still close to on schedule, but they still needed to push a good march. They had chosen Berges rock as the meeting place for their first messenger relay, because it was where they were scheduled to be and the fact that it was a commonly known landmark. Common folklore has it that a red dragon used to live in a cave at the top of the rock pedestal. Some even believe he is still there, just sleeping for his thousand years, that some dragons need to increase the powers of their magic. No one really knows, but for now it was unimportant.

"I'm glad Shiheel gave us maps of this area, he has more detail than we ever had." Talmorg said to Saphrine. "Once we get past Berges rock, there is a slight ridge along here running straight north for quite a distance, it will be a good landmark."

"You mean Tolegus Ridge, we can use it for a landmark, if we travel on the west side of it." Saphrine looked up from the map, "It was named after my great grandfather. He never returned from his exploratory scouting trip, up onto that ridge when, our ancestors first moved south from the Elven forests of the Uklian.”

“Why can’t we travel it?” Talmorg gave her a curious look, “It can’t be too much different from the rest of the area.”

“Oh, but it is. It isn’t supposed to be too wide, an arrow shot, nor is it too high, it barely reaches above the tops of the trees in the lower forest. The problem is, it is nothing more than sheer rock cliffs, broken up and down. You can’t go more than two steps anywhere, without having to climb up or down smooth rock walls.”

“You seem to know a bit about it.”

“Grandfather talked about it a lot. He believed it was some kind of protection around a great treasure and the trick was finding a way in.”

“I wouldn’t tell Freebic about this, until the return trip at least,” Talmorg chuckled, “otherwise we might lose him to a treasure hunt.”

“You have more confidence in our return than I have.” she gave Talmorg a very serious look, “Not that I doubt Eric’s ability or Shiheel’s and I do believe our fighting skills are as good as any, but we are walking into the middle of a war against an unknown enemy, with allies that are losing, almost twenty days before Eric reaches his destination. According to Shiheel, Eric needs to take out the Scaldorian’s power source before they can be defeated. I lack some of your confidence that we will all live through this, forgive me for that, but I am determined to do everything I can for my people.”

“My dear Saphrine, your concern is justified, but you must

understand our primary purpose will be to slow down their advancement." Talmorg too, now had a serious look, "We will fight a retreating battle, incurring minimal losses, until Eric has succeeded, at which time the ebb of the battle should turn to our favor. All we need to do is survive long enough to be there when the battle turns around."

"You do make it sound reasonably possible." Saphrine was now smiling again slightly, "I'm glad you are our leader." she leaned forward and kissed him.

Caught off guard, Talmorg blushed slightly, but was too late when he thought to return the kiss. Saphrine had turned around and was facing the rest of their encampment. Talmorg also looked out over the small ocean of tents, everything was already set up for the night.

"They have gotten quite efficient at setting up and breaking down camp." Talmorg commented, looking again at Saphrine, her kiss had stirred his inner passions and he felt a deep yearning desire. "Shall we adjourn to the tent?"

"Sure." Saphrine turned her beautiful green eyes to him, "You can help me with my cleansing lotion, you could use some too." She was also feeling great desire for Talmorg. If she had thought about it, she would have been surprised at herself, for not having Eric on her mind, while admiring Talmorg. At last the twinges of love in her heart were turning to Talmorg. "We have a little time before dinner." she whispered as they slipped out of sight into the tent.

Bonny woke up early the next morning, before Darset or Elisha.

She was becoming almost comfortable in this alien world. Darset and Elisha had become very good friends, even Saphrine and Talmorg, though Bonny hadn't been as close to them. She wrapped in her cloak and stepped out into the crisp morning air. The sun wasn't up yet and the blue glimmer of her protective dome shield obscured the stars that still shone. Discreetly she slipped into some brush and relieved herself. As Bonny was returning to the tent, she noticed others stirring around the encampment. The halo of light to the east, indicated that the sun would be up soon and with it the entire army for breakfast.

"Good morning, Bonny." Darset said as she reentered the tent.

"Good morning, Darset."

"Are we still under that blue dome?"

"Yes, it's still up there."

"Well, at least we won't get wet if it rains."

"I wonder what we're having for breakfast." They all got dressed as they talked.

"Ha, like there should be variety. We would need to double the wagons, just to accommodate breakfast." Darset laughed, "Nice thought though."

Elisha sat up and yawned.

"Good morning sleepy head." Bonny jeered.

"You're in a good mood this morning." Elisha mumbled through a stretch, as she rolled out of bed, "Looks like it's rubbing off on Darset too." she smirked, "You'll have to teach me that trick."

Darset mocked a scowl, "Watch your manners, or I'll have ya fed to the dragons."

"It's too late for that."

"Oh, and why is that?"

Elisha sneered, "I'm not a pure sacrifice any more, I've been contaminated from being around you."

"You two can squabble this out, I'm going to go eat breakfast." Bonny turned and walked out of the tent. As she walked toward the meal wagon, she was intercepted.

"Bonny, Bonny," A young Elven assistant came running up to her, "Bonny you are needed back at our tent."

Bonny followed as the young Elven girl turned around, "What is it Dorney?"

"Oh, Kerb tripped over one of our tent stakes and knocked himself out on a rock, the clumsy cad." She glanced over her shoulder, "It does look nasty though."

"Well let's take a look at him."

Dorney held the tent flap open for her, "He's in here."

Tarish another Elven medic was cleaning the injury. She looked up as Bonny entered. "He really gave himself a bad knock this time."

Bonny knelt down opposite Tarish and looked at Kerb's head. He had taken a solid blow, just forward of his temple, on the left side of his head, "It looks like he might have fractured that thick skull of his." she said as she opened one of his eyes and noted it was fully contracted, "

Wipe it clean with your herbal ointment and wrap it when we're done. She pictured in her mind's eye, his head completely healed and held the image in focus for a few moments. Bonny's confidence in the power she possessed had greatly increased with use. Almost immediately Kerb opened his eyes and looked at her, it had worked again.

"Thank you."

"Don't mention it, just watch where you're going a little better." Bonny smiled and got up, "Watch that he doesn't go to sleep on us for about eight hours and Kerb make sure you stay warm. You are also not to do any heavy work today and let me know how you're feeling tomorrow."

On her way to the breakfast line, she was joined by Darset and Elisha.

"Where'd you go, Bonny?" Elisha asked, "I thought you'd be done eating by now."

"If you two don't want to eat with me, just say so, you don't have to try to avoid me." Bonny faked a little indignation.

"Oh, no we enjoy your company." Elisha said, then realized Bonny was jeering and just giving her a hard time, "but really what happened?"

"Oh, Kerb just tried killing himself." she answered lightly.

"Are you sure?" Darset looked worried.

"No, no, I see you both are still asleep. It was an accident; he tripped and fell on a tent stake." Bonny smiled and shook her head at their slow-witted grogginess, "He will be just fine." They each grabbed a bowl of breakfast mash. It was a cereal made from grains and a variety of nuts and dried fruit, the result was a very nutritious and still tasty meal. When they were done eating went back and packed for the continued march.

CHAPTER 19

Reaching the Uklian

Talmorg woke up with a yawn, he had fallen asleep talking to Saphrine. Her head was still tucked on his shoulder and they were stretched out on top of his bedding with their dinner plates still on the floor next to them. She stirred when he tried to move, so he relaxed and gazed into her face. She was beautiful, he thought to himself, looking at her fine yet sharp Elven features, dancing in the light of the tallow lamps. He pondered her for a while, then his thoughts drifted back to their mission. Looking out the tent flap, Talmorg could see the light of predawn, as commander of the great army, he did not have time to dawdle.

"Saphrine, honey," Talmorg lifted her head, with a gentle nudge of his shoulder, "It's time to get up." He kissed her forehead, she opened her eyes and smiled up at him.

"Good morning." she stretched a little, "Can't we stay here all day?" Saphrine smiled a very seductive smile.

Talmorg resisted melting in her gaze, "It would be grand; however, we have responsibility as leaders of our people."

Slowly they got up, a little stiff and still dressed from the night before. "I do hope we stop near water tomorrow; I am in desperate need of a bath."

Talmorg nodded, "We will." he said. His mind was already on the day ahead, "We will catch up with the hunting party today. We can use magic to clean for now."

"That's good I'm sure fresh meat will lift the spirits of the troops, but so will a fresh stream of water." Saphrine knew the day had begun now and Talmorg needed her support, intimacy would have to wait. They walked out together.

Talmorg looked up and said, "You would think that Bonny's magic dome would have dissolved by now."

"She has more power than she knows, or we've imagined. It may prove useful later, if it can stop arrows and weapons."

"This is quite true. She focused on this for less than an hour and look how it has lasted almost three days already."

Calbork walked up, "Good morning sire, breakfast is ready and we have already begun to break camp."

"Very good Calbork. Did the night watch have anything to report."

"No, sire."

"It is too quiet. No morning birds. I haven't even seen a mouse for three days. It's a bit eerie."

"It could be the shield, sire."

"This is true. Thank you. Saphrine, shall we eat?"

"By all means, my liege." she gave him a stiffly addressed answer, then smiled.

As they set out the terrain rapidly changed, from flat open plains with low brush, to waves of shallow hills and dark heavy forest. The trail they followed, was barely wide enough for the wagons to pass through. Talmorg actually wondered whether they were following a trail or making one. They pressed on until shortly before midday, when they approached Berges rock. Freebic and Browman were seated at the base of the monumental red rock, that towered skyward. They called a halt and Freebic walked up through the blue dome that separated them.

"It was a great hunt, cuz, should have been there. We have enough meat to last a couple of weeks."

This is good news, Freebic. I presume it is already divided amongst the hunters, according to company. "Talmorg looked around the hunters camp."

"You can be sure a that, cuz."

"Well then, have the hunters return to their respective companies, with their portions."
Freebic turned and went back to the hunters.

"This is good news sweet prince, and it seems to top off a good day." Saphrine stated in a voice of regal authority.

"Yes, indeed it does." Talmorg was obviously in a good mood.

The hunters started filing by, heavily laden with cleaned and butchered meat, carrying them back to their respective companies. Freebic and Browman approached last, leading their mounts, which were overburdened with meat, carefully wrapped in hides made into giant saddlebags, draped across the horses' backs. Freebic like the rest of the other hunters, passed freely through the dome, but Browman stopped as though he ran into a solid stone wall and even stumbled backwards.

"What!?" Saphrine was caught off guard. Browman tried to pass through a second time, with a little more caution, but no more success.

"Strange." Talmorg commented, then after watching Browman make a third attempt, he turned to his guards, "Calbork, would you go get Bonny. It seems Browman can't pass through her protective barrier."

"Yes sire." Calbork reined his horse around and bolted back through the ranks.

"Why just him, it let him pass the other way?" Saphrine asked, her voice echoing shades of his own doubts.

"I don't know." Talmorg looked at her, "I have an idea, but I can't say right now." Pondering he glanced around at everyone there. It is a protective bubble he thought and there could be only one reason it kept anyone out. That was a hasty conclusion though and he would keep it to himself for now, besides Browman has been a loyal guard at Efra for years.

*   *   *   *   *   *   *   *

"There it is." Elisha said pointing through a hole in the tree tops ahead.

Bonny looked and saw the rock towering up at least fifteen stories above the tree tops, "What is it?"

"It's just Berges rock." Darset answered, "Legend says it was raised up out of the ground by a dragon's magic. Personally I aint never seen a dragon, or anyone who has."

"That rock means we'll stop soon and Browman will be back here again." Elisha was almost jumping with excitement.

"Yeah, the lout who never even sent word to you for two years." Darset retorted.

"But he was ready to explain." Elisha said softly. She really did love him Bonny thought.

"They always have an explanation." Darset shook her head, "But he's the scoundrel, not you."

"We really should hear it out, before we judge harshly." Bonny defended Elisha.

"Alright, I would like to hear this myself. It should be a good story." Darset answered, sarcasm still lingering in her voice.

They had not gone much farther, when they came to a stop. Immediately preparations started for lunch. Bonny, Elisha and Darset all went over to the meal wagon. They were still there when the hunters started arriving, bringing a portion of the catch to the wagon.

Elisha looked anxiously at their approach, then concerned, "Is Browman coming back here?" she asked one of them.

"Don't know, my lady." the leader of the small group shrugged his shoulders and dropped his load in the wagon.

"Relax." Bonny put her hand on Elisha's shoulder, "No need in worrying. Remember he is with Freebic."

"Thanks." Elisha turned and smiled up at Bonny, "You're right."

"Bonny." she turned to see who called her. Calbork came to a stop in front of her.

"Yes?"

"Talmorg, requests your presence. It seems, Browman cannot pass in through your magic bubble."

"Why not?" Elisha asked, worry etching her face, and reflected again in her voice.

"We don't know that. I believe that question is the very reason Talmorg requests Bonny to come up front."

"I am going too." Elisha stated.

"Very well," Calbork signaled a guard who brought two horses over to them.

"Let's go then." Bonny said, hopping on the first horse. Elisha hopped on the second horse and they started forward, following Calbork's lead. The ride forward was much longer than Bonny had expected, but made sense when she remembered she was traveling with a group of over thirty thousand. Finally, however they caught up with Talmorg and Saphrine, who were now standing with their mounts tied to a nearby tree.

"Ah, here is Bonny." Talmorg began, "Maybe we can find our answer now." He stepped over and helped her dismount. "It seems our bubble of comfort, has singled out Browman and disallowed him to reenter and join the rest of us for lunch." He looked Bonny square in the eyes, "Can you explain this?"

"I am sorry sir," Bonny blushed, "but I cannot. I only know I did it to protect the encampment, when it rained."

"I didn't think she could." Saphrine said.

"Neither did I," Talmorg looked now at Saphrine, "but why did you doubt it."

"Simple, Eric doesn't yet understand the magic he has and he explained to me, they have no magic like this on Earth. So, this is all new to them. Logically we should understand it better than them."

Turning to Calbork, Talmorg asked, "Why did Elisha come along too?"

Her and Browman were friends, before she left Efra, my Lord." he answered simply.

"Very well, no one else is to leave the bubble, until we can figure out why Browman can't get back in." Talmorg ordered, looking at Elisha, who quietly nodded her understanding. "We will eat lunch while we discuss the matter."

They all grabbed a plate of food and Calbork pushed a plate out to Browman. They sat and ate in silence. No one understood yet, why Browman could not walk in through the barrier.

Finally, Talmorg spoke, "I have an idea." He cleared his throat, "The blue shield was made to protect us. It is possible, I am only guessing, that Browman carries something that might be a threat to us. Maybe an object of evil, or even a sickness."

"That seems to me to be a logical presumption, Sire." Calbork responded.

Saphrine looked away from Talmorg and turned to Bonny, "If it is a sickness, Bonny can cure him and if it is something he carries, touched by dark magic, he could take it off."

"Bonny, can you open the shield?" Talmorg asked.

"Maybe, I really don't know."

"Please try." Bonny walked up about ten feet in front of Browman and knelt. Then pictured an image of a door opening in the blue wall. She didn't know how long she sat there trying to open a way for Browman to enter, but the longer she did, the more she felt the presence of evil. Finally, she opened her eyes, not willing to bare any more of the evil sensation, got up and turned back to Talmorg, sweat pouring down her brow.

"I cannot do it." She shrugged, "I was overwhelmed with the feeling I would be letting evil in." She looked over to Elisha, who was scratching at the dirt with a stick, "I'm sorry Elisha, I really have no idea why it feels that way."

Elisha looked up, "It's not your fault, you acted out of goodness and didn't know this would happen."

Talmorg noticed a strange expression come over Calbork's face when he looked at what Elisha was scratching in the dirt. "What's wrong, Calbork?"

"It might be nothing, Sire, but I recognize the symbol she has drawn in the dirt." He looked up at Talmorg and shook his head in a disturbed manner.

"What is it you have scratched in the dirt, Elisha?" Talmorg inquired of her.

"My Lord," she said apologetically, "it is the symbol from an amulet Browman used to wear, when we were together in Efra. Seeing him again brought it back to mind. Though he would never tell me where he got it, he would never take it off either."

Calbork's expression quickly turned to icy anger, "Prince Talmorg, my Lord, that is a symbol of the Scaldorians. The only explanation is he is a spy." Browman shot to his feet, while Calbork pulled a strange green tube from his belt. "Almost anything he has heard, the Scaldorians already know. They are expecting us." He pointed the green tube at Browman and Browman let out a yell as the front of his garments burst with flames.

Browman immediately turned to run, but Freebic, who had just returned from putting meat in storage, was on top of him in a flash. Browman turned about on Freebic, with his sword drawn, leaving a bloody gash in Freebic's left arm, as he jumped back drawing his own sword. Freebic leaped forward again bringing his sword downward in a mighty stroke. Browman saw it coming and brought his sword up to meet it. sparks flew, where the two blades met. As though unimpeded Freebic pulled his blade through looping it around with another blow. This time Browman was a little slow and the blade came down between his right shoulder and neck, snapping through his collar bone. Freebic pulled the swing through and stood there in a ready stance to strike again, but Browman had collapsed to the ground.

Bonny turned from the carnage and looked around. Talmorg and Saphrine stood fast and watched and so did Calbork. Elisha was in a state of shock with her mouth wide open. She kept turning back until her eyes met those of King Erron, who was seated on a nearby rock. His face showed her understanding and compassion, as if he knew she had never seen anyone actually slain by the sword before. She looked quickly back. Freebic had disarmed Browman the rest of the way, leaving Browman's sword on the ground and now carried him back. To everyone's surprise, he came right through the blue shimmering wall with Browman in his arms. Bonny ran up to meet them.

"I'm afraid you cannot help him." Freebic looked at her, "That burn on his chest must have slowed him down. My intent was to bring him only into submission, not kill him." Freebic laid Browman on the ground.

"Your arm though, I can help that."

"Please do." Freebic grinned, this time Bonny could see the pain he tried to hide in his face and set to work.

Talmorg now turned to Calbork, "How did you recognize a Scaldorian symbol and what is that green tube."

"Sire, I am your chief of guard, it is my job, to learn what I can of your enemies, so I came to an agreement with Hesheil some years back and he has been teaching me. As for this tube it is for the destruction of Scaldorian trinkets, that is all it works on."

"I am surprised, by your dealings with Hesheil, at the same time I am thankful, but why have you kept it secret."

"Very few trust the out-worlders. Though I am convinced of their loyalty to us," he looked at Talmorg, "even you would have let your distrust carry over and you acknowledge their advice."

"We will discuss this farther in private, Calbork."

"Yes, Sire."

"Mean while, get some soldiers, to give a proper burial for this Elf." Talmorg commanded.

Saphrine spoke up, "Use soldiers from my ranks. He is, or was a citizen of Efra." she turned to Talmorg, "I don't understand, he was born and raised in Efra. He was still young. How did he become a spy, a Scaldorian spy at that? I mean he was even one of my top guards, he was in the Royal Guard."

"Calm down dear." Talmorg put an arm on her shoulder. "How and when could he have met the Scaldorians?"

"I have no idea."

Elisha spoke up, "My Lord and Lady, twelve years ago he went on a journey. The journey of youth, which is a practice of all lands. Though it is optional, it still helps keep all of us aware of each other."

"You see, Saphrine," Talmorg took over, "The Scaldorians are vicious and a formidable foe for Hesheil and Shiheel. There is no telling what they did to Browman or offered him to get his allegiance. It is possible, that they somehow even gave him the ability he needed to rise up into the elite guard."

"Quite true, Sire." Calbork spoke up, "The Scaldorians have given the Milmorgs the ability to fight against the Elves. The amulet he was wearing could have served a few purposes, including controlling Browman's allegiances and sending messages back to the Scaldorians."

"Calbork, you must tell me more of your dealings with Hesheil. We will set up camp here, it has gotten late in the day. How is Freebic's arm, Bonny?"

"It will be as good as new in no time at all." Bonny answered. She knew the magic she had would heal him over night. It was however a very nasty wound, that would otherwise have taken weeks to heal.

"Is but a skin scratch, cuz. Ya need not worry about me." Freebic smiled at Talmorg, with a childish grin.

"It wasn't you I was worried about; it was the women of the kingdom." They both laughed.

Camp was quickly set up. Bonny and Elisha were given escorts back to the medical support section of the encampment. Talmorg called Calbork into the tent with himself, Saphrine and King Erron, his father, where they were all seated on mats on the ground.

"Now Calbork, tell me in detail your involvement with Hesheil." they all looked with interest at Calbork.

"Well, he approached me several years back, before I became involved in the Royal Guard."

"You have been in the Royal Guard for twenty-six years." King Erron interrupted.

"Yes, Sire." Calbork looked at his king before going on, "I have never done anything disloyal to the Royal Family, or my people. Hesheil provided me with special weaponry, made by both him and Shiheel. Hesheil started teaching me about his people and their enemies. He has even taught me how to use some of their magic. One of the things he taught me was a way to increase my ability to learn and refine my skills.”

“Is that how you got promoted to the Royal Guard?” Saphrine asked.

“In part maybe. I became skillful in the arts of fighting, by applying what he taught me. I also became more disciplined in the rest of my life. Over the years, I learned we could trust the Eftites, they are uniquely loyal to good, generally even at the sacrifice of personal gain. I don’t know if you have noticed, but in our history, since they arrived there has never been an Eftite arrested and they have proved to be a vital part of our cities defense.”

“This is true, but that does not mean we can give them blind trust.” It was Talmorg who interrupted this time, “What has he gotten out of this relationship?”

“I don’t know. He seems to be solely interested in the protection of our kingdom. Though he has shared with me the knowledge of a complex network of spies he has, even given me free access to the information they gather. He told me that he has this network so he can help in any situation where trouble arises. His life and business are safe as long as our kingdom is safe.”

“Ah, his business I knew there had to be a selfish reason for it!” King Erron emphasized his own distrust.

“But a good reason to trust them, in looking out for our best interest.” Talmorg added with a chuckle.

Calbork shook his head, "Their lives and safety are not the reason that they look out for our good. The only reason they do that is because they believe we are good. Why is it you have taken to trusting Eric and Bonny? Have you considered why they stand with us? Do you think they are looking out for their own good? Of course not, if that was all they were about they would have gone back to their own world long ago. But no, they are placing their lives in danger for our good. Look at the device Eric has gone to destroy, Hesheil could use a device of the same sort. He won't though because it endangers everyone and throws off the balance of existence and could result in more problems than the Scaldorians."

"Calbork, it is obvious you have a great deal of trust in the Eftites. Which may be good, but I believe your true loyalties are still with me. So, I will trust your judgment to keep me informed of anything I need to know." Talmorg knew that it was strictly his decision how to deal with this situation and no one would challenge it.

Conversation turned to less significant matters and the afternoon drew closer to evening and evening to dinner.

*   *   *   *   *   *   *   *   *   *

"It's been two years anyway," Elisha was saying, "It was a nice thought while it lasted, but I don't think I'll lose my grasp on reality over it."

"I'm gonna keep an eye on ya anyway." Darset said.

"Well, it won't help to dwell on it." Bonny sighed, "I need to take a bath, Darset, do you know if there's a stream near here."

"Oh yeah. Freebic came by and told me about it when you were gone. I need one too. I'll show ya to it."

"I'm going too. I feel like a cleaning rag." Elisha stood up, "We want to be back before dinner though."

"That's not for over an hour, girl," Darset laughed, "and it's not that far away."

Bonny picked up her bag of dirty clothes, "Might just as well clean some laundry too."

"Now that's a good idea." Elisha grabbed hers too. Darset didn't say anything, but joined them in the plan.

"Well let's go." Darset led the way. The stream was not more than forty feet away, through the trees near where they were set up. It was still within the shelter of the protective magic dome, so Bonny figured they were quite safe from danger, especially after what happened to Browman.

"There's a nice pool right here." Elisha said. They stripped and climbed in.

"Wow! The water isn't cold." Bonny was surprised, it was just a little on the cool side, but still comfortable. The early morning air was cooler than this she thought to herself.

"There are a lot of streams here, fed from underground sources." Elisha said, "Sometimes you even find places in the streams that are too hot to stay in."

"That sounds wonderful." Bonny smiled, grabbed her clothes and started washing them.

Shiheel had set off on foot, he wanted to find Talmorg's trail and follow it until he caught up with them. He headed straight for Keltoe, the red dragon's layer, he might even find them right there at Berges rock, as they called it. He generated a beam of energy and rode the beam; it was faster than walking. Some called similar techniques wind walking, but he called what he did riding the light. It would normally take four days to walk the distance he was traveling, but it would only take him about a day. He would be there the following evening, with one stop to regenerate his energy supply. It only took a few moments and he was on his way again.

As he neared Berges Rock he slowed down, a strange blue dome covered a large area at the base of the rock disappearing into the trees. Shiheel had never seen anything quite like it, but recognized it as a magical field. The energy fields were not stable from a scientific point of view. He wondered for a moment what its origin was. It was not of Scaldorian origin or the medallion Hesheil had given him would have given warning. Keltoe could not be responsible, it was not within the realm of the red dragon's abilities to create a field of that size or nature, besides it was very doubtful anything awoke Keltoe.

He reached the perimeter of the field of energies. Shiheel reached out his hand to touch it and it was as if nothing was there. He could hear the voices of women not far away, on the other side of the energy-field and he thought he recognized them. It sounded like Bonny and the heads of the medical support team. They were obviously not worried or alarmed and they had to know that the strange energy field was here, so Shiheel decided it must be safe and passed through it without effect. He headed straight for the voices he heard and quickly saw the three ladies through the trees and bramble, that stood between him and the stream. The ladies were bathing. Without hesitation or thought he pushed his way through the brush and to the edge of the stream.

With a slight gasp for air, Bonny, Darset and Elisha, all looked up startled by the noise and movement of the brush. After a brief moment of silence, Darset spoke first, "Have ya no manners at all, ya act like some stupid beast just walkin up on us like that with outa care."

Shiheel spoke quickly before the others could voice their complaints. "My apologies, Ladies. Please excuse my intrusion, but do not be alarmed. I have come only out of concerned for your well-being and that of the whole army. It is obvious you must be aware of this strange energy dome that surrounds you. How long has it been there?"

They all laughed at Shiheel's concern over their protective dome and to shake off their nervousness at standing in front of him naked, except for whatever articles that they had been washing now being held protectively in front of them.

"Three days." Darset managed.

"Has anyone come to harm by it?" Shiheel inquired.

Seeing it as a joke on Shiheel and with a quick look at the others, Elisha said, "Oh, yes, one Elf is now dead." referring to Browman, "Do you know what it is?"

"No, not yet," Shiheel said, "But don't worry, I will find out."

All three women laughed again, only this time it was at Shiheel.

Shiheel was puzzled, they were not taking him seriously. They must know something he did not. "Do you know what it is?" he asked, "and how did someone come to harm?"

Elisha and Darset glanced at Bonny, then Darset started an explanation, "Browman couldn't get back in, so Freebic killed him."

This time Shiheel knew the answer was not complete and Bonny had something to do with it. Then his thoughts started making sense. In Dragoncove, Bonny had used protective magic and saved life of an infant, with a blue barrier that existed too briefly for him to analyze. It must have to do with her magic. Now Browman, Freebic must have had good reason if he killed him and that must have been with a good fight first. He had his answers without them telling him. Then he realized he had put them in an awkward position, barging in while they stood naked, something to do with their morality perceptions. He deserved to be the brunt of their joke.

He crossed over the stream, "Excuse me again, I will leave you to your cleaning and speak with Talmorg." he said as he turned about, then headed toward the rest of the encampment.

"Strange little one he is." Darset said as they returned to their cleaning.

"I most definitely agree with that." Bonny added her support, "It is hard to believe someone like that is even real."

"They are very small," Elisha threw in, "but their power is quite awesome and their ways are still strange to me."

"Eric trusts them though and I have always been able to rely on Eric's judgment of character." Bonny smiled, paused and added, "I'm ready to head back whenever you are."

*   *   *   *   *   *   *   *   *   *

Talmorg had called a meeting of the war counsel. He wanted to be sure all of his combat leaders were familiar with the fighting methods Eric had introduced to them. He also wanted them to know the land as well as possible from Shiheel's maps of the area they would be fighting in. Before they split up, he had instructed the others to do the same, several times in route to their rendezvous point. Talmorg knew both Prince Ashkin, the stately Dwarf and Hanser Schultzmann, Lord of the defense forces of Harmosk were well organized and see to it that their troops would be ready. The question that lingered in his mind was whether the Elves of the Uklian would receive this new form of warfare, while already at war.

In the center near the campfire so all could see them, sat, Talmorg, Saphrine, Freebic, Erron, Calbork and spreading out from there the leadership, by descending rank.

"We need to send ahead an elite messenger party to alert the Uklian Elves of our coming to join them and the nature of our party." Talmorg continued explaining why he had called them together. "Calbork has recommended Breckheart, his and my diplomatic right hand, to lead the party, because of his diplomatic abilities. I want four of our best protectors and our best medical healer to go with him, to insure a safe and hasty journey. I have made the decision to send a party of ambassadors, for though we are of common blood, we have had no communication for over a thousand years, since before any of us were born."

Discussion opened and with time and debate, four protectors were selected. Freebic was a little disgruntled not to be included, but conceded to being more needed at the head of his army. The final selection was, Shirken an Eftite protector, the most efficient they had, Tsarca a female Elven protector, who was titled the Invisible Warlord, Epraphil an Elven protector, who earned the title Master of Combat and Shark another Elven protector, titled The Sword Master.

Just as they started to discuss who would be the best Healer, Shiheel showed up and sat by the fire.

"I think our medical heads would be best suited," Saphrine interrupted, "to select the best from their people."

"You are right," Talmorg agreed, "Borak, go bring Darset, Elisha and Bonny here." He looked at Shiheel, "We will take a break until they get here."

Relaxed conversation broke out and Talmorg stretching and standing, walked up to Shiheel, "You have information or questions?"

"Yes, both." The two of them exchanged information for a short while. Shiheel first inquiring about the dome and then Talmorg learning of Hanser and Brask. Finally, Borak returned with the heads of their medical support team. The meeting came back to order and Talmorg quickly briefed them on what was going on.

Darset shook her head, "Yep, think Bonny would be the best for it."

"Bonny?" Talmorg thought for a moment, "Why would you say Bonny?"

"First seems no matter what happens she can fix it and then her healing is fastest, plus she could help protect such a small group."

"Your logic is good, Darset, but Bonny, I cannot tell you to go, because you are not of our world. If you go it must be of your own choosing. Will you accept?"

"I will do whatever I can to help." Bonny stated flatly and thought to herself, she must be crazy.

"It is settled than." Talmorg turned his attention to Calbork, "You and Borak see to their provisions and horses. Borak, you help Bonny with whatever she requests."

Saphrine stepped up, "I think we should have dinner before we go over the review of battle strategies, hunger clogs the thinking."

"I'm for that." Freebic remarked.

"Very well, we will take one hour." Talmorg turned back to Breckheart, "You will embark, one hour before sun up."

"Yes, Sire."

The gathering broke up and Shiheel went with Talmorg and Saphrine, departing shortly thereafter. Borak escorted Bonny back with Darset and Elisha.

"I will need two medium size bags, for my medical supplies."

Bonny said, gesturing to Borak the size, "I will pack them and set them on the front of our wagon, so you can strap them to the horse."

It was a quiet evening and Bonny went to sleep early, so she would be well rested in the morning.

CHAPTER 20

Convergences

"Keltoe, are you awake?"

"Who wants to know?"

"Do you forget me so soon?"

"Step forward where I can see you."

"Is this better?"

"Ahh, It's the little blue flame sucker." Fire sputtered out as Keltoe spoke, "What is it two years since your last visit. Just can't let a dragon get a good millennium of sleep can you."

"It's about time you got up anyway. Your energy level is at about its maximum and your scales are regenerated flawless."

"Let me snooze a couple of more decades, okay, then maybe I'll even go into business with you."

"With fire in the sky the lost prince shall return,

Heir to all Elves with victory to spurn,

Yielding the rights of King to none akin,"

"An old poem, very nice, but tell me now is this advice, or need I ask twice is it poem or device?"

"Your time has come to fly in glory, for an Elven victory, Keltoe. You are the fire in the sky."

"Device, Hurmph." Keltoe shifted, "You aren't even going to give me a month or two to play with my new wings."

"You are the greatest and oldest of Dragons, you knew this time would come. You were there when the poem was first given."

"A silly poem, you little blue thing, it says, fire in the sky, not on the wings of dragons, I may be the oldest does that mean the greatest or boldest."

"Keltoe remember in the poem, does it not describe your home. From a tower of rock that stands alone, he lifts up his wings with a groan. The breathless one shortens his sleep, red wings to the air he goes with a leap." Shiheel sat down, this might take a while.

"It is true, Shiheel, I have known for some time that, that refers to me. I did not know however that you were breathless. Have you traveled every corner of Ethar yet?"

"No, not yet, I've only been around now for six hundred ten years, two months, seven hours and thirteen minutes."

"Have you seen Greperp lately, he too was there you know, him and his female companion Gerpep."

"Now Keltoe, you know Gerpep was trapped on Earth when they lost contact with Ethar, but I deal with Greperp on and off."

"Ah then the time has not come yet."

"Why do you say that."

"The greatest wizard born on Earth,

Did not have magic from his birth,

Passing to Ethar he goes through change,

Granted powers of unlimited range."

"You should be happy to know he has arrived and right now is in route to accomplish his first task here."

"He is a dangerous man you know, if he knew the full extent of what he has. He could even change the nature of our existence."

"He has a conscience."

Keltoe rose to his feet and blew a blast of flame out the cave entrance and stretched out his wings, "I will join with Talmorg, son of Erron, son of Talmorg, fourth son of Bracken, in six days."

"Why so long?"

"I wish to first become used to my new skin." With a hiss Keltoe sprayed the sides of the entrance and they dissolved back from the acid, "I'm a bit larger than when I came in to metamorphosis, However I have assimilated all the treasures I acquired. They plated and scaled out well."

"Your crystals are in a new arrangement too; I presume they generate more power now."

"I'll know how much, when I use them. I should have twelve times the power I had before, plus whatever your advice added to that." He held out his front claws and generated a brief electrical arch filling the air with ozone, "Glad you came before the hardening was complete, spinning the metal fiber has made my scales seven times harder to penetrate and much more durable with that composite blend you suggested."

"You give me too much credit. It was nothing you wouldn't have figured out before your next sleep cycle." Shiheel now stood also, "besides, you taught me a lot of Darkon history. I would visit your home world, if your sun hadn't disintegrated the three-star systems."

"How did the Earth man get here, Shiheel? Our planets no longer overlap."

"I developed a door, or a portal if you will."

"I see. Are you sure it wouldn't be better for me to wait until the Scaldorians arrive before I show up."

"I see you've been talking to Hesheil."

"How do you know?"

"I never told you about the Scaldorians. No, don't wait that long, you can wait until the armies of the south lands engage, but you are our cover. They don't know any Eftites are here yet."

"How do you know that?"

"They would take us as a primary threat and search us out first."

The two of them talked about a vast number of different things the rest of the afternoon, all night and until midday the following day. Finally, Shiheel took his leave.

*　　*　　*　　*　　*　　*　　*　　*　　*　　*

They separated from the main force five days earlier and now had a three-day lead. Breckheart was determined to reach the Uklian Elves as quick as possible, however looking down the valley in front of them he seemed a little apprehensive. Fog filled the valley.

"It's a beautiful view." Bonny commented.

"Yes, it is, but what is down their?" Tsarca who rode next to Bonny, added, more as a statement than a question.

"I don't know," answered Breckheart as if she were asking him, "but it is too big to go around." He started down the slope and the others followed cautiously, as they approached the fog.

"We better use a rope, so we don't lose each other if we enter that fog." Shirken stated, as they approached the wall of white, that stood before them, "I'll lead, I can use alternate radiations to see in the fog, as though it weren't there."

"Sounds like a plan." Breckheart said, I'll follow you, then Epraphil, followed by Tsarca, Bonny and Shark, in that order. They lined up and passed a rope from one to another, tying it around their waists.

A feint alert was going off in the back of Bonny's mind, and she thought about how the protective barrier had faded and then vanished during the night before they left Talmorg. Then an idea struck her, the dome was small, but it encompassed the six of them, pushing the fog aside as they rode forward. She put it up at the last minute before they entered.

"Nice, that helps a lot." Breckheart commented, "Will it last as long as the one you put over the main force."

"I don't think so." Bonny answered, "I only focused on it for a couple of minutes."

They only went about forty feet and they were out of the fog. The valley below was a spectacle of beauty, from where they were they could see across the entire valley under the ceiling of the low cloud. The forest had a sparkle to it and in the middle was a large waterfall, spilling into a small lake with a continuous geyser in the center, that fanned out into a beautiful fountain.

"It smells like the work of Fairies." Said Epraphil with a snarl, "That means only one thing, trouble."

"I'm with you on that." snapped Shark.

"Not all Fairies are the same as those in the forest of dreams." Shirken stated flatly.

"I have yet to meet one who wasn't a prankster." stated Breckheart, in pensive thought, "and I'm sure, that they already know we are here, if they were set on our demise, it would already be over."

"A creature that can make the land this beautiful, cannot be all bad." Tsarca answered their reproach, "besides it was a Fairy that taught me my vanishing techniques."

Breckheart stopped and turned his mount, "What association do you have with Fairies?"

"I saved the life of one trapped in the web of a Murkin spider." She held a cool glare on Breckheart, "and he in exchange taught me the vanishing techniques, without which I would never have escaped the Murkin Flats."

"Tsarca, have you still any association with Fairies?" Breckheart pursued.

"No, that was it two months of learning, forty-three years ago, are you questioning my loyalties?" Her glare was now one of hot anger. "I have stood in defense of Efra for over seventy years, but these are not yet an enemy. Should we deny them a chance at friendship?"

"Forgive me my haste, however it was not your loyalty I question, but protocol. We know nothing of Fairy culture, or ways, because of their secrecy." Breckheart relaxed slightly, "I had hopes you could educate a diplomat in diplomacy."

Tsarca laughed, "Forgive my haste in judging your intent. No, I did not learn their social ways except, how a student greets his teacher."

Breckheart thought for a moment, "That might help."

"I hope so, we're surrounded and they are approaching quickly." Bonny said.

"Do as I do." Tsarca said, quickly dismounting, the others following her example, "Form a circle, facing outward and draw your swords, poised."

Bonny not having a weapon, pulled a scalpel from her medical bag as she turned from her horse, just in time to see a Fairy bounce off the defensive bubble.

"Put your weapons flat across your chest and bow, but don't lower your face or take your eyes off of them." Tsarca instructed, as she did the same, "That's it, the rest is up to you Breckheart."

When they stood back up, they were surrounded by hundreds of Fairies. A voice came from the direction they had traveled, "Clear a hole the prince is coming through." The Fairies spread apart near the ground. A large Fairy, about fifteen inches tall came through and walked up to Breckheart, as if the defensive bubble was not there. He wore a crown and carried a scepter.

"Who are you that you should greet us as your teachers. Do you come to learn the secrets of quiet valley, or steal them?"

"Neither, your eminence," Breckheart began, "We are but a messenger party and seek safe passage through your valley."

"You should go around."

"Sire, we are urgent and lacking for time."

"How did you pass through the cloud of disorientation, with no effect."

"A magical protective field, that you see about us."

"I see that it effectively stopped my warriors from reaching you."

"Narco?" Tsarca asked, everyone watched as she walked up next to Breckheart.

The Fairy prince had an expression of surprise and delight. "Tsarca? Tsarca, how did you come to be here? but never mind. If you seek passage, I am still in your debt." With a slight wave, all the rest of the Fairies vanished.

"I guess that means we have free passage." Breckheart stated, "You have more association than you thought, you didn't tell us you saved a prince."

"I didn't know he was a prince."

"Leave a purse of gold, a token of our appreciation." Breckheart ordered. Shirken dropped a bag on the ground as they mounted and continued forward.

The valley was truly rich with beauty and fruit hung on every tree.

They ate the fruits they recognized as they passed. Bonny's protective bubble dissolved not long after their encounter with the Fairies and she thought the valley looked so much better, without the bubble, it was like a change from black and white to color. They were all caught up in the rapture of the fairyland beauty, when the roar of the waterfall caught them by surprise, as they rounded a bend in the path they followed.

The mist from the falls hit them in the face, it was cool and refreshing. The falls towered above them as the waters rushed down to fill the lake they now looked across. Breckheart brought them to a stop. They all felt a little light headed and had smiles plastered on their faces.

"I need a bath." Tsarca broke the long silence between them.

"We all do." Breckheart added as they dismounted from their horses.

"It is said," began Epraphil, "that Fairy water can added years to your youth." he laughed.

Everyone was dropping their clothes at the edge of the water. Bonny as if out of nowhere said, "Now this is fantasy." and laughed. Her next thought however was, 'We're being drugged.'

"Fantasy fills the mind," Epraphil was quoting from some old writings he had read once, "like the mist fills the air from the Fairy falls." he laughed again, "The magic of dreams is the Fairies delight."

Dreams and reality blended into one as they walked into the water. Streaks of color followed every movement and they laughed and talked about everything as they played in the water. Conversation led nowhere, but they all talked, sharing everything and anything with each other, loosing track of time and purpose.

Bonny woke up first, lying on a soft skin. She looked around and found they were on the other side of the lake about thirty feet from the shore and out of the mist. Then Shirken sat up looking out over the water, his back to her. The others were all still asleep. They were naked and uncovered, but their clothes and belongings were all neatly piled nearby. Bonny's thoughts on what had happened were unclear. She had a feeling she had given her body to one or maybe all of them, but nothing was clear.

She sat up, sorting her clothes from the neat pile at her feet. She started to dress as the others woke up, with the same confusion.

When the rest were up and dressed, Shirken stood up and turned to face them. "The Fairies brought us across the lake. They know what is happening and wish us a safe journey. Only one hour has passed since we first reached the falls."

"What do they know?" Breckheart asked, concern reflected in his voice.

"Our mission, the army that follows and why." Shirken said, "They might even join us in battle."

"Did you tell them?"

"No, we all did. We talked about it while we were under the influence of the mist of the falls. Our conversations were all with the Fairies."

"They knew that would happen." Breckheart said, with disgust.

"We should have known too." Epraphil said, "We know the stories around Fairy water."

Breckhearts momentary anger faded, "Okay, where are our horses?"

Shirken pointed up the slope behind them, "They are grazing in a small clearing, just up the path."

"Well let's head on and let these good Fairies have the tranquility of their valley back."

They all followed Breckheart. Tsarca and Bonny both lagged a little behind, walking together they exchanged wondering looks.

"Do you remember any of what happened, Tsarca?" Bonny whispered.

"I don't know?"

"I mean, I feel like I might have, uh, well, you know, done it with someone, maybe all of them." She pointed to the rest of the party ahead of them.

"I don't know, I feel strange about it too, but we haven't been getting any looks. Maybe we did, but it was the Fairies working, whatever happened."

"But, Tsarca, wouldn't we remember something like that."

"Maybe not, I wish I knew. I'm fertile right now and, Bonny, a different time I wouldn't care, but right now, I would choose not to."

"Shit."

*   *   *   *   *   *   *   *   *   *

It was the third day since their departure from Berges Rock, since they sent their messenger party ahead. The morning was becoming routine, everyone was up at daybreak and moving in less than an hour. The morning went with almost no incident. It was about the fifth hour. Freebic who was scouting ahead had stopped and they were approaching him.

"Something is wrong." Talmorg said to Saphrine, then indicated a halt to the rest of those marching behind them. "What is it Freebic?"

"We might have trouble." Freebic pointed out some broken twigs, branches and smashed impressions in the ground. "There were at least five Ogres through here this morning. They seem to be following the trail of our messenger party."

"There is no chance they will catch up with Breckheart, is there?"

"I would say not, but there is the possibility that we might catch up with them, or they might circle around on us."

"Alright, Thank you, Freebic. Calbork, alert the side ranks and have troops reinforced around the medical support group."

"Yes, Sire." Calbork turned at once and went to carry out his lords instructions.

"Talmorg, since we are already stopped, why don't we break for a meal, before moving on?" Saphrine gently inquired.

"My Dear, You're true in wisdom. I will have Freebic see to it."

"You got it, Cuz. I am always ready to eat." Freebic slipped off into the ranks.

"Calbork, order up the ranks, we're moving on!" Talmorg

commanded. The meal was finished, packed and they were ready to go. They moved forward, more alert, on the watch for further signs of the Ogres.

Freebic and Corba, one of his personal guards, scouted ahead. Talmorg could see the tracks of the scouts' horses in the Ogres' trail. A breeze picked up blowing northward and this worried Talmorg. If the Ogres were close enough, they might pick up the Elven scent and either double back or circle around. The nape of his horse's neck twitched in alarm, and he gave Calbork a hand signal.

The march came to a halt, Calbork and about twenty Elven guard vanished into the woods ahead. Almost as soon as they vanished, Freebic and Corba came racing back, dismounting and arming themselves, before they hit the ground.

"Ogres." Freebic barely got the words out, when the loathsome creatures came into sight.

At the sight of the Elven army the Ogres slowed down, but kept approaching. Arrows flew from the surrounding forest, raining down on the Ogres in several waves. The foremost of the six Ogres reeled in pain, his screaming piercing to the marrow as he let out his death cry. Freebic and Corba charged the next one while others came charging on horseback. Freebic somersault through the air, avoiding the deadly blow of the Ogre's stone club, severing tissues in the Ogre's neck on the way past. To find himself landing directly in front of another swinging club. He tumbled between its legs, striking for both Achilles tendons on the way through, downing his second Ogre, before the rest were taken out by the mounted guards.

Corba had not been as lucky as Freebic, he suffered three broken ribs and a sprained ankle. He would still be able to ride, however with a minimal amount of pain, after his ribs were wrapped. One of the mounted guards suffered a broken leg, from his horse falling, when an Ogre's club left the horse headless. One of the other guards was the only casualty, being left inseparable from his horse. It was over quickly; Corba and the injured guard were rushed back to the medics and the army was back in motion.

*   *   *   *   *   *   *   *   *   *

Shiheel looked out over the water. Time was running short. He had been unsuccessful in convincing the lordships east of the Torak of the danger their world faced and there was still too much rivalry and tension between them, so none would risk any of their forces and weaken their defenses. The only exception was Darkalon, named after the home world of the dragons, the largest and strongest city kingdom of the east south lands. They had gotten word from their cousins, the Borken Dwarves and had already sent over half of their armies north to fight in the Rackenwolf, one of the strangest forests Shiheel had ever seen. Most of the standing forest was dead trees, because at twenty years of age the trees all would just die.

The water was calm, but offered no answers, though he could see it was full of life. He knew very little about what lie beyond the water.

Yes, he had traveled there, but quickly and only once, to choose in the end Fire Islands as his private sanctuary and this land a suitable start for his breekkatt, or hatching. This world was now their home. The next breekkatt would hatch in less than one year, in safety, only if the Scaldorians were stopped. The future generations depended on their success. The whole world of Ethar did. Would he be alive to know? He hoped so.

Their only true hope now lay with Eric, there wasn't time to turn anywhere else for help. When Shiheel brought Eric here, he had counted only on Eric teaching what he could among the Elkinshanes. Since the Elves seemed to be losing their magic, they would have great need of technology to replace it. But then Mistav happened and now this. And then to find the Barrier and the Ancients or gods of Ethar have granted Eric power that no one fully understands, or knows the extent of. Shiheel had to wonder if Eric had the full power of one of the Ancients, or even maybe one of the Old Ones who came before the Ancients.

It was time to head north again, or they might start without him. Shiheel knew now however, when this was all over, he would explore the rest of this world much more, if he lived. If the Scaldorians had landed this close and he didn't know until now, who knows who else has come to this world.

    *   *   *   *   *   *   *   *   *
*

They set out through the caves again in the direction of the catlings. Shortly after lunch Eric felt a sudden change in the walls of the caves around them, and stopped.

"The enchantment is gone." said Stalina, "We have stepped out of the lost caves."

Lady Moor padded off ahead of them. Kedd was checking out the walls, "These aren't the same kind a caves alright. Much cruder diggins. we better be watchful ah cave ins."

"I'll just be glad to be out from under the ground." Brent complained, "Caves are for Dwarves, Nobs, Gnomes and Trolls. We Elves were made for open space, as the paths of the Ancient Ones set."

"We better be more cautious, if these are no longer the magical caves, no telling what we might run into." Hans added to bring Brent back to things at hand.

They lit another torch and continued with more caution and less talk, though without incident. Later having found a more open chamber in the cave, they made ready for dinner and sleep.

Eric was up again as usual, before anyone else, except for the last watch, and went to find a quiet space to sit. Hans was practicing fighting forms while keeping watch in one direction and while Garth kept watch the other direction, he was carving on a translucent green stone, he had found some days before they entered the caves. Eric felt a strange tugging in his mind from the barrier and closed his eyes. Immediately he felt lifted up and light burst forth around him, then a vision formed in the light. There was a man seated on a low limb of a tree, beckoning him closer with a wave of his hand and a voice of music. He swept towards the image like riding on the wind. When he got closer, he could see it was not a man, but had the sharp Elven features, much sharper than those he had met, but distinctly kindred. His voice captured all of Eric's attention, with beautiful music. Somewhere in his mind Eric felt he should know who this was.

"You are counted amongst us and also have the barrier at your call. I am Gaharias Emarlandestria elder of Elvendom, servant of the Lord of the Ancients. You are one of mine from your ancestry. In me you will find yourself."

Eric started to speak and his voice came out in the same musical manner, before Gaharias motioned him to be silent. In what seemed like a few brief moments Eric saw and understood the history of the Elven people and then he was back with Gaharias. Gaharias stood holding a sword and scabbard out to him. He took the sword and the vision started fading, but just before he came back to himself, Eric noticed Gaharias had Eric's coat of arms on his tunic. The coat of arms for his family on Earth had been handed down as descendants of Gaharias.

When Eric opened his eyes the rest of his traveling companions were sitting around talking and eating and Charlie was curled up in his lap.

"He's back with us." said Jahar from somewhere on the other side of the fire pit.

"Well, nice to see you're back." Hans stated, lifting whatever he was drinking as if in a toast, "We've been sitting here for a day and then some. Want some lunch?"

"I tell you; he was tranced by the Ancients." said Brent, "I have never seen it before, but I have heard of it."

"I didn't know men served the ancient ones." Kole was eying Eric with doubt, "I thought they followed something called gods from their world."

"Men know nothing of the ways of Ethar!" Stralina spoke up, "Nor should we tell them! We have been instructed not to discuss that in their presence since our births." She glared at those who had spoken for a moment and then relaxed. "I am sure you are hungry, Eric?"

"Yes, thank you." Eric felt the music he had heard in his vision, remained somewhere in his voice, ready for him to call upon if he chose. He started to get up a little awkward from sitting too long and Brent gave him a hand. When he stood up, there was a difference in the weight or balance of his sword belt. He shifted his belt, until it was comfortable, without thinking twice and grabbed a bowl of soup and a chunk of bread. No one said anything else about what had happened, but Eric did not stop thinking about it. What he could remember, had still not completely sorted itself out in his mind, but he knew with time he would remember it all with clarity. There was much more than just the history of the Elves he had learned. He had also learned the history around his heritage and lineage, along with the histories of the other races of Ethar.

The original old ones each formed a race after their likes, spreading them in an orderly fashion, where they were allotted place on Ethar, which was much more vast then the exposed portion of this northern continent. After that came the chosen from the races, which are now called the ancient ones, or Ancients by the present races, or the elders. Among the Elves the ancient ones were governed by a guardian, Gaharias Emarlandestria. The ancient ones had the ability to exercise great power and some to draw on the power of the barrier, without disturbing its balance. Later there were three major wars. The first one wasn't a war with weapons, but politics, peace was maintained, when the ancient ones gave the choice to follow their rule, or for the races of the land to set up their own governmental systems. Only a few of the races stayed with the rule of their ancient ones as a whole, the Elves and Dwarves were among these, though all of the races of Ethar turned to worshiping the Ancients after one form or another. This left a large portion of the ancient ones dissatisfied or angry.

A few of these ancient ones stirred up trouble, leading a few of the races into believing they should rule over the other races. That was the first-time real evil was found among the ancient ones and the second set of the wars was not political, but long and bloody. The Ancients who caused the war managed to keep their positions when it was over, only stripped of authority, the thinking being that, that would be the end of it. Yet words were passed in secret and cunning ways among the Ancients and increasing unrest and dissension grew over the next three hundred years. Then began the third and last set of these great wars, with the councils of the ancients split almost down the middle. The guardians of the ancients worked together and still failed to bring an end to the war, or turn the hearts of the Ancients who had turned to evil.

Finally, seeing no end to the war, the guardians called upon the Old Ones, who came down to intercede, separating out the Ancients to an ethereal kingdom apart from Ethar, not allowing them to act directly on Ethar, but rather limiting them to working through their followers only. Not being allowed to walk on Ethar was severe and exercised on all of the Ancients, compelling them to sign an accord. It was deemed that the powers of the immortals were too great in a world of mortals.

The largest part of the Elves, chose to continue following Gaharias and so Terrikai was established as the first Shane of the Elkins or the first Elf lord and his cousin Relchies was established as the first Barh Hallah, or disciple caller. Each lineage of Elves was granted certain powers, that would be passed on to their heirs.

Eric knew this was a sketchy summary and there were still pieces he could not readily recall yet. After that it was quite a confusion of events, for the mortal Elves could not remain totally united in their governing where they were separated on different continents and by oceans. Gaharias delegated his authority among the other Ancients and the sons of Terrikai divided the rule of the other Elf lands into separate elkinadoma, the adoma being the living heart of each kingdom. Somewhere in his mind Eric knew that with time he would grow into the full knowledge of Gaharias and that it had already been given to him. It saddened him that he could not share is experience fully with his companions, nor its implications.

They stopped just short of the catlings caves, to break for dinner and to sleep. Lady Moor came and went through the caves. Everyone else was uncommonly quiet and Eric felt they were waiting for him to explain what had happened. Finally, he looked up and they were all watching him. "The other day I was beckoned by Gaharias, guardian of the Elven Ancients. If you know who that is, you will understand, that I can give you no further explanation, at least not at this time."

Brent stood up and said accusingly, "He would only speak with Elves, only an Old One could deviate from that rule."

"Not just Elves." Garth said leaning back in thought.

"No, but Elven blood," Brents face was intent, but unclear, "and the Ancients can talk to each other too."

Stralina laughed, "Then he is either an Ancient or an Elf blood."

Brents face relaxed a little, he was surprised that he had not considered that possibility himself, knowing their worlds had met before. "Maybe He is descended from Elf blood," he shook his head, "but he is still more human than Elf."

The tension released around the fire, but conversation was a little more than the idle chatter of previous nights. Another night's travel and they would be back in the open again, this too was entered into their casual chatter.

CHAPTER 21

Uklian Elves

"After today we will be seven days march from the rendezvous. Schultzmann should be two days behind us and Prince Ashkin three." Talmorg finished, as they looked over the maps after lunch, "Form them up Calbork."

The scouts passed on ahead heading out from both flanks, then they started forward. They had not gone far, when they caught up to one of the lead scouts.

"Kurelian, what do you report?" Freebic called to the scout.

"Small party of three passed through here going west, looks like yesterday." Kurelian paused, "Light footed, I would guess, carrying no load, possibly spies, or rangers."

"Any identifying traces?"

"No, my Lord."

"Very, well dismissed."

Kurelian vanished, back into the woods ahead of them.

"What do you make of it, Freebic?" Talmorg asked.

"Well, cuz, we can't even tell which side they are on, if either. Could be anything, from fugitives, to thieves, scouts, or assassins, but they did not turn to follow our advance party."

"I agree. Nothing we can gain by it and using any kind of identifying magic could draw attention. Not that the movement of this force can be hidden."

"As evening came, the lead scouts sent back word, that Quiet Valley, was a drill field ahead. They stopped and set camp, Talmorg had no desire to march through and camp overnight in the land of Fairies.

The next morning, they kept all of their scouts in and moved forward. When they reached the fog bank, it parted before them and the prince of the Fairies approached.

"Greeting from Quiet Valley, your messengers precede you and your plight is known." he flew right up to Talmorg, "I am Narco and this valley is my princedom. You have passage, only do not stray, my guards will guide you. We would also join you; your quest is one of concern to us also."

"Greetings Narco of Quiet Valley, I am Talmorg of the Walled City of Talmorg in the south lands, for the sake of time I will dispense of the full formality and introductions. The war has already been started and we are pressing forward, if you are ready to march with us you can join, or you can follow after." Talmorg answered, "meeting up with us when you are ready. I am sure no help or support will be refused, when we arrive."

"We have had four days to prepare, while waiting for you, since your messenger party passed. We shall form up behind you, as you pass."

Prince Narco gave some orders to the other Fairies that were with him, before coming up beside Prince Talmorg, "You can continue passage through the valley, I will travel with you."

They marched forward into the valley in an eerie silence. The valley pulled all the sound out of the air, so they could barely hear their own horses move across the ground. At midday they were moving around the lake in the center of the valley. The Fairies had built a bridge four columns wide, at the lower and of the lake.

"These falls must be the adoma of this valley." Talmorg said to Saphrine. Prince Narco had gone to his own people when they stopped for lunch.

"Indeed, the water itself seems to live and fill even the rock with color." She paused as they both stared for a few moments. Then she started to sing in the old Elf tongue, the first two verses of the song of healing, that told of the life-giving power the ancients had given to the adoma in the Uklian. The sounds on Talmorg's ears flowed through him with a feeling of refreshment. When she stopped all those who were near enough to hear had stopped to stare at the bridge. The wood, that had been hastily put together for the bridge, had come to life, rooting and budding with spring growth. Talmorg looked into Saphrine's face. He thought he could see a slight sharpening of her Elven features, but was unsure.

"You never told me you had the old magics, that have been lost to the south land Elves."

"I don't." She said with a look of surprise, that changed to delight, "or didn't. I felt the adoma and it wasn't even elkinadoma."

"Our people have suffered being away from their adoma."

"But how could I, here...., I mean..., this is Fairy or Iempishadoma, set by Isiseristin, Guardian of the Fairies, not for Elves."

"True, my love, but the adoma itself is the life-giving heart of the land, brought to focus by the Ancients, not to be ruled, but rather nurtured and loved by its care takers. It must have felt the love in your music." Talmorg smiled at her, "Maybe the Ancients will help us bring such life to the south."

By evening they were out of the Iempish or Fairy Princedom and set up camp two hours march away. They had dinner and followed it with a meeting of officers.

"Father, the old customs and formalities of our people are endless." Talmorg went on expressing his concern for all but forgotten traditions, "but we are Elves coming in alliance with Elves of common ancestry and we should all know and follow them."

"It is not all tradition, Talmorg." Erron was giving him a pensive look, "They have helped the Elves for thousands of years, to keep order and peace and a true will for the good of the land. When living in touch with the adoma, every word and action can carry power."

"Yes, I understood that from our records, but there are many in our kingdom who cannot even feel the adoma."

"That is how, or why much of the old tradition was lost in the south lands and not forced upon the other races." Erron to the others, "However different things are from the south, everyone must show the utmost courtesy to the Elves in the Uklian, is that clear?"

They all responded in a positive manner, understanding the nature of the situation. Erron was about to go on, when they were all overcome with sleep and suddenly were out.

Kurelian was standing guard, one moment, outside the Kings tent. The next thing he knew, he was being awaken by a monstrous red dragon, lifting him onto his feet.

"Fetch Talmorg, Guard." Came the bellow, that should have alerted everyone. Before he knew what he was doing, he was shaking Talmorg by the shoulder. Talmorg jumped to his feet.

"What is happening here?" Talmorg grabbed the hilt of his sword and looked half dazed at Kurelian, "What...?"

"A red dragon, sire," Kurelian said shakily, "The whole camp is asleep and a red dragon is standing out there and asks your audience."

Talmorg subdued his trembling anger and with a gesture toward the door of the tent, said simply, "Lead!" He followed Kurelian out of the tent.

When he stepped out, he came to an immediate stop, not more than ten paces in front of him stood Keltoe, who did not have enough room to sit without leveling several tents.

"Keltoe at your service, prince among Elves."

"What?" asked Talmorg in surprise.

"I came to offer my services, Shiheel sent me." Keltoe looked around the camp, "Had to put them all to sleep. Wouldn't have done much good to fight my way in to talk to you."

"I thought dragons spoke in riddles." Talmorg felt foolish as soon as he said it.

"We do normally, but we're not stupid either. This is an urgent matter and simple understanding is necessary, however if it pleases you, I should make it more difficult."

"No, no pardon me Keltoe," Talmorg said slowly regaining his composure, "Your aid will be much appreciated, I am sure." Talmorg shook his head with thought, "This will not do, I need to prepare my men to meet you."

"I will return in the morning before you march." Keltoe lifted his wings and took to the air in one motion, swirling winds stirring light materials in miniature tornadoes from the ground.

Talmorg watched the ancient giant depart. Five hundred soldiers could march in formation under each wing. This was a very old dragon. Red dragons were one of the good dragons back during the great wars. It is said to that their guardian had turned evil, but good to know at least some of the race was wiser than their guardian and served the elders directly, elders that were not even of Ethar. Dragons according to Talmorg's research, were actually as independent in thought and ways as humans. Right now, Talmorg just wished he knew more about them.

The camp started waking up, immediately. Talmorg realized he had felt no fear, he had just been startled and angry. He returned to the tent, filled with waking officers and informed them of their new alliance. They were filled with awe, but not surprised when the massive creature appeared in the air the next morning, wandering the sky and staying abreast of their forward progress.

*   *   *   *   *   *   *   *   *   *

They had just started off again after breakfast, with Tsarca and Shark in the lead, Epraphil and Shirken guarding the rear and Bonny and Breckheart in the middle. Suddenly out of nowhere, twelve Elven archers and six Elven swordsmen, appeared out of the trees, surrounding them.

"Declare yourselves!" demanded the Elf directly in front of them. Bonny noticed he had markings on the shoulders of his leather tunic, that covered his chain mail, probably rank she thought. She also noticed his face had much sharper features looking far less human than the Elves she was traveling with. The voice of the other Elf, also carried a musical tone she had not heard before.

Breckheart moved his horse to the lead of their small double file and dismounted. "We are a small messenger party. I am Breckheart, this is Tsarca, Shark, Bonny, Epraphil and Shirken."

"Enough diplomat, declare your message!" the Elf added quickly, "We are soldiers of a people at war and have little time for diplomacy and formalities, among soldiers they are waved during this war."

"Indeed!" Breckheart seemed offended, but it did not reflect in his voice. "We precede the armies of the south lands, coming to make alliance with the Lord of Elves."

"Who leads this army?"

"Talmorg Elkinshane."

"Impossible!" The Elf glanced at those surrounding their party, "You will disarm and come with us. You will answer to our captain and we shall learn soon enough if your story bares any truth."

"We choose no quarrel with you."

Breckheart gathered their arms and turned them over to the other Elves.

"We will travel straight through and arrive at camp in the morning."

The Elves led them at a steady pace, not stopping for meals. Bonny was thankful for the trail food in her saddle bags. The Elves kept their word, at nightfall and did not stop, sometime later in the night they stopped and the lead Elf blew a small horn he was carrying.

A challenge came back and a light appeared ahead of them. "Declare your business."

"Emarialt, with unknown captives, possibly friendly."

"Are you coming up the river?" asked the voice in the darkness.

"No, passing to the east." Emarialt answered, Bonny figured this was part of their password or something.

"Step into the light and lead your party through."

After this they traveled some more, until the suns began to glow in the sky. They were challenged again and then escorted into a makeshift camp.

They were sat down outside, by a campfire and given a meager breakfast, while Emarialt disappeared into what looked like a main tent. Bonny was thinking about the extended reverberation in the voices of these Elves, that made them almost musical, when the voices rose in the main tent.

"Don't they know that the Elkinshanes were killed in one fell swoop, by this evil, when the dark kingdom first started forming, some two hundred years ago?!"

A pause.

"You don't know, they must be scaldo spies, or agents. Do any of them wear the mark?"

A few moments later Emarialt came back out of the tent, with an older Elf, whose face had much harder lines. He looked over the group and pointed to Bonny.

"You come with me." he said with absolute authority.

Bonny rose and followed him into the tent and sat down in a chair when he pointed to it. He made a series of musical sounds and Bonny found herself relaxed, even though she knew she was being faced by his anger.

"You are enchanted and cannot lie to me now." he said, "I am the Lord Kerrikai Barhallah."

Bonny could not help laughing, "I would not have lied to you anyway and I am Bonny Harrison of Earth, my lord Kerrikai Barhallah."

Her laughter took him off guard, he looked slightly surprised and the anger faded a little in his voice, "But the message I received cannot be true. These scaldos, or whatever they are, are leading great powers of darkness and evil, bringing war to our land, when they first started their thrusting effort to rule, they laid traps and killed all the Elkinshanes of the Uklian. They left no Elkinshanes living and now the Barhallahs of my cousin's family rule. Now you come along and tell us an Elkinshane is marching an army to our aid." He paced the confined space for a few moments, "Are you coming as our allies?"

"Yes."

"Is there really an army following you and how big is it?"

"Of course, there is. It is approximately ninety-four thousand strong, split into three forces for traveling. They are also supported by a large medical support team, of which I am a part."

"Who leads this army?"

"It is led by Talmorg Elkinshane, son of Erron Elkinshane, son of Talmorg Elkinshane, who traveled south with Tolgus Barhallah."

A fire of anger danced in Kerrikai's eyes again, "I know our family lost one of its sons in our history, named Tolgus, but no songs ever came back and they completely vanished. They have been presumed dead for years now. I shouldn't be angry with you; I should have realized you would not be able to tell if you had been lied to. Unless of course another family has taken on the name. Well, for now don't be nervous, go back to your friends." He walked her to the flap of the tent, "And by the Ancients, I hope, though I cannot believe it, that what you have told me is the actual truth."

Emarialt was standing by outside the tent, when they stepped out. "Lord, your disposition of these matters?"

"Treat them as guests, no weapons and limited freedoms, until we can confirm or deny their story. They have their own tents, set them up in that area over there. Send word back to my uncle, that we might have a large army coming up from the south, being led by an Elf lord."

*   *   *   *   *   *   *   *   *   *

After they ate Eric split them into two groups, just in case the catlings proved aggressive, he was counting on them behaving like a pack. This way the second group would be able to attack the catlings from behind, after they attacked the first group, if they attacked. Himself, Garth, Kole and Stralina would go first, the others would follow. As they moved their way through the crudely dug caves, Eric used what he knew, to feel his way ahead as they approached.

Another ten steps and they would be in the first chamber of the catlings. He grabbed the hilt of his sword, it felt strange in his grip, but he didn't have time for that now. They had stalked halfway across the chamber, when with a sudden yowl, the catlings leaped toward them. The four of them pulled their swords, a sudden blaze of blue light filled the air and the catlings were turning in mid leap to escape from it. It took Eric a moment to realize the blue blaze was coming from the sword in his hand. The rest of their companions joined them, with their swords drawn and they pushed their way through the caves and out into the open moonlit night. The light of the twin moons made seeing almost as easy as broad daylight. Eric looked at the sword, it was not his, it was the sword Gaharias had given him in his vision. He sheathed it quickly, his own swords still hung next to it on his belt.

"Nice blade," laughed Brent, "Did Gaharias teach you the secrets of his sword? Your sword didn't do that before." Brent was sure he recognized the significance of the particular glow, but did not add comment.

"Many of the old Elven blades glowed like that in the hands of an Elf. " Said Garth, " Though that was quite brilliant. I would say, we have an Elf blood, in Eric."

The night air was crisp and they walked on at a brisk pace, making a brief stop for lunch and kept moving. No one else said anything about the sword, so Eric just let it drop. Then Lady Moor came up next to him, with Charlie riding on her shoulders.

'The Lady here was told by the catlings, you drew a blade of the Ancients, or gods if we were on Earth.' Charlie's thoughts entered Eric's conscious thoughts, *'The baser beasts can see the difference between an Elven blade and one forged by and for the old Ancients.'*

'The old Ancients?'

'Yes. That sword was forged for Gaharias to give to a guardian of the future, who had not even been born yet at the time of its forging.'

'A guardian? Then he must have given it to me as a temporary loan.'

'No,' before their conversation could continue, Lady Moor took off ahead of the rest of them.

The small party slipped on through the mountain forests in the cover of darkness as shadows in the night, avoiding moonlit clearings.

396

They stopped under a rock outcrop for lunch. Lady Moor and Charlie showed up with perfect timing. Somewhere above the tree covering they heard the crackling of giant wings.

"Darkwatchers." whispered Calhan, "agents of the scaldos."

"Mutants they have made with evil magic." Jahar answered the unspoken question.

They finished their light meal and continued in silence till morning. The darkwatchers flew by overhead five more times, before the early rays of sunshine caste their light through the forest. They pushed on for a little over an hour, before picking a place to eat and sleep. Hans and Stralina took the first watch. Eric curled up with his cloak wrapping him and his head on his pack.

Sleep did not come quickly. Eric was unsettled, why hadn't Shiheel mentioned the darkwatchers, and yet they were apparently not new to Ether? Then Shiheel was not of Ethar anyway and not as knowledgeable as he had thought. This was for some reason disturbing in the back of his mind. The sagely alien that brought him to this world was not as knowledgeable as he fist seemed?

*   *   *   *   *   *   *   *   *   *

Corenestral Ekberghestia gave the proper signals relieving his fellow sentries and his stem (squad) was posted, hidden along the three southern ridges of their mountain. They would see anything coming from the south along their stretch of the border patrol. This stretch of their frontier border, was important, facing two valleys that swung around from the east and either one could accommodate any army that might try penetrating the back lines. Coren, as he was known for short, knew the rumors of what the message was the strangers had brought to their camp, but he had been warned it could be a devious enemy plot sending an army in under a Glamor Spell. Their chief wizard said there was powerful enough magic among the advance party and they may not have been subject to the truth enchantment, but if they were allies, they were greatly needed.

He was glad his Elves were on a rest from the front lines, his battle group was down, now little over one twelfth of what they started with, seventy-six Elves he now commanded to be exact. They were being called a stem, though a stem actually referred to seventy-two. They had been one of the best Battle Groups of the Uklian and the remnant were now hard-core battle trained fighters. Next week they would start training to form a new battle group, eight hundred and sixty-four strong. The border patrols were also training camps. Each of his men would train their own column, with the exception of his five spooks, he would get seven more.

The wizards would spend the training time working up spells and coordinating their use for battle.

Coren's thoughts were interrupted, when a wisp of smoke turned into Shadoweaver, his best wizard, perched on the branch next to him. "They're coming."

"Who?"

"The rumored army from the south."

"Is it a trick?"

"Can't be those with power have not mastered it. Even you have done better than they have." Shadoweaver smirked.

Coren had studied a little and been told he could become a master, but had chosen to be a leader in what had been thought of as an obsolete border patrol, "How soon will they be in sight?"

"Two hours at the most."

"I should have sent you out earlier, go tell Kerik, I mean Captain Kerrikai Barhallah, his 'king and cousin' are arriving." Shadoweaver turned to smoke and was gone, "Blaster stand ready." the other smiled viciously from the next tree and his eyes and hands turned to a red glow.

An hour had lapsed when Shadoweaver finally returned, "Coren, they travel under the wings of Keltoe, it is foretold in the song of the Ancients."

"Blaster, no show."

Blaster frowned and shot Shadoweaver an accusing look.

*   *   *   *   *   *   *   *   *   *

The crisp autumn air was refreshing and to Talmorg's pleasure they were in motion before the sun crested the horizon. Soon they would reach the rendezvous point and meet their northern cousins. He was confident Breckheart had smoothed the way with the northern Elves. He looked over at Saphrine and she smiled a big beautiful smile and asked, "Do you think they'll send an envoy out to meet us?"

"Who knows, we must remember they are at war, formalities may, or may not be in order. Word may not have yet reached the Lord of the Elves yet.”

“Is it true that we are still subjects of the Elkinshane King of all Elves?”

“According to the laws of the Ancients, yes, but who knows where we stand with Gaharias Emarlandestria, we may have been disowned for lack of piety, but according to the old records of our grandfathers, they were following orders.”

“I don’t think we have been disowned, look what I did with the Iempishadoma.”

“Yeah, look at it, Elves are not supposed to be able to work, other than their own adoma. Do you have Iempish blood?”

“No.” Saphrine was a little surprised she felt insulted, but what if they had been handed off to another Ancient, that could explain why she has not been accepted to lead the priesthood yet.

“Maybe Gaharias has given us to another of the Ancients and we are no longer true Elves.” Talmorg echoed her thoughts.

Saphrine frowned, “We must still be true Elves.” After a few moments of silent thought, she added, “The high priestess has the power to work the ways of the adoma anywhere, maybe Gaharias is showing us a promise for the south.”

“You speak boldly, should I be the Elf lord, by rights of being a distant relation.” he thought for a moment, “Maybe it is true for the south, but why hasn’t he come to you?”

"The promise can only be true, if we win and live through this war, to return south. Perhaps my fate is not yet clear, after all if it were not for Eric, I would already no longer be a part of the future of this world."

As they rode on, towards lunch they discussed their ideas on a unified southern kingdom. They stopped for lunch, with Talmorg slightly disappointed that they had not yet been greeted by the Uklian Elves. They rested and ate lunch around small fires. Talmorg, Saphrine and Erron discuss, with their top officers, the possibilities they faced in the war that lay ahead of them. When they put the fire out, Talmorg noticed a strange puff of darker smoke, seemingly self embodied, leave in a different direction than the rest. Odd as it was, he shrugged it off.

They mounted and led their armies north and then west, through the valley and back north again as it curved around another mountain of the low reaching foothills near the river.

*   *   *   *   *   *   *   *   *

Coren heard the approaching armies, before he saw them, they sounded massive and all on horseback. First came the forward scouts, then he saw the front of six columns, with three leading the way. One of those in the lead could be the rightful heir of the Elkinshanes, he started down the hill to meet them, with Blaster on his left and Shadoweaver on his right.

As they advanced forward, Talmorg watched the three forms appear out of the forest in front of them. Their sharp features could be seen from quite the distance and if he had not already known they used the magic of the elkinadoma, singing, he would have known it from the sharpness of their features, especially the two on the outside. When they were close enough Talmorg called the columns to a halt and he and Saphrine dismounted and stepped forward to greet them. Noting their attire and mannerisms Talmorg knew they were not a welcoming envoy, but rather in the ranks of the military.

"Greetings, I am Talmorg Elkinshane, Prince heir to the throne of the Walled City of Talmorg and Lord commander of the combined armies of the south lands." he said with a slight bow and the open right hand of friendship, then added, "This is Saphrine Barhallah, princess and heir to the throne of Efra, my betrothed and assistant commander of the combined armies." Saphrine gave a slight bow, with the open hand of friendship.

"Greetings, I'm Corenestral Ekberghestia, captain of the third battle group of the Uklian Elves." Coren spoke curtly, "This is Shadoweaver and Blaster. Your armies by far exceed what we were expecting when your messengers arrived, not that they didn't properly warn us. We'll need you to camp in this valley for tonight. I will escort you and your top officers to our headquarters, to confer with the Lord Kerrikai Barhallah. After a pause he said to Saphrine, "My Lady, you have a resemblance."

"Calbork set camp, Freebic, Father, I need you with me." Talmorg yelled this over his shoulder, then turned back to Coren, "I must tell you captain Ekberghestia, what you see here, is a little over thirty-one thousand fighters and about six thousand medical support and it is only about one third of the total combined armies coming to join with your forces against the threat to our continent and world. The next force should be arriving in two days, dominantly human and in three the final third, dominantly Dwarves."

"That is roughly one hundred and twenty nine battle groups." Coren said with one eyebrow raised in impressed thought, "This is pertinent information for Lord Barhallah. We need to make haste and arrive at camp before dark. Is Keltoe coming too?"

"He does as he wishes." Talmorg answered, looking with respect at the massive winged reptile circling like a hawk high above the armies making camp in the valley.

As they walked Talmorg wondered about the Lord Barhallah he would shortly meet. He knew from his histories, that the Barhallahs were the priests to the Ancients and the Elkinshanes were the Lords of the Elves, "How is it, Captain Ekberghestia, that one of the priesthood is in the position of an Elven lord?"

"Please, My Lord, excuse me for any rudeness in this matter, but there is doubt and concern as to who you really are and until that is settled, I am not at free liberty, to indulge you with the state of affairs in the Uklian." Coren was truly apologetic, then shrugged and added, "This much I will tell you, the Elves are filled with sadness and mourning, however their efforts are not lulled in the least. Also, while I'm thinking of it, if you would please just address me as Coren, I feel more comfortable thinking my comrades in battle are also my friends."

"Very well, Coren," Talmorg paused, changing the direction of his thoughts, "I will direct my questions and inquiries at Lord Barhallah. Your directness shows your trust in my integrity and your discretion shows your loyalty to the Uklian and the Elkinadoma."

Talmorg, Saphrine, Freebic and Erron went the rest of the way with their escorts in silence, and on foot. It took them almost an hour to reach the well concealed encampment and they were taken directly to the command tent of Lord Barhallah.

"Wait here one moment." Coren instructed them as they reached the tent and then slipped in. He was out of their sight for but a few moments, when the tent flaps were opened from both sides. Standing about five steps in front of them, was an Elf in priest robes, with the mantel of an Elf lord draped over his shoulders.

Talmorg's look of cynicism did not go unnoticed by Lord Kerrikai, before he greeted them, "Welcome, Talmorg Elkinshane and welcome to the comrades of the Elf lord. I am the Lord Kerrikai Barhallah, son of the priests of Gaharias Emarlandrestia. Forgive our discourtesy and meager accommodations, but please do come in, a hearty meal awaits us over which we can talk."

"Thank you, Lord Barhallah, I understand the conditions of war." Talmorg said as they entered the tent, "Allow me to introduce you to, my father King Erron Elkinshane, Freebic Elkinshane and Saphrine Barhallah."

"Please accept my welcome and apologies, for the way we dealt with your messenger party. I had doubts about your identities, after all we are at war, so I called upon Gaharias Emarlandrestia, as is the rights of the priesthood and he has established for me, who you are."

"It is well that your doubts are cleared, but how is it that a priest is also a lord?" Talmorg inquired, considering that his ancestral family might be too small to hold all its proper positions, but even then they would have avoided adding the extra responsibility to the already burdened priesthood.

"It happened before we knew we had an enemy, before we were at war. The enemy is led by three wizards of another world, that descended out of the sky. They are known among their minions as Scaldorians. They sent out into our midst a beetle like bug, that went undetected, until it was too late. These scarabs slew all of the Elkinshanes in one night, taking from our peoples the powers of the Elf lords. Since then, we have called upon the powers of the elkinadoma to ward off any similar attack. We believe they thought to throw us into internal turmoil and disorder by their action. Instead, our people turned to us the priesthood to take the seat of rule, until the power of the Elkinadoma can be found in another. If you know history, Talmorg, then you know, that the types of magic of the Elkinadoma are divided among our peoples. The Elkinshanes were given the ruling powers over the Adoma. It will deteriorate, without at least one, to keep its heart of life. Erron sire, you and your son Talmorg are the heirs and bloodline of this power."

"It is near time for me to transfer my inheritance," King Erron stated flatly, "to a son and it is Talmorg here, who has proven most apt. Let him speak as the last son, but he has never practiced the magics as you can see by the roundness of his features. I have brought with me the Scepter of Elkinshane, we can transfer the title of Elkinshane if we need to."

"Very well, my lord." Kerrikai looked thoughtfully, wondering if this was the giving of the inheritance to another, from the ancient song. There was a pause in conversation while they all ate involved in their own thoughts.

After several minutes, Talmorg broke the silence, as much thinking out loud, as addressing the others with him, "We have come to help in a war that threatens the world. We don't know the war and the warriors we join, don't know us. I believe we should leave the politics alone, at least until the war is won, but I say now, I have a responsibility, laid upon my shoulders, to see to it the Elves of the Uklian Elkinadoma have the best leaders. The Elkinshanes, or Elf lords and the Barhallahs, or called of the barh, the Ancients also known as priests are a division of power set with wisdom, that neither should be corrupted by their power. The present arrangement is not good in the long scheme of things; however, it is not best to disrupt it in the midst of war and your family does well in their service to Emarlandestria and the Elves. Our people though, will also need lords they know and trust, so when the time comes to make decisions, I will have thought it through. For now, I shall give new life to the heart of the Elkinadoma, but I will exercise her massive powers under your current structure of command."

Kerrikai took a long deep breath and carefully let out a deep sigh,

"You have the wisdom of Terrikai. It would be an honor to serve you, but you are right it would breed doubts in loyalties at this time, and that would be an added weakness."

Tension that had hung in the shadows like cobwebs dissipated and their conversation flowed more freely. Kerrikai and Coren filled them in on the battle lines of battle and strategies being employed. They discussed at length alternatives including what Talmorg had learned from Eric and the powers of the Elkinadoma and the nature of Talmorg's armies. Hours passed with the whole group in deep conversation, decisions were made and plans were set.

Coren would not be training a new Battle Group this time. His command would be attached to Talmorg, because he knew their battle field. It was his field and he knew every tree and bush, and most importantly, he knew the ways of their enemies. He would start mixing his men with Talmorg's armies in the morning. They would not resent missing their rest from battle, there was some comfort in joining with already trained troops with some experience. It was much more likely that this would turn the war to their favor and possible victory.

CHAPTER 22

War

Talmorg would be gone for three days, that was how much time he would need to give new life to the Elkinadoma and speak with Arimith Barhallah, Kerrikai's distant uncle and high priest to the Elves. He had chosen to take only three companions with him, Saphrine to sing new growth, Bonny for her healing powers and Ziph an Eftite wizard, one of Hesheil's understudies. They were now preparing for departure. The Elkinadoma still had sufficient power to transport them to its heart and Talmorg had been given the Staff of Elkinshane.

"Are we ready?" he asked and they all nodded. He lifted the staff over his head, a blue aura surrounded them and he spoke, almost sang, three words in the ancient tongue. As if they had been a mirage, they vanished from the sight of those who stood by to see them off.

When the blue glow faded, Bonny could see they were standing atop a knoll within a circle of stones. There was a wooden throne in front of her, it looked like it grew that way, for that matter the strange stump was completely grown over with bark, as though it was somehow still alive. Looking around she felt some disorientation, though the circle of stones seemed somehow familiar, yet she couldn't quite place it. Outside the stones that hedged them, was a field that spread for over a hundred yards in every direction. There was something about the stones..., the pattern..., she had seen something similar before. Closing her eyes, she could sense great power where she stood, the living power of the Elkinadoma. On an urge from within, she reached out and touched the living wooden throne. Bonny didn't notice but under her touch, split, chips and cracks in the bark healed and smoothed over. She felt the surging of power, course through her very soul, and heard her mind sing songs in a language she had never heard before.

Bonny opened her eyes, not realizing she had closed them until they again beheld the view around her. A tall Elf was approaching them and Talmorg and the others were walking up to meet him. She quickly moved to join them.

Talmorg stopped, slid the staff through the side of his belt, then extended both hands, palms forward in the ancient greeting of open friendship, "I am Talmorg Elkinshane, I bring with me Saphrine Barhallah, Bonny Harrison, and Ziph the Eftite. We greet our Elven brother."

The other Elf took one more step and placed his palms against Talmorg's, "I am Arimith Barhallah, High Priest of the Uklian. I have been waiting for you. I bid you welcome with gladness that as foretold you made it on time." He then welcomed each of the others in turn, "Welcome Ziph the Eftite master of magics from the stars, healer of stone... Welcome Saphrine Barhallah, voice of springtime gold... Welcome Bonny Harrison, healer of the Ancients and Ancient of the new order. No one has ever ministered healing to the heart throne before. If you look around the edge of the clearing, you will see seven great trees that stand high above the rest." She looked at each as he pointed to them, "They are the guardians

and the throne is their common heart root." This surprised Bonny a
little because each of the seven trees was of a different kind, though she
recognized none of them, they looked like great guardians. "Talmorg your
time for now is short, I have a special meal prepared and then we will give
service to the Elkinadoma."

They walked out between the stones and followed Arimith into the
forest. The homes of the Uklian Elves were grown out of the forest. The
trees grew to form the walls, floors, ceilings and roofs, within the forest
canopy. They could not be seen from the outside, unless you knew exactly
where they were. The meal they ate was herbs and teas, consumed as part
of a ritual.

Once they started, they were to talk and think about nothing but
the renewal of the Elkinadoma. Bonny was to be continually ministering
to the guardians. Ziph was to heal the stones. Saphrine was to walk
around singing to everything in the circle of the guardians. Talmorg would
summon strength to the heart and Arimith would be given to the care
of the grounds, with three other priests. The ritual lasted for two days,
nonstop, after which they all slept. The third day Bonny woke up early,
the two days prior were unclear in her memory, distorted images she could
not put to order or purpose. She decided that the herbs they had eaten must
have had psychedelic effects, that aided in the workings of their magics.
Her most amusing memory was running naked, laying hands on and
singing to the guardians. She dressed and found breakfast on a table in her
room, so she ate before stepping out into the main hall of her Elven host's

abode.

"Good morning, M'Lady." a young Elf greeted her as she stepped out, "The Elkinadoma is restored and they are saying it has greater power than ever before and you had something to do with it. My apologize, I am babbling, Adriel, I am your guide and servant. Lord Talmorg is in conference with the Barhallahs."

Adriel was the first black haired Elf Bonny had seen. He had a big bright smile and the sharp features of the Uklian Elves. The cuffs of his sleeves were blue with stars, he was a wizard at least in training. Bonny smiled back, "I would like to see the heart of the Elkinadoma again."

Adriel knew what she meant, "This way, follow me." They walked back through the forest, with Adriel overflowing with energetic conversation, causing Bonny to wonder if he talked to himself when no one else was around. When they stepped out Bonny was awed at the change. First the grass was no longer a wild field, it was fresh even growth, no more than three inches tall. The Guardian trees looked like they had grown another ten feet taller. The stones, to her eyes they were living stones, they were glowing. Then it hit her, Stonehenge, their patterns were similar to a circle of stone she had seen when she visited England, except this formation was also complete, she wondered in amazement. The whole thing was beautiful. Bonny sat down, had there been an Adoma on Earth once, or could Stonehenge be a mimic of this splendor. She asked Adriel if he knew.

"I'm not sure, some of the old songs almost mention such, but we have little knowledge of Earth, outside of its historical effects on Ethar."

"Let's go back." Bonny said standing up.

* * * * * * * * * *

Balak was irritable when he walked into the room. Salgek and Drogeshus were already there. He had been the one to call this meeting.

"What is the meaning of this?" Salgek asked.

"Fools, you said only one family had the power to keep the Elkinadoma alive. Well, it's back and neither of you knew it. On top of that, when we got here you said the south had no real magic of consequence, nothing to worry about. No unity and just little weak armies. Well, your minor kingdoms that we'll conquer or subdue later, one at a time have reinforced our enemies on the west, with over a hundred thousand strong and almost as much to the east. We now fight a greater war than we planned. How did our enemy grow without you two even seeing it? Do I have to do everything?"

"I told you when we got here, the ancient magics of this land were of great power, possibly even equal to our own though different." Drogeshus snapped back at him, "If awakened, they would be a true test of our continuous power source." Bringing his temper back under control, he continued, "I told you we should be patient and more subtle, cultivate a base source of food among the lower creatures and let the next generation rise up and conquer the world."

Slamming a tentacle on the table, Balak went on, his anger no less than when he started, "But you also assured us of no major magical powers on this continent, just two families to worry about. One we got rid of, but you, Salgek blundered with the dwarves, giving us two major battle fronts prematurely."

"Maybe we should vanish, go into hiding, like brave warriors for a while." Salgek sarcastically gestured, "A smart cat runs from too many mice, right?"

"Alright, alright, we've made mistakes. We need to rethink." Balak sat down with the others, "So far we have been able to pit these animals against each other. The minds of the scattered tribes were easy to manipulate, but if things escalate too much more, too fast, we will wind up directly involved. We need to mind link."

"By the way, three more of the night watchers haven't returned." Drogeshus commented, "The last one started to curse the smell of a dragon before it died. I think we need smaller probes, less conspicuous."

"Agreed. Mind lock begin."

Balak paced the floors. The mind lock had been disturbing. The battle was progressing well, with the night watchers commanding and leading the mixed forces. Nightwatchers were magical demons from another time, who had submitted to them in exchange for a rebirth. There was something out there that continued to elude them, something more powerful than the demons. The only hint they had was one of the night watchers cursed the smell of dragons, but dragons supposedly vanished over a thousand years earlier, if they were even real to start with.

Then, there was the south lands to consider, their spies had never reported back from the southeast. On top of that the entire south had somehow been warned, united and was joining the enemies in battle. He wondered if surviving Eftites had also reached this far away world. The thought alone chilled him through every nerve, remembering the destruction of their home worlds. He blamed the Eftites and found consolation only in believing they were now extinct. Balak and his mates were a remnant of their civilization, where survival had depended on ruthlessness, until they were of age to mate. Only once they were mated did they start to learn to work together. Balak himself like his mates had scattered offspring in the form of worms across the mountains, but none were yet old enough to surface. They would not be a resource or learn civilized ways for several years. He was a brown shell, Drogeshus was red-brown and Salgek was a yellow-brown, together they became a Scaldorians, a hope for survival of truly the highest life form.

Yet there were things out there that eluded them and threatened the establishment of their new world. Was it possible that something else approached their evolutionary equal? No, he could not believe that for a moment, the food is always lower on the evolutionary level than the feeder. The Eftites had come close to equal, but they were no more. Yet what was out there now? The magics here were foreign to them and at first much had gone undetected. Now he wished he had some of the old devices they had used back on Scaldor for locating magical powers in use. The less effective spells they used proved their faultiness, for now many unknowns joined in the battle against them. Now their spies the darkwatchers were being picked off quite effectively, and everything indicated that the enemy had somehow raised a dragon out of nowhere.

*   *   *   *   *   *   *   *   *

*

Talmorg set his command camp fifteen miles behind the front lines, along with the medical support encampment. He was sitting in the command tent with his select advisers. In general, their plans of action were set. They were in charge of the southern third of the Elven battle field, and acknowledgment messages had been received from all of the field commanders.

He had selected his own advisors and others had been selected for him by those he selected. Among them were Saphrine, Prince Ashkin, Brask Scaller, as military advisers of his own. Shiheel, Darset, medical adviser, Hesheil, and Keltoe who took on human form now for their meetings, Coren and his inseparable spooks, Shadoweaver and Blaster, were also among his private counsel.

"The Adoma is in readiness." Talmorg continued, "The silent retreat is to be tonight." He turned to Saphrine, "Each of us has our part." He then looked each of them in the eyes around the circle, "Tonight the Black River will conceal the land in heavy fog to hide its changes. Is there any further discussion?"

All that were seated there asserted their readiness, each in their turn including the messengers back to the other command centers. The meeting was adjourned, leaving Talmorg and Saphrine alone as the others

415

vanished into the dark of the late evening. Talmorg felt the power of the Elkinadoma pulsing through him with life, it was as if he and it had always been one. He could feel the history of his Elven homeland, feeling the memories of the Elkinadoma as though they were his own, yet separate and new to him, a storehouse of knowledge to serve a wise and powerful ruler, readily there to draw from. Talmorg would know when the battle lines withdrew into the Elkinadoma, when the fog covered the land and when the enemy advanced. He smiled up at Saphrine, "We should sleep while we can, soon we will have little time for sleep."

Coren went to the river with Shadoweaver and Blaster, where they started upstream. Coren led his spooks as they sporadically issued forth murmurings, accompanied by ritualistic motions, causing the river to start billowing forth thick mist as they passed. It took them two hours to reach their designated turn off point. They headed north and spread a line of some black stuff as they went, to Coren it looked like no more than dirt. If he had not been familiar with Blaster's handy-work he would not have taken them seriously. By the time they finished they started encountering retreating forces, being joined by the forces of the south lands, setting up a new front line. The troops were concealing themselves no more than a hundred yards from the line of Blaster's magic dirt they had been spreading.

Suddenly Blaster signal a stop, bent over and picked up a small red rock, "We've reached Karias' line." They turned and joined the new line vanishing into the trees just as the forest started weaving with a strange new life.

It was a couple of hours before sunrise when Talmorg and Saphrine stepped out of their tent. Talmorg closed his eyes and reached out with the Elkinadoma and pulled in. He felt the land separate just below the rooted network of the ground surface, leaving a concealed, seemingly bottomless trench between his people on the line and the enemy, no less than twenty yards from the newly formed lines.

Saphrine began to sing, unlike her previous use of her new found magic, she had purpose. Her voice reached out in an eerie wail that slipped out into the night causing a shift in the forest, as the trees moved to form a defensive barrier about ten yards closer than the hidden trench. They finished their work as the first rays of the sun started burning off their fog cover.

Five Darkwatchers had been brought down during the night, three by Keltoe, one each by Shiheel and Hesheil. If all went as planned, all they needed now was to wait for the Scaldorian forces to advance. They were starting, Talmorg could feel it.

Bonny and Darset were busy setting up the medical camp and organizing, between handling the injured and wounded. Over half of the medics had already been dispatched to the front lines. As night settled in so did their camp. It was in the early morning when they started receiving the war injured from the retreated front line.

It seemed to Bonny that the magic enhancement of her medical arts increased with use. A few times she thought she actually saw flesh mending as she worked on the injuries. When she sat down to breakfast, she thought of her mom and then of Eric, wondering when she would see them next.

*　　*　　*　　*　　*　　*　　*　　*　　*　　*

Eric looked out across the mountains ahead as they descended from the Gnar Pass. The snow and ice caps were majestically jutting up into the clouds. Lady Moor was their guide now, leaping up and down ledges, where they needed ropes. The mountains here were barren open rock and they were still alive with geothermal activity. Streams, steam and smoke were scattered throughout the black and white panorama giving Eric the feeling he was walking across the skeleton of a mountain range, unable to sustain life of any sort. It also left them openly visible to anything that might be scouting the area, which did not set well with Eric, though he did not feel any immediate threat.

The party had become sullen and morosely quiet since their first encounter with the darkwatchers. Eric had denounced the use of any magics unless they should absolutely need it, considering the possibility of its detection and exposing their secret approach to Darval Keep. Eric was not without his own misgivings, starting with Shiheel who apparently knew less than he made out to know, and he set to evaded the enemy's knowledge of the presence of his kind. The enemy according to Shiheel, had destroyed his home world. Supposedly Shiheel had just brought him into this world for the resolution of the lesser war, but had he been simply holding back the real truth? Maybe Shiheel did not even know why.

Then there was the matter of the ancient ones, Gaharias had told him he was counted among them, yet they were forbidden to act directly in the affairs of the races. Was he an exception or a criminal against the forbidding of the older Ancients, which seemed to him to be, no more, or less than gods of the gods in this world? With gods and lesser gods how do they fit into the scheme of good and evil. How much was hidden from him and he had not missed the fact that his own last name was a part of the last name of Gaharias Emarlandestria's. Was it just a coincidence? Even their quest to Darval Keep bothered him, who had abandoned it to begin with and why had no one else taken it up sooner? Who was or what was Darval?

'*Charlie.*' Eric thought to the Gerpin, who was riding on his waist pack again.

'*Yes.*' the answer came clear in his mind.

'*Who was Darval?*'

'*He is Gaharias' twin brother.*'

'*A member of the council of the Ancients?*'

'*No, he disappeared during the great wars, along with others of the dark pact, just before they lost.*'

'*But the keep?*'

'*It has been emptied for over five thousand years; it had been sunken into the mountains. Somehow the Scaldorians resurrected it.*'

The entire group paused briefly to eat their midnight meal, halfway up the other side of the barren stretch of rocky valley. Eric realized they had traversed, but a narrow part of the naked, dead ground, when they were back in the forest cover by sunrise. Some tension lifted with dinner, but silence prevailed for the next two days. Then on the third day Stralina dropped back with Eric on the narrow trail, marked only by odd rock piles.

"The home of the mountain Ogres is not far from here." She told him, "They are the smartest of their kind and they are not flesh eaters."

"Are they friendly?"

"You jest. A friendly Ogre. Of course not, though they are less aggressive and more organized. They actually form tribes and have a developed social order. I am sure we are avoiding them, but we need to watch for traps."

"We should already be keeping our eyes open for anything unusual; we have no idea what we will run into next." Eric said with a smile. This area was known only by Stralina and Lady Moor, and right now the huge cat was off gallivanting around somewhere in the forest. "Are you comfortable letting Garth and Kedd lead the way?"

"I needn't be up there all of the time, we're in the company of good trackers." She smirked, "Besides, I left good instructions and told them what to watch for.... and I would know if we started to get off track."

Hans Spardic, who was following Eric, spoke up, "You speak of Mountain Ogres, do you forget we are already in Scaldorian ruled lands, any Ogres are probably already impressed in the scaldorian army. I doubt they would leave any resource untapped. We have more to watch for than mountain Ogres."

Jahar spoke over his shoulder in front of them, "Yeah, in addition to the Darkwatchers, mounted patrols scout everywhere continuously, plus their magic eyes can see different places in the kingdom, and they wander the land."

"But if ya know how to avoid them ya can do it pretty easy. They can see only an area of about fifteen feet in diameter and you can tell when they're look'en about from a good distance off. They cause a circle a wind, like little dust devils around what they'r look'en at." Calhan added.

"Sounds like a defective crystal ball." Eric snickered to himself, "or maybe a mercury dish, or a magic mirror. Would you happen to know if they use any tool or object to see with?"

"Turks thunder, I would never want ta know the other end. those cursed scaldo's are there. We'd be eaten alive." Calhan said, "at least rumor has it that's how some a us has disappeared.,. Mostly prisoners though."

Garth suddenly brought them to a halt, causing them to bunch up. He pointed to the ground ahead of them, and said, "Ten fifteen Ogres, thirty Milmorgs, five rackenwolves, and maybe even a darkwatcher."

"They're movin west, could be they're leav'en from the east, er headed to the west front, but my guess'd be a scout'en party, do'in the area." Kedd suggested, "If they haven't already crossed our trail, them er another party will. If they got a darkwatcher we can't hide our pass'in from em, might even draw they're attention with our ability fer magic. They can detect it, when it's around."

"Then we need to move more quickly." Eric said and started forward.

Hans stopped him, "Booby traps." he stated simply, pointing at the ground ahead, "Some form of magic. See those red balls."

"Alright, caution is needed." Eric conceded, "How do we get through?"

"It appears that the only way to disarm them is with magic." Brent said, "All they are is alert signals. You would never know it if you stepped on one, but the darkwatchers would know something passed by. If we disarm them, we would use magic and alert the darkwatchers that something with magic passed by."

"Or we go after them before they go after us." Kedd suggested with a wicked smile.

"No, I think we should rest a day here first," Eric said, "then we can devise a plan of action."

They decided not to pitch a camp and to stick with cold rations and traveling food. Charlie managed to supply them with an abundance from the land. They set up guard duties and rested. Eric sat and meditated.

*   *   *   *   *   *   *   *   *   *

Coren sat ready, holding light tension on the string of his bow, with an arrow between his fingers. Blaster had treated all Coren's arrow tips with magic, so they would work on the darkwatchers. Shadoweaver had flashed him a hand signal a few moments earlier indicating the enemy's approach, now he could hear the movement ahead.

The first Milmorgs appeared and started across the root network that webbed over the trench, Talmorg had formed with the Elkinadoma. They were followed closely by Ogres. Scattered infrequently among the armies that approached them, were darkwatchers and other demons summoned by the Scaldorians, to command the other minions. When the first of these crossed the trail, he had laid with Shadoweaver, Blaster threw what appeared to be a rock at first, until it burst with multicolored flame. Suddenly a blast of fire erupted out of the ground, slicing through the enemy, taking with it everything including Milmorgs, Ogres and demons. The wall of fire stretched in both directions, impenetrable, trapping a smaller portion of the enemy on their side of the fire line and preventing any further approach of the rest of the assaulting forces.

What happened next caught Coren's breath for a moment, even though he was expecting it, even counting on it. Before they realized they were in a trap, the root network dropped out from under the Scaldorian minions, dropping them into the depths of the ground. Most of the surviving darkwatchers and winged demons, took to the air, avoiding the trap before Ethar's mouth slammed shut. That was when Coren and the rest of the archers let loose their first volley of arrows.

Coren's magic arrow flew true and one darkwatcher burst into a black cloud of smoke and dissipated. Looking for his next target, he saw only two darkwatchers and one demon left, one of the darkwatchers within his range. Before he could release his next arrow, and Coren was quick, lightening flew from the darkwatchers hands in eight directions, one bolt hitting the tree he was in. He remembered falling and never knew if the arrow he let go hit its target.

Talmorg drew a deep breath and opened his eyes. He needed rest, so did the Elkinadoma. As long as he was within its realm, they were one, him and the land. He would sleep, but he would first visit Darset, Elisha, Bonny and the medical camp.

He sipped the now cold broth, sitting a few moments longer, before he stood up and walked to the tent flap. He stepped out. The camp was quiet but alert, as Talmorg walked through. Activity picked up as he approached the medical camp. He located Bonny first, in the kitchen tent, sitting at a table sipping some herb brew.

Bonny looked up from the table as she sipped the strange tea. "Greetings, Lord Elkinshane." she said acknowledging Talmorg's approach.

"Hello, Lady Bonny Harrison," he winked with an exaggerated mock bow, "I suspect you shall be quite busy soon; we have met the enemy and they suffer great losses, yet we have not gone unharmed. We should start seeing casualties arriving soon."

Bonny half smiled a pained smile, "It is expected in war my liege." She took his hand as he sat down across from her, "In all that has happened, we have done well and we shall do well. If my touch really does heal, let it grant you the rest you need."

To Talmorg's amazement he felt renewed in strength and revived power running freely through the Elkinadoma. It felt good. "Thank you. Be ready for anything." Talmorg stood up, he still had to see Darset and Elisha. "Where would I find Darset?"

"She'd be in the hospital tent right now."

"Thank you again." Talmorg turned and headed back out of the kitchen tent.

Bonny stared down into her tea. She pondered how busy they would get and the nature of their facilities. To her it was more primitive than meatball surgery, yet somehow more advanced. Maybe it was just different, she decided.

As she stared at her tea, the surface rippled and a face appeared. She caught her breath, it was Shadoweaver. She heard his voice in her head, "Oh wise and sacred ancient ones, call to safety Coren and Blaster, my brothers in battle, they have fallen defending our homeland and all of Ethar from evil. Call them to you and tend to their needs." Shadoweaver repeated his plea, with a few variations. Her heart went out to his pleas and Bonny decided he was casting some spell and needed her to call them to finish the spell.

She spoke softly to her tea cup, "Coren, Blaster, come to me, come now." She could feel her face turning red with embarrassment, feeling foolish as she repeated herself, talking to a cup of tea.

Coren and Blaster appeared on makeshift litters, on the ground next to her. Coren lay unconscious and Blaster had both legs mangled and a burn across his face. Blaster looked up at her in disbelief, but said nothing. Bonny called to a handful of attendants, who were also in the kitchen tent, "Quickly, come here and take these litters to the main hospital tent."

"Yes, Lady Bonny." One of the attendants answered as they got up from their table. She did not know them, yet, but they knew her. There were four that came over and picked up the litters. Bonny followed them out of the tent, staying with them as they carried Coren and Blaster through the camp and into the hospital tent.

Darset saw them enter the tent and rushed over, "That was quick, Talmorg just walked out. How did these two get here?" she asked glancing around.

"Put them on those first two tables." Bonny said to the litter bearers, pointing to the back of the tent, then answered Darset, "Shadoweaver had something to do with getting them here. He appeared in my tea cup and told me to call them."

"Whatever," Darset shrugged, "They need help and their here. Shareen, Elseirra start taking care of this one, Bonny you and I will tend to Coren first."

After thoroughly examining him, Bonny looked up at Darset, "He has taken a blow to the back of his head, I haven't located any other injuries, other than minor scratches and bruises."

Darset agreed and they worked on him for almost an hour, with two Elves assisting, by keeping him alive with their magic while they worked. They worked with meticulous care, comparing techniques and methods of operating. When they were finished, they wrapped his head and the Elves placed a pulsing green amulet about his neck. Bonny was learning to feel the magic she imparted, she knew that the only hope Coren really had was that magic.

The others were finished with Blaster about the same time. He had remained awake the entire time and was still staring at Bonny when she turned to face him.

"You answered it, Shadoweaver's call to the Ancients." Blaster stated, unable to change the bewildered expression on his face. Other Elves that heard, gave rather odd glances at Blaster and Bonny.

"I only did what he asked." Bonny answered. Darset seemed to move intentionally away from their conversation, while other Elves were trying not to make it obvious they were listening in. "Should I have ignored his plea and not called you?"

"Oh no, we appreciate your help. I am just confused by the fact that you were able to answer such a summons." He shook his head and looked away. "You don't even know what you did, yet it has profound significance on the future, for the human race will then have access." When he finished the enigmatic statement, he fell asleep.

Bonny turned not understanding what Blaster was talking about and followed Darset. She caught up with her at the sterilizing table, where she dropped off the few tools they had used.

"Well, Bonny, that was just the beginning, soon we will be too busy to think in here."

"I know that Darset, but what was Blaster talking about that it bothered everyone so much?"

Darset moved as though she was going to ignore what Bonny had asked her, then turned back and faced her full, "He spoke of the Ancients. Humans are not supposed to know about them, they are the lesser gods of this world and the old ancients are gods of the gods..., But they are not supposed to be known to, or spoken of to humans, who are not of this world, or of its gods."

"Shadoweaver was calling upon the Ancients, to take Coren and Blaster to safety, 'take them to you'. Shadoweaver pleaded for the Ancients to call Coren and Blaster. Finally, I decided he was trying to tell me to call them, so I did and here they are."

Darset looked at her with doubt filling her eyes, but simply said, "Maybe you were just the safety the Ancients brought them to."

"Maybe." Bonny said, though neither of them were satisfied or believed that was the answer.

*   *   *   *   *   *   *   *   *   *

Shiheel and Hesheil rode their tensor disc, battling the winged demons with Keltoe and the three other dragons that had answered Keltoe's summon for aid. Only two of the other dragons had survived when they reached their rendezvous behind the rocks of the second defensive retreat line. The third had been a younger green dragon, Cugen, took down by five darkwatchers, before the black dragon, Shelock and the

Silver dragon Darcose could come to his aid.

"Nothing it seems can get past you two, yet, you little blue fire suckers." Keltoe said, "and I have held my own, but we need more air support, and I have a way."

"It would take too long to get our brethren here." Shelock stated.

"The great Rocs are not capable of fighting the demons," Shiheel added, "and even if we had enough wizards to ride them, they would still be weak against the demons."

"Have you not heard of the magic that can make dragons from men?" Keltoe asked.

"It was lost before my birth." Darcose countered.

"Ah not lost," Keltoe rumbled, "and not before my birth. It was a magic despised by the races, because it resulted in great wizards among the humans, such as Merlin and Margose. It was stopped out of fear, because some of the men became too aggressive. I have long saved twenty-five of the old dragon amulets. They take three hundred years to make and then only one out of four turns out right. They were too valuable to destroy. We will need volunteers from among the humans, if we are to use them, however. Unfortunately we do not have the time to first examine the character of each of the volunteers we get."

"I can seek them out from among those I already know." Shiheel said, "Shelheen can ride in my place in the interim."

"We have less than an hour before the wall of fire falls." Hesheil warned.

"I entrust you with these amulets, Shiheel." Keltoe said, pulling twenty-five stone carvings of dragons out of the air, hanging from fine silver chains. "They shall return to me should I call them."

Shiheel took them and parted their company.

Shadoweaver was now field commander to Coren's men and acting adviser to the southern armies. From what he had seen of the reports he had received; he was quite impressed. The strange Eftites had taken down several Darkwatchers and demons with strange powers, they claimed were not magic. The rest of the south land armies also seemed familiar with non-conventional means of warfare and camouflage. Casualties and injuries were much less than he had expected and he now estimated that better than two thirds of the enemy demons in their sector had been destroyed. They were dug in now at their secondary retreat line and set to wait.

Shadoweaver had a little time to think and his mind went to his friends. It puzzled him how that human woman had been able to answer his call to the Ancients. He would like to think that Gaharias had orchestrated it, but he knew it was not true. In fact, the only possible answer he could think of, was that Bonny was now one of the Ancients by some means beyond his understanding. This would mean that Ethar had excepted humans as its own people and now the races could not argue it. It would be declared to and made known by all of the Ancients. How would the dark council take this? Times were strange, was this the beginning of another series of great wars?

A messenger of Hanser Schultzmann approached him, "What news do you bring friend?"

"The horsemen are ready." the young man with overly decorated light armor stated.

The horsemen were a glory to watch, all over dressed with plumbs and decorations, but quick and ruthless. They were prepared to make lightning strikes and keep the Scaldorian minions confused.

Shiheel had come and taken twenty-eight men and fifty-six Eftites out of their front lines. From what Shadoweaver understood, that meant eighty-four of the best fighters taken out of the ground troops, to fight up in the air. He felt as though he was of little use in the token position as adviser to an army so mixed, whose resources he did not know or understand. Strange new strategies, magics that are not magical, devastating an enemy by running away and a kingdom with not just Ancients, but human Ancients in its service. He had to concentrate on what he did know and could use to help in his part in this war, as he watched a new age of magic coming into play. He already missed Blaster and Coren and he ached to have his friends back at his side.

"Keltoe," Shiheel was saying, "two Eftites on the backs of each of the dragons, will increase firepower and provide better look out, nothing can sneak up from behind. I will vouch for their accuracy and with three limbs grappled on, they will not fall off."

"Very well, your argument does seem to bear wisdom." Keltoe turned to the small horde of dragons, "As the Eftites mount take to the air, the wall of fire is starting to lower. Remember to rely on your reflexes, you will have no time to think through your counter attacks!"

As they took to the air Keltoe sent up a request to the old ones, who had created dragons long before the Ancients, to watch over and protect these men of courage, who took on the form of dragons. He did regret that the amulets were now a part of these men and for all practical purposes these men were now dragons with the ability to transform back and forth at will. Keltoe would have to answer to the world council of dragons, for the amulets now, but this he did not regret as he lifted up into the air.

As Shiheel and Hesheil rose in the air behind Keltoe, the first exchange of fire and lightening burst into the late afternoon, early evening sky. Two dragons were descending in a semi guided fall, injured and no longer able to maintain stable flight. The number of demons had been cut in half and those that remained were falling back out of the dragon's range. The Ground battle seemed to move in waves back and forth from the glances from above.

CHAPTER 23

Closing In

Salgek was pacing again, stopping each time he reached the end of the room to stare out the window of Darval Keep, across the rocky mountain wasteland. He wondered briefly about the prior residence of the keep. Why had it been laid hidden totally intact, in a dimensional abyss, as if left waiting for them, or its previous owners intended to return. The Scaldorian magic brought it out of hiding with no problem, yet whoever was there before would have been a formidable enemy. Salgek believed there was no entity greater than himself, Scaldorians believed in no gods and nothing greater than themselves. Even the demons they raised from the dead were no match for them.

Things were not as they should be, the eastern front was being slowed by a uniting of the enemy kingdoms and a half a million reinforcements that appeared out of nowhere and their battle strategies were improving with experience. Then the disaster in the west, first the armies from the south show unity and come to join the battle and all spying attempts failed. Then the Elven magics coming back to life. There was also evidence of other greater magics and the sniping of the darkwatchers just added to the growing list. Now the entire western front had fallen into a trap. The front had moved forward thirty miles, a quick gain at the expense of over eighty percent of the darkwatchers and demons and a third of the ground troops. Yet at virtually no expense to the enemy.

The southwest corner was the worst with only twenty-five darkwatchers and demons surviving out of four hundred fifty and only half the ground force. On top of everything else there were dragons, dragons with men riding on their backs full of surprises and magic.

They would have to go into that sector of the battle themselves, to turn the war back in their favor. It would take too long to bring enough demons back to life to fill the gaps and to get ones powerful enough to fight dragons even longer. What Salgek and the Scaldorians did not have was time.

Balak and Drogeshus stalked in, they were both just as irritable. Balak was their voice and in a sense their leader when they were together, though they thought of themselves as one with a common ego. It took the three of them to make one Scaldorians.

"The guard of the keep is formed up and ready to start their march as soon as they see our winged chariot leave the tower." Balak stated, "We will seal the keep first."

They filed out of the room, one of the lower chambers of the tower, and turned right down the corridor. Through a door at the end of the corridor they came to a stairway and started up. At the top of the tower after finishing the sealing of the tower, a strange ritual no one of this world would have recognized, they climbed into their simple battle chariot and took to the air. The guard of the keep, a small army would catch up with them a week and a half later.

*　　*　　*　　*　　*　　*　　*　　*　　*　　*

Bonny, Darset and Elisha had been busy, but not as busy as they had expected. Bonny was kept on the most severe cases where her magic saved several lives. Most of their patients were treated and sent back to the lines. Coren had still not gained consciousness, which had them concerned, though he seemed uninjured aside from minor bruises. Blaster on the other hand insisted on using magic to help. He could not walk around, both legs were in birch bark castes, but he had talked two assistants into ushering him around on a makeshift litter, doing what he could for those he could help and entertaining others. Bonny noticed he made no further mention of the incident that had brought him there, so she dismissed it from her thoughts also.

"Bonny, go wake Elisha and get some sleep," Darset yelled over to her, "I'll wake you when it's my turn."

"I bet you will." Bonny smiled and turned to walk out.

The injured had all but stopped coming in. Apparently, the enemy had stopped attacking, or was held at bay with their present defense line. Talmorg had mentioned something like that last time he had been by, but warned that it was not over, "So far we have only fought the minions, not the real enemy." he had said. Darset continued her rounds, changing dressings and checking her patients.

Elisha was working with the Elves preparing potions and balms to replenish their supplies. There were a few healers from Coren's battle group that were teaching some of the old healing techniques and magic. Elisha like the other Elves could feel the living elkinadoma and was growing more in tune with it, feeling her bodies response and sensing the changes in her voice. She had new harmonies and felt the magic of the land carried on every word she spoke. She understood the reason now for the older Elven formalities, words carried power, and any power could be used for good or evil, even if by accident. Even healing could be used at the wrong time or in the wrong way, like it would not be wise to heal an enemy that was trying to kill you.

She had been raised thinking that the old magics had been lost to the Elves, instead it had been a sacrifice made when they had moved south, a sacrifice she did not understand.

*   *   *   *   *   *   *   *   *

Coren remembered falling. Then the voice of Gaharias Emarlandestria, "Corenestral Ekberghestia future Shane of the Uklian" He was without his body, yet he was there. *'I'm dead,'* he thought, *'and the Ancients now call me.'*

"No, Coren, you are not dead." Gaharias laughed. He was before Gaharias now, without physical form, "I have summoned you and your body has been safely removed from battle."

"But why have you summoned me? I am a simple servant among Elves, with a duty to help protect the free Elves and their freedom."

"Exactly and I have chosen you to be their next Shane. As king of the Uklian Elves your duty will be the protection of the Elves and their freedom. You see Talmorg will not stay, he has a duty as king of a new kingdom in the south, which is now his true home and he cannot properly rule both. So, I have chosen you. Talmorg will choose you also, in honor to my choice, he is a very wise Elf. He and his heirs will always stand with you, but I am needful of this time to teach you in the full ways of the Elkinadoma. You will be one with it just as Talmorg is now. That is where I am sending you now, my voice will stay with you, instructing you, but first let us clear up your questions and doubts. I want you to see my great grandson, eleven generations removed."

Coren found himself in the air somewhere above the Mother Mountains. Somewhere below him he saw an enemy party of thirty-five, stalking through the forest. Their leader was a darkwatcher supported by two demons, seven Ogres and twenty-five Milmorgs. His attention was drawn to a much smaller party that was tracking them not more than a mile and a half behind, yet unnoticed by the darkwatcher.

It was the oddest-looking group he had ever seen. They were accompanied by a moor cat who seemed to be in the lead at the moment. There were ten others in the mixed party, no, as he got closer, he saw to his amazement another, a gerpin, riding on the shoulder of a human. He would have thought they had come from the south lands, if there had not been a Moorcat, a Jinn and two Milmorgs, that seemed to also be members of the group. Again, if they were not tracking the darkwatcher he would have questioned their alliance.

Then he found himself floating next to the human, "Meet Eric Marland. His last name was shortened on Earth, E-Marland-Estria, which is his full name and true identity."

"A human?"

"In part, but still my blood line."

"But the darkwatcher will destroy him, with the rest of his companions."

"No, fear not, his power is greater than mine, though he doesn't know it yet. He will prevail and reach my brothers keep and once there, destroy the Scaldorian machine. Now we must return to the adoma." Gaharias paused, "The Old One Elkero said he will operate outside the bounds of the council, yet will sit on the council when he chooses. I wonder if he has more power than the old ones."

Coren was caught by surprise, Gaharias spoke to him almost as an equal and for the first time ever he heard one of the names of the old ones. He knew that if he had been in his body, he would have gone white with shock. Then the implications of what was just said struck him, this distant son of Gaharias had the power to change his world. He was shaken at the thought of the future riding in the hands of a human.

*   *   *   *   *   *   *   *   *   *

They had slept in brief spurts over the span of about an hour, before giving the idea of rest up. The trail was fresh enough that Lady Moor said she could smell it, so Eric let her take the lead. They all had their senses working at peak efficiency, lest they should come upon the darkwatcher to their own surprise. Eric thought he felt the presence of Gaharias somewhere in the air watching him and then it was gone.

They tracked silently and quickly for about two hours when Lady

Moor suddenly slowed down. Eric felt her thoughts, they were close now, a hundred yards and closing. Suddenly Lady Moor stopped and looked back at Eric.

'They are stopped just ahead, to give the Milmorgs a rest.' The image formed thoughts came to him.

They had made a plan before they set out, but Eric had doubts of its effectiveness, magic would be used. Eric would circle to the other side; Lady Moor would take the front and Brent Kelch would take the near side. The rest would attack from behind. Eric gave the signal and in less than ten minutes they were in place. Eric sent Charlie, quicker than the eye could see. Sudden commotion in the camp, signaled the attack.

As Eric had hoped, when he rushed from cover full attention was focused on a cloud of volcanic dust in the center of the camp. Unseen he charged the darkwatcher, sword of Gaharias drawn. The darkwatcher had been most alert and turned on the glowing sword and its invisible bearer, before Eric reached him, lightening spewed from its talons. Eric lifted his shielded arm protectively and the lightening spider webbed on the blue transparent field he unconsciously threw in front of him. The darkwatcher registered fear for but a brief moment of realization before his demise. With a glance he saw Lady Moor wrenching a demon back and forth with a death grip around its neck from behind, so he continued turning to see Brent in an open fire fight with the other demon. Eric headed towards its back, he almost did not see the lunging Ogre, turning with barely enough time to slice it in half and dodge the plummeting stone club.

Brent leaped to the open with fire blasting from his hands, too obvious to bother using the invisibility ring. The demon he struck turned on him, returning the fiery favor, but he was ready with his wall of ice and enjoying the freedom to show off. Amidst the back-and-forth exchange, it was not until the third try he successfully threw the Esberkian web, which squashed the demon into the dimension of chaos, where nothing had form or substance. Through the vanishing demon he saw Eric's image in the cloud of black smoke from the destroyed darkwatcher, sidestep the plummeting top half of an Ogre.

Stralina leaped into the air, dropping a ring of fire that took out three Ogres before she hit the ground, as Hans ran through eight Millmorgs, leaving them dead to fight at her back slaying whatever came at him, while she spewed forth liquid fire.

Kesker simply went head-to-head against two Ogres, bashing it out quite effectively. Kole, Garth, Kedd, Jahar and Calhan went in formation against the Millmorgs.

As the dust settled, they had won, but Lady Moor was still violently wrenching the tattered and suffering form of the demon back and forth.

Brent laughed, "It takes magic to kill a demon, although that one may be ready to submit." he stated as a spear of ice shot from his fingertips, impaling the demon and leaving it limp in Lady Moors grip.

When they took account of themselves, Jahar was dead and Kole lay on the ground with a fatal gash, just below the ribs. Under Erics touch the bleeding stopped, but that would not be enough to save his life.

"Bonny could save him." he said. The rest were silent.

After a moment Stralina said, "I could send him to her, if I knew where she was."

Eric looked up into her eyes, "I can feel where she is. Open your mind and I will try to show you."

More passed between them than Eric had expected. He learned a lot about her, though she gained exactly what he gave her. Then she crossed her arms over Kole and he vanished, with a cloud of smoke. Her magic was innate, she was born with the magic of a Jinn, a wish magic. It did not have the control or predictability of other magic; it could affect things unintentionally. It was however a very powerful magic never doing less than the wish, but costing the user, Stralina needed to eat and rest now, though she did not show it outwardly. Eric knew her need, but he also knew they could not stay where they were.

"Stralina," he called her to the side, "here eat this." He pulled some high energy bars out of his pack and then held her hands in his closing his eyes. "This will help." He felt the energy pass through him to her.

"Thank you." she said with a humble whisper, and they rejoined the others.

"We need to move away from this area." Brent stated. It was a statement of the obvious, they were at the end of an obvious trail. A search of the bodies lying around turned up very little, some coinage and a little jewelry was about all. They gave Jahar a proper burial although expedient and brief. They set out tracking their way along the opposite side of their enemy's trail.

*   *   *   *   *   *   *   *   *

The minions of the Scaldorians had stopped attacking, but the south land armies and the Elves maintained continuous lightning strikes on their encampments, from horseback and from the air. Hanser Schultzmann was enjoying the battle, charging in through and out of the encampments, doing as much damage as possible in the least amount of time. The horsemen avoided the demons as much as they could, whereas that was the focus of the air attacks. Shiheel and Keltoe had organized the dragons in strike forces, with the sole purpose of eliminating the darkwatchers and demons. They coordinated their attacks with the horsemen and enjoyed their success for the few days that it lasted.

It was a snap decision by Hanser to grab a couple of the higher ranking Milmorgs in the middle of battle and bring them back as prisoners. The captive's morale was broken with fear and they were babbling before Hanser ever got them back to camp.

"The Scaldorians themselves will be arriving in the morning." one of them blurted out, crying out with defiance and fear.

Hanser did not know how anyone could live with such fear and he was more than slightly amazed when it registered, that it was not a fear of death or being captured, but rather of the Scaldorians. He sent word back to Talmorg immediately and an alert went out to all the battle units.

The sudden attack wave still caught them by surprise. The

Scaldorians appeared in the sky annihilating the seven northern most dragons and devastating ground troops as they flew by. Their minions attacked with renewed vigor and reinforcements from the north. The entire length of the front was shaken into retreating battle. It took the combined efforts of Shiheel, Hesheil, Keltoe Shelock and Darcose to slow the Scaldorians down and help cover the retreat of the armies, yet the Scaldorians were still not stopped. The battle of power in the air was more intense then when the Ancients had done battle, ripping at the very substance of time and space between them, leaving magical fallout in their path. Keltoe had doubts, for the first time he could remember he was in forced retreat.

Bonny had been on her sleep shift when the activity picked up, with the beginning of the new influx of injured. A massive variety of burn injuries, but all seemed to have an infection of a magical nature and the number of injured was growing faster than they could handle. Rumors had siphoned through things had turned bad and their armies were all in retreat. Morale was not good and Bonny felt very irritable. Time went by without measurement. Bonny received a little rest, when Darset insisted. Her body ached and she felt like an assembly line worker, putting bodies together to go back into battle.

How much time had passed, she had no idea, when Talmorg stepped in. "They have severed us from the rest of the Uklian." he said, fatigue lines showing in his face, "The elkinadoma is taking all I can do to fight off the infectious fallout from the battle of magics. We lost Darcose this morning, the Scaldorians are pushing faster with less resistance and what seems to be an unlimited source of power.”

Darset saw his weariness, “Come and sit down a minute.”

He sat where she moved him to sit, “Then they received more reinforcements. A captive told us it was the last of their reserves. They believe if they beat us, they will have total victory.” He paused and looked at Bonny, “Eric, has not yet finished his mission. If he doesn’t make it soon, it could be too late.”

Bonny forced a smile, seeing Talmorg’s need for support, she placed her hands on his shoulders and passed her healing magic through him, “We will win.” she whispered. She knew it, she did not know how, but she did.

Talmorg was visibly restored, “I need to see you more often.” he smiled, “I needed to let you know the Scaldorians are pressing their way toward our camp. The way things are going they’ll be on top of us in a day or less. I must return to our command post now.”

“How is Saphrine?” Elisha asked.

“I don’t know, she went out to the front lines and I have received no word of her whereabouts. She missed the battle group she was supposed to join in their retreat.” He stood up and left without another word.

*　　*　　*　　*　　*　　*　　*　　*　　*　　*

They peaked the next ridge and Stralina pointed to the north, “That is Darval Keep.”

Eric could barely make it out, it stood like a shadow in darkness, several peaks away. "Still quite a way off."

"It looks abandoned." Brent stated.

Eric pulled out his binoculars to get a better look. "It is still too far away to get a good look."

"We won't get a closer look." Stralina said, looking into the ravine ahead, "We will be headed back into the caves soon."

"I feel this would be a good time and place to set camp." Eric said. After their battle they had stopped worrying about whether they traveled by day or night. They had all lost track of how long they had been traveling and time seemed unimportant, except that they did not waste it. There was a growing urgency to get to the inter-dimensional generator.

They shared the mixture of vegetation and fruit that Charlie had gathered. Charlie continued to be a great asset to the small company, no one else had to consider scavenging for food, with the exception of Lady Moor, who took care of her own needs. They were all weary of their adventure and purpose is what kept them moving in unity. Seeing Darval Keep had brought a quietness over them knowing that was their goal and not knowing if they would return.

Sleep did not come easy for Eric and when he did get to sleep, he had dreams. He dreamed of Bonny handling injured from battle and then he dreamed of her in battle, but he could not remember his dreams when he woke up, just bits and pieces.

It was still dark when he woke up, Eric walked over and took

Brents post at guard, facing the keep. Looking toward the keep he perceived by means other than his eyes a stream of energy flowing out from beneath the keep, flowing as water towards the west. He thought about intercepting it, but knew that would bring the Scaldorians back before he was ready. He also considered again the power that had been given him, he still did not know its limits or if it had any. His brief exchange with Stralina, taught him how to exercise the magics she had, and he wondered if there was a limit to the magic he could use. Eric also wondered if the change was permanent and if any of it would carry over when he returned home, some of it would have to, unless he forgot everything that had happened, but then he would have forgotten the first time he returned and he had not. Some of the magics he realized were forms of science and chemistry, others still required physical preparation ahead of time, yet the ones that fascinated him the most tapped into realms of energy science had never touched. It was these that he wanted to study, to find a scientific way of approaching them. If Earth scientists could tap these sources of power, they would not need fuel for space travel.

He was on Ethar now and heir to the powers of an Ancient Gaharias. He was a god or at least a demigod. Eric wondered if his inherited power was magic, or if the power of the gods, Ancients, was a different kind of power. With time he would find out where he fit in the scheme of this world. The fluttering of a passing bat drew his attention back to his surroundings.

Looking around Eric could not locate what he heard, but

everything seemed normal enough. Turning back to look at the fortress he got the sensation that someone was watching him, but the rest of the party was asleep and he shrugged it off as paranoia. He was sure that the armies of the south were involved in battle by now and wondered how they were faring. Bonny was with them and he missed her very much, but he needed to keep his thoughts on the things at hand and what he had to do.

The sensation of something watching him persisted and became irritating when he found himself searching the shadows for hidden eyes. Finally, he gave in and used the power within him to search his surroundings. He was unsure however of what he found, something small, a nonliving self-contained energy form, that seemed born of magic. It was about twenty feet to his left, on the lower limb of a tree. Eric opened his eyes and started over to investigate. The sky was getting lighter with a predawn glow and he could barely make out a darkened lump on a large lower limb. As he approached, the shadow took to the air on bat like wings, but as it passed over his head, it took on the distinct form of the demonic darkwatchers. Before he gave it a thought, Eric whipped out his arm and hurled a blue fireball at the flying thing and blasted it out of the air. The flare of the explosion woke the rest of the companions he was traveling with.

Startled awake they all sprang to their feet, grabbing for their weaponry and looking about aggressively. Eric laughed, and the rest turned toward him with glaring gazes. He held up his hands to abate the barrage of questions that started to burst forth.

"I apologize for waking you all" Eric said looking upon their faces, "However it was necessary to stop spying eyes from returning to their master. Brent, stir up a fire, we'll have a hot breakfast and an early start today. Our presence is known so we will need to maintain a more defensive posture and try to find a way to disappear from watching eyes."

"That will be easier said than done," Brent mumbled, "just ask Calhan."

Calhan stepped up, "That is quite true. The Scaldos have many ways of spying on their enemies. I am sure I don't know all of them" Calhan tried to keep it to himself, but he had become much more pessimistic, having lost his companion Jahar.

"We can hope, that they are too preoccupied with the battle at the front to be concerned with us," Garth piped up, "but we can't count on it!"

"We could try to use a decoy." Stralina added, "If they can't spend much time or energy on us, that could easily throw them off our trail."

"Phantasm, that could be very effective," Eric pondered the idea, "Let's do it, we need to stop talking about it for sake of secrecy. Stralina, come over here with me, it will be easier if we both work on this. Cancel that fire, Brent, we'll be leaving in about twenty minutes."

While everyone else picked up camp, Eric and Stralina worked together to generate a phantasm of their entire party. A phantasm, was more than an illusion, it has actual physical substance and is capable of a certain amount of interaction to include doing battle. The spell was one Stralina knew, but had not mastered, yet Eric understood how it work from his brief merge with her mind. When they were finished, the only way they could discern the difference between the phantasm and their own party was a red shoulder patch they generated on the phantasm for that purpose.

They sent the phantasm on a direct path to the castle. If the phantasm made it all the way they would provide an even further ruse than they were really hoping for. The phantasm had been instructed to enter the castle and seek out to destroy the source of power for the Scaldorian magic. The phantasm would be quite capable of accomplishing their mission for them if nothing got in the way, but Eric was confident that the Scaldorians had it defended at least well enough to stop the phantasm.

They formed up, everything ready, and head off in the direction they had planned, keeping a low profile and a watchful eye. They still had a substantial journey ahead of them. Stralina was in the lead, because she knew the way to the cave entrances they sought. Eric went back into pondering his purpose in this world, and on Earth for that matter. Among other things he wondered if he would become corrupted by his new power and status, not that he honestly believed that he would, he just knew the old saying about power corrupting. He wondered, considering the fact there were gods, or Ancients as they were called here, how absolute his power and authority might be.

Eventually he would have to have a long chat with Gaharias to learn more about who he was and who his Ancestors were, and what he actually was, and what that meant. In the meantime he would have to go along groping, and guessing what he was doing. Off in the distance he

could feel another one of those strange little spy things of the Scaldorians,
it was following the phantasm. Eric decided not to tell the others, he
did not want them to drop their guard in the slightest, their first being
discovered was bad enough. The ruse might not work a second time.

*   *   *   *   *   *   *   *   *   *

Saphrine had gone out alone so as to be undetected on her
rendezvous with the secondary field command controlling the activities
of the northern most section of their part of the front lines. She slipped
through the forest totally undetected by anyone, avoiding skirmishes she
heard in the passing. she reached the area of their rendezvous hours ago
and shimmied up into the lower branches of a tree for cover while she
waited. They were late, but everything in war does not always meet its
schedule, so she waited. It was Tsarca and Eprarhil that she was supposed
to be meeting. The more time passed the more she wondered what might
have gone wrong until finally she climbed back down and set out to
investigate. She headed in the direction she thought the front line should
be. The princess had not traveled far when she almost stumbled into a
Milmorg camp. She realized immediately that the front line must have
shifted much more than anticipated, and the retreat had already taken
place.

As long as she was there, she decided to spy out the enemy camp,
to see if she could learn anything. This group was on a lunch break or
something, there were Ogres and Milmorgs gathered in groups around
camp fires, and they seemed to be cooking something. Saphrine assumed

it was food. There were three Darkwatchers near the center of the camp torturing someone, at first glance she thought it was an Elf, but then realized it was one of the Milmorgs. She felt bad that she could not help the poor fellow, and wondered why he was not screaming or making any noise. Then he turned around and what she saw made her stomach turn, the front of his neck was missing. It was more than she could stand by and watch, taking the bow which Eric had given her, she pulled back and pictured an exploding blast of fire aimed at the center most of the Darkwatchers, and let loose the string. The arrow formed and flew true, causing a great explosion of flame when it hit its mark, taking out all three of the Darkwatchers along with several others in the camp that were too close to the blast. The extensiveness of the damage surprised her, the weapon had carried the intensity of her thought with it, and turned the whole camp into confusion, fighting one another.

Saphrine slipped away totally undetected, and started working her way back to the medical, and headquarters camp. It was hours before she reached the sounds of the battle lines ahead, and evening was setting in. She was going to have to spend the night behind enemy lines, so again she found her way up a concealing tree, where she got some sleep.

She worked her way through the tops of the trees the next morning, following the progress of the enemy lines, every so often sniping out one of the enemies, neither side knowing where the arrows came from when they hit. She had just taken down number thirty-seven an Ogre, making it three Ogres, two demons, a Darkwatcher, and thirty-one Milmorgs for the morning, when she heard the strange whining sound coming closer in the air behind her.

Looking up she saw three insect like creatures riding up in the air, in some kind of metal chariot. Somehow, she knew that they must be the Scaldorians. Then out of nowhere from the other side came Hesheil and Shiheel on their energy disc followed by several dragons. Flames and lightening flew back and forth, and the armies from both sides cleared out from the area underneath, leaving a major hole in both lines, where flames and splattering of green and multicolored glowing slime formed. As she watched they pushed each other back and forth through the sky, but the Scaldorians seemed to be making the better progress. Grabbing again the Bow of Nester, she pictured a great ball of fire and took aim at the metal chariot, it was a true shot, but Saphrine did not get to see the chariot rock and sputter backwards from the blast. The reflected blast had knocked her to the ground, and by the time her vision cleared the Scaldorians were pushing forward again. When she realized she was sprawled out on the ground directly under the air battle, she got to her feet and ran through to the Elven side of the battle lines, where she collapsed into the hands of a couple of medics.

Saphrine awoke, and after a few moments of disorientation realized Tsarca was the one, who was shaking her. It was not an Ogre spitting her over a fire, she had been dreaming. She held down the urge to scream, and then to cry, she was the Princess Barhallah and had to maintain at least a minimum amount of composure. Then she remembered what happened the

blast of fire, crashing against the ground, and then running for the safety
of the Elven side of the battle lines. A voice started coming through the
ringing in her ears. It was Tsarca she was saying something it was gentle
but urgent, she could tell by the tones of her voice. Saphrine looked hard
at Tsarca and tried to concentrate.

"Saphrine, we're in retreat we need you on your feet, wake up,
please snap out of it." Tsarca was saying, "Your dazed nothing broken, we
need everybody we can get to defend the retreat. If you can walk, we need
you to walk."

"Her eyes are starting to clear, Tsarca," It was an Elven medic
leaning over her, she could tell by the green leaf sown on as a breast
emblem, the leaf of life. "She's coming around now, she's got good
fortune I dare say this ethereal armor saved her life, in more ways than
one. That slime we cleaned off her was contaminated waste from the
battling magics. The effects of that kind of thing are totally unpredictable."

"Enough we are also fortunate she is here if she is able to come
around well enough to boost our soldier's morale." Tsarca turned for a
moment like she was about to walk away, then turned back, "Saphrine can
you give me a response yet?"

"Yes, I think so." she managed to mumble, her words sounded
slurred to her, but her head was clearing and that was a start. She tried to
sit up, and was only successful with the help of Tsarca and the medic. The
world seemed to be swimming around her, she knew however that she
would be all right in a few minutes with the exception of the throbbing

headache she was starting to feel. "How long was I out?"

"Not too long," Tsarca answered, "maybe about twenty to thirty minutes. It is fortunate I saw you running out of that blasted area. I sent those two medics to meet you after that blast. What was that blast anyway, it almost knocked those cursed things and their air chariot out of the sky."

"I am not really sure," she shook her head, "something I got from Eric. It's got more power than he told me about."

"Maybe you just have more power than you thought you did." the medic added, "remember you are in the Elkin Adoma now were the full power of the Elves lives."

"That is true." Saphrine nodded, then shook her head gently from side to side to try to clear it.

"We need to be moving," Tsarca added, "before we are overrun by the front and you're not in any shape to be fighting right now."

"I just need a little time, and then I will stand with you. It might be good for morale especially under these conditions. It would not be good for me to show up hurt, and then rush off ahead of the retreat."

"You will get no argument from me, but be ready to move on a moment's notice." Tsarca started to walk away, but paused and said over her shoulder, "You might try singing." then she walked off.

The thought surprised her, but she remembered the power she held in her voice at Quiet Valley with the fairy adoma. She started humming to herself and felt the energy of the adoma pushing its way into her, strengthening her and healing her. The adoma filled her with waves of joy and strength. She started after Tsarca who had not gotten too far ahead. She sang as she started to run, her strength fully returned, but before she reached her, Tsarca made a strange motion and vanished altogether from her sight. That did not matter though, Saphrine could still give strength to the troops. She kept on singing and heading towards the battle line, feeling a power and joy she had never felt before.

As she approached, she felt the power being carried on her voice to the other Elves, and she walked with confidence, which gave a renewed confidence to those who saw her. She sang with all her heart, but she also had her bow at ready, which she had grabbed before running after Tsarca. She moved in and took a place among the archers, as she drew back her bow this time, she pictured a spray of lightening. When she let loose the string a shining bolt flew forth and split into a shower of lightning bolts blasting a hole in the enemy line, resulting in a brief backward motion in the enemy lines. The Elves rushed in to take advantage of the surprise. Almost immediately a Darkwatcher and two demons appeared out of nowhere spitting forth fire and lightening, and the tide turned back against the Elves.

It took one arrow, to take out the darkwatcher and the blast knocked down the two demons, putting another flaming hole in the enemy troops. Saphrine knew if she was not careful the next arrow could give her position away to the surviving demon and she would not get a third shot. She decided to try ice and a single arrow to minimize detection, hurriedly she got it off before the demons got to their feet. The arrow flew and hit its mark, freezing the demon like a statue in its half-risen position. As she

fought, she kept on singing, but when she turned to the other demon it

was already facing her and raising one hand in her direction. She quickly

drew again, only this time letting loose a wall of ice arrows, knowing

she had no other shield. The ice and the fire met about halfway between

them, resulting in multicolored, glowing slime splattering about the battle.

A scattering of fire traces got through injuring the Elves around her, and

some of the ice arrows got through, both injuring the demon and other

troops around them, but she did not have time to evaluate her next move.

Almost instinctively her singing went shrill and directed itself against

the last demon and he went up in flames with his hide falling away like

shredded pieces of paper. When the smoke cleared, she could see over half

of the enemy troops were either laying down their arms in surrender or

running from the battle. Those that kept on fighting were disorganized and

being forced into retreat. When she looked up through the air battle was

not faring as well.

The ground battle here was slowing down, as the Elves were

ordered not to advance, lest they should get cut off from the rest of the

army. Saphrine wondered how the rest of the army was faring, but she

directed her attention to the sky, that battle of magic was much more

intense than the ground battle, so much so that neither side was paying

attention to the ground war. Aside from the Eftites and the Scaldorians

there were dragons and Darkwatchers and demons. Neither side seemed

to be exactly winning, however the Scaldorian side was pushing the combined forces back slowly but surely.

Suddenly Tsarca seemed to appear out of thin air to be standing right next to her. "You have helped us win this battle, but I don't think we should let that battle get to far behind us." she said pointing to the sky where Saphrine had been just looking.

"I could not agree with you more." Saphrine said in singing tones, "Sometime I'd like you to teach me that disappearing trick you have. If I knew that I might be able to help them up there without leaving myself as a total sitting duck."

"I'll have to think about it. I did swear to keep it a secret when Narco taught it to me." Tsarca gazed into the distance distracted by something of the past, "It is a secret of the fairy folk you know."

"Why did they teach you?" Saphrine was curious.

"Oh, I just saved the life of Narco the crown prince of fairies," she smiled, "I didn't know who he was at the time, but if he had not taught me that one secret, I might not have survived the Murkin Flats."

"That sounds like a story for a long evening around a camp fire." She looked with respect at Tsarca, "I would like to be at that storytelling, so little is known about the ways and customs of the fairy folk. It is always interesting to learn anything new about them."

Another Elf approached them, Saphrine recognized them as an officer by their insignia.

Tsarca also saw his approach, "What news have you Guardsman Carn, are we ready to move back?"

"Yes, my lady, but we will have to move faster than we planned. The rest of have not fared as well as we have. They have already been pushed back much farther than we have, and we could get cut off if we don't hurry. The runner is over by our command flag."

Tsarca thanked him, he turned and bowed to Saphrine before leaving. "You may be needed back at the central command camp, Saphrine. I can send a couple of guardsmen with you as an escort."

"You are right I should head back, but I don't need an escort." Saphrine gave a slight smile, "I am sure that Talmorg is worried about me, you did send word back when I arrived?"

"No, we were in the midst of battle, I had no one to spare as a special messenger. That information is going back with the routine reports."

"Okay, it has been an honor standing with you, but I will depart without further ado." Saphrine gave her head a half bow.

"The honor is mine."

*   *   *   *   *   *   *   *   *   *

Shiheel had no idea where that blast from the ground came from, but it had a major effect in cutting down the Scaldorian attack power. They had to divert some of their magic to staying in the air the effect probably saved many lives. Now though they were still being forced to retreat they were able to defend themselves more successfully. Shiheel figured that this would work to their favor the Scaldorians could not generate any more demons and Darkwatchers while engaged in combat themselves. The dragons were having great success in reducing the numbers of Darkwatchers and demons, though they were still in forced retreat. He and Hesheil were also fully engaged in combat and had no way of knowing how the rest of the war was going. The only real enemy however was those three Scaldorians they were battling now; the rest was a consequence.

He also knew that the only way that they could possibly defeat the Scaldorians was if Eric and company were successful. Otherwise, this one battle could go on long after the war was over possibly for hundreds of years. They had an almost perfect match of power as long as the Scaldorians had their power generator. Actually, the Scaldorians had a little more power, which was why they were forced in retreat, but they could keep retreating around the world for years. What bothered him most about that thought, was how much damage the energy fallout from their battle would do to the ground below their travel. Neither side had to stop for eating or any other necessities they could both survive on energy they grabbed from the surroundings they passed, although the Scaldorians would have to actually produce food and eat which might slow them slightly. They would turn into a passing nemesis to all that lived on Ethar.

Even worse if the Scaldorians had already gone through a reproduction cycle than more would rise up in the future and eventually destroy this world as they did their own. Eventually they might even eliminate the rest of the races on Ethar. Scaldorians were ruthless and the races of Ethar could never be that ruthless, and it was ruthlessness that would grow up into power.

Shiheel found an ironic sadness in it also, because he knew that it took that ruthlessness for the Scaldorians to survive the harshness of their home world. An attribute necessary for survival on their home world made them incompatible with life forms on any other planet. To Shiheel this was an unwelcome extension of the war that had destroyed the home worlds of both of their races. The thought of extinction of any race even Scaldorian saddened him. He did have one ace in the hole however, he had left instructions with the unborn hatchlings of his own and they would know the full history around the Scaldorians at hatching. They might be the salvation of this world even if the Scaldorians were to win this war now.

They battled with the Scaldorians for days retreating more and more, until Shiheel noticed that they were retreating directly towards the command center and medical camp. The implications were numerous it seemed that possibly the Scaldorians had some control over the direction of their retreat. It also seemed that maybe the Scaldorians felt they could engage a more extensive battle without pushing them further back. Shiheel wondered what other ploys the Scaldorians might have up their sleeves. The barrage that they were throwing at the Scaldorians already would be enough to exterminate life on many a planet. It would take years for the ground to recover from the magical waste that was littering from their battle, but that was better than not fighting and giving the Scaldorians free run to destroy the planet.

He also knew that the Scaldorian magic was stealing energy from some other dimension or time, or both, not to mention the damage it was doing to whichever barrier they were violating. The consequences of their abuse would not easily be corrected if at all possible and the imbalance would have effects for years to come, even beyond his life.

The Scaldorians had no concern for that they sought only their own needs and wants without any regard for anything else. They maintained the basic nature of insects, even after attaining their greater intelligence. They were proof that intelligence and experience do not give conscience, wisdom or cure the ills of a society, but rather goodness if it could be called that came from a source of its own without regard to knowledge and experience. That in truth the battle of good and evil could not be solved by science, but was a matter of the nurturing of the heart, not even by deeds, for evil can hide behind good deeds. Not to say that this excuses us from the doing of good deeds because the only way for the mortal mind to know anyone is by their deeds. Shiheel snapped back from his pointless thinking.

Shiheels glance over his shoulder had cost them, and forced them back a little further, but he increased his attack to a pace he did not know if he could maintain and they briefly gained a little ground. An increase in the numbers of depleting demons and Darkwatchers indicated they were not the only battle front converging on the main camp. Why hadn't Talmorg ordered a retreat of the main camp, the Scaldorians must wonder that to. The Scaldorians could not have expected them to remain there like sitting ducks in a pond waiting to be destroyed from the air, or run over by ground troops. Talmorg must also know something he didn't Shiheel took some comfort in that thought.

*   *   *   *   *   *   *   *   *   *

Talmorg paced the entire camp when he wasn't involved in more specific coordination. He felt the flow of the Elkin Adoma no matter what he was doing at the time. He knew where all of the front lines were and how the retreat was moving, it did not please him things were closing in faster than he had expected. He considered retreating the main camp, but dismissed it too much preparation had already been made to meet and stay the encroachment where they were. He had learned a lot from the homeland Elves during the brief time he was here. The last time he had talked to Bonny and Darset most of the injured were back on their feet and ready to fight. Talmorg was holding them back to entrench themselves for a hard resistance line, and screen the retreat to give short relief to the retreating troops. The entrenched troops would be fresh while the attacking troops would be battle worn, on top of that over half of his magicians would be in that entrenchment, they had been injured in the first major onslaught of the demons and Darkwatchers.

While laid up the magicians had learned how to enhance their power with the Elkin Adoma, doubling or better their power, giving advantage and surprise at their greater power. The workings of the Adoma were also prepared for the ground battle, he was going to have to rely on the Eftites and dragons to handle anything in the air. He would provide any firepower he could afford to assist the battle in the sky if they came close enough, but that was the best he could offer. He did not personally have wings to hand out, and it takes Jinn months to make flying carpets, if the ones fighting with them even knew how. Talmorg could not count on any more support coming from the Uklian Elves, the troops they had designated for this corner of the war had been split up elsewhere when they arrived. The next wave of recruits would be at least another week in the coming, and very green. The entire known world to them was already involved in this war, so there was no hope of another kingdom coming to the rescue either. Another pipe dream also passed through his mind, and that was the return of the ancient wizard Starnook, but he vanished centuries ago.

Bonny was an unmeasured asset, whose value could not be known at this point or counted on. It would be nice if her power field work in full against the coming onslaught, but it was also unknown, even if it does work, how long she could keep it up, or how much area she could protect with it. They would start learning sooner than he expected, or wanted. He had told her that, she just nodded and kept on working on healing the injured. She showed no indication of concern one way or the other, but what had he expected she was busy and would be either way, there was no reason for her to show anything. Though he could also tell that she was not getting enough sleep, and magic only went so far to make up for that. They all needed more sleep.

Where was Saphrine, no one knew, Tsarcas last report had no news of her whereabouts. The best Tsarca could provide was there seemed to be someone snipping off the enemy, from behind the enemy lines with a powerful weapon. He felt pessimistic about that, but something had called on the power of the Elkinadoma since then, from her battle group. That could be any stray Uklian Elf discovering their power however, Talmorg could feel them calling upon the power of the Adoma in faraway battles. It also could have been one of their own who chanced on how to use that power. No matter what or who was using the power it was to their advantage and that was what really counted right now.

His pacing brought him back to the command tent the next reports would be coming in soon, and he wanted to be there when they arrived. The messengers would be turned around and sent back with any new instructions. Talmorg went inside and sat down shutting his eyes to get a little rest while he waited.

CHAPTER 24

Fallout

Saphrine and the messenger slipped quietly into the forest. Staying under cover, they traveled as much as possible through the branches of the trees, so as not to leave a trail. They were both experienced and the traveling went quickly. They passed with the secrecy of the wind, without disturbing even the wildlife, continuing with ease until the messenger indicated a stop. They used a complex nonverbal communication, and he indicated that they were waiting for another messenger and would continue when she arrived. The young Elf showed up before they had time to finish their jerky, and Saphrine noticed she wore the Barhallah insignia on her hunter scout uniform. Immediately they set off again, arriving at the edge of the command camp much quicker than she had expected. The battle was closing in too fast!

"Halt who seeks passage?" they were challenged as they approached the perimeter of the camp.

"Brecken messenger of Tsarca, Sheleica messenger of Epraphil and the Lady, Princess Saphrine Barhallah returning to command post."

"Pass quickly, Lord Talmorg has been pacing incessantly awaiting news, honor be with you!" the guards vanished from their path.

Saphrine headed straight for the command tent leaving the others to follow. She went in without announcement and smiled seeing Talmorg sleeping half sprawled across their makeshift command desk. Letting her smile fade she awoke him by name, "Talmorg."

He snapped alert, and a smile of great relief passed briefly across his face when he saw who it was, "It is good to see you alive and well! How come I got no message? or word concerning your welfare?" He asked with some irritation, which Saphrine knew only came from worrying about her.

"You, have been worried. By the time I caught up with Tsarca, I was on the wrong side of the battle lines, and they were still fully engaged when I got through. I did not have her send a special messenger; I simply came myself." She looked at their planning table full of maps and implements, "By the time I got there it was obvious that plans had already been changed. I gave them some aid while I was there...I used the power of the Adoma. It was like a reflex, some old instinct that manifested itself, or maybe the Adoma used me in its own defense. I understand that it is alive."

"No, you used it I could feel it, but I did not know who was using it." He gazed for a moment into her eyes.

"The messengers are waiting for you to give their report, they are just outside."

Talmorg yelled toward the tent flap, "Borak, send in the messengers!"

The meeting was relatively short. Everyone learned of the power that Saphrine had manifested, and she suggested that every Elf in battle should try singing. Any of them might have the power to manifest or the ability to use the Adoma. The only way of knowing was to try. Talmorg added to that, that the Adoma was strengthened by use. This concept seemed to boost the morale of the messengers at least. The idea that they might be able to bring back to their comrades something that might help them in battle was good. They all had just reported an increase in casualties.

Talmorg issued orders for everyone to try using the power of the Adoma, and gave them plans for a slightly accelerated retreat to try to reduce the number of dead and injured. Their supply of arrows was also dwindling, and new supplies were not expected for at least three days. He told Borak to search out and find whatever craftsmen could make arrows from the camp. He would use the Adoma to get them the raw material that they needed; he could get any kind of tree to grow at an accelerated rate where they needed it. With an effort, they could start producing their own arrows by tomorrow, at least he would like to hope, because an army needed weapons and ammunition. As long as Blaster was in camp he would put him in charge of enchanting the arrows for effectiveness, he had already taken care of the stock pile they already had.

"Calbork, where is Shiheel's understudy, is he around?"

"He is with Freebic's group. I can summon him for you if you would like, my Lord."

"Yes, please do I would like him to make us more metal arrows, Shirken can do that too if I remember correctly." Talmorg looked at him and he nodded, "that will be all for now."

Calbork went out leaving Talmorg alone with Saphrine, "It is good to have you back, you were right I was worried."

"Thank you, but I think I could better serve our peoples if I mix with the troops, I can help in battle and it does boost their moral."

Talmorg knew she was probably right, but was not ready to admit it without some protest, "You are quite useful here."

"Doing what sitting around while you make decisions, all I can do here is give you moral support. You have others more experienced than me to give you any advice you need. It is nice to be here, but not most practical for our needs."

"You are right. If that is what you want to do I should not as much as I would like to, stop you."

Saphrine got up, walked over to him and gave him a kiss, "It is best, besides if you didn't have to be here, you would be on the front lines also, but I will concede to standing with the troops that you are entrenching."

Shadoweaver, had not liked the accelerated retreat order when he got it two days earlier, and he had thought the order for all of the southern Elves to try using the power of the Adoma was a waste of time, when he got it. Now however, the only thing he did not like about it now was how concentrated their armies would be when they reached the entrenchment. He had one arm wrapped from elbow to shoulder, a dressing around his waist and one leg wrapped with a splint, but refused to go back to the medical camp without a replacement he approved of. The change in strategy had reduced the number of casualties and allowed them to march the enemy through more traps. As it turned out there were several of the southern Elves with the power to call on the Adoma, and now the enemy no longer faced his command with Darkwatchers or demons, and when one did show up it was quickly eliminated. His biggest problem now was what to do with the defectors from the other side. Even though they were pressed by overwhelming numbers of the enemy the ground battle was starting to look like it might turn back to their favor.

He knew also from the reports he got that they were also faring a lot better than most of the other commands. They would pass the entrenchment today and by the winds of all the great wizards that would surprise the Scaldorian minions to be brought to a stop. His troops would get a brief rest, he was proud enough of the southerners he now commanded to call them his troops. He would however be glad when he could relinquish his command over to Coren and go back to being just a spook. He was wondering why Coren had not returned when someone tapped him on the shoulder.

"So, who told you, how to take command, spook?" it was Coren's voice and he almost knocked him down turning around. "You have reached the trench start moving them back in groups, we need your singers, and you can return as soon as you're ready, only after you report to Bonny and get fixed up, I don't need a broken old spook hanging around my neck if I am going to get anything done here"

"Coren, thank the Ancients you are back, and well. How could all you guys take off and leave a bungler like me in charge anyway?" they both laughed. Then with a more serious look Shadoweaver said pointing over his shoulder, "They could use a short rest, I will start at once." and with the blink of an eye he was gone.

*   *   *   *   *   *   *   *   *   *

Talmorg sent for Bonny, the retreating troops had started crossing the entrenchment hours ago. He could not let the remaining demons and Darkwatchers make an attack on the main camp, if they should realize they are close enough, it was time to try her protective barrier. While he was rifling through logistics, Shadoweaver was announced and came in.

"Good to see you again, Shadoweaver, please sit over here for a minute." Talmorg instructed him to a chair at his side, "I need you to coordinate our magical resources. We need to balance out our defense lines as I am sure you already know we have some lines substantially weaker than others in the magic department. You need to coordinate those efforts; you have the most experience in that area."

He handed Shadoweaver about thirty pages of paper they had gotten from Eric written on in the old Elven script. Shadoweaver gave them a curious look and started reading them. "This is a general listing of who can do what, I take it."

"Yes, but it is not complete, I believe the power of the adoma has also produced additional magic for the Elves." Talmorg pulled out another sheet, "Blaster is enchanting the arrows we are making with two others they are here; you can change that around with others if you need to but we need them enchanted to be effective against other magics." As he was speaking Bonny walked in.

"Consider this taken care of." Shadoweaver said glancing up at Bonny, "anything else?"

"Actually, Yes, Bonny will be putting a protective field up, you may be needed to help at times, so stay in touch."

They stood up, and after words of greeting to Bonny the three of them walked out. Shadoweaver went his own way, while Bonny and Talmorg headed to the center of the camp.

"We are going to erect an open tent here and we will have someone here at all times to tend to your needs. I would like to see if you can extend the shield far enough to protect the trenches also. I hope it is not asking too much, but it would save a lot of lives."

"I will do my best Lord Talmorg. I may not have to tend to holding it up constantly, but if I should sleep someone needs to be here to wake me before it drops."

"As I said at least one person will be with you at all times, you may well be the difference between winning or losing. All we need to do is establish a stand off until Eric accomplishes his task, then Shiheel and Hesheil will be able to overpower the Scaldorians, with that done victory is ours."

"Let us hope he does not take much longer." Bonny lifted her arm pictured in her mind's eye a barrier reaching out to encompass their defensive trenches and immediately it was there, with far less effort than she had expected, "Lord, I have but eaten only once today, if you would be so kind." She left the words hanging there.

"It shall be taken care of right away." as he spoke the open tent was being put up. She would have referred to it as a lean-to, but it was sufficient, and she was somewhat relieved to rest. It was far less work to hold up her defensive wall, than to work in the field hospital, less mental stress also. For the first time she had a chance in the late afternoon sun to see how busy the rest of the camp was, not to mention what it looked like.

*   *   *   *   *   *   *   *   *

*

Shiheel had his full focus on the battling at hand, so he had not noticed when Bonny's protective bubble went up or they might have backed through it sooner. It surprised them, when suddenly the Scaldorian attacks were cut off, impacting the barrier with a distortion of the applied magic, creating rips and splatters of color and energy. Shiheel was sure he saw at least one rip in time and dimension, which gave some concern for possible side effects. Anything could wind up passing through a rip in the fabric of time and space, and something as small as gas or bacteria had the potential of destroying the entire planet. It was unlikely, but still possible. Quickly he explained to Hesheil what was happening and determined he would examine anything that came through for hazardous repercussions. They needed to maintain a steady attack on the Scaldorians at the same time. The Darkwatchers and demons still outnumbered the dragons by about two to one, but now the dragons too could take refuge from attack.

Only two Darkwatchers and one demon slammed against the barrier before they all realized they could not pass through.

The Scaldorians paused in their attack before they threw what Hesheil recognized as a portal spell, it failed, but all of a sudden there was a massive hole in the air through which among other things a tyrannosaurus fell, but nothing as far as Shiheel could tell, that threatened any high level of destruction. Aside from squishing a few Milmorgs it landed on, the dinosaur ran away immediately from the battle field. The Scaldorians intensified their attack, Shiheel could measure a deterioration in the field, but before it got too far, they stopped their attack altogether and started to circle the protective dome, presumably searching for weaknesses. He was confident they would find none, but they followed the circling from the inside dropping off their own fruitless counter attack.

Bonny gave the protective barrier a concentrated effort for about twenty minutes and then stopped while she ate. If it held up as well as it did on their journey to get here, it would hold for as much as a full day. She did notice however that this time it was subject to a steady assault, which she guessed would reduce its duration. She watched the steady beating that the Scaldorians were giving to the barrier concentrated on one area, she saw them pause and the giant lizard fall from the sky, but she felt the massive attack they concentrated on it before they stopped. It felt like an extension of herself getting shot at with a squirt gun full of warm water. She paused in her eating long enough to reinforce the barrier, but after that attack she could continue to feel the energy field like it was a skin somehow her own. It was a strange sensation to her, quite new and different from the feel of the adoma. She did not think of it as unpleasant, but it was not pleasant either, just different.

Bonny realized if all she did was sit there, she would very quickly get bored, so she requested that patients with minor injury be brought or sent to her. She liked being able to heal by touching, how nice it would be to be able to do that in the real world. She wondered though if this could be a real world also. She had trouble believing this to be something Eric made up, but she had trouble believing it was real too. What she did know was that she could not tell anyone at work about it they would think she was kidding or crazy, or both no one would ever believe anything this outlandish. It felt real.

Coren and his troops were intense in the middle of battle, when the barrier went up stopping any more of the enemy from getting through. A portion of the enemy on the inside already threw down their weapons and gave up when they realized they no longer had any back up, but most were killed before they knew what was happening. The Scaldorian minions were force to back up, not being able to get through they were just target practice for the southern archers unless they were back far enough to avoid the shower of arrows. An undeclared cease fire was forced into effect, and both sides sat quietly watching the other.

Coren smiled inside, as long as that barrier remained in place they were winning. Between the Eftites ability to convert matter and energy and the Adomas power to produce food, all their needs were met whereas the enemy had a supply problem, resulting in the falling of moral and desertion. The enemy was losing by attrition and attitude, and they were winning without more lives being lost. Although pleased with what was happening, Coren was amazed at how well the strange barrier was working. To think a human had this much power, the race that had never been granted natural magical ability in the past, considered too violent a race and alien to their world.

Coren remembered having a vision while he was unconscious after the fall, but it was not all that clear. He dreamed Gaharias had come to him and made him the future Shane of the Elkinfolk, king of the Elves. Dreams had meaning to the Elves no matter how they came about, but this one troubled him. Of course, the Never Ending Poem did say that when the long lost prince returned he would give his kingdom to another. Gaharias was also the only one who could give the power over the Adoma to another blood line, and he had started to feel it since then. He could feel the shifting on the surface of it and knew when its power was being used in part, sometimes even who was using it. He wondered if he could make new things grow out from it, but now was not the time to find out. That would have to wait until he was chosen if it were true.

*   *   *   *   *   *   *   *   *   *

Calhan had been nervous the last few days and quite withdrawn, Eric knew it was because of how close they were to the keep which he and a good friend had so recently escaped. Lady Moor was also a little more on the alert. To Eric's comfort however Charlie had remained quite at ease.

Both Garth and Kedd agreed that there were no new tracks in the area with the exception of those that belonged to wild animals. They were following Stralina's lead, she seemed to have total confidence that she knew exactly where she was going, the rest of the party with the stubborn exception of Brent had totally given up their mistrust of the Jinn. Brent simply professed not to trust anyone and was still very critical of anybody else and their ideas, but they all saw right through his front and humored him when they could by arguing their point, even if there was not a point to argue. They were now one day out from the maze of caves that led under the keep.

'*Eric!*' Charlie interrupted his thoughts '*Something large is approaching*'

Eric noticed that Lady Moor had vanished again, '*Any idea what it is* ' he thought back to the Gerpin

'*No*' Charlie's answer was short and simple.

Eric hand signaled the small company to a stop and whispered once he had their attention, "Something is approaching, take cover." then slipped into the concealment of some underbrush himself. He was barely hidden when he felt the ground shuddering from the approaching footsteps of a large or at least massive creature. He used his mind to reach out and investigate the situation, and was surprised at what he found. He started picking up mind images not from Charlie or Lady Moor, but the giant creature that was approaching. The images were confused and tainted with fear bouncing between what Eric would think of as prehistoric scenes and those of a battle he had seen in his dreams of Bonny.

Eric judged the approaching creature intelligent, but entirely out of place, hungry and afraid. Then he saw its head above some trees in the distance, he could not believe it, it was as best he could figure a tyrannosaurus. The closer it got the more he felt it was in pain, but fighting to keep his pain and anger under subjection to reason. It was worth a try he decided and sent out a strong thought image *'Hello stranger to these lands, can I help you.'*

The giant lizard came to a stop and looked around and answered back in the language of thought, *'Who and where are you.'*

'I am smaller than your arm and, on the ground, ahead of you.' Eric thought his exact location to the creature as he stood up and stepped out of the brush.

The dinosaur looked down at him, Eric could feel it subdue a laugh, *'Little one how could you possibly help me, I was at meal with my family, when a hole opened up out of nowhere and I fell to the ground on this strange world in what seemed to be the middle of a war, so I ran. I now have a broken arm and am lost in a world I know nothing about, hopeless of return to my home'*

'Well I could start by seeing if I can fix that arm of yours, then we could take it from there' Eric paused than continued *'Show me what you would normally eat. I see that you are hungry and I could help you there also.'* Eric's mind was filled with the image of lightly steamed fish meat in a large bowl with something he took as an eating utensil. He focused on

the image and felt the power rise up within him making the image a reality setting halfway between them. *'Eat and then I will look at your arm.'*

As hungry as the large one was, he used great restraint, to eat by what its customs considered good manners. Using the eating implement with its left hand. Eric looked at the right arm obviously the one normally used for this purpose, it seemed broken in the lower section and dislocated at the shoulder. The rest of Eric's small company began showing their faces from out of hiding. Eric directed his thoughts to the creature once again, *'I am called by Eric, may I inquire as to how to address you?'* Its eyes lifted from its meal, *'I go by Aargar, I will not bother with title, for it may never have meaning again if I cannot return to my home. My first born shall carry it on.'*

'I am going to set and mend your arm.' Eric closed his eyes and pictured the arm whole as the other one, again feeling the power welling up inside of him and releasing into the great lizard Aargar. *'It is done, Aargar.'*

He felt the shock, wonderment and then appreciation. Aargar returned, *'Where I come from your kind, healer that is are held in high regard, and worthy of great respect.'* He looked over his arm, *'and you must be one of the best, worthy of the highest respect.'*

'Respect life, respect skill, but do not give honor to one who has not earned it, lest you should fall in an evil snare.' Eric surprised himself, because he did not recognize the thought as his own, but his next statement was his own surmising, *'I think you must have fallen through a rip in*

time and space, possibly caused by the clash of powerful magics. I am not sure if I can help you in that area yet, it could be a matter of several days or longer before I can give you an answer on that matter. I will need to consult with some others that I know. There are fish in the oceans of this world. It seems your kind is civilized; can you find the means to survive for a while. I must finish a mission that is near its end before I can look into giving you further help.'

'I will be alright, thanks to you, you have been more than kind to a total stranger, who might intimidate others. Thank you, but be on your way and do what you must.' Eric turned to the others, and suppressed their questions with a look. "Form up we are ready to move out of here." Again, they were following Stralina's lead, leaving the stranger to finish his meal in peace.

Before evening they reached the mouth of the cave, through which they would reach the depths of the keep. There were no signs of anything occupying the cave, but they checked out the inside anyway. It was clear, and they set up camp for the night in the entry of the cave. When they settled around the fire, Eric, after a little persuading, shared with them what had happened with the giant lizard, and then they set guard and went to sleep.

*   *   *   *   *   *   *   *   *   *

How much time had passed he had no idea, he had been trapped in this magical prison for a long time, but had still found no way to escape. He had been tricked into the trap, not that it was totally uncomfortable, or maybe he was just used to it by now he did not really know. Actually, he had been there long enough he could not remember exactly how he had gotten there. His memory was a little jumbled and sanity felt like it was escaping him, if he did not get free soon, he might lose it altogether. His only hope was that someone would come upon him by accident and bring about his rescue, for there was no escape from the inside out.

He was Merlin Starnook, a great wizard of different names in different worlds. Merlin Starnook was his real name though, that was one of the bits of drifting thoughts he clung to. Time without purpose had stripped much of the meaning away from thinking, but shear stubbornness had kept him from giving in completely. Time had long since taken those who had imprisoned him, but he would never know how. He was in an eternity of neither sleep nor wake, but he had not aged one second in its grasp and time had become unreal. When he was first imprisoned Merlin had spent much time or the distortion he now recognized as time to sharpen his skills, at the time unmatched by any other. He had dreamed of escape and vengeance, but vengeance no longer had any meaning.

He had been a good wizard and would like to keep it that way, if he were to find the freedom to practice once again. There were times when he could feel what was going on in the world outside, but he did not know if it was real or not. For some time now he had felt an oppressive evil power not too far away, the evil seemed to have left, though a tremendous flow of power continued. The energy flow however was neither good nor evil, but he suspected the evil he had felt was using that power. He thought he felt the subtle presence of something good approaching, but he had doubts, it could all be illusion in his own mind, generated by his own moods and feelings.

The feelings though had been a stimulation, and he used it to bring his mind back into focus. He searched the menus of his mind for what he wanted, until he found it, then he stopped pacing the room and sat down to meditate. This would take a little bit of time, but he would do it. If what he was feeling out there was not an illusion than this was the only hope he had of escape, and regaining his sanity. He closed his eyes and started humming quietly to help hold his focus.

*   *   *   *   *   *   *   *   *

Eric woke up before anyone else as usual, only he did not relieve any of their posted guard as he had made a habit of doing. Instead, he found a secluded corner and sat down to meditate, what he planned on doing was searching the caves and tunnels ahead of them, but what happened was quite different. When he relaxed and closed his eyes, he felt a tugging calling him, whatever or whoever was calling him did not know who he was. A warning came from his deductions, they were approaching an enemy strong hold and the calling could be a trap or part of a security set up by the Scaldorians in their absence. The calling persisted but he did not sense any evil at its source, it was not even coming from the right direction. The calling was coming from somewhere in the depths below the caverns they would be traveling through.

After analyzing the situation, he allowed himself contact with the calling in such a way as to not reveal his location or identity. He projected himself much closer to the source and sent out a simple thought, '*Hello.*'

A strange thought came back, '*Have I lost the last edge of sanity or are you real?*'

'*I am quite real, but who and what are you?*'

'*Merlin Starnook, a wizard of old.*'

'*I was told you disappeared a long time ago, hundreds of years, and presumed dead.*'

'*That long is it, I have had no way of knowing. I have been entrapped in a web of magic, that I cannot break from the inside. You are the first one I have been able to reach, no one else has ever answered my call. Whether they could not hear it or could not answer I do not know. Either way it will take power to help me, to break the spell which binds me, time itself has not weakened it. I only hope you are both able and willing to try. You may be my last hope.*'

'*If you are Starnook, by what magic did Suan defeat Deassheema?*'

'*That is easy, Suan's family never had any real magic, they were tricksters, and good at it. He burned the lock blocking the gas from the death pits, then put on a good performance resulting in the gas killing Deassheema, well done job. Unfortunate he died at the same time. Nobody could know that story though I hid his diary, nobody could have found it without me.*'

'*I have read that diary. You must be Starnook, you finished the diary for him.*'

'Thank you, for that much. Will you help me?'

'How?'

'I am not sure. I am not even sure exactly where I am.'

'I can probably find you. Just stay in touch.'

'I hope you are a fairly powerful wizard.'

'Some have compared me with you. I will have to see what I can do when I get there, but I have confidence I can get you out of there. I am several times farther away than I seem however, so stay calm and we will be there.'

Eric reached out with his mind and located the energy generator, that penetrated the dimensional barrier. Then he established a route that would take them past Starnook to get there. After close examination, he realized it was the shortest route anyway, shorter than the one Stralina had described she took. He rose from his meditation the others were up and eating a sparse meal. He joined them. When they were finished eating and ready to continue, Eric called them together, "I am going to lead the rest of the way in, we are going to take a different route than we planned."

"But I am the only one who knows the way," Stralina interjected. "I thought that was already agreed."

"It was agreed, but I found a shorter way while meditating." Eric paused, "There is also someone who needs our help on the way."

Hans asked the question everyone was thinking, "Who could be down there that needs our help?"

Eric watched to see their reactions, "Merlin Starnook."

"Anyone else I would not believe," it was Brent that broke the silent suspense, "though I have my doubts, you have proved yourself enough that I will trust you." The support of their number one doubter brought the rest into agreement to follow after what they all thought was impossible.

Eric turned and they started winding through the dark tunnels, using glimmer spells to light their way. They traveled for what seemed like the most part of a day, and nerves were on edge, after all they were not all cave dwellers and through some of the lower and tighter tunnels brought on minor claustrophobia. For the most part however they kept totally silent which helped them get along without quarreling. They had gone a long way down and some of the travel had been quite steep even bad enough that crude steps had been cut in the stone a long time ago, indicating that at some time these caves had been more regularly used.

They had gotten close enough to Merlin that Eric could feel his presence not far away and slowed down a little, "Not too much farther, we need to be careful. Merlin is in some kind of magical trap and we don't want to get caught in it too."

They turned a corner and Eric stopped. He could see an old wizard sitting on the floor in a chamber ahead. The entry to the chamber was about fifty feet away and the chamber was filled with light.

Brent spoke up, "There is a magical field that starts about five feet from the doorway, I would guess it completely envelopes the room. It is an ancient kind of magic, from before even Merlin's Day. It will be dangerous to remove even if we can, it will result in the release of a tremendous wave of magic, possibly cause tremors." he went silent they all knew the implications of tremors this far down in a network of tunnels.

"We must try though." Eric started carefully forward.

Charlie caught his attention, '*I know this magic it is set up with a crystal pattern, we have to be fast. There should be a white crystal in the wall near where the field begins, and there must be four other entry ways to this chamber, each with an identical crystal. Turning this crystal will open the field, but then the rest need to be turned before the energy of the crystals starts to reform and rips the rock apart around us. I am the only one who has a chance of moving fast enough. When I signal after you find this crystal, turn it.*' The Gerpin hopped down on the ground in front of him and stopped just short of the invisible wall, studying the other entrances to the chamber. '*I have located the other crystals.*'

Eric found the crystal in the wall and put his hand on it, '*Found this one, I am ready when you are.*'

'*Now!*'

Eric turned the crystal immediately, and Charlie moved fast enough to vanish to the eye. It seemed almost as quick as he had vanished, he was back in front of Eric, yet with all his speed it seemed he was just a little slower than needed. The rock under their feet shook knocking them all off their feet. Even though he had fallen to the ground, Eric saw the old wizard levitate off the floor and raise one hand silencing the shake.

"That was close." Merlin said rising to his feet. "Much more of a shake and we would need to dig our way out of here. Ah, and who am I indebted to for my own rescue." When he stopped speaking he turned and looked into Eric's face, "The son of Gaharias and mortal man, you have returned. More time has passed than I had thought. If you are here than the first of the second great wars has begun, destruction and remaking are at work and the coming of new order. Powers are at play that out reach the ancients. It is my honor to make your acquaintance, but if I am correct the Elves need my help now. I cannot tarry or I will be too late."

"They may have more power with them than you know," Eric said, "but if you seek to give them help do not let me slow you down."

The rest of Eric's company simply looked on in silent awe at the legend from their past, returned from among the dead.

"I do have a question for you though, how did you escape Deassheema's ambush, and why did you leave your death recorded in Suan's diary?"

"First, I could not change his diary, it is a record of history from his point of view and helps give an understanding of things that happened to a student of history. I did not escape the ambush, I was mistakenly left for dead, it took me quite a while to recover from the extent of injury, for that matter I was even buried, considered dead by those who knew me. How is it you come to know so much about that diary?"

"I wanted information and it, or a magically created copy of that diary came to my bidding."

"The power to summon what you wish, even if you don't know

what it is. You have much more than that the power of the Ancients indeed, be careful for some will envy how much power you have been granted, and that among the Ancients themselves.”

“I only know one of them, Gaharias. He has given me guidance, but does not know the extent of power I have, nor do I.”

“Some of the Old Ones might even be jealous” Merlin laugh and wisp out of the cavern on a windwalk spell. Eric knew where he went and did not give it a second thought.

Hans Spardic stepped up and asked, “Where did he go?”

“To help Talmorg.” Eric gave a simple answer. “Let’s move on.”

Stralina commented as they filed behind Eric out another door, “We will need to stop soon and rest, it took me three days to travel out through these tunnels the other way.”

“I agree,” said Eric, “but this chamber is no longer safe after that tremor.”

They traveled for about another hour before they found a suitable cavern to spend the night. Eric decided that they needed a good hot meal to pick up morale a bit, so he willed a full steak dinner all set up around a wooden table in the middle of the cavern. It worked quite well giving them all a temporary break from what they were doing, except Eric who used his magic to keep watch for anything approaching them. He did however get relief from seeing, the others unwind, and even though he would know if anything approached, he had no problem relaxing.

The next morning was very quiet, they all knew that they would reach their destination, before the day was out. What was ahead now was totally unknown and promised to be the most dangerous part of their entire journey. They were all determined in their mission, knowing that Eric was the only one who could disable the energy generator, they were of a mind not to allow anything to get in his way. The first couple of hours went without incident, Eric probing ahead to see the way was clear. They had two minor encounters before lunch, a cavern with a creature that seemed to be a cross between a large bat and a blood sucking misquito and about twenty giant rats they slipped by in a side tunnel. After a brief lunch stop, they started out again with Hans and Brent in the lead. Eric picked up on a patrol of Ogres shortly after they started up again, and passed the information on to Lady Moore, who disappeared and caught up with them about an hour later after taking care of them.

Finally, they pushed their way through a hidden door into the lower level of the keep. Eric could feel that the keep was almost empty, with scattered small patrols. He wondered why the Scaldorians would leave the keep so unprotected especially when their source of power was hidden here. He probed the keep to where the power generator was being kept, it was completely walled in. Not only was it all walled in, but there were several castings of magic around it to protect it, though he did not yet know exactly how they worked. They managed to avoid most of the patrols, but when one became unavoidable Hans slipped ahead and finished them off in silence.

Eric directed them around turns and down halls, finally bringing them to a stop in the middle of one hall he pointed to a wall, "The device is the other side of this wall. There are several protective spells caste about it and we don't know what they do until we try to penetrate them, so be ready for anything. Kesker, would you see if you can knock some of these stones loose?"

Kesker stepped up and slammed his double clenched fist against the wall and the stones shifted in their mortar.

Brent stepped forward, pointing up the wall, "Don't touch it again that is poisonous slim running down the wall."

Stralina reached forward and threw some dust on the wall, instantly it went up in flames, burning until the slime was completely gone. "That should take care of that." she said, "try again."

Kesker swung again shifting the stones a little farther.

"Gas." Calhan piped up, "coming out of the floor."

"More poison." Kesker said, a spray of sparks flew from his fingers and the gas was gone.

Kedd stepped up and handed Kesker his battle hammer, "Here try this it might be a little quicker, it is enchanted to shatter stone, among other things."

They were all forced to jump back when the wall burst into white flame. This time Eric froze the wall, countering the flames, and stepped up to look through the hole in the wall where the hammer hit, the stone had turned to gravel. He could see one side of the machine they were looking for.

When he stepped back patrols were coming at them from both directions, attracted by the commotion they had caused. Eric decided the easiest way to deal with it was to put up a wall like Bonnys, and with the thought it was up. The patrols slammed into it before they saw it and wound up sprawled on the floor in confusion. Kesker broke out a couple more stones giving them room to fit through. Brent stood there for a minute then started casting spells to counter the Esberkian protection spells that had been caste on the room.

When he was done, he turned to Eric and said, "There is one more spell on the room that I cannot break, it is a bad one, if we try to enter that room we'll be zapped out of this dimension."

Eric took a hand full of the powder he was still carrying from his backpack, and summoned the energy of the barrier within him into the powder and through it into the opening, saying, "Here goes nothing." There was a flash of white.

Brent was impressed, "That did it, you jammed the spell."

They all slipped into the small room. The strange mechanism was right in the middle of the room with pipes and tubes coming out of a large central sphere. There was a large pipe that extended down towards the floor, but seemed to fade out of existence before it got there, that was the one Eric wanted to destroy and where he needed to seal the hole in the inter-dimensional barrier. Eric pulled out one of the bags of volcanic powder he had left and set it on the floor, then he pulled out his samurai sword and sliced clean through the large energy conduit. He put the sword away. Picking the bag of powder up, he called upon the power that was within him channeling it into the powder he held in one hand. With his other hand he pushed down on the lower part of the conduit he had cut, it gave so easily that he pushed it much more than he intended, driving it completely out of sight and exposing the raw flow of power into the machine.

He reached out and felt the alternate barrier with his mind, he had driven the conduit right on out the other side. Quickly he threw a handful of the powder in the energy flow, causing it to stop then he took the rest and shoved it down in the hole in the barrier, reaching out with his mind and helping the barrier knit itself back together.

While he was helping the barrier knit itself back together, he communicated with it in a strange way. He felt as though it was becoming a part of him also or at one with him and he knew that somehow the power he had increased and he already did not know its limits, but now he had the power of two barriers dividing different dimension at his disposal. The barrier felt like a life to itself and his help was appreciated and he was trusted.

When the barrier was fixed Eric stood up, "We must destroy this apparatus leaving nothing left together."

They all set to work cutting and pounding till there was nothing left but a pile of scrap on the floor. When they were finished Kesker pounded a hole through the opposite wall from which they had come in and they started up through the keep.

*   *   *   *   *   *   *   *   *   *

The horseman units had made at least seven lightning strikes per day since the barrier went up, doing major damage and returning before enemy had a chance to counter strike. It had been working out well, but now the enemy camps had moved too far out to make the tactic worthwhile. They were now at a total standoff, neither side effective against the other. Once the protective field faltered and there was a brief hard engagement in the air, but Bonny had it back up before there were any casualties and the battle immediately ceased, neither side wanting to waste their energy.

Saphrine was back with Talmorg, there was nothing for her to do out on the front lines now, though they both had a habit of mixing with the troops. They were having dinner with Bonny, when an old gray wizard appeared out of nowhere in a cloud of dust about ten feet away, stumbled a couple of steps then laughed.

"Out of practice on that landing I guess, long time since I wind-walked. You must be Talmorg, you look a lot like old Lacrane's son, his name was Talmorg too, come to think of it. Excuse my babbling, I am Merlin Starnook, been out of circulation for a while."

Several of both Talmorg's and Saphrine's personal guard were now gathered around the old wizard. Talmorg addressed them, "He can't be an enemy or he would not have been able to get through the barrier, I will at least hear him out. Come closer, if indeed you are Merlin, I could use your help. The least I know of you is you did not come as an enemy; therefore,

I shall try not to make you one. I can also see you have some kind of power to appear so in the middle of my camp."

Nice setup you got here that barrier and all." Merlin said walking towards them, "Seems to me you got yourself in quite the stalemate here, shall we see if we can stir things up a bit, aye?"

"I am impressed by your entry, but how am I to know that you are indeed Merlin Starnook, and how do you propose that we stir things up 'a bit'?" Talmorg inquired "You must know that Merlin went down in history as dying in a battle with Deassheema centuries ago."

"Indeed, the record is faulty, I was left for dead, but you can take me for whoever you want, that's not too important. What is important is winning this battle, and war. I am experienced at dealing with demons, and I was here when those wretched Darkwatchers were first fought and eliminated from the face of Ethar, I know how to fight them."

"Oh, and how is it best to fight them?" Saphrine asked obviously skeptical.

Merlin laughed a sarcastic snicker at her skepticism, "With the weather, a mild lightning storm. The world from which they were summoned to begin with has no water, they cannot caste their lightening or fire in the rain, it messes them up. Then they also attract lightening and it will destroy them if they are wet." He then took his staff and struck it to the ground, lifted it up drawing three circles in the air. Immediately dark clouds started forming and dropping a gentle rain outside their protective dome, followed by flashes of lightening in the sky.

From where they sat, they could see the Darkwatchers bursting with a brief flash and turning into clouds of black smoke, dissipated by the rain. The steady elimination and flight of the Darkwatchers, freed the Dragons up to focus on the other demons which were already far fewer in number and with all the eyes from both sides on the ground watching the air, the dragons made short work of the demons. The tide of the air battle was turned completely against the Scaldorians and they started retreating immediately to avoid being surrounded, the entire air battle group pursued. An uproar went up from out of the entire camp at the sight of the retreating Scaldorians.

Shortly after the Scaldorians were out of sight, reports started coming back of abandoned enemy camps and surrendering enemy units. To Talmorg it meant that the war was coming to an end, but it was not over yet, not until the bonds of peace were reestablished. The Scaldorians had lost some of their power though at least the power they had over their armies.

CHAPTER 25

Dividing the Crowns

Shiheel and Hesheil led the pursuit, fighting as they went. The
Scaldorians now stood alone no minions at their side. Still Shiheel
felt caution was needed, he knew that they fled only to avoid being
surrounded, not out of fear, but by decision. They knew where they were
retreating to, and it would work to their advantage. They were probably
headed back to Darval Keep. Shiheel was worried about Eric, whether he
would be finished when they got there, but near the end of their first day
of pursuit, the Scaldorians suddenly dropped off their fighting and sped
off faster than the dragons could keep up, leaving only the Eftites and
Merlin on their tail. Shiheel knew then that Eric had just severed their
dimensional power tap and left them high and dry, unable to maintain the
intensity of battle.

By the next morning the keep was in sight. The Scaldorians made
a semicircle and disappeared into one of the towers. The Eftites descended
to the roof inside the parapet and followed in through the door and down
the stair with the old wizard at their sides. They had to catch up with the
Scaldorians before they managed to open another bag of tricks, or maybe
did repairs to their disabled power source. They stepped off the landing
at the bottom of the staircase into a hall with doors lining both sides. The
Scaldorians could have gone through any one of them. The hot trail was
lost but escape could not be allowed, it would only result in future disaster.

They would have to go one room at a time keeping a watch on the hall at the same time.

*   *   *   *   *   *   *   *   *   *

The small company followed Eric through the keep, the patrols they happened upon ran at the sight of them, now. Word of what they had done must have spread fast. None of them asked Eric where he was going or what he was doing, they just followed. They eventually turned down a hall where there was a guarded door, but the guards too ran at the sight of them. It was into that room, Eric turned.

The room was filled with alien gadgetry. There were metal implements hanging on the walls, most of which Eric interpreted as simple hand weapons, others he could not identify. There were several tables in the room with a wide array of alien equipment, most of which he had no understanding of. Brent seemed to recognize some of it, so Eric listened to his explanations, some sorcery, some science. Finally, they decided it would be best to destroy all of it, to prevent the Scaldorians from gaining advantage of it if they returned.

About the time they were done, Calhan, who was on watch at the window gave them the alert, "They are coming back, they just landed on the far tower."

"Okay, every one stay calm and take cover. Conceal yourselves in the closets under the tables and stay quiet." Eric took a quick look around the room, while the rest of them vanished from sight. Then he hid himself in a wall closet of obviously more recent construction. They had already emptied its contents on the floor and he left the door ajar so as to be able to observe the room.

It was not long, when the door opened and Eric saw what at first looked like large insects enter the room. They were about two feet tall and with a closer look Eric, noticed their bodies and heads were armored in what looked like beetle shells. The face of the one he saw looked like it was painted on a smooth ball, with the exception of the eyes which were protruding with independent motion like some kind of lizard. It had three legs and four arms which gave it the first impression of an insect, but they were more like octopus tentacles with four opposing fingers at the end of each one and the feet looked just like the hands only heftier. They were ugly as they rushed into the room slamming the door behind them.

They stopped briefly and looked over the destruction in the room. Then the three of them, differing only in the color of the shells that protected their heads, scuttled across the room concealing themselves from the door, behind a table right in front of Eric. They settled on the floor and began working what Eric could feel was very powerful magic, then turned as if ready to pounce on something they were expecting to follow them.

Only few minutes later the door opened again, to Erics surprise Shiheel stepped in and he could see Hesheil and Merlin standing in the hall. Eric could feel the power of the magic rising from the Scaldorians as Shiheel started around the room, oblivious to the fact they were lying in wait for him. Eric knew he would have to do something or this could well be the end of Shiheel. He hesitated only a moment then reached down into the depths of the power within him and with a full exertion let it loose. A translucent sheet came forth from within him moving in a wave through the air about four feet high and square, moving toward the Scaldorians. They turned and saw it just before it hit them. As the odd apparition passed through them the Scaldorians vaporized leaving nothing behind. The casting of the magic had caught Shiheel by surprise and he instinctively turned and blasted in the direction it was coming from barely missing Eric, and only missing because at the last possible moment he realized what was happening.

Eric stood up and stepped out from where he was hiding. The Scaldorians were gone, totally defeated. Shiheel stepped up to him, "Nice job, Eric. A little overkill maybe, but the job is complete."

Hesheil and Merlin stepped into the room and the rest came out of hiding. Hans shook his head, impressed by what he had seen. "Remind me not to make you mad at me." he laughed a hollow laugh of nervous amazement.

"I would say we should get back to the front and see if Talmorg needs any more help there." Shiheel said looking around with satisfaction at the situation.

"I have some other business to tend to not far from here first, a friend in need you could say and I could probably use you guys' help." Eric said pointing to the Eftites, "We have a dinosaur that wants to go home, you might have seen him?"

"No actually, we were a little busy for sightseeing, when we flew

498

in." Shiheel answered, Eric could not tell if he was being sarcastic or not.

"We will probably find him, to the southeast of the keep, not more than a couple days travel away on foot." Eric looked out the window, "Can you carry all of us back on your disc?"

"No, I don't think so, but Hesheil can get that chariot of the Scaldorians operating, then we could carry everyone except the moor cat. She probably wants to go to her own home anyway." Shiheel walked up to the window next to Eric.

"I'll ask her." Eric said, "Do you think that we can work this portal you gave me to get Aargar, that's the dinosaur back to his home."

"It may be possible, but we will need Hesheil's magic also, Or possibly Merlins. The mechanics of the device will only serve their designated purpose without the help of magic." Shiheel paused, it seemed to him unlikely, but worth a try for Eric's sake, "We will have to make some of its fixed matrix patterns adjustable, hopefully we can find some way to get a fix on where he came from."

"His kind communicate by thought, I should be able to get information that will help with that from him." Eric turned from the window, he wondered if the dinosaurs of old Earth had really been intelligent. He felt brain size had nothing to do with intelligence, but rather its mental activity. He also considered that it was possible that some of the mental facilities might be handled in other areas of the nervous system. "Well let's get out of here and see what we can do." he headed for the door.

As they walked down the hall Eric communicated with Lady Moore and Charlie, '*Lady Moore, are you returning directly to the Elves with us, or are you returning to you own first. I understand that your children are still in the south, but you could meet us there if you wanted to bring report of what has happened back to your own people first.*' Eric felt like he was trying to dump her and he did not like the feeling.

'*My people, need to know what is happening, but it will be quicker if I travel alone.*' Lady Moore answered, '*I will be able to stop and tell them on my way south. I will see you again there.*'

Eric marveled at how well she communicated in images rather than words, though he had gotten to the point with her that it was not as foreign as it was to begin with. '*That will work out best for all of us than.*'

Charlie who was following their conversation interjected, '*It will also be safer, for Lady Moore not to be slowed down. She can out run anything if she has no one to hold her back.*' Then he changed the subject, '*About our friend, Aargar the rex, you have the power of two of the dimensional barriers. I assure you, that you could return him home by yourself. You need to follow his thoughts back to his place of origin, then you have the power to bend the portal yourself.*'

'*I always thought magic was a learned skill, which I know very little about.*' Eric was realizing that the power he had did whatever he wanted with little or no forethought, which was quite different from everything he thought he knew about magic. '*How is it I am able to bend the portal when its maker isn't even sure it can be done?*'

'In actuality you don't even need the portal, now that you have been empowered by two of the dimensional barriers.' Charlie did what Eric took as snickering, *'You are more powerful than any of the old Ancients now, and they are not allowed to act directly in the affairs of the races on Ethar because of the extent of their power. I find that humorous, however you may not want to abuse that power or you might find yourself limited to living on the same plains of dimension as them. Not that it is bad, just different.'*

'It sounds to me like an exile of sorts,' Eric knew that it was indeed an exile, one he would rather not face. They were there because of a war that almost destroyed Ethar. He had no desire to abuse his power. *'I shall be careful, but I will need your guidance and that of my ancestor, Gaharias.'*

'I can assure you of both, Gaharias is one of the best, almost not even sent away from Ethar with the rest. He has more liberality than the others, but he rarely uses it.'

'Am I able to visit them where they are?'

'Any time you want, however it would probably be easier to see him through meditation. Not all of the Ancients would be glad to see you.'

They got to the door, that marked the entrance of the tower through which the Scaldorians and the Eftites had entered, Lady Moore interjected, *'There is no need for me to go up with you I will take the stair down and be on my way.'*

'Fair well for now then friend, I will see you at Dragoncove.'

In a single motion she was gone and Eric explained simply to the others, "She is going to her own and will meet us again at Dragoncove." and they started up the stairs behind Shiheel.

On the roof the Eftite tensor disc and the damaged Scaldorian chariot were just where they had been left. The Eftites stepped up to the Scaldorian chariot.

"I can still make this thing fly; the damage can be compensated for with just a little magic. I'll have it running in a flash." Hesheil stated in his totally matter of fact manner, "Figure out how we're going to split up, anyone queasy about flying had best ride in the chariot where there is something to hold on to."

While Hesheil worked over the chariot, the others decided who would ride where. Brent as Hesheil's student in Esberkian magic chose the chariot. Kesker also chose the chariot, wanting to sit down hold on and not see when they were off the ground. Calhan chose the chariot and Kedd was put on the chariot, because he was the only other one who would fit. The rest were happy to ride on the disc each for their own reasons.

In a few minutes they were ready to lift off. As they took to the air, Eric reached out with his mind and located Aargar. He gave directions to Shiheel who flashed them in a beam of light to Hesheil and they headed south and slightly east of the keep. The keep would again be abandoned until someone else came to claim it, hopefully next time it would house a more benign lordship that would make it a pleasant place to visit. Eric realized that with its history it would probably be left unclaimed for a long time.

What would have been a couple of days travel on foot took less than an hour in the air. Eric did not examine how Shiheel did it but he managed to protect them from any wind as they flew. That made the flight much more pleasant than he had anticipated. There was no conversation during their flight aside from Eric giving Shiheel directions. They were all involved in their own private thoughts about flying, none of them had done it before, with the exceptions of Eric, Shiheel, Hesheil, Merlin and Stralina.

Stralina did not find it much different from the flying carpets her people had learned to make and use. For Merlin, it was like wind walking on a strange disk. Eric however found it quite different from his flying experiences, but was more involved in where they were going than how they were getting there.

Eric made contact with Aargar when they were about half way there and projected mind images of what to expect when they arrived, so he would not be too surprised when they showed up. Aargar was still amazed at what he saw, but glad Eric had shown him ahead of time. Eric had managed to convince Aargar that it was not going to be a problem getting him home, before they reached the clearing where they met him.

Aargar was standing at the south edge of the field watching when they landed, '*I have never seen anything fly that did not have its own wings.*' Eric could not read his facial expression, but he could feel Aargar's disbelief in his thoughts.

'When we are done, I hope you will be able to look back on this as a bad dream.' Eric was curious how Aargar would deal with what was happening when it was over, but he did not ask, *'You will be able to forget all this and return to your normal life?'*

Eric was the first one to step off, when they landed. Shiheel was right behind him. "The first thing we will have to do is try to get some fix on where he came from, then we will have to try to adjust the portal as close as we can. After that, Hesheil will ...." Shiheel started saying, but Eric interrupted him.

"For the sake of expedience, I can handle it myself." Eric said to him, catching Shiheel totally off guard. "I have been learning more about what I can do, and it will be quicker and easier if I do it myself this time."

Shiheel was stunned and did not know what to say. Eric's sudden decision to make such a great display of power, left him standing there questioning, even doubting Eric's wisdom, but there was nothing he could do to stop Eric. For the first time Shiheel doubted his own wisdom in bringing Eric to Ethar to begin with, the willingness to use this much power so casually could be very dangerous. If Eric starts solving all their problems with simple whims, he could wind up causing more problems than he solved. Great wizards would become a mockery and the people could soon lose the ability to defend themselves without him and the people needed that sense of self-reliance. He would have to talk to Eric about this and bring it to a stop before it went too far. The Eftites themselves withheld a lot from the peoples of this world, to allow them to develop in their own manner and time.

Eric was totally oblivious to the reactions of his comrades as he walked towards Aargar. He had already engrossed himself in locating the origin of Aargar's thoughts, and feeling his way to their place in time, space and dimension. The quickness of his actions when he reached Aargar caught the dinosaur off guard also, and he was stepping through the opened portal before he really understood what he was doing.

Eric felt good about being able to help Aargar so quickly and easily, he had great power to use as he saw fit. Eric stepped back on the tensor disc and they returned to the air. He did not notice anyone else once he sat down, he did not notice how they looked at him. The next thing Eric knew after sitting down was that he found himself standing face to face with Gaharias, with the sensation of having done something on the verge of being wrong.

"I am not disappointed; it is as much my fault as any. I should have given you better instruction a long time ago." Gaharias paused, revealing nothing in his expression, "You have the power to turn the world upside down, but there are rules you should follow. They are the same guidelines that the rest of us have to follow."

"I take it I violated one of those rules somehow with Aargar?" Eric was very uncomfortable, "Charlie started to tell me a little about limitations, but no details."

"It is too bad he did not tell you more. There are a lot of things we can do, like when you eliminated the Scaldorians, that was on the borderline of acceptable, but under the circumstances it was at least something to overlook. It was possible for you to have done that with the weapons you carry, or regular magic, so the use of power in that situation was acceptable." Gaharias pointed to a table Eric had not before seen, with chairs pushed under it. "Come sit down we have some things we need to discuss, and this may take a little time."

The two of them went over and sat down, and Gaharias handed him a glass of golden hued liquid. "Drink and relax, I need to teach you the laws of the Ancients, though to be honest, I do not know which if any actually apply to you."

"That is good, but can I know first what I did wrong?" Eric could not seem to get comfortable with the feeling that his actions were being judged.

"That would be as good a place to start as any. Aargar's presence was the consequence of the normal flow of events and actions of the peoples in this dimension and on Ethar. With an anticipated flow of events the Eftites would have figured out how to return Aargar to his own world, in the meantime there would have been an exchange of information. Now it will be some time before they develop their skills in inter dimensional transportation any further which will add to the growth and development of their society." Gaharias paused sipping on the golden liquid that was some form of wine. "Your action obstructed normal development in the society, by an erroneous display of unnecessary power. It is a minor indiscretion. You could have accomplished the task by helping Shiheel and Hesheil, thereby accelerating the development of their knowledge, with no harm done. Merlin would have also needed to help and so he too would have received some of the glory and knowledge. If you had done something like ending the war by yourself or taken actions on your own that could change the order of the future of Ethar by your own decision."

"That could be anything I do." Eric was getting frustrated.

"Not exactly, you are also a part of this world, and some of your abilities are in the category of normal on Ethar and you can use them to their full extent at any time. The operation of any of the magics that are common or known to the peoples of Ethar, no matter how you learned them, like the magic of the Jinn, you have at your full disposal. Gifts such as those you gave to Saphrine, they are totally acceptable for an Ancient to give to his people. What you do not want to do is take away their independence and self-reliance."

"Maybe, when we are done, I will understand," Eric said enjoying the flavor of the wine, which was helping him relax, "Basically what you are telling me is that Eric the wizard I am a part of the people of Ethar and the flow of events, but as Eric the heir of Gaharias the Ancient, I should try to follow the rules that now govern the Ancients, though they once walked as a part of the people of Ethar themselves."

"You perceive true. Now you need to learn the rules that govern the Ancients, but to understand those rules I will first teach you the history of the Ancients. It is because of our history and the mistakes we made, our failure to govern our own actions, that we were brought under a set of rules to govern them for us. It is also not the actions of all of us that brought the restrictions about, minor mistakes like the one you have made would never have brought about any real problem. There were some among us who were not pleased to give the peoples of Ethar free will to function as they chose, but rather felt that they should be completely subject to the will of the Ancient they were fashioned after. The result was a war that almost destroyed Ethar. There was actually a series of wars, but before the end of the last war, Darval, my brother, and the dark pact vanished, they were not there when the rules were laid down and accepted. They did not accept them, not having been there the dark pact is not yet subject to those rules. You are not yet subject to them in truth and do not have to accept them, yet I hope you do. When I am done you will have the choice whether or not you will be subject to them, but I would advise you to accept most of them." Gaharias shifted in his seat and pulled out a pipe.

"You are aware that Charlie was the one who told me I could sent Aargar back without anyone's help?" Eric pointed out. "You are recommending I generally follow these rules, but not necessarily subject myself to them?"

"If you were following information Charlie gave you, I can not be as critical, but what I said still applies in concept. Just because you can do something does not mean you should." Gaharias continued in conversation with Eric, sharing what knowledge and information he could with suggestions that might help him avoid making more enemies than he needed to among the Ancients of the Old Ones.

None of them had noticed until they landed that Eric was in a trance, but when they did, they guided him to a secluded part of the command tent after Merlin levitated him, and Shiheel requested that he be notified as soon as Eric came out of it. It was shortly after noon when they landed and they were informed that Talmorg was calling for a meeting after dinner and he wanted them to be there.

Kerrikai Barhallah had come into camp the day before, the war was basically over and the Elven empire had to be set back in order. It was expected that Gaharias Emarlandestria would appear and give them his advice, and guidance. The decisions would remain theirs however and tomorrow's meeting would set their future and effect the future of the south land peoples also. A lot rested on the decisions that Talmorg would have to make, he was heir to the throne in the south and to the Uklian crown. If he chose to return to the south than he would have to choose another family to rule the Uklian and receive the power of the Adoma. If Talmorg chose to stay he would have to learn the ways of the Uklian and gain the respect of its people who were still strangers to him.

Talmorg fought a war with his people of old, yet he did not really know them. As he paced the floor of the command tent, he wondered how they would take his decision. He knew nothing about how these people lived outside of war except for what he read in the old records in his father's archives. There were only a few of the native Uklian Elves that he knew and he had to make decisions based what little he knew about them, he hoped that Gaharias would help him in the choices he had made and that the Uklians would agree to his decisions. He could make them mandates without their consent, but he felt that they had the right to have some say in their future. To accept his decisions, they would have to first accept his authority and his position as the heir to the throne. Their acceptance may very well depend on his judgment of the character of those he chose to fill the positions he had to appoint them to.

Saphrine stepped in to see Talmorg pacing the floor, and noticed Eric still in a trance in the corner, with Charlie sleeping in his lap. Saphrine gave Talmorg a warm comforting smile, "You're nervous about the meeting and how they will react to what you have to say."

"A little maybe." Talmorg tried to play it off.

"I have a suspicion, that Eric is in audience with Gaharias right now." Saphrine said, "Your wisdom will not be questioned, I stand behind your decisions so don't be nervous. Remember you haven't been the greatest ambassador in the south, without having learned how to read people and understand their character."

"That is true but those are people we have been dealing with for years," Talmorg stopped pacing and sat down "not just one war."

"These are the people of our ancestry; they are not that different from us and I am sure they have like passions. You must realize by now that wisdom is wisdom regardless of where it comes from, trust they will see the wisdom of what you are doing."

"You are right, and nothing would be gained by worry either

way. Calbork has already seen to all the physical arrangements, so we are ready. I hope Eric is back before the rest start arriving." As Talmorg spoke, Calbork entered the command tent and started lighting the candles, removing all the shadows.

About the time Calbork lit the last candle, Talmorg saw Eric stand up out of the corner of his eye and turned with some relief. He started in Eric's direction, inquiring, "Are you all right, I was starting to think you wouldn't make this evening's meeting."

"I wouldn't miss it, Talmorg. This meeting will indeed mark an important day in the history of Ethar." Eric smiled, his eyes showing he knew things Talmorg did not, which made Talmorg a little less comfortable. "You have nothing to worry about."

"That's what I'm worried about." Talmorg let out a little chuckle, and an almost mocking smile.

"That's more like it, I knew there had to be a smile in there somewhere. I have to go see Bonny and change out of these grubby clothes."

"Hurry back, we'll be starting soon." Talmorg watched Eric go and turned back to Saphrine. She was proud of him, he truly cared about his people and anyone who knew him, knew that. As soon as Talmorg got seated he stood right back up to greet Kerrikai Barhallah as he walked in and the others started to follow. Calbork would take care of greeting the rest however, so Talmorg returned with Kerrikai to the table at the head of their tarp meeting hall.

All of the top staff involved in the Uklian battle front, were present. There was some murmuring about humans being present at a high Elven meeting, but Talmorg was pleased when Kerrikai put an end to it by stating that Gaharias would not turn aside any who helped save the Elven kingdom and the Elkin Adoma. The attitude of the meeting improved and things quickly came to order. There was still tension in the camaraderie between the Elves and the south land companions that had fought this war against a common enemy, they all realized that it would not have been won without the armies of the south. Kerrikai brought the meeting to order he was still the temporary reagent of the Elves, in the absents of an official king.

"Fellow Elves and comrades in arms, our enemy has been defeated and their armies have fled before us scattering themselves in the mountain forests. Our land is again safe and we have no need to pursue the disorganized remnant of the army that stood against us. They were not our actual enemy, and they will eventually make a much stronger ally.

As most of you are fully aware just before we were attacked agents of the Scaldorians slipped in and slew the entire royal family in the Uklian. We the Barhallahs the leaders of faith among the Elves were asked under emergency conditions of impending war to fill their shoes also, but it is not right for us to maintain that position. Two families were set up in different leadership positions a long time ago to maintain a peaceful balance in our Elven kingdom and ours is that leadership in the understanding of the ways given us by Gaharias. The physical leadership belongs in the hands of a king and his family, as it was set up to begin with, having the power to command the Adoma and the responsibility for the care of the Elven lands.

A faction of the Elkinshane family returned to us after the war had already progressed for some time, this being Talmorg the heir to a kingdom in the south. He has the rights and responsibility of the Elkinshane rule according to the laws of our land and the response of the Elkin Adoma to his will, yet he is not a family large enough to fill all the leadership positions throughout the kingdom and will have to appoint reagents to those positions, if he accepts the position as our king. Allow me to present to you Talmorg Elkinshane, that we might hear what he has to say." As he finished Kerrikai turned to Talmorg.

Talmorg looked about the gathering, "Thank you Kerrikai. My friends this is a matter of a decision I have given much thought to since I arrived. I have had to make this decision only after much careful thought. I cannot be the king of two kingdoms, so far apart, and living according to such different rules and ways of life. That leaves me with having to choose between two kingdoms, one of my ancestry my birthright to claim, the other I was born to and lived to help in its forming. I am sure that either one of these can do well with another on their thrown, I am not irreplaceable in either kingdom, it would be foolishness for anyone to think that way of themselves. I do however know the ways of the people I was raised with and though I have knowledge of the ways of the Uklian they are not my own.

I believe that it would be best for all involved for me to maintain my position in the south were I know what I am doing and chose one from among you who knows your ways to take my place here and hope Gaharias accepts my choice and grants them power of the Adoma. If not, then I will have no choice but to remain and learn the ways of the Uklian, because the Elves need the Adoma and someone needs to have the power to care for it." Talmorg paused and looked around, some of the looks he saw seemed surprised, yet more seemed to be expecting what he said even to appreciate it. He watched now for their reaction to his next statement. "It has not been easy deciding who should receive the honor of a king among you. I have with careful consideration chosen Corenestral Ekberghestia. He is of a large and well-respected family and not lacking in wisdom and leadership ability. Further appointments will be his if he is found worthy by Gaharias and anything else I might have to add will wait until after that. I would like to know, whether you of the Uklian will accept my appointment of Coren as your king?"

Kerrikai spoke up in answer, "I believe I can speak for all of us, that is not just acceptable, but we are ready to endorse the wisdom of your decision. Some of us were expecting you to leave, after all it was written in the Never Ending Poem, 'He will give his rule to another'. Corenestral is an excellent choice, he has proven unselfish and impartial in judgment in the past. I personally applaud your wisdom and judgment." As he finished speaking an apparition started to take form in front of the table. It was Gaharias in full formal apparel, chain mail under green cloaking and a plumbed helmet. He had green leather gauntlets to his elbows and his coat of arms was displayed in three places, on the breast of his armor, the collar of his cloak, and stamped into the back of his gauntlets. The coat of arms was identical to Eric's, gold on black.

The room took on an expression of reverence at his appearance. After a pause Gaharias stepped up to the table and addressed them, "Kerrikai, Talmorg, Elves of the Uklian and friends of the Uklian be at ease. I know all that has transpired here and have already prepared the way. Corenestral Ekberghestia has already been granted the power of the Adoma and his family. The power cannot be taken away from the Elkinshanes, nor is that necessary for they have not broken their trust, but Authority in the Elkin Adoma is granted to the Ekberghestia family, to be the new Shanes of the Elkinfolk." He paused and turned to Talmorg, "You shall be, Talmorg, the ruler of a great kingdom that shall stand for many generations. It does not fall under the authority of only one specific ancient, for this purpose is Eric Marland of common blood to me, counted among the Ancients. Let it be known now, that the Ancients may be spoken of among men, because Eric is an Ancient to all races. He is in the old form, able to walk among you as one with the people of Ethar. He shall give the south land its own Adoma and grant its power as he sees fit in accordance with the ways of the Ancients. Eric's coat of arms shall be wreathed in garland that you shall know his from mine." He finished and vanished.

At Gaharias' last statement there was an astonished gasp heard from the Elves, Eric did not understand it, but Talmorg did. From his reading Talmorg had learned that, Darval had altered their family coat of arms by adding an edging of garland half way around the coat of arms. The similarity was suggestive, but it was not the same, the garland is the crown of a champion and an honorable part of a coat of arms. At the same time Talmorg was sure that it was not by coincidence that it bore similarity to Darval's self-proclaimed honor. He wondered if Gaharias might be using Eric to try to pull Darval out of hiding. If this were so than this could have been a small war in preparation for those that were still to come. It was an uncomfortable thought and Talmorg could not seem to shake it, but as Saphrine had labeled him he was a worrier, and he tried to play this off as just another of his stray worries.

Eric was oblivious to the reaction to Gaharias statement, he was still wrapped up in thought, concerning the things he was to do, and the rules he was to operate by in this world. He knew what Gaharias had just told them, but he was thinking about their prior conversation. He did not have all of the restrictions the others had, he had barely conceded to enough of the agreements the Ancients had worked out, to be accepted. He had been ready to sign to all of them but Gaharias stalled and caused him to reconsider signing, but rather agree to giving consideration. Eric knew that Gaharias did not want him under the restrictions, but could not tell him, nor had he showed him why. It really did not matter right now though; he was taking Bonny back to Earth as soon as they got back to Dragoncove. Gaharias had told him that Jaffro Jamis was going to choose to stay on Ethar and not to try to make him return. That was his decision to make, Eric could not make it for him.

CHAPTER 26

Home for Dinner

With things settled in the Uklian the march home had been simple. The majority of the southern armies had been sent ahead, the Elkinshane armies were the last to leave. Dragoncove had a royal reception waiting for them when they got there and the party lasted for three days, with dancing in the streets. Announcements were made, before a month would pass Talmorg would be crowned and Saphrine would be queen Elkinshane. Jaffro, Hans Spardic did decide to stay and Bonny and Eric were ready to leave, after Eric Worked out details for forming an Adoma centered in the city of Talmorg, one that could be tapped by those with ability from any race. The adoma would extend to the reaches of the areas influenced by the Walled City of Talmorg with focus points at towns and cities within the kingdom. Eric would also be returning regularly, at least for a while.

"Are you sure you need to leave immediately?" Talmorg was asking Eric as they strolled down the streets of Dragoncove. "We have not yet had a chance to show you the true hospitality of the south lands."

"Friend Talmorg, Bonny and I have things we need to take care of in our own world." Eric clapped his arm around Talmorg's shoulders, "We will be in the Walled City for your wedding, you can show us your hospitality then. That is also when we shall call to life the Adoma of the south lands, your wedding shall indeed mark the beginning of a new life in the south."

"Good news, cuz," Freebic ran to meet them, "We have received letters of allegiance from every town and city west of the Torak and they will have ambassadors to swear their loyalty to you at your wedding and coronation. That is with the exception of the fairy folk of the forest of dreams, of course."

"This is good news; we will have strength and security in this unity and renewing our strength will go more quickly. We must not overstep our authority though; every member of the alliance will have their say in all aspects of this arrangement." Talmorg gazed off ahead, as though he were looking into the future, and in fact he was trying to project in his mind what lay ahead of them. He had not been able to shake the feeling that the war they had just won, marked only the beginning of events to come. In the shadows at the corners of his mind Darval threatened to return.

"Where ya at cuz?" Freebic asked, taking a firm grasp of his elbow. "Something bothering you, with that look of gloom on your face. Why don't we stop for an ale, then you can tell us about it?"

They turned in to the tavern they were about to pass and over the next hour Talmorg unburdened his mind on Eric and Freebic. When they were finished Talmorg felt much better, but they all agreed that they should do what they could to prepare for whatever might lie ahead and Eric agreed to learn what he could from Gaharias.

It was late afternoon when Eric and Bonny walked in the front door. The T.V. was left on and they recognized the weekly show that was on, it was Sunday, and if Eric was right, it was still the same weekend as when they had departed. The fragrance of coffee filled the air from the kitchen where it had been left a few hours earlier, when Bonny and Jaffro accidentally stepped into the Ethar world.

Looking out the window Eric could see the snow was still deep though there was light coming in the western side of the house. Eric walked into the kitchen and poured two cups of coffee and shut the coffee maker off. Setting them down on the dinner table he pulled up a chair and sat down. Bonny sat down across from him and took one of the cups.

"We need to go see my mom," she said looking out the window, "she is expecting us, you know."

"We can leave as soon as we change out of this middle age attire." He looked at the kitchen clock, it was four P.M. "She is not expecting us for a few hours anyway. We have a little time to clear our heads before we go."

"It will take weeks or even years to do that." Bonny laughed, and then smiled at Eric. "I don't think I will mention any of this to mom."

"She would never believe it. She might even think you were mocking her." Eric paused, and looked at Bonny seriously, "We are changed, you know, she will notice a difference even if she can't explain what it is."

"I think we can probably play it off."

"Maybe, it will be overshadowed by the fact that we are actually getting married this time." They sat quietly and finished their coffee, each in their own world of thought.

Neither Bonny nor Eric knew how much power they had brought back with them. The lives of the people they touched would become healthier and unusual things would begin happening around them as they started to perceive the beginnings of the power, they had brought back with them. They healed Bonny's mom when they visited her, but did not let her know nor did they try explaining anything, except that they had finally both agreed to be married. Bonny decided to delay telling Eric they were going to have a child until after their wedding, it would be soon enough.

Later that evening when they sat down to the dinner Bonny fixed at home, they started planning their return to Talmorg and Saphrine's wedding.

"The time distortion factor in the portal has been altered." Eric stated, "When I sent the rex home, I altered the time distortion factor. I think I have some control over it, but I don't know how much and I don't want to miss the wedding."

"Eric, I have to go back to work tomorrow." Bonny gave him a serious look of warning, then started laughing.

"How about, we leave early in the morning, making sure we can get back here a couple hours before you have to be at work. We can get a good night sleep there before we come back again."

"You mean leave at three in the morning, why not just leave now and get there a few days early and help with the preparations?" Bonny asked mocking him.

As it turned out they decided that was a more practical idea and they returned to Ethar before midnight.

The Walled city of Talmorg was crowded and filled with the activity of preparation. It was two days before the wedding when Eric called the adoma of the south lands to life, according to the ways of the Ancients. Talmorg gathered selected leaders from throughout the kingdom and their high priests and all were instructed in the use and maintenance of the life of the land. All races had access, but they had to follow the proper rituals, so some control could be kept over who used its strength for what.

The wedding was a gala spectacle and Talmorg and Saphrine were crowned King and Queen of the south land kingdom of Talmorg in the same ceremony. As part of the ceremony, Eric gave them each a staff of rulership and all of the appropriate runic tokens, due to a ruler of an adoma. Eric also gave them several other gifts to help them in many ways. It was not until after a couple of days of farewells, that Eric and Bonny finally returned again to their home on Earth.

It was the next day after Bonny had gone to work, when Eric sat down at his computer. The interactive game he had designed had his server monitoring program running. When he brought it up and examined it, he noticed a series of requests made to Eric Emarlandestria had been answered by his game program, under the game subprogram for divine intervention. After reviewing them he realized to his surprise they were requests from people in the south lands of Ethar. Turning to the statistics page of the program for divine beings in the game under the subheading;

Eric Emarlandestria he started reading:

Name: Eric Emarlandestria (Ancient of the new order)

Alignment: Nuetral

....

Before he got too far he noticed the back reference to the previous

heading: Bonny Emarlandestria (Ancient of healing of the new order)

9 781966 954484